'*The Curator* is like a bar fight: you're in it so **fast**, you're **breathless**, your **adrenalin** is through the roof and you're just waiting for the next punch'
Mark Griffin

'Craven more than deserved the CWA Gold Dagger for *The Puppet Show*, and this novel is just as **dazzling**'
Holly Watt

'Witty, clever and **shocking**, *The Curator* is excellent at **jolting your eyes** onto the next page'
Cumbria Life

'Genuinely **nail-biting**'
Crime Review

'Poe and Bradshaw are a **memorable duo** no crime fiction fan should miss. M. W. Craven is an **impressive** writer, and *The Curator* demonstrates why'
Mari Hannah

'What a ride . . . compelling and **wonderfully devious**, with a dash of **dark humour**. Lock yourself in with *The Curator*'
Alison Bruce

'This series is really **something special**'
Morning Star

'**Pacy, gory** and **clever**, this is our new favourite duo'
Crime Monthly

'M. W. Craven **grabs the reader** by the scruff of the neck and drags them bodily over the grit and grimness of this **expertly crafted** tale'
Matt Wesolowski

'Sharp, flawless, compelling . . . the **best in the series**'
Louise Mullins

'Disturbing'
Woman Magazine

'A series that keeps on getting **better and better** with every new volume. The Dagger judges got it right'
Crime Time

'A compelling, **suspenseful**, powerful read. Craven knows how to take the reader on a **gripping ride**'
T. F. Muir

'So twisty and turny and just so **brilliantly clever**'
Woman's Way

'Elite entertainment from a **crime maestro**, which had me **astonished** and **thrilled** from start to finish'
Rob Parker

'A superbly plotted, **witty**, **violent** thriller'
The Tablet

'The **brilliance** and **unpredictability** of Poe and Bradshaw propel the storyline'
Deadly Pleasures Mystery Magazine

Also by M. W. Craven

Washington Poe series
The Puppet Show
Black Summer
Cut Short (short story collection)

Avison Fluke series
Born in a Burial Gown
Body Breaker

THE
CURATOR

—

M.W.
CRAVEN

CONSTABLE

CONSTABLE

First published in Great Britain in 2020 in hardback by Constable

This paperback edition published in Great Britain in 2020 by Constable

ISBN: 978-1-47213-194-2

Typeset in Adobe Caslon Pro by Initial Typesetting Services, Edinburgh
Printed and bound in Great Britain by Clays Ltd, Elcograf S.p.A.

Papers used by Constable are from well-managed forests
and other responsible sources.

Constable
An imprint of
Little, Brown Book Group
Carmelite House
50 Victoria Embankment
London EC4Y 0DZ

An Hachette UK Company
www.hachette.co.uk

www.littlebrown.co.uk

To my late mother, Susan Avison Craven.
You weren't with us when I finally realised my dream,
but none of this would have been possible without
your enthusiasm for reading.

A Black Swan event is unprecedented,
impossible to predict and has a huge impact.
Afterwards, it is rationalised by hindsight as if
it should have been anticipated.

Nassim Nicholas Taleb

'The player who understands the role of the pawn, who really understands it, can master the game of chess,' the man said. 'They might be the weakest piece on the board but pawns dictate where and when your opponent can attack. They restrict the mobility of the so-called bigger pieces and they determine where the battle squares will be.'

The woman stared at him in confusion. She'd just woken and was feeling groggy.

And sore.

She twisted her head and searched for the source of her pain. It didn't take long.

'What have you done?' she mumbled.

'Beautiful, isn't it? It's old-fashioned catgut so the sutures are a bit agricultural, but they're supposed to be. It's not used any more but I needed the "wick effect". That's when infection enters the wound through the suture. It will ensure the scar stays livid and crude. A permanent reminder of what has happened.'

He picked up a pair of heavy-duty rib shears.

'Although not for you, of course.'

The woman thrashed and writhed but it was no use. She was bound tight.

The man admired the exacting lines of the surgical instrument. Turned it so the precision steel caught the light. Saw his face reflected in the larger blade. He looked serious. This wasn't something he particularly enjoyed.

'Please,' the woman begged, fully awake now, 'let me go. I promise you, I won't say anything.'

The man walked round and held her left hand. He stroked it affectionately.

1

'I've had to wait for the anaesthetic to wear off so this is going to hurt, I'm afraid. Believe me when I say I wish it didn't have to.'

He placed her ring finger between the blades of the rib shears and squeezed the handles together. There was a crunch as the razor-sharp edges sliced through bone and tendon as if they weren't there.

The woman screamed then passed out. The man stepped away from the spreading pool of blood.

'Where was I?' he said to himself. 'Ah, yes, we were talking about pawns. Beginners think they're worthless, there to be sacrificed – but that's because they don't know when to use them.'

He removed a coil of wire from his pocket. It had toggles at each end. He placed them between the index and middle finger of each hand. In a practised movement he wrapped the wire around the woman's neck.

'Because knowing when to sacrifice your pawns is how the game is won.'

He pulled the garrotte taut, grunting as the cruel wire bit into her skin, severing her trachea, crushing her jugular vein and carotid artery. She was dead in seconds.

He waited an hour then took the other finger he needed.

He carefully arranged it in a small plastic tub, keeping it separate from the others. He looked at his macabre collection with satisfaction.

It could begin now.

The other pawns were in position.

They just didn't know it yet . . .

Chapter 1

Christmas Eve

It was the night before Christmas and all wasn't well.

It had started like it always did. Someone asking, 'Are we doing Secret Santa this year?' and someone else replying, 'I hope not,' both making a pact to avoid mentioning it to the office manager, both secretly planning to mention it as soon as possible.

And before anyone could protest, the decision had been made and the office was doing it again. The fifteenth year in a row. Same rules as last year. Five-quid limit. Anonymous gifts. Nothing rude or offensive. Gifts that no one wanted. A total waste of everyone's time.

At least that's what Craig Hodgkiss thought. He hated Secret Santa.

He hated Christmas too. The yearly reminder that his life was shit. That, while the colleagues he outwardly sneered at were going home to spend Christmas with their families and loved ones, he'd be spending it on his own.

But he *really* hated Secret Santa.

Three years ago it had been the source of his greatest humiliation. Setting himself the not unreasonable Christmas target of shagging Hazel, a fellow logistics specialist at John Bull Haulage, he'd wangled it so he was the one who'd bought her Secret Santa gift. He reckoned buying her a pair of lace panties would be the perfect way to let her know he was up for some

3

extracurricular activities while her husband long-hauled across mainland Europe.

His plan worked.

Almost.

It *had* been the perfect way to let her know.

Unfortunately she was happily married, and instead of rushing into his bed she'd rushed to her husband, who was between jobs and was having a brew in the depot. The six-foot-five lorry driver had walked into the admin office and broken Craig's nose. He'd told him that if he ever so much as looked at his wife again he'd find himself hogtied in the back of a Russia-bound shipping container. Craig had believed him. So much so that, in front of the whole office, he'd lost control of his bladder.

For two years everyone had called him 'Swampy'. He couldn't even complain to Human Resources as he was terrified of getting Hazel into trouble.

For two years he hadn't made a dent in the girls in the office.

But eventually Hazel and her brute of a husband had moved on. He took a job driving for Eddie Stobart and she went with him. Craig told everyone that Hazel's husband had left the company because he'd caught up with him and given him a hiding, but no one had believed him.

Actually, one person seemed to.

By Craig's own standards, Barbara Willoughby was a plain girl. Her hair looked like it had been styled in a nursing home, her teeth were blunt and too widely spaced, and she could have done with dropping a couple of pounds. On a scale of one-to-ten Craig reckoned she was a hard six, maybe a seven in the right lighting, and he only ever shagged eights and above.

But there was one thing he did like about her. She hadn't been there when he'd pissed himself.

So he'd asked her out. And to his surprise he found they got on really well. She was fun to be with and she was popular. He

4

liked how she made him feel and she was adventurous in bed. He also liked how she only wanted to do things at the weekends. During the week she would stay in and study for some stupid exams she was taking.

Which suited Craig just fine.

Because, after a few weeks of dating Barbara, he'd got his swagger back. And with it he began carving notches again.

To his amazement he discovered it was actually easier pulling the type of woman he went for when he told them he was in a long-term relationship. He reckoned it was the combination of his boyish good looks and the thought of doing over someone they didn't know. Which gave Craig an idea: if those sort of women enjoyed the thrill of being with someone who cheated, they'd go crazy for someone who had affairs . . .

So Craig Hodgkiss, at the age of twenty-nine, decided he would ask Barbara to marry him. She'd jump at the chance. She was in her early thirties, had some biological clock thing going on (but was unaware he'd had a vasectomy two years earlier) and would almost certainly be left on the shelf if she said no. And then he'd reap the rewards. A faithful doormat keeping his bed warm and a succession of women who'd happily shag a man wearing a wedding band.

And because he wanted everyone in the office to know he was about to become illicit fruit, he'd decided to put past experiences behind him and propose during the office Secret Santa.

Arranging it hadn't been straightforward. He'd got Barbara's ring size by stealing her dead grandmother's eternity ring, the one she only wore on special occasions. While Barbara turned her flat upside down looking for it, he'd been asking a jeweller to make the engagement ring the same size and to recycle the diamonds and gold. The whole thing had only cost him two hundred quid.

The next thing was to think of a cool way of proposing.

Something that would get the office girls talking about how romantic Craig was. A rep like that could only help. He decided on a mug. It was the perfect Secret Santa gift as it met the five-quid limit set by the office manager and, although half the gifts under the cheap fibre optic Christmas tree looked like they were mugs, half the gifts under the tree didn't have 'Will You Marry Me?' printed on the side.

When Barbara read the message and then saw what was inside . . . well, he reckoned she'd burst into tears, shout yes and hug him for all she was worth.

The office floor was strewn with cheap wrapping paper. All reindeer and snowmen and brightly wrapped presents tied with ribbons.

Barbara was next. She picked up her parcel and looked at him strangely.

Did she know?

She couldn't. No one did. Not even the girl he'd persuaded to swap with him so he was the one buying for Barbara.

Tiffany, Barbara's best friend, began recording it on her mobile phone for some reason. That was OK, though. Better than OK actually. He'd be able to post it on Twitter and Facebook and keep a copy on his phone. Ready to show girls at the drop of a hat. Look at me. Look how nice I am. Look how *sensitive* I am. You can have some of this . . . but only for one night.

Craig caught Barbara's eye. He winked. She didn't return it. Didn't even smile. Just held his gaze as she lifted the wrapped box from one of his old gift bags.

Something wasn't right. The wrapping paper was thick and white with black pictures; he thought his had been cheap and brightly coloured.

Barbara ripped it off without looking at it. The mug was in a polystyrene box. He'd taped the two halves together to increase the suspense. Barbara ran a pair of scissors down the join before separating them.

She pulled out the mug and Craig's confusion intensified. It wasn't his. He hadn't seen this one before. Something *was* printed on the side but it wasn't proposing marriage. In inch-high black letters it said:

#BSC6

Barbara didn't know she'd opened the wrong parcel, though. Without looking inside the mug, she glared at him and upended the mug's contents.

'Cheating fucking bastard,' she said.

Craig didn't protest his innocence. He couldn't. He was unable to tear his eyes away from the things that had fallen on the floor. They were no engagement ring.

He recoiled and gasped in revulsion.

A familiar and unwelcome warmth began spreading from his groin.

And then the screaming started.

Chapter 2

Boxing Day

Someone else who hated Christmas was Detective Sergeant Washington Poe.

As a committed grouch he was against all forms of enforced joviality and, up until today, he'd managed to shun all festivities, organised or otherwise. He usually worked through the enforced Christmas break, spent it alone or found a pub full of like-minded misanthropes and drank until it was over.

But not this year. This year he'd been well and truly 'Bradshawed'.

Because, instead of being in the pub or hunkered down in his two-hundred-year-old shepherd's croft, with beer in the fridge and leftover roast potatoes in the oven, he was in a penthouse flat in a village on the outskirts of Cambridge.

His friend and colleague Matilda 'Tilly' Bradshaw had dragged him to a baby shower.

Initially, he'd point blank refused.

She'd looked upset, but that was OK, she'd have got over it. She might be his best friend but a baby shower at a rich person's house was his special kind of hell.

She'd stamped her foot.

He'd ignored her.

But then she'd used her most deadly weapon against him, one he was powerless against: incessant logic.

He'd told her that baby showers were for women.

She'd shouted at him in front of the whole office. Everyone in the Serious Crime Analysis Section, the National Crime Agency unit charged with investigating emerging serial killers and apparently motiveless murders, stopped to listen.

And giggle.

'Washington Poe, you might have a penis but that doesn't mean you get to use the social privileges of the patriarchal society to get out of doing things you don't like.'

Poe had been about to ask her what the hell she was talking about when he'd heard someone snigger, 'What does she mean, "*might* have a penis"?'

He'd tried saying he couldn't leave Edgar, his springer spaniel, on his own for that long.

She'd replied that Edgar could stay with Victoria Hume, his neighbour. 'You know, like he does all the time.'

He tried the truth – that he didn't want to go.

'Well, gee golly, mister,' she'd countered, 'since when did Washington Poe always get what he wants? Our line manager, DI Stephanie Flynn, is having a baby and her sister has been kind enough to host a baby shower – we're her friends, we're invited, we're going, it's as simple as that.'

So Poe was at a baby shower, sulking in a corner. Up until then he'd avoided catching anyone's eye. He planned to do that until he'd been there long enough to leave. His glass of Champagne had gone warm forty minutes ago but it gave him something to do with his hands.

Jessica Flynn, the boss's elder sister, lived on the top floor of a renovated brick factory. It was an open-plan, loft-style apartment, more suited to Manhattan than semi-rural Cambridgeshire. There were at least fifty women there. Poe was the only man, a fact he was reminded of every time someone gave him a weird look.

9

He'd barely spoken to his boss. Flynn had said hello when he'd arrived but had been dragged off by a succession of women. She was now seated on one of her sister's large couches, surrounded by them. She looked angrier than he felt miserable.

He watched as someone reached over and patted her stomach. 'Will you pack that in!' she snapped, pushing the hand away.

Flynn wasn't a stereotypical pregnant woman, if there were such a thing. She scowled rather than glowed, wore leggings and New York Dolls T-shirts rather than the Laura Ashley maternity dresses Poe knew her partner, Zoe, had bought her, and she flat out refused to take any leave. The only giveaway was that she had a massive belly. Everything else about her was the same: her blonde hair was still tied back in a severe ponytail, her makeup was subtle and her work mobile was never away from her ear.

Flynn glared at the woman who'd touched her. 'The next person who pats my belly is getting punched in the fucking throat.'

The woman smiled nervously, unsure whether Flynn was joking or not.

Poe knew she wasn't.

Because, although Flynn was trying to act as if everything was the same, pregnancy *had* changed her in one small way. She had a rare pregnancy-related cortisol imbalance, the hormone that sends the body into fight or flight mode.

And Flynn didn't back away from fights. Every new experience and challenge had to be beaten into submission. Before she'd got pregnant she'd been a considered and courteous manager. Now she was a foul-mouthed ranting loony. Whereas before she would stay calm, even when up against the most intransigent, obnoxious moron that SCAS occasionally had to deal with, now you risked her wrath if you typed too loudly.

Poe thought it was hilarious, although he never acted like it was to her face.

He'd spoken to Zoe earlier but they had little in common.

Zoe worked in the City profiling world oil prices and he worked anywhere he was needed profiling serial killers. She earned seven figures a year, he earned . . . considerably less than that. They didn't dislike each other but they had an unspoken agreement that they shouldn't have too much contact.

Poe glanced at Bradshaw and smiled. She was wearing the dress she'd bought when they'd attended a charity gala during the first case they worked on together – a mosaic of thumbnail-sized comic book covers. She'd marked the night's occasion by doing something different with her hair. Usually it was tied back and fastened with pigtails; now it was piled high like candyfloss. He wondered idly if she'd had it professionally styled or just followed an online tutorial. His money would be on the latter.

Bradshaw caught him looking and gave him a double thumbs up. She hadn't been to a baby shower before and had attacked it with her usual mixture of enthusiasm and research.

She'd spent a small fortune on gifts – some, like the Spider-Man onesie, were cute and appropriate; others, like the electric double breast pump, were not.

'It's so you can express milk in the most time-efficient way, DI Stephanie Flynn,' she'd said in front of everyone.

Poe envied Flynn her present. She wouldn't have to use it for long, whereas he knew the state-of-the-art pasta maker Bradshaw had bought him for Christmas would torment him for years. He didn't like pasta. Didn't care that it would lower his cholesterol, that it was a 'gateway to a whole new cuisine' or that making his own pasta was cost-efficient.

But that was Bradshaw all over.

Despite being in her early thirties, the Serious Crime Analysis Section was her first real job. In academia since she was a teenager doing degrees and PhDs, then working on the research grants organisations were throwing at her, she'd had neither the time nor the inclination to develop any social skills.

11

SCAS was her first step into the outside world and she'd found communicating with anyone with an IQ lower than 150 a challenge. She was naive, literal and painfully honest but, although Poe had been initially wary of her, he'd recognised that she had the potential to be SCAS's greatest asset. She specialised in mathematics, but was so intelligent she would know more than anyone else on a subject in a matter of hours when she put her mind to it. She could spot patterns in data when no computer could, she could devise bespoke solutions to intractable problems without breaking a sweat and she was intensely loyal.

Pasta maker aside, she was Poe's best friend and he was hers. Bradshaw softened Poe's harsher edges and he helped her plot a course through the outside world. They were a formidable team, which, considering the amount of trouble they frequently found themselves in, was probably for the best.

Jessica Flynn was a rich woman with rich friends, all of whom worked in the City. They would have been called yuppies in the 1990s. They'd taken Bradshaw into their collective bosom and before long she was the centre of attention. Poe would have stepped in if he thought they'd been taking the piss but it was clear they weren't. Bradshaw was so honest and agenda-free – the opposite to the people they usually socialised with, people for whom backstabbing, double-dealing and flat-out lying was a way of life. Having a conversation with someone who answered the question you asked, rather than the one that gave a tactical advantage, must have been a breath of fresh air to them.

Poe looked round Jessica Flynn's penthouse. It covered the top floor and there were huge windows on all four sides, at least ten feet high. Although it was dark, Poe could see that the windows facing the countryside and the windows facing the car park at the rear had large balconies. The front one was set out with wrought iron seats and benches. An upside-down ice bucket was on a small table.

The internal décor was open brick with expensive furniture and fittings. Jessica was obviously a mountaineer. Photographs and memorabilia adorned a whole corner. A shelf, filled with a collection of mountaineering curiosities, was the centrepiece of her collection. In pride of place was an old ice axe. It was on a beautiful teak plinth.

There was a brass plate on the bottom. He could see it was inscribed but it was too far away to read.

He wandered towards it.

A woman joined him.

'I see you've found my little obsession,' she said, sticking out her hand. 'We haven't been formally introduced – I'm Jessica Flynn, Steph's sister.'

They'd been introduced earlier in the evening but it had been quick and perfunctory.

She was tall and cat-like, lithe and graceful in her movements. She had Flynn's golden hair although hers was cut much shorter, possibly because of the mountaineering. Poe had served three years in the Black Watch so was aware that personal hygiene was difficult to maintain in the field – anything you could do to make it simpler was not to be ignored.

She was well dressed, but not over the top like the others. Jeans and a cashmere jumper. Her only piece of jewellery was a delicate golden chain.

Poe studied the photographs. Jessica was in most of them. Ropes flung across her chest, a string of carabiners on her belt, huge smile on her tanned face. He leaned into one photograph and squinted. He recognised what she was climbing: a rock called Napes Needle in the Lake District. It was thin and tapered and looked like a missile.

'That was taken a few years ago,' she said. 'It was afterwards, in a pub in Keswick, that we began planning for the big one.'

'Scafell Pike?' Poe said. Scafell Pike was the tallest mountain in England but it hardly needed expedition-type planning; on a nice day you could walk up it in shorts and trainers.

She pointed at a photograph of the most famous mountain in the world.

'Everest?'

Jessica nodded. 'Everest.'

Poe whistled. 'Impressive. Dangerous.'

She shrugged. 'Everything's dangerous.'

'When are you going?'

'They go next May, when the jet stream isn't hitting the summit at one hundred miles an hour.'

'They?'

'I won't be going with them, I'm afraid.'

'Oh . . . what happened? You don't seem the type to abandon difficult goals.'

'I was diagnosed with Addison's disease, unfortunately,' she said.

'I'm not familiar with it.'

'You're lucky then. It's a long-term endocrine disorder. Means my adrenal glands don't produce enough steroids.'

'It's treatable, though?'

'It is. I'll have to take tablets for the rest of my life but it won't affect how long I live.'

Realisation dawned on him.

'But for someone attempting an Everest summit expedition it's problematic?'

'Altitude sickness. My condition means it would have a greater impact on me, and as Everest's summit is 8848 metres – the cruising altitude of a 747 – my diagnosis would have invalidated the group's insurance.'

He gestured to the ice axe and read out the inscription on the brass plate: 'Tenzing Norgay's mountaineering axe. Mount Everest Expedition, May 1953.'

The axe had a wooden handle and was a more basic design than the ones Poe saw in the Lake District's plague of mountaineering shops. The shorter end was wide and flat, like a pickaxe; the longer end was pointed and curved. The handle ended with a tapered metal spike.

'The axe Sherpa Tenzing used to reach the summit is a pretty decent consolation, though,' he said.

'The one he used to reach the summit is actually in a Nepalese museum. This is a replica of the axe he used to save the life of Sir Edmund Hillary earlier in the expedition when he fell down a crevice. It was why Hillary chose Norgay as his climbing partner when he made his summit attempt.'

'You never thought about trying to get the real thing?'

Jessica snorted. 'Way out of my league, Sergeant Poe. Artefacts like that cost hundreds of thousands of pounds.'

He looked at his surroundings. 'You seem to be doing OK, though. This place can't be cheap.'

She burst out laughing.

'The bank owns the apartment, Sergeant Poe, I just pay subsidised rent. I'm expected to entertain at home and investment banking is all about projecting an image.'

'And is that what you do? Investment banking.'

'It is, and it's not as much fun as it sounds,' she said with a grin. 'Walk with me?'

She opened the double doors. A blast of chilled air filled the room. She stepped outside. Poe followed.

She turned and leaned against the balcony's glass and metal guard.

'Stephanie tells me you're a bit under the weather?'

'Bit of a bug,' he said.

'Bug' was an understatement. He'd been laid up for almost a week now. The grandparents from *Charlie and the Chocolate Factory* had spent less time in bed. It had started as a headache but had evolved into a hacking cough that had turned his throat red-raw. He felt he was through the worst but it hadn't been nice. Winter bugs never were.

'I've got a fine single malt that'll sort that out,' Jessica said. She disappeared inside, returning a minute later with two crystal tumblers full of amber liquid.

Poe sniffed it, then took a sip. The whisky was like fire and ice. Beautiful, smoky and unlike any hard drink he'd had before.

'Why are you here, Sergeant Poe?'

He was tempted to say, 'Because Tilly made me,' but it seemed flippant. He decided on the truth.

'Steph's a good friend. We've been through a lot together.'

Jessica nodded thoughtfully. 'I need you to do something for me.'

Poe said nothing. Jessica seeking him out had been no accident.

'I need you to talk my sister out of this ridiculous career path she's chosen for herself.'

'And why would I do that?' Poe said carefully.

'In the next month or so she's having a baby. My nephew or niece. She'll have responsibilities she hasn't had to consider before. Being a police officer's fine when you're young and single but she can't keep putting herself first any more. People are relying on her now and this job you do isn't conducive to sensible decision-making. She needs to quit playing cops and robbers and rejoin the real world.'

'It's not like that,' Poe said. 'Most of what we do is office-based.'

She raised an eyebrow. 'Didn't you nearly burn to death in a house fire last year?'

'Yes, but—'

'And weren't you arrested for murder recently?'

'Yes, but that was a misunderstanding. What happened, was this man had—'

'But you'll agree what you do has its . . . unnecessarily exciting moments?'

Poe didn't know what to say. It was true they had been in a few scrapes recently. He blamed Bradshaw — she kept finding new and inventive ways to get closer to the bad guys . . .

'Is this not something that the two of you should discuss?' he said.

'Stephanie doesn't listen to me, Sergeant Poe. She used to. Used to hang on her big sister's every word. Not any more.'

But Poe had stopped listening. Flynn was talking on her phone and she was frowning. She caught his eye and nodded. He drained the whisky, grimacing as it burnt his raw throat.

'Duty's about to call,' he said. 'Sorry.'

'Go,' Jessica sighed.

By the time Poe got to her, Flynn was already reaching for her coat.

Zoe walked across and joined them.

'Steph, your absence is conspicuous,' she said.

'Sorry, Zoe. We're going to have to leave, I'm afraid.'

'Oh no!' Bradshaw cried.

'Oh no,' Poe said.

'Thank fuck,' Flynn muttered.

Chapter 3

'Our analytical support will be here this afternoon,' Flynn told the group that had assembled in Conference Room A of Carleton Hall, Cumbria Constabulary's headquarters building in Penrith. 'We were at a social function last night and Tilly had to head back to Hampshire to collect her computers. Sergeant Poe and I were able to leave immediately.'

Poe had got back to Herdwick Croft, his secluded home on Shap Fell, in the early hours; Flynn had booked into the nearby North Lakes Hotel and Spa. It was now 8 a.m. and it looked as though Poe wasn't the only person who hadn't had a full night's sleep. There were around forty people in the room, a mix of senior uniformed officers, senior detectives and essential support staff. The atmosphere was sombre.

Flynn had taken a seat at the front. Poe was standing at the back, next to the freestanding banner displaying the Constabulary's and the Police and Crime Commissioner's logos. When the briefing was finished the last rows of chairs would be reversed and the room would be set up for press conferences, the first of which was scheduled for later that day.

'We have computers here,' Detective Superintendent Jo Nightingale said.

'Not like hers you don't,' Flynn said. 'Trust me, what Tilly Bradshaw brings to the investigation can't be overvalued.'

Nightingale nodded, satisfied. She was a serious-looking

woman in her early forties. Cropped dark hair, black trousers and a white shirt. Eyes green enough to start traffic.

Poe had met Nightingale only once. She'd taken over the vacant detective superintendent position when Ian Gamble had retired after the successful conclusion of the Jared Keaton case. Poe had returned to Herdwick Croft one afternoon to find her waiting outside.

She'd introduced herself and said Gamble had advised her that Poe was an asset if used properly. She'd brought a case file with her. A murder. After the 2015 floods, when Carlisle had been flooded for the second time in a decade, a lot of buildings became all but uninsurable. People had a choice: pay for the repairs themselves or cut their losses. Several chose the latter with the result that there were abandoned buildings all over the city. A body had been found in one of them.

The victim was an economic migrant from Poland, and Nightingale had asked Poe if SCAS could add value to her investigation. He'd read the file while she waited then said, 'You don't need us – you'll catch the perp using the investigation strategy you're already following. He'll be from within the Polish community and he's probably already returned home. He'll be known over there and your forensic evidence will be enough to extradite and convict him.'

She nodded.

It felt like he'd passed some sort of test. That she'd needed to reassure herself that Poe wasn't going to invent drama just so he had an excuse to leave Hampshire. It had been unnecessary anyway – Poe lived in Cumbria full time now. At the end of the Jared Keaton case, Detective Chief Inspector Wardle, a cop Poe had had a run in with, had done the dirty. Realising that the Lake District National Park's new boundary included Shap Fell, the prehistoric moorland where Poe's croft was situated, he'd asked the local authority, 'purely as a concerned citizen', if Poe had been granted permission to convert the two-hundred-year-old building into a dwelling. Poe hadn't and they'd issued a legally binding instruction to return it to its original condition.

Although he was fighting it in court there had been an upside. In the law of unintended consequences, Wardle had done him a favour: Poe's solicitor had said it would be helpful if he could demonstrate that Herdwick Croft was his sole residence.

Poe, who up until a couple of years ago wouldn't have cared if he lived in a shoe, had asked if he could work from home when they weren't out in the field. Director of Intelligence Edward van Zyl had immediately agreed.

'You're like a caged animal down here anyway, Poe,' he'd said. 'The open space up there has cleared your mind and brought a clarity to your work – I don't want to lose that.'

'I'll send the SCAS guys videos and photographs of the crime scenes when we're finished, but it'll be helpful for me to summarise,' Nightingale said. 'Some of my colleagues were away visiting family over Christmas and aren't up to speed.'

She tapped her laptop's keyboard and a photograph of a building appeared on a wall monitor.

'This is the first crime scene. These are the admin offices of John Bull Haulage in Carlisle. On Christmas Eve a cargo administrator called Barbara Willoughby opened her Secret Santa present. She was supposed to be getting a mug with an engagement ring inside. Instead she got this.'

The photograph changed from the outside of the drab building to a close-up of a scuffed beige carpet tile, the hardwearing type found in offices up and down the country.

Two fingers lay in the middle.

They'd been severed close to the knuckle. The cuts appeared neat. The bloodied ends were clotted and dry and snagged with

20

fluff. One of the fingers still bore a ring. It was thin, almost certainly a woman's wedding band.

The photograph changed again. This time a mug appeared onscreen.

#BSC6 was printed on the side in large black letters.

Flynn said, 'What's that mean?'

'We have no idea,' Nightingale said. 'We can't find any reference to it online.'

'If it's on the internet, Tilly will find it,' Poe said.

'We also have no idea how the mug ended up under their Christmas tree,' Nightingale continued. 'It wasn't the one that Barbara was supposed to open. The paper used to wrap the mug is interesting too.'

She brought it up on the screen. Four pieces of paper. Crumpled and torn by Barbara Willoughby when she had opened her gift, then flattened by CSI so they could be photographed. A4 size according to the forensic ruler that lay beside them. Each piece was patterned with silhouettes of a black water bird. A swan, or possibly a duck with an elongated neck. Nothing else. No words, no message.

'These sheets of A4 appear to be bespoke. We think they were produced on an ordinary household printer. Other than the bird symbol, there was nothing of any forensic value on them. Detectives are interviewing staff at John Bull but we don't think anyone from the firm was involved.'

'How can you tell?' Poe said.

Nightingale didn't answer. Instead, she tapped her laptop again. The exterior of a church appeared on the screen. It was constructed from red sandstone and had high, arched windows filled with stained glass. A tall steeple towered above an imposing ironbound oak door.

'Crime scene number two: Saint Luke's on the outskirts of Barrow-in-Furness.'

The photograph changed.

It was a close-up of the church font. The bowl was made of brass or copper, and was ornately carved with religious symbols. Two severed fingers lay in the middle of it.

Poe stared at the image, burning it into his brain. This was his first impression and he needed to see it as the killer had intended him to. The horror would have to wait.

The fingers were clearly female again. One of the fingernails was pierced at the end with a gold stud. Nightingale displayed a close-up. The stud was in the shape of a teddy bear. Poe thought the fingers looked younger than the ones found at the previous crime scene.

The next photograph was of a hymn board. It was light oak and had five rows for the service's hymn numbers to be slotted into. The middle row held a piece of folded-up A4 paper. #BSC6 was written on it.

'We don't know how this deposition was achieved either. The fingers definitely weren't there during Midnight Mass. The warden found them at 6 a.m. when he went in to turn on the heating for the Christmas Day service. There's no sign of forced entry and only he and the vicar have keys.'

Poe raised his hand.

'Sergeant Poe?'

'Can you bring up all the images you have of the inside of the church, ma'am?'

Nightingale did. There were several.

Poe studied them. Saint Luke's was like most churches Poe had been in. A Bible lectern on the left, a pulpit on the right and an altar front and centre. The stone floor looked well worn and uneven. Ornate candleholders and offertory boxes flanked two rows of oak pews. Wrought iron curtain rods framed the back of the door. A pair of heavy curtains were tied back, no doubt ready to be used as draught excluders during a service.

He made his way to the front of the room.

'Creeping round in the early hours of Christmas morning is too risky; anyone out then has burglar written all over them,' he explained. 'Any copper worth their salt will give them a pull. Even if it's just out of boredom. A quick search to check they're not going equipped, and instead of a screwdriver or crowbar, the cop finds severed fingers? I don't think so. This isn't how our guy likes to play.'

'What are you saying?'

'Midnight Mass is the one service of the year that's packed with non-regulars. I think our perp will have attended the service, slipped away at the final whistle when everyone was wishing each other merry Christmas, and found somewhere to hide. Churches like this have cubbyholes everywhere. The warden would have been so eager to get home I doubt he checked for stragglers. Probably just a shout out that he was about to lock up.'

Nightingale nodded. Poe saw others were nodding too.

'Thoughts on how he broke back out?' Nightingale asked.

Poe pointed at the front door and the thick draught curtains tied back beside it.

'He didn't. All he had to do was wait until the morning and hide behind the curtains when the warden came to turn on the heating. He'd only have been popping in so I doubt he'd have locked the door behind him and it would have been too dark to see what was in the font. The perp only had to wait until the warden was in the back before walking out the front door.'

Nightingale stared at him.

'That's how I'd have done it anyway,' Poe added.

'I want the Midnight Mass crowd interviewed,' Nightingale said. 'All of them. Today if possible. I want to know if there was anyone there they didn't recognise. Helen, can you arrange?'

'Will do, ma'am,' a woman in a suit said.

'Let me know if you need more people. Paul, CSI is still processing the crime scene, right?'

'They are,' a man near the front said.

'Get them to check anywhere someone could have hidden for a few minutes after Midnight Mass ended. It's possible he slipped up and there was some forensic transfer.'

'I'll phone them now, ma'am.'

CSI Paul left to make his call and Nightingale tapped her laptop again.

The screen changed.

'The last crime scene: Fiskin's Food Hall in Whitehaven. They open for an hour each Boxing Day to draw the meat raffle.'

It was the interior of what a lot of old-fashioned butchers had had to diversify into. Big pieces of meat still hung on hooks, dark red haunches and forelegs marbled with tallow and suet. Steaks and hams and streaky bacon were still displayed on artificial grass. But there were also tables piled high with jams and biscuits and olive oils and balsamic vinegars and other things Poe thought had no business being in his favourite type of shop. There was even a salad bar.

The screen changed again, this time to the cooked meat counter. It was glass fronted and full of sliced ham, fancy coleslaws and pies. And right in the middle, nestled between the sausage rolls and the sliced black pudding, was yet another pair of fingers.

These ones were podgy and the nails were bitten to the quick. The amputation looked less clinical than the previous crime scenes. The ends of the bones were splintered and the skin was torn and messy.

Poe thought they looked male.

The perpetrator had affixed a folded A4 sheet, displaying the now familiar #BSC6, to a white plastic price tag. Nightingale's next photograph, of the A4 page unfolded and straightened and next to a CSI forensic ruler, could have been mistaken for the one from the church – they seemed identical.

'The killer was caught on the shop's CCTV but his face was

24

well covered. He waited until Mick Fiskin was drawing the raffle and simply walked behind the counter and placed the fingers in among the cooked goods. Bold as brass. He then walked out with the crowd when it was all over. It's a good fifteen minutes before anyone notices what he's done. We have someone trawling through the CCTV in Whitehaven but it's not saturated. We aren't hopeful.'

Nightingale turned off the monitor and everyone settled in their seats.

'Obviously we have hundreds of photographs and CSI are at all three scenes, but these are the highlights. Questions?'

'The fingers, are they from one person or six?' Flynn asked.

'We think three. We'll confirm soon but the pairs seem to match visually. We're fairly sure one is male and two are female.'

'You've been referring to the perpetrator as "our killer", ma'am,' Poe said. 'I assume you don't think this is just a sick prank?'

Nightingale shook her head.

'The pathologist found one finger on each pair had something called "vital reaction" – that's what happens to living tissue when there's trauma. Inflammation, clotting, the presence of a range of chemicals that wouldn't be there if they'd been removed after the victim had died. The other finger *didn't* show vital reaction, which means it was taken some time after death.'

'Assuming the fingers in each pair are from the same person then, this man wants us to know these are murders,' Poe said. 'If the fingers were all removed before death, they could have potentially been stolen after a legitimate surgical procedure. If they were all removed after death occurred, it could have been medical students or someone messing around at the mortuary or funeral parlour.'

Nightingale nodded. 'That's our assessment too.'

'You've not found or identified the victims yet, I assume?'

25

'No victims, no IDs,' Nightingale confirmed. 'Any more questions?'

Poe had several but he'd wait until he'd read the file. He kept his hand down.

'OK, then. If the SCAS guys can stay behind, everyone else can get back to work.'

Chapter 4

'Can I make a suggestion?' Poe said after the room had emptied. Flynn also stayed behind. 'When we do find a body, there's a pathologist in the north-east you should ask to take a look. Estelle Doyle. It looks like we might need the best and, trust me, she is.'

'I've heard of Professor Doyle,' Nightingale said. 'Will she be available? And do you think she would look at the six fingers? The attending pathologist was a locum.'

'I'll call her when we're finished here.' Estelle Doyle was the weirdest person Poe knew – even weirder than Bradshaw. He'd be surprised if she did something as vanilla as celebrate Christmas. Black Mass maybe.

'Good,' Nightingale said.

Flynn said, 'Putting writing on the side of a mug takes specialist equipment. How's that lead going?'

'We're following up with businesses who do digital printing but we're not optimistic. There are thirty who can do it in Cumbria alone, and if you include UK-wide mail order businesses and people who've bought home kits, the numbers are six figures.'

Poe had guessed as much.

'The A4 pages he leaves with the fingers are curious,' Nightingale said. 'When we processed them the tech noticed that a different printer had been used for the note left at each scene. Apparently each printer drum has flaws as unique as fingerprints.'

'That's odd,' Flynn said.

'Unless he's using printers in libraries and internet cafés. Making sure he never goes to the same place twice,' Poe said. 'Might be worth checking their CCTV.'

'Already on it,' Nightingale said.

They discussed it for a while longer. It was clear Nightingale had hit the 'golden hour' hard and was conducting a thorough and intrusive investigation. She'd got in early and had ensured that evidence wasn't compromised, lost or destroyed, witnesses hadn't yet drifted off and there'd been no time for alibis to be constructed. Her primary role was to develop lines of enquiry for her team to follow. It was a responsibility that Poe had never sought – the wrong decision could waste hundreds of investigative hours – but he knew when it was being done well. Nightingale knew what she was doing.

'What do you want from us, ma'am?' Flynn asked.

'Large investigations move at the speed of logistics,' Nightingale replied. 'And that's how they should. It's how every-thing gets done. But with this I think I'd also like a smaller, independent investigation running parallel to the main one. It can be reactive, maybe even proactive, in the way that the main one can't.'

She turned to face Poe.

'Would I be right in saying that a Venn diagram of the people you know and the people you've upset would closely intersect?'

Flynn snorted. 'A Venn diagram of the people Poe knows and the people he's upset would be a fucking circle.'

'Ha ha,' Poe said.

Nightingale smiled. 'Don't worry, Sergeant . . . look, can I call you Poe? Everyone else seems to.'

'Poe's fine.'

'Someone like you, with no ties to the investigation, with no real worries about upsetting the political hierarchy, could be invaluable. If you're OK with it, DI Flynn, I'd like SCAS to work independently. You'll report directly to me and if you need support I'll arrange it.'

'Suits me,' Flynn replied. 'And I know it suits Poe. Upsetting the political hierarchy is his particular area of expertise.'

Chapter 5

'Poe, darling,' Estelle Doyle said. 'Don't tell me you've found some online mistletoe?'

'Er . . . no,' Poe replied. 'No mistletoe here . . . only cold weather.'

In the grim world of forensic pathology, Estelle Doyle was, as Bradshaw would have described her, an outlier. Even in the mortuary she dressed like she was off to an S & M club. Black hair and even blacker makeup. Fishnet stockings and stilettos. More tattoos than David Beckham, lip gloss redder than arterial blood. Poe found her extraordinarily beautiful and utterly terrifying. But she was unrivalled in her field and that was enough for him to keep going back to her lair.

Pathology was only part of her expertise. All forensic disciplines came naturally to her and she divided her time between forensic pathology, forensic science and lecturing.

And for some reason she had a soft spot for him. Poe didn't know why. Her contempt for police officers was never understated, but with him she would find the time to make sure he understood everything. Earlier in the year, she'd said it was because he was the perennial underdog and that he had Capraesque qualities. Poe had been too scared to ask what she meant.

Doyle paused and Poe forgot to fill the silence.

'It's the twenty-seventh of December, Poe. Surely even someone as adamantine as yourself can find someone to spend the festive season with?'

'Adam Ant what now?'

'Don't worry about it, Poe,' she replied. 'What is it you desire of me?'

Poe was sure she spoke like this just to make him blush, even over the phone.

'I have a finger for you,' he replied.

'Do you now?' she drawled.

'Lots of fingers.' He knew he was making it worse but for some reason, whenever he talked to her, he became a right chatter of shit.

'Well, aren't you just the gift that keeps on giving, Poe?'

'We have three separate crime scenes,' he said, recovering some dignity. 'A pair was found at each one.'

'Same victim?' She was all business now.

'No.'

'I'm visiting friends in Haltwhistle so I can be at the Cumberland Infirmary in thirty minutes. How soon can you get everything to me?'

Poe glanced at his watch. Assuming Nightingale agreed, he reckoned he could have them there within the hour. He told her.

'See you soon then,' she replied. 'You do bring me the most fabulous gifts, Poe.'

The line went dead and Poe went looking for Nightingale.

Chapter 6

It had been six months since Poe had seen Estelle Doyle. She'd helped enormously in the Jared Keaton case. She'd given them the early break and then overseen the recovery of evidence in one of the most complex crime scenes anyone in law enforcement had ever had to deal with.

Poe trusted her. It was as simple as that. She stood up to senior investigating officers and interpreted the evidence as she saw it. She had no interest in following the narrative the SIO was trying to present. Some detectives preferred malleable pathologists but Poe wasn't one of them.

'I hate these gimmicky killers,' Poe muttered to Flynn as they walked down the stairs to the mortuary in the Cumberland Infirmary, Carlisle's major hospital.

Flynn had insisted on coming with him. She wasn't quite waddling yet but she wasn't far off. Naively, he'd asked if she'd wanted to stay in the car.

'I'm not the one who's fucking ill, Poe,' she'd snapped. She'd ignored the lift and taken the stairs to prove her point. She could be just as stubborn as him sometimes. By the time Poe had caught her up he was wheezing so hard it sounded like he'd swallowed a whistle.

Flynn smiled in satisfaction. Point proved.

The fingers had been sent ahead and Nightingale had tracked the order and confirmed delivery with them.

It was the 27th of December and this part of the hospital was quiet. Their footsteps reverberated along the sterile corridor.

At the end was the mortuary.

Poe knocked on the door and entered.

Doyle was bent over an inspection table. At first glance it looked empty. It wasn't. Two fingers were in a small tray. Doyle was working on them.

She straightened when she saw them.

She was wearing a lab coat, a hairnet and goggles. Standard attire when the metal met the meat. Her eyes were ringed with black eyeliner and her lipstick was crimson. Poe didn't know if she always looked like this, whether it was a work thing and she dressed like Mary Poppins when she was on her own time, or if she did it just to watch him squirm.

'Merry Christmas, Poe,' she said huskily. She had a smoker's voice although Poe knew she never touched them. 'Good grief, you look dreadful.'

'Estelle,' he replied. 'Bit of a cold.'

'Suit yourself,' she said. 'Good to see you again, DI Flynn. What has Cumbria's answer to C. Auguste Dupin got you into this time?'

'We were hoping you could tell us, Estelle,' Flynn replied.

'This mortuary's a bit basic compared to mine and you haven't given me much to go on.'

Poe and Flynn waited.

'OK, here's what I can tell you for certain: these are not medical samples as they haven't been flushed. The blood types prove they are from three different victims and your initial assessment is correct: one finger from each pair was removed ante-mortem, the other post.'

So far Nightingale's locum pathologist hadn't messed up.

'So we do have three murders,' Flynn said.

'The facts cannot be disputed,' Doyle said. 'It's up to you to interpret them. I'll know more when my LC-MS results are back.'

Doyle had used liquid chromatography-mass spectrometry in their last case. Poe didn't understand the science behind it but he knew it separated and analysed biochemical, organic and inorganic compounds and was considered the Rolls-Royce of chemical analysis. If there were anything in the fingers that wasn't supposed to be there, the LC-MS would find it.

'I am also prepared to say that, in my professional opinion, different methods of amputation were used with each victim. One pair of fingers was removed neatly and quickly. The blades were different sizes and didn't meet so shears were used. Possibly bone snips, possibly rib shears.'

Poe didn't ask how she knew these things. If she said that's what had happened, then that was what had happened.

'The second pair were removed more crudely. There are tiny flecks of blue paint embedded in the wounds. I'll have them analysed to confirm, but I suspect they are from a hacksaw. Probably a coping saw, as he'd have had to grip each finger with one hand and saw it off with the other. Under the microscope you can clearly see scars on the proximal phalanges, the bones between the knuckle and first finger joint. They were made by the blade's teeth.'

Poe frowned. That was odd. Why use a saw when you had rib shears?

'The third pair is the most interesting, though,' she continued. 'This is the male pair and he made a right mess of it. I'm almost certain your killer snapped the fingers then used a pair of scissors to cut through the skin and tendons. Blunt blades, judging by the incisions.'

'And he was alive for the first amputation?' Poe said.

'Possibly not conscious, but definitely alive.'

'No time of death?'

She shook her finger in admonishment. 'Keep that up and I'll have to spank you, Poe.'

Doyle never gave a time of death. She said that any pathologist who did was guessing. There were too many variables with liver temperature or lividity. Even insect activity was all smoke and mirrors. Yes, flies *do* behave in a certain way, but what the forensic entomologists never admit is that flies have to be present to begin with.

'Anything else?' he said before Flynn picked up on the being spanked remark.

Doyle walked over to an open laptop. They followed her.

She brought up an image of a finger and pointed towards some scarring.

'It was underneath the wedding band,' she explained. 'At first I thought it was a long-term epidermal surface reaction to gold, but it was too inconsistent. I removed some layers and found this.'

She changed the picture.

Poe leaned in and frowned. 'What's that?'

'She's had a tattoo removed,' Doyle said.

The markings were faint but visible. Three scars the size of a grain of rice were separated by two the size of a grain of sugar in a big/small/big/small/big sequence.

'Care to hazard a guess?' Doyle said.

'It's a date,' Poe said. 'And if it was under her wedding ring then it's almost certainly her wedding date.'

Doyle nodded. 'I think that too.'

'And we can't recover it?'

'No. It was professionally removed with cosmetic lasers.'

'But, if she's had the date removed, why the hell was she still wearing her wedding ring?' Poe said.

Doyle said nothing.

Chapter 7

Flynn put Nightingale on speakerphone as soon as she had a signal. She updated her on the scar Estelle Doyle had found.

'That's helpful, DI Flynn,' Nightingale said. 'We can use it as a control filter when we go public.'

'What do you want us doing?' Flynn asked.

'I'm concentrating on finding the bodies. Do you want to go over the first crime scene and see if you can work out how he did it?'

Poe nodded to Flynn. That was exactly where he wanted to start. He thought he knew how the killer had deposited the fingers at the church and he'd been on camera at Fiskin's Food Hall, but so far no one had figured out how he'd got them into a Secret Santa mug at John Bull Haulage.

Craig Hodgkiss, the man whose Secret Santa present had been swapped, was on police bail. He'd been charged with a public order offence after his initial arrest as the responding officers hadn't known what else to do with him. He had to report to Durranhill, Carlisle Area's headquarters building, at 2 p.m. every day, and Poe and Flynn were waiting there for him.

He was led into one of the modern interview suites and they all took a seat.

He was an over-groomed man. Gelled hair and fake tan, bleached teeth and designer stubble.

'I gather you were the only one in the office to piss yourself?'

Poe said. May as well annoy him straight away. Put him off any script he'd prepared beforehand.

Hodgkiss stiffened. 'I most certainly did not.'

Useful information, Poe decided. Attacking his ego was clearly the way to go. He'd spoken to Nightingale before they'd started and he concurred with her overall impression of him: he was a dickhead but ultimately harmless.

'Show him the video, boss,' Poe said.

Flynn opened the laptop she'd brought in with her. It had a video set up. She pressed play and span it round so Hodgkiss could see.

Barbara's friend, Tiffany, had taken it. It included the moment Barbara opened her Secret Santa present, but they'd also recorded a prologue.

They were in the work toilets. Tiffany was doing a mock interview with Barbara. She must have been using a selfie stick as they were both on screen.

'Barbara Willoughby, today's the big day,' Tiffany said. 'The great Craig Hodgkiss has selected you as his woman. In a few minutes he'll ask you to marry him in the most romantic way possible: a cheap stunt in front of your workmates using your dead grandmother's eternity ring.'

Barbara nodded. 'I am indeed truly blessed, Tiffany.'

Tiffany snorted.

'And will you be receptive to his magnificent gesture?'

'Well, Tiffany, as you know I've given this a great deal of thought and, what with him having cheated on me several times, I was only too happy to acquiesce.'

'And would you like to record a message for your future husband?'

'I would, Tiffany.'

'I'm sure he'll treasure it. I know I will.'

Barbara composed herself.

'Craig, being asked to be your wife is the most singular honour in my life so far. I'm struggling to express my feelings so I apologise if this reply is shorter and more direct than I would have preferred. In answer to your upcoming question I would like to say this . . .' She paused as both she and Tiffany raised their middle fingers to the camera. Together they shouted: 'Fuck you, you cheating bastard!'

'I get the point!' Hodgkiss snapped.

'Wait, this is my favourite part,' Poe said.

Barbara continued, 'Craig, you limp-dicked, weak-willed fuckwit, I'd rather shit in my hands and clap than see your stupid girly face one more time. The clothes you left at mine are at Age Concern, your iPad's at Barnardo's and the spare key to your flat I gave to three homeless people this morning. I think they're there now.'

'Feeling better?' Tiffany asked.

'I'm a whole new woman,' Barbara replied. She looked at the camera again. 'Oh, one last thing: if I don't get my grandmother's ring back I'm going to the police.'

Flynn pressed pause.

Hodgkiss looked like he was going to be sick.

'Who-who's seen this . . . thing?'

'Me, my boss here, most of the investigation team,' Poe said.

'No one from work?'

Poe shrugged. 'I don't know. I'm not really up on social media.'

Flynn reclaimed the laptop and opened another tab. Facebook was already set up. The video was on Tiffany's page. It was called 'The Rise and Fall of Craig Hodgkiss'. She'd posted it before Barbara had opened her present.

'You tell me?' Poe said. 'What do all those likes and shares and comments mean?'

Hodgkiss burst into tears.

'She-she-she can't do that!'

38

'She has and it's not a bell that can be unrung.'

Flynn pressed play again. This time it was footage of the Secret Santa. Tiffany had recorded Barbara opening the present, holding up the mug without looking inside then turning it upside down. The screaming started immediately. Tiffany had followed the fingers to the floor, presumably because she'd thought it would be the ring. She held it for a few seconds before panning across to where Hodgkiss was seated.

He was wide-eyed in shock. His light-coloured jeans darkened at the crotch.

'I don't believe it, he's fucking pissed himself again,' Tiffany said off-camera.

Flynn paused the video. 'I think we've seen enough.'

'I understand it was your Secret Santa gift she opened,' Poe said.

Hodgkiss was staring aghast at the paused screen.

'Mr Hodgkiss, were you involved in this?'

'What . . .? No, of course I wasn't,' he replied. 'Is what those two bitches did legal? If it isn't, I'm pressing charges.'

'Grow up,' Poe said. 'They were mean to you, that's all. I suspect it was less than you deserved.'

'But . . . they've ruined my life. Who's going to want to have sex with me now?'

Poe slammed his fist on the table. Hodgkiss jumped.

'Enough!' he said. 'You can whine on your own time.'

'If this wasn't the gift you intended to give, Mr Hodgkiss, where's the one you *did* intend to give?' Flynn asked. Her tone was more moderate, more measured. Kinder. Just like they'd discussed before they went in. Good cop/bad cop was clichéd but occasionally useful.

'I-I-I don't know,' he replied. His brow furrowed. 'Actually, where *is* my mug? It still has Barbara's engagement ring inside.'

'The one you stole?' Poe said.

Hodgkiss nodded then realised what he'd done. 'It was the only way I could afford a nice one.'

Flynn clicked on a different file on the laptop. This time she showed Hodgkiss some CSI photographs. The first was of the paper the #BSC6 mug had been wrapped in, the four sheets of A4 with the bird design.

'Did you use bird pictures to wrap Barbara's mug?' Flynn asked.

It was an important question and one that had been missed so far. If Hodgkiss had used the same design, then he'd been selected. And, as most mugs came in the same size polystyrene protective boxes, if the killer had known what paper Hodgkiss was going to use, he could have swapped it anywhere and used him as an unwitting mule. He wouldn't have had to go anywhere near the John Bull Haulage office.

But, if he *hadn't* used the same bird design, then the killer would have had to risk entering the John Bull Haulage office in Carlisle. He'd selected Hodgkiss's mug at random, copied Barbara's name onto his own label, left his mug under the tree, and left with Hodgkiss's original.

Hodgkiss shook his head. 'That's not my paper.'

'You're sure?' Flynn said.

He nodded. 'Absolutely. My wrapping paper was from Celebrations on Bank Street. It had snowmen on it.'

So . . . the killer had been in all three crime scenes.

Chapter 8

Poe and Flynn arranged to meet Barbara Willoughby at her home. She lived in a flat in the centre of Carlisle. Tiffany would join them. Barbara answered the door in her pyjamas, a dressing gown and fluffy slippers. She wore no makeup and her hair was wet and slicked back.

Tiffany arrived shortly after. The two women hugged each other. They'd only worked together for a few months, but they'd been best friends since school.

'Tough times,' Poe said when they were seated.

'Tougher for him,' Tiffany said.

Poe nodded. 'No doubt.'

'Have you spoken to him?'

'We have.'

'How's he doing?' Barbara asked.

Tiffany said, 'You're kidding?'

'I don't wish him harm, Tiff. He's a shallow, shallow man, and his life was shit enough before all of this. I don't want to come to work one day to find out he's hanged himself.'

'Wouldn't bother me one fuck—'

'He'll survive,' Flynn cut in. 'The public order offence has been dropped and, unless you do actually report the theft of your grandmother's ring, his part in this is over.'

'The jeweller melted it down apparently,' Barbara said. 'I'm not pressing charges.'

'He did tell us the parcel you opened didn't have the same

41

wrapping paper as he'd used though,' Flynn said. 'That means that your Secret Santa gift was probably selected at random. Whoever did this must have broken into your office and swapped Craig's mug for his own.'

Barbara shook her head. 'If I didn't have bad luck I'd have no luck at all.'

Tiffany frowned. 'I doubt he broke in. The industrial estate has some high-value warehouses and businesses, and security is tight during the night. Dogs, mobile and static guards, the works. I know because we pay a percentage of their fees and I do their invoices.'

Barbara nodded. 'She's right.'

'And, although the office is open eight-till-six, the guys on the wagons don't keep those hours,' Tiffany said. 'The depot is open twenty-four hours a day. Breaking into the office would be next to impossible.'

'Could someone walk in unnoticed during the day?' Poe said.

Barbara and Tiffany considered it.

'Probably,' Tiffany said. 'We don't carry much petty cash and everything else is pretty much logistics for the guys downstairs. Tachograph filing, manifests, sales and the like. Nothing of value so we don't need strict security during the day.'

'How would they do it?'

'They'd have to check in with reception but they wouldn't be escorted upstairs.'

'Would a stranger hanging around the Christmas tree be noticed?' Poe said.

'Definitely,' Tiffany said.

He thought about it for a minute. 'Then he must have hidden in plain sight.'

The Newtown Road Industrial Estate was a five-minute drive from the flat. Rather than making Barbara get dressed, Tiffany said she would take them. CSI had finished with the office.

Tiffany let them in.

'That leads to the warehouse,' she said, pointing to a secure metal door. 'We're up here.'

She led them upstairs. The admin offices for John Bull Haulage were nondescript. A box-shaped main office had smaller individual rooms at the far end. Tiffany led them to a drab artificial Christmas tree. There was nothing underneath – Nightingale and her team had seized all the unopened presents.

'Talk me through where everyone was sitting,' Poe said.

Tiffany did just that. She asked Poe to be Hodgkiss, Flynn to be Barbara and she played herself. She didn't have a phone as it had been taken into evidence, so she held a stapler instead. They were seated in a horseshoe shape. She stood and told them what had happened.

'I kept switching between dickhead's face and Barbara's. I wanted to get her telling him to fuck off but I wanted his expression more. I filmed her opening it, his response to her tipping the mug, then I caught the fingers falling out.'

Flynn checked the laptop to make sure the video Tiffany had recorded matched with what she'd told them. It did. Poe sat back down and looked around, searching for anything out of the ordinary.

He saw it immediately.

He also knew everyone else had missed it.

'What's that?' he said, pointing at a chair away from the tree. It was loaded with cheap books and even cheaper toys.

'Oh, that's just the book man's stuff,' Tiffany replied. 'Every now and then people come in and leave samples of heavily discounted stuff for us to order.'

Poe knew what she meant. The SCAS office was cursed with the same thing. There was always a table or a chair filled with tat. The modern-day equivalent of the travelling salesman would turn up hawking a load of shit, dump it in a designated place, leave an order form then return a week later to collect the money and leave behind what had been bought.

He removed rubber gloves from his pocket and picked up the order form. There were a couple of names written down. An envelope was stapled to the back. Poe could feel the weight of coins inside.

'What is it, Poe?' Flynn asked.

He held it up.

'What's wrong with this?'

She frowned. She knew him well enough to know he'd found something. She also knew he'd give her the chance to make the connection.

Tiffany got there first.

'What type of weird-ass book man has a delivery date *after* Christmas?'

'Exactly.' He shook his head at the audacity of it all. 'Who is this guy?' he said.

Nightingale confirmed that the company the book man was from didn't exist. It looked like he'd bought some books from a bargain bookshop, knocked up an order form and walked into the offices of John Bull Haulage unchallenged. Book men went where they wanted at Christmas. It was possible he'd tried other businesses before he found one with an easily accessible Secret Santa tree with at least one mug-shaped gift underneath.

Nightingale put two detectives on it; the rest were re-interviewing anyone who'd been in the office the day the fake book man had dropped off his stuff.

Poe didn't hold out much hope. Eyewitnesses were notoriously unreliable. Attention is fleeting, recollection short-lived and memory is vulnerable to suggestion. And even if someone did remember him, the human brain isn't equipped to move from a mind's eye picture to an accurate verbal description.

Chapter 9

Poe wanted to see the food hall next. He wasn't expecting to get anything new but he wanted to keep moving. They'd just passed Cockermouth when Flynn's phone rang.

It was Bradshaw.

'You've arrived then? I need you to . . . What? No, the baby's fine, Tilly. Stop worrying. As I was say . . . Yes, Poe's fine too.'

Poe chose that moment to start coughing.

Flynn glanced at him. 'Well, fine-*ish*.' She paused to sigh and roll her eyes. 'I don't know if he's eaten fruit today, you'll have to ask him.'

Another pause.

'No, I won't put him on, he's driving. Ask him tonight.'

Poe blew his nose and suppressed a grin.

'OK, you do that,' Flynn said. 'We're going to Whitehaven now to see the crime scene.'

Another pause.

'Check into the North Lakes Hotel then book a small conference room we can work from . . . Yes, just the three of us . . . Yes, we'll need teas and coffees . . . If you want to get him some then order it . . . Just do what you think is best, Tilly. You know what we need.'

Flynn listened for a bit longer then said, 'OK, we'll see you soon.'

'She OK?' Poe asked.

'Yep. She's going to read up on everything then sort out a room we can meet in.'

'Good.'

'And she's ordering you some fruit.'

Poe knew and liked Whitehaven, a large coastal town in West Cumbria. It was the last place to be attacked by American naval forces during the War of Independence. Its port used to be the centre of the British rum trade. It is picturesque, crammed with Georgian buildings, and where the spree-killer Derrick Bird wreaked havoc in 2010.

It was where the real spirit of Cumbria could be found. Tough, no-nonsense men, and practical, unaffected women. A place where problems are solved with fists not solicitors, and rugby league is more important than football.

Fiskin's Food Hall was near the bus depot, at the port end of the town. Poe parked in their dedicated car park and they got out. The freezing sea air hit them immediately. A trawler must have just docked as he could smell fish. It was beginning to snow again and Poe didn't want to hang around. Whitehaven was in a natural cove and in extreme weather liable to be cut off. He had a maxim: if it was snowing *anywhere* in Cumbria, it was definitely snowing on Shap Fell, and Poe wanted to get home tonight.

They were about to make their way inside when Flynn's phone rang.

'OK, we'll be there,' she said after listening for a few seconds. She put her phone in her pocket. 'That was Nightingale. We're to go to Whitehaven nick and join a videoconference. You know where it is?'

'I do. You OK to walk? It's about five minutes away.'

She nodded.

'What's the conference for?' he said.

'Estelle Doyle has found something.'

46

Chapter 10

'OK, Professor Doyle,' Nightingale said, 'everyone who needs to hear this has managed to put themselves in front of a computer somewhere.'

Poe and Flynn watched Doyle nod in the jerky stop-motion way everyone did on videoconferences. Cops across the county would be watching the same thing.

'I know you're all very busy so I'll get straight to it,' Doyle said. 'I've found an anomaly: both female victims had minuscule traces of midazolam in their blood work.'

'Which is?' Nightingale said.

'It's a benzodiazepine commonly used to induce general anaesthetic.'

'They were asleep when their fingers were removed?' Nightingale asked incredulously.

Doyle shook her head. 'Definitely not. The amount I found indicates it had all but worn off. Whatever the reason for the anaesthetic, it wasn't anything to do with their fingers being removed.'

'What the hell is going on?' Nightingale said after Estelle Doyle had left the videoconference. 'Why does he put his female victims to sleep? What does he do to them while they're asleep? And why does he wait until they're awake to mutilate them?'

She paused.

'They weren't rhetorical questions!' she snapped.

'Sadist?' someone said.

'Only explains why he mutilates,' Nightingale said. 'Come on, people, we need ideas.'

If it weren't for the laptop's fan, the silence would have been absolute.

'Anything,' she insisted.

More silence.

'Hashtag BSC6 then? Are we closer to figuring out what that means?'

The only reason Poe had expected more silence was because he didn't know Bradshaw had just joined the videoconference.

'It's supposed to look like a social media tag, Superintendent Jo Nightingale,' she said, 'but if it is, it's *sui generis*.'

Poe couldn't see her – when Doyle had left the videoconference their computer screen had switched to Nightingale – but he'd recognise her voice anywhere.

'Who is this, please?' Nightingale said.

'Matilda Bradshaw,' she replied. 'I work with Detective Sergeant Washington Poe and Detective Inspector Stephanie Flynn of the National Crime Agency.'

'Ah, you're the analyst. Well, ma'am's just fine, Matilda.'

'OK, Detective Superintendent Jo Nightingale.'

Nightingale rolled her eyes.

'Tell us what you have, Matilda.'

'I get called Tilly.'

'Tell us what you have, Tilly. What does *sui generis* mean?'

'A hashtag is used on social media to draw attention to, or to facilitate a search for, a message or keyword. I've searched and there's nothing on any of the major platforms. It is therefore *sui generis*. One of a kind. Unique.'

'Perhaps our High-Tech Forensic Crime Unit will have more luck.'

'They won't.'

'If Tilly can't find it then it can't be found,' Poe said. 'You'll get used to her, ma'am, and then you'll be glad you did.'

'We'll revisit this later,' Nightingale said. 'Poe, you've got to grips with this quicker than anyone else. You must have a theory?'

'I can't begin to connect these dots, ma'am. All I have are questions.'

'Go on.'

'Estelle Doyle thinks he used rib shears to remove one pair of fingers. Yet he chose to use a hacksaw and scissors on the others. Why?'

No one said anything.

'And who the hell are the victims? It's Christmas; someone must be missing them. Why haven't they been reported AWOL?'

'I've asked all police stations in the north-west, north-east and south of Scotland to inform me the moment someone rings up about a missing loved one,' Nightingale said. 'I don't want anyone fobbed off with the "wait twenty-four hours" protocol. For now I think we need to focus on—'

The door to Conference Room A burst open and one of Nightingale's detectives ran in. He was out of breath.

'Ma'am,' he said. 'We've DNA-matched one of the victims.'

Chapter 11

The victim was called Howard Teasdale and he lived on the top floor of a townhouse in the higher part of Whitehaven. As they were already in town visiting Fiskin's Food Hall, Poe and Flynn arrived at Teasdale's address at the same time as the Whitehaven CID. Nightingale was being blue'd and two'd from Carleton Hall but she'd be another hour.

'Can't let you in yet,' the cop on the outer cordon said. 'It's an active crime scene and we're still securing it.'

'Were you first here?' Poe asked.

'Second.'

'What can you tell us?'

'Only that he's inside and it isn't pretty.'

Poe would have liked to question him further. The first officers at the scene often saw, smelled or sensed things that had disappeared by the time CSI and CID got there.

But the machine that is a large-scale murder investigation was beginning to be assembled. Pretty soon they were in the way. Poe and Flynn moved a few yards down the street and, after clearing it of snow, sat on a low garden wall. It had good views of the harbour below.

Sailing boats and fishing trawlers bobbed and creaked, tugging at their moorings. Some harbours are bitten from the land by men, deep channels dredged and cleared and deepened wherever they were needed. Not Whitehaven. Whitehaven harbour was naturally occurring. Until ports with larger shipping capacities, such as Liverpool and Bristol, began to take over its main trade, Whitehaven had been one of the most important ports in the country. It had been renovated as part of the millennium developments and was quite beautiful. Even in December people were sitting on benches sipping coffee and eating chips.

Seagulls the size of chickens wheeled overhead, flashes of white in the dark sky, occasionally swooping down to brazenly snatch food from the unwary. Although they could be a menace, Poe liked seagulls. Without their squawks and cries, the air above the harbour would be empty, the same way the fells had been when the 2001 foot-and-mouth crisis had decimated whole bloodlines of sheep.

'Come on, let's go and get a brew,' Flynn said. 'This wall's playing havoc with my haemorrhoids.'

An hour later Nightingale called to say the video walkthrough of the scene and the crime scene manager's evidence recovery strategy were complete. She could allow them in.

'What do we know?' Flynn asked when they got there. They were both out of breath. The road from the harbour to the townhouse had been steep.

'It's a bit different in there,' she said. 'His name's Howard Teasdale and he was a freelance website designer.'

'Why was his DNA on the database?' Poe said.

'He was convicted of making and distributing indecent images of children earlier in the year. Got twenty-four months' probation, a sex offenders' course and a SOPO prohibiting him from accessing the internet for anything other than work.'

Poe nodded. Sex offender prevention orders were a commonly used tool to manage DBs, or dirty bastards to give them their full name. He didn't know much about web design but he knew you couldn't do it without the internet.

'You think we're looking for a vigilante?'

Nightingale shrugged. 'I'm not prepared to rule anything out.'

CSI had put anti-contamination stepping plates down. They were transparent plastic with a slip-resistant tread. The rubber pads on the bottom of each foot would be removed and bagged as evidence when CSI had finished.

Poe took his time and followed Nightingale into Teasdale's dining room. Flynn trailed after them both. He was surprised. It was one thing to insist she was fit to work while heavily pregnant to make a point, another thing entirely to fall off a footplate because she was less certain on her feet.

'See what I mean about it being different?' Nightingale said.

Poe did.

Teasdale had been secured to a wooden chair with zip-ties. He had been a fat man – the kind who could have used a sports bra – and the ties had dug into his fleshy wrists and ankles. One of his hands was clenched into a fist, as if he'd been in pain when he died. The other was open. It was missing two fingers.

His mouth was partially open, his lips were covered in shiny cold sores. His T-shirt was stained red. A pair of bloodied kitchen scissors rested in his lap. Poe wasn't surprised to learn that Doyle had been right about the method of amputation.

Flynn retched. She rushed out before she could contaminate anything.

'Women, eh?' a CSI man laughed.

'It's pregnancy-related chronic indigestion,' Poe said, 'and if your face is still here in ten seconds I'm punching it.'

'Excuse me?'

'You heard.'

Nightingale gave Poe an appraising look.

'I'd leave if I were you, Andrews,' she said. 'Apologise to DI Flynn on your way out, then go back to Carleton Hall and wait for me.'

After the CSI tech had left, Poe said, 'I can't see the wound that killed him.'

Nightingale gently lifted Teasdale's head and showed him a thin ligature wound around his neck. It had cut through the skin, hence the blood-stained T-shirt.

'Looks like he's been strangled,' she said.

'Garrotted more like,' Poe grunted.

'You think?'

'Estelle Doyle will be able to confirm it.'

He studied Teasdale's bedsit, looking for inconsistencies. It was filled with the debris of a lonely life. Takeaway containers, pizza boxes and empty energy drinks were piled on the kitchen counter. Coffee mugs with green mould at the bottom had been abandoned in the sink. The bin was overflowing and smelly. The tiling at the back of the cooker was covered in grime.

The only things Teasdale appeared to care about were his video games. He had hundreds of them. They were neatly stacked on two bookcases. A third bookcase held his controllers. Poe looked for the consoles and found them. A PS4 and an Xbox.

'He was in breach of his SOPO just by having these,' Nightingale said. 'They're both internet-enabled. Anything?'

'Maybe,' Poe said.

'What?'

'The smell, it's unusual.'

'Why?'

'What's the dominant one?'

Nightingale sniffed the air the same way Edgar did.

'Faeces,' she said. 'He voided his bowels when he died.'

Poe shook his head. 'He's been dead a few days, why doesn't he smell gamey?'

'I don't know.'

'It's because he was on an electricity meter and the money's run out. That's why it's so cold in here.'

'You're right,' she said.

'He obviously never left his bedsit so he'd have needed his heating on permanently. Coupled with his electricity-heavy entertainment choices, he'd have been putting coins into it like a fruit machine.'

'What's your point?'

'All this took time. Hours probably. The killer had to secure Teasdale then wait to make sure he hadn't been overheard. Cutting through his fingers with those scissors will have taken an hour at least. Although the actual killing wouldn't have taken long, he'd have been covered in blood. No way did he leave Teasdale's bedsit without cleaning himself up.'

'You think we need to check the shower?'

'I think you need to check the electricity meter,' Poe said. 'Unless the killer did all this and then cleaned himself in the dark, it's entirely possible he'd had to put some money in just to see what he was doing.'

'And we might get a fingerprint.'

'Why not?'

'Do electricity meters even use coins any more?'

Her phone buzzed.

'We'll check it out, Poe,' she said before answering. 'Superintendent Nightingale.'

She frowned as she listened.

'OK, thanks.'

She turned to Poe.

'We may have identified another victim.'

Chapter 12

Not found. Identified.

A man called Andrew Pridmore had called 101, the police non-emergency number, and said he couldn't get in touch with his ex-wife. He was supposed to arrange a drop-off time for their kids and he was worried she'd done something stupid. The family court judge had given her less access than she'd wanted and she'd taken it hard. He lived in Reading and wanted uniform to go round to her house in Carlisle to check she was OK.

The woman in the control room at Carleton Hall had been briefed on Estelle Doyle's findings and knew that one of the victims had had a finger tattoo removed. She asked Pridmore if his ex-wife had any distinguishing features.

'She had our wedding date tattooed on, then lasered off her finger,' she'd been told. Pridmore then added that she still wore her ring when she was with their children as it upset them when she didn't.

Nightingale had to stay with the dead man – a corpse at a crime scene required her attention more than what might just be an unrelated missing person's case – so she asked Flynn if she and Poe could attend. Uniform had already secured the woman's house and CSI were processing it.

Poe was pleased when Flynn readily agreed. He rarely got to see fresh crime scenes these days. It wasn't what SCAS did.

Rebecca Pridmore lived in Dalston, six miles west of Carlisle. It was an affluent village with a population of two and a half thousand. The inappropriately named 'The Square', which was actually a triangle lined with shops, pubs and a church, was the beating heart of the village.

Her bungalow was on The Green, Dalston's main thoroughfare. It was three hundred yards from The Square. Opposite was a field and the River Caldew. To the rear was another field. The bungalow was set back from the road and had a large gravel drive. The front was bordered by a chest-high stone wall.

Dalston rarely saw serious crime and the presence of so many police vehicles was causing a commotion. Villagers had lined up to stare. A uniformed cop kept them from getting too close. He was wearing gloves, had red ears and was stamping his feet against the pavement. Sentry duty in the cold sucked.

Although the drive would have fitted five cars comfortably, all police vehicles were parked on the opposite side of the road. Poe pulled up behind a CSI van.

A detective called Pearson met them at the gate.

'Anything?' Poe asked.

'Nothing,' he said. 'No sign of a break-in.'

'How'd you get in?'

'Smashed a window.'

'No sign of a struggle?'

Pearson shook his head.

'And she's not just out on the piss with the girls?' Flynn asked.

'Until we get a DNA match, all we're going on is that she's had a finger tattoo removed and she isn't at home.'

'Fair enough,' Flynn said. 'Can we go inside?'

'I'll get you some suits.'

Rebecca's front door was rustic and huge. It was painted white and hung from three iron hinges. Pearson was right: no way could it have been forced. Poe doubted even the battering rams the police used would have had any effect on it. It had an old-style keyhole, stark black against the white paint. Above it was a modern deadbolt lock. The windows were double-glazed, the type you can't force from the outside without leaving a mess of evidence.

Poe hadn't seen the whole of the house yet but he knew the back would be just as secure as the front. He wasn't surprised by the level of security – Nightingale had told them that Rebecca Pridmore was a Ministry of Defence contracts manager at BAE Systems in Barrow. BAE was one of the largest defence and security companies in the world. They had fifty sites in the UK alone. The site at Barrow had produced all but three of the Royal Navy's nuclear submarines.

When they were suited and booted, Poe and Flynn walked into Rebecca's bungalow. It was the polar opposite of Howard Teasdale's bedsit. Whereas his had been a glorified man cave, this was a home.

It had country charm but with the modern conveniences of city living. Modern paintings hung from the wall in the narrow hallway. It bisected the bungalow. A door on the left led them into an open kitchen and lounge area.

The kitchen was at the rear. It was lit by wall-mounted, half-globe lamps and had stainless steel appliances, an American-style double-door fridge and a polished marble counter. Utensils hung from ceiling hooks; an island in the middle had a large chopping board and a professional knife set. Fresh herbs lined the windowsill and a spice rack was fixed to one of the walls.

The only nod to the past was the Aga. It was squat against the wall, in between the double sink and the Bosch dishwasher. Peeling cream enamel but cared for nonetheless. Heavier than the car they'd arrived in. Solid and dependable, you didn't get an Aga if you wanted to do precision baking: you got an Aga when you wanted the kitchen to be the heart of the home. If Poe had had enough room he'd have bought an Aga years ago.

The floor was tiled but the stepping plates had rubber feet and didn't slip. Poe opened a few cupboards but nothing stood out. The fridge was stocked, but not in the way most fridges were this time of year. There were no leftovers, no drinks chilling. No fancy cheeses or chocolate truffles. If Rebecca Pridmore had celebrated Christmas, it hadn't been at home. He made a note to check her computer for hotel bookings.

The lounge area was at the front of the bungalow. It was a room for living in. Seats and a sofa pointed at a wall-mounted LCD television. Her glass coffee table had a Jo Malone diffuser and some silver coasters on it.

A beautiful mahogany desk with a closed laptop in the middle was clearly her home office. The stepping plates only went up to the front of the desk but Poe wanted to check the drawers. He waited for CSI to put down more plates.

The desk had six drawers, three either side of the leg space. Poe pulled them, only the top right was unlocked. It was empty save some foam lining.

'May I?' he asked, pointing at the laptop.

'It's been photographed but the contents haven't been checked,' Pearson said. 'We're not even allowed to move it. The MoD are sending someone to collect it tomorrow.'

Poe picked up the laptop, turned it upside down and studied the foam in the drawer. He nodded in satisfaction then turned to Flynn.

'Please tell Superintendent Nightingale that Rebecca Pridmore *has* been abducted.'

'You sure?'

'The drawer's where her laptop lives when it's not being used.' He pointed at four round indentations in the foam. 'You can see the witness marks from the adhesive feet. No way someone this security conscious leaves her laptop out when she's away.'

'It does suggest abduction rather than a spa break,' Flynn admitted. 'I'll call Jo now.'

Poe studied the family photographs on the mantelpiece. They were mainly of her kids mugging for the camera. Some were of their birthdays, some were school portraits. Others were fragments of their lives. Rebecca was in all the family ones, Andrew, her ex-husband, was in a few. Probably included him so the kids didn't get upset.

Poe stepped into the kitchen area and looked out of the back window. Flynn walked in, eyes down as she navigated the stepping plates. She was still on the phone.

'That's what he thinks as well,' she said.

Poe raised his eyebrows and Flynn gestured towards the laptop.

He glanced over to the mahogany desk. He hadn't looked at the lounge area from the back of the house. The angle was different and this time he could see the shadows of indentations in the carpet. Four of them, square-shaped, not unlike the indentations in the foam in the drawer.

He frowned. There was nothing obvious in the lounge that could have caused them. But there was from where he was standing.

'Hard to say at this point,' Flynn said, giving him a 'what's up' reverse head nod. 'She's been reported missing by her ex-husband and the laptop indicates she left suddenly. On the other hand, there's no sign of forced entry. And believe me, this isn't a place you can get into without leaving evidence.'

Poe carried over one of Rebecca's high-backed kitchen stools and held it above the indentations. The legs matched exactly. He tried to look out of the front and rear windows. He couldn't – the stool had been positioned so it couldn't be observed from outside the house. He studied the stool but saw nothing obvious. He brought it back to the kitchen bar and checked the other one.

There was a one-inch scuff mark on the varnish on each arm and the front two legs. If someone had been struggling while zip-tied these were the marks they'd have left.

It looked like the killer *had* been in the house. But he'd then waited before moving her somewhere else. Why take the risk? Why hadn't he moved her straight away?

His thought process was interrupted as a tractor rattled its way past the front of the house. The silence it left was immediately filled with the sound of people chatting. Poe walked over to the window. He could just see the top of a bus-stop sign. The bus must be due soon.

And that, of course, was the answer: he hadn't been able to move her, not during daylight. Dalston was a busy village – if he'd tried to move her during the day he'd have been seen. But, if he'd had the balls to wait until the sun had set and the buses stopped running, he'd have had a better chance of getting her out unobserved.

Flynn was still talking to Nightingale. 'I'd say she *could* be who we're looking—'

'Boss,' Poe interrupted.

'Just a minute, Jo. What is it, Poe?'

'I'm almost certain Rebecca Pridmore *is* one of the victims. Our man found a way to get inside, zip-tied her to this kitchen stool and held her captive until nightfall.'

Chapter 13

Flynn got a lift with uniform to go and meet Nightingale.

Poe stayed behind. He couldn't work out how the killer had got inside. The door locks were anti-snap and drill resistant and, although an expert could have picked them, it would have taken time. From what Poe knew of the killer he didn't expose himself like that. He preferred to blend in.

He could have bluffed his way into her house. Pretended to be a utilities man or a courier service with a parcel. Certainly doable, but with someone as security conscious as Rebecca it would have needed supporting logistics. A van with the right markings, a uniform and ID card. And a utilities or courier bluff would have had to be carried out during the day on a busy road in front of nosey neighbours with nothing else to do but remember things.

Poe retraced his steps. He left the lounge and went outside. The wind wasn't strong but it was biting. Ice crystals had reformed over the footprints they'd left on the doorstep. Poe reckoned the temperature was still a few degrees below zero. He hoped whoever was in charge of securing the crime scene took that into account and put everyone outside on shorter shifts. Nothing sapped vigilance like cold feet.

He checked the windows on the side of the bungalow. They were all closed and undamaged. There was no access to the back garden from the front, not without climbing a six-foot wall. He was wondering what to do next when the house phone rang.

Poe made his way inside, removing his BlackBerry as he did so. He began recording. He checked his watch.

'House phone ringing at 15:05. Detective Sergeant Washington Poe answering it.'

The house phone was wireless and slim. Poe pressed the green button and held it and his BlackBerry to his ear.

'Hello?'

There was a pause.

'Er . . . hello, who's this?'

Poe told him.

'This is Andrew Pridmore, Rebecca's ex-husband. I called the police earlier today. I didn't think you'd take it this seriously.'

'Why's that?' Poe said.

'Well . . . she's not been missing that long. I thought the police had to wait forty-eight hours or something before they investigated.'

'We take all calls of missing people seriously, Mr Pridmore. Is there anything you can tell us that may help? Anything we might not know.'

'I'm not sure.'

'What contracts did she manage at BAE?'

'Something to do with the strategic weapon systems on the new nuclear subs, I think.'

'Did she ever talk about her work?'

'Wasn't allowed to. I doubt I would have understood anyway.'

'Had she mentioned any new relationships or friendships recently?'

'She hadn't.'

'Would she have?'

'We had a rough time when the family court judge gave me custody of the kids but she's quite pragmatic. She has no family in Cumbria and works incredibly long hours – in her heart she knew she couldn't offer them the home they deserved. She'd have told me if she was seeing anyone.'

'So you get on?'

'Better than we did when we were married. The pressure was off to impress each other all the time, I think.'

Poe took a moment to gather his thoughts. 'Did she have any interests outside work?'

'Not unless feeding birds counted. If she wasn't at work she was reading about work.'

'Birds?'

'She liked to feed the birds in the garden. She would sit in the kitchen with her laptop sometimes and watch them. Spent a fortune on seed, mealworms and fat balls.'

Poe hadn't been in the utility room yet. If Rebecca kept bird food it would be in there. He couldn't see how it was relevant but he would check anyway.

He finished with Pridmore and hung up.

CSI hadn't yet put stepping plates in the utility room and Poe called them in to do so. Pearson, the detective in charge, followed them.

'What's up?' he asked.

'Probably nothing,' Poe replied. 'Just dotting an I.'

After CSI had readied the utility room and completed a cursory search and video walkthrough, Poe and Pearson were cleared to enter.

The room was narrow and an obvious extension to the main building. A large bench ran the length of the wall with the windows. Underneath sat a washing machine, a tumble dryer and two closed units. Coat hooks lined the wall that – pre-extension – would have been external. Some had jackets on, most didn't. Underneath were wellies and outdoor shoes. The door to the back garden was on the right. The wall on the left had a wall-mounted ironing board.

Poe opened the unit next to the washing machine. It contained washing powder and fabric softeners, two bottles of bleach and spare toilet rolls.

Pearson watched without comment.

Poe opened the other unit. He'd been right. It was where she kept the bird food. There was enough to suggest it was a serious hobby. She had pre-bought mixes but also Tupperware boxes with handwritten labels: finches (winter); wood pigeons (breeding season); high fat (extreme cold).

Poe counted ten boxes, all with different concoctions. There were spare plastic feeders and books on garden birds and wildlife. There was also a pair of binoculars and a notepad recording the species she'd seen in her garden. Poe flicked through it. She had been visited by over one hundred species, it seemed, from the humble sparrow to a goshawk.

'What's it mean?' Pearson asked.

'Nothing,' Poe said, putting everything back. 'It was just something her ex-husband said. Thought it was worth checking out.'

Poe looked into the back garden. The light was fading but he counted eleven feeders hanging from trees and shrubs, and another seven on the dedicated bird feeder she had. More fat balls than anything else – fat was what the birds needed at this time of year.

A large, stone birdbath dominated the middle of the lawn.

With the birdwatching hobby a dead end, Poe followed Pearson back into the kitchen.

'What do you think happened here, Sergeant Poe?' Pearson asked.

'I'm not sure. Nothing makes sense. If he's selecting victims at random, why choose a hard target like Rebecca? Security conscious and lives in a village with high foot traffic. And why take her, but leave Howard Teasdale in situ?'

'Teasdale was a fat man. Perhaps he was too heavy to abduct. Or he could be adapting,' Pearson said. 'Maybe killing Howard Teasdale didn't do for him what he thought it would.'

'Possibly. Although we can't assume that the order the fingers were found is the order the victims were killed or abducted.'

'Maybe Rebecca Pridmore is the only one that matters then. He's hiding her murder among two others?'

'Maybe,' Poe agreed. He'd heard worse theories. He thumbed Bradshaw a text asking her to profile BAE. He also told her that she would be with him in the morning. If he wasn't allowed to remove Rebecca's laptop from her home, Bradshaw would have to forensically examine it where it was.

Before he read her immediate response his phone rang. It was Flynn.

'They've identified the third victim, Poe.'

Chapter 14

The third victim was called Amanda Simpson. 'Mandi' to her friends. She was twenty-five years old and worked as a retail assistant in Barrow. Her boyfriend was in the Duke of Lancaster's Regiment. He was serving in Cyprus and hadn't heard from her over the Christmas period. He'd called her estranged family and asked if they would check she was OK.

They couldn't find her.

Her boyfriend then emailed a mate he'd gone to school with who was now a cop. The cop had called it in and Nightingale had sent two of her team to check it out. Amanda lived in a one-bedroomed flat in a part of Barrow with a large student population. Poe knew the area but not well.

After they'd established that she was missing, the detectives checked the photographs on her fridge and the borders of her dressing-table mirror, searching for anything that could identify her as a potential victim. There weren't many photographs as she lived her life online. Nightingale hadn't sent two idiots, though. They contacted the boyfriend and got the passwords for her electronic devices.

It was in a photograph on her iPad that they found what they hoped they wouldn't. Amanda and her boyfriend were having a meal out somewhere. Abroad, judging by their clothes and suntans.

She was holding a glass of fizz.

And one of her fingernails was pierced with the same teddy

bear stud they'd found in the font in Saint Luke's Church in Barrow . . .

As soon as he ended the call with Flynn, Poe's phone rang again. It was Nightingale.

'How you getting on at Rebecca's house?'

'I'll be back with Tilly tomorrow to check her laptop, but otherwise I'm nearly done.'

'And you're OK?'

'I am.'

For several moments she was silent.

'What are you after, ma'am?' Poe asked. No way was this just a welfare call.

'I'm a good superintendent, Poe,' she said eventually. 'And that means I know when to say I'm struggling.'

Poe said nothing. That couldn't have been easy.

'I'll follow the murder manual and I'll call in all the special ists I can think of. I'll run a thorough, methodical investigation and if that's how we catch this bastard then great, but me and you both know there's something odd going on here.'

'To put it mildly,' Poe agreed.

'How has he chosen his victims? Why did he abduct two of them? And why did the female victims have anaesthetic in their system? Why use a surgical tool on one but not the others? Why stage body parts over three consecutive days and then go quiet? Is he sending a message? Has he finished? Is he only just getting started? And what the hell is hashtag BSC6?'

Poe let her vent. It was useful to hear someone else voice what he was thinking anyway.

'What can I do for you, ma'am?'

'DS Ian Gamble told me you're the best he'd ever seen at finding what doesn't want to be found. At following the evidence, not the story.'

'I'm sure he was exaggerating,' Poe replied.

'I'm bloody not. He said you're a contrarian but I think that's what I need right now. My team and I will continue to investigate but I want you . . . I want you to do the things we won't. Talk to the people we can't, look for the things we'd miss. In short just do what you did in the Immolation Man case.'

'I hardly—'

'Find me something I can fucking use, Poe,' she snapped, and hung up.

He stared at his phone for almost a minute. He then sent a text to Bradshaw saying he would pop into the North Lakes Hotel soon and could she meet him in the lobby. He sent another to Flynn asking if she had time to meet when she was finished with Amanda Simpson. Finally, he sent a text to his neighbour, Victoria, asking if she could keep hold of Edgar for an extra night.

Within a minute all three had said yes.

Chapter 15

Flynn had arrived at the hotel an hour after Poe. She looked exhausted.

She must have had the same conversation with Nightingale as he'd had, as she said, 'Where do you want to put yourself tomorrow, Poe?'

'I want Tilly to examine Rebecca's laptop, boss.'

'Why?'

'It'll be protected with MoD encryption. No way the High-Tech lot in Cumbria will be able to open it.'

'You ever consider that we're not *meant* to open something like that?'

'Not for a second,' Poe replied. 'And I'm not interested in her work. There's nothing to suggest that's how the victims are being chosen.'

'Then why examine her computer?'

'Amanda Simpson's abduction would have been simple enough. Straight in and out in an area with a low population at this time of year. And Howard Teasdale's murder, well . . . he was a registered sex offender with an Xbox. Total recluse by the looks of things. If he wasn't at the takeaway the chances were he'd be at home whacking off.'

'What's your point?'

'I can see how he did it with Amanda and Howard but I can't with Rebecca. I don't know how he broke into her house and I don't know how he knew when she'd be in. The front of her house is on a main road and a six-foot wall protects the rear. All her doors and windows have modern, burglar-proof locks.'

'So?'

'So I need Tilly to see if she'd emailed anyone her work schedule or any other appointments she had,' Poe said. 'The only way I can see it happening is if the killer knew exactly when she'd be leaving her house. It's possible he simply rushed her and bundled her back inside.'

'That doesn't sound like the man we're after.'

'It doesn't,' Poe agreed, 'but it's all I've got.'

'Do it then,' Flynn said.

She then talked them through what they knew about Amanda Simpson. It didn't take long. They had a three-day window for her abduction – the time she was last seen and the missed Skype chat with her boyfriend. The working theory was that she'd been taken from her flat. Because students went home for Christmas, only Amanda and an old man on the top floor had been in during that period. CCTV didn't cover the flats but Nightingale had a team combing through the town's cameras anyway. They weren't expecting anything. This killer was only seen when he wanted to be.

Flynn said, 'Estelle Doyle's scheduled Howard Teasdale's post-mortem for the day after tomorrow. Perhaps we'll know more then.'

'Perhaps,' Poe said.

'What have you been working on, Tilly?'

'I've been profiling Howard Teasdale, DI Flynn,' Bradshaw replied. 'I've emailed you both my initial report but I'm not sure how helpful it is. He spent more time playing online games than I do.'

'OK, I'll look at it later tonight,' Flynn said. 'Are you going to draw up profiles on the other two victims now that we know who they are?'

'I will.'

'After you've examined Rebecca's laptop you'd better base yourself here. It'll save you traipsing across Cumbria with Poe.'

'I *like* traipsing across Cumbria with Poe.'

Poe stifled a grin.

Flynn sighed. 'My feet are fucking killing me and my ankles are twice the size they normally are. Can we skip ahead to where we've had the argument and I've won but Tilly does whatever she pleases anyway?'

'Sounds about right,' Poe said.

'Good, because I need to lie down for a while.'

When Flynn had left, Poe said, 'Go and get some rest, Tilly – we're gonna Sherlock the fuck out of this thing tomorrow.'

Bradshaw giggled.

'Classic Poe. That's so going on Twitter.'

'No it bloody isn't,' he said.

It was dark when Poe got back to Herdwick Croft. It was cold and empty. He wished he'd stopped to get Edgar. The spaniel brought the croft to life the same way seagulls did at the coast.

He'd collected his mail from reception at Shap Wells Hotel. Because the ancient stone cottage was inaccessible by car and, as the postman had point-blank refused to yomp over two miles of rugged moorland to deliver it every day, he'd come to an arrangement with the hotel to have his mail delivered there.

Poe flicked through it while he swigged a bottle of beer. The last letter was a copy of one sent to his solicitor by the council's legal department. They wanted Poe's availability for court.

They were pressing ahead with their eviction.

Poe had been fleeced with the purchase of Herdwick Croft. Victoria's father, Thomas Hume, had told him it was for sale because of an unexpected council tax demand. He'd offered it to Poe at a knockdown price. Peaceful, isolated, simple – it had everything Poe had ever wanted and he'd turned it from a derelict shepherd's croft into a home he thought he'd never leave.

But the real reason behind the sale was that Thomas Hume's planning permission to convert it into a home had been refused. It was worthless. Poe had applied for retrospective planning permission, but since the Lake District National Park had been extended to include Shap Fell, and more recently been given UNESCO status, the chances of success were lower than sheep shit in a tyre track.

Poe's time at Herdwick Croft was borrowed.

He twisted the letter, put a match to it, and used it to light his wood-burning stove. He finished his beer, made himself a beef sandwich then sat down with his notes. He couldn't shake the feeling that he'd missed something at Rebecca's bungalow. Something had either been there that shouldn't, or wasn't there that should have been. He reran his steps and studied the photographs he'd taken but he saw nothing out of the ordinary.

He knew how his mind worked and it was pointless trying to force it. It would either come or it wouldn't.

When his eyes started to tire he decided he'd be serving the investigation best by getting some sleep. He tidied up then put some water in his espresso maker so it was ready to go in the morning.

He frowned then picked up one of the photographs of the kitchen. He saw the discrepancy immediately.

'Where's her bloody kettle?' he muttered.

Chapter 16

The journey to Rebecca's bungalow the following morning took longer than expected. A freezing fog was suffocating Shap Fell and the dips and sinkholes simmered like witches' cauldrons. It was impossible to judge how deep they were and, despite knowing the route well, Poe exercised caution – if he came a cropper he would likely die of exposure before anyone found him.

By the time he got to the outskirts of Carlisle the mist had disappeared and the sun was low and dazzling. It was the type of weather where you needed sunglasses but felt silly wearing them.

Bradshaw was waiting for him at the side of the road. CSI had finished processing Rebecca's bungalow during the night and their vans were no longer parked outside. A lone uniformed constable stood at the entrance of the driveway. He watched them approach then bent down to retrieve a clipboard protected by a clear plastic sheet. Poe and Bradshaw showed him their IDs then waited for him to radio it in. When he received authority, he told them they were free to go in.

'Door's not locked,' he said as they walked past.

Other than the millions of particles of fingerprint dust that hung in the air, the bungalow looked the same as it had the day before. Poe walked Bradshaw over to the laptop. Before she could open it and get stuck into its guts, he gave her a bit of context.

'The laptop has been left for you to examine, Tilly. Rebecca Pridmore was a senior contracts officer with the MoD and was currently working on some sort of strategic weapons system for nuclear submarines. On her laptop there will be any number of interesting things – most of which will lead us down blind alleys if we let them. Your job is to separate the interesting from the important.'

He paused to let it sink in.

'Jeez, Poe, and you say *I'm* a dork . . .'

'Just tell me if she was hacked, will you?' he said. 'The killer was on a tight schedule and I need to know how he knew when she'd be at home.'

The laptop was password protected. Bradshaw opened one of her own laptops and before long she had cables running between them. In two minutes Rebecca's MoD-encrypted laptop was unlocked.

Poe left her to it. She was oblivious to him now anyway.

The day before, when he'd been searching the bungalow, he'd been restricted in where he could look by where CSI had put down their stepping plates. Now that the scene had been processed he could go anywhere he wanted.

And he had a kettle to find.

Which he failed to do.

'What are you looking for, Poe?' Bradshaw said.

'I can't find her kettle.'

'There's a café not far from here. Shall I go and get you a black coffee?'

'I meant it's bothering me that I can't find it.'

'Lots of people don't have a kettle, Poe.'

'I don't know a single person who doesn't have a kettle,' he said.

'You don't have one.'

'I have a pot I use.'

'Maybe she has a pot she uses.'

'Perhaps,' he said, looking round the sleek, modern kitchen, 'but I doubt it.'

The sound of clacking stopped.

Bradshaw said, 'There's nothing obvious on her laptop. If she's been hacked then my program hasn't been able to spot it. And as I wrote the program I'm confident in saying that she hasn't been hacked.'

'Bollocks,' he said. He'd not expected to find anything but he was still disappointed.

'I'll run the program again using slightly different search parameters, but . . .'

A tall man had entered the room. He had a stiff walk, like he'd eaten some bad prawns. He didn't see Poe so approached Bradshaw.

'I'm looking for Detective Sergeant Washington Poe,' he said.

Bradshaw looked up, flashed him an on-off smile and said, 'OK.'

She went back to her laptop. Poe grinned. Sometimes Bradshaw appeared normal, but it never lasted long.

'Excuse me, young lady!' the tall man snapped. His throat rattled cancerously when he breathed in. 'When I ask you a question, you'll answer me!'

Bradshaw looked up in astonishment. Poe nipped out from the kitchen area and stood in front of the man. He had a blotchy face and ears like a gremlin. He looked startled by his sudden appearance.

'Apologise,' Poe said.

The man's blotches became more pronounced. 'She's touching MoD property; I'll speak to her any damn way I choose!'

Poe took a step forwards. Put his nose six inches from the man's. 'Look into my fucking eyes.'

The man backed off and held up his arms in supplication. He turned to Bradshaw and said, 'I'm sorry.'

Bradshaw shrugged and went back to the laptop.

'He didn't even ask a question,' she muttered. 'How was I supposed to answer him?'

'I'm afraid I'm going to have to ask you to stop doing that, miss,' he said. He flipped open a black wallet and showed Poe an ID card.

'Malcolm Sparkes. Ministry of Defence. Security,' he said.

'You're here for the laptop?'

'I am. And there's no point trying to unlock it – it has military-grade security.'

'How long did it take you, Tilly?' Poe said.

'Ninety-seven seconds, Poe.'

'Nonsense,' Sparkes said.

Bradshaw turned the laptop around and showed him a clearly unlocked screen.

'But-but how . . .?' he said.

Bradshaw ignored him.

'What can you tell me about Mrs Pridmore?' Poe said.

'Other than she's in big trouble when she gets back to work, nothing.'

'Why's she in trouble?'

'She's obviously not using our security.' Sparkes couldn't stop staring at the unlocked computer.

'She was.'

'She was what?'

'She *was* using the laptop security. Tilly is just better than the people who designed it. And she isn't in trouble because this is a murder investigation.'

'Murder? I thought it was a missing persons case.'

'Not any more.'

'You're sure?'

'We are. We're trying to find out how the killer knew she'd be at home.'

Poe talked him through what they knew so far.

'Hashtag BSC6?' Sparkes said.

'You don't know what it means, do you?'

'No idea.'

'Are you going to let us do our job?'

Sparkes nodded. 'But can I ask that I supervise what your analyst is doing, and if I think she's getting into sensitive areas can I ask her to stop?'

That didn't seem unreasonable, and Poe said as much. Bradshaw had probably got everything she needed by now anyway.

'What can you tell me about her job?' Poe said.

'Not everything, obviously, but basically Rebecca was our man on the ground, as it were. Contract management is done at a pretty high level but we still need people to work on site.'

'What exactly did she do?'

'The contract she was managing was for the strategic weapons system on the new SSBNs being built.'

'SSBN?'

'Ship Submersible Ballistic Nuclear,' Sparkes replied. 'Submarines basically. The navy has two types of nuclear-powered subs – those that are armed with Trident and those that aren't. SSBNs are the former. The Dreadnoughts being built now are replacing the current Vanguard class. As well as managing the contract, Rebecca was responsible for liaising with everyone involved.'

'Everyone at BAE?'

'As well as the Royal Navy and the MoD. Even the Yanks.'

'The Americans? I thought BAE only built British subs,' Poe said.

'They do, but the Americans own the design for the Trident D5 missiles and they need to know that our subs will be compatible with theirs.'

Poe processed what he'd been told. He still didn't think Rebecca was murdered because of her work but it seemed she interacted with far more people than he'd first assumed. He briefly wondered if DC Pearson had been right: that the other murders were to disguise the one that mattered. Hiding her murder in a serial killing investigation. It had been done before. It was something to keep in mind.

'Which program did you use to breach her computer?' Sparkes asked Bradshaw. 'I'd better report we're vulnerable to it. Make sure our tech-heads can write in a fix.'

Bradshaw shrugged. 'It doesn't have a name.'

'Where did you get it then?'

'I wrote it.'

'So, you're good at this computer stuff?'

'I'm good at everything,' she said. And with that she lost interest and went back to what she was doing.

Poe pulled Sparkes away. 'Better to let her get on with it. If it's any comfort there won't be another program like hers and she assures me Rebecca wasn't hacked.'

'That's a relief, I suppose.' He kept glancing over at Bradshaw. 'I'll still need to make a phone call.'

'That's one way to get rid of him,' Poe said after he'd left.

Bradshaw nodded without looking up.

'There's no kettle but I can get you a drink of water if you want?'

'Yes, please, Poe.'

Poe turned on the tap and stared out of the window while he waited for the water to get nice and icy. When you drew it directly from the ground like he did you kind of got spoiled when it came to meat locker-cold water.

A bunch of starlings flew in and settled on the largest tree in the garden. It was stripped of foliage and colour, little more than a skeleton. Winter was the comma in the year. It stripped the land of colour and joy but without it there would be no spring – the plants and trees needed time to rest.

There was nothing wrong with helping the animals through

the colder months, though. He did it at Herdwick Croft by leaving out bacon rind and Rebecca did it here with fat balls. Poe watched as a starling hung upside down and pecked at one. Before long there was a mass of feathers and confusion as ten more joined it.

A wood pigeon flew in and landed on the edge of the stone birdbath. It pecked in vain at the solid ice, desperate for something to drink.

At the *solid* ice . . .

Poe straightened.

He knew how Rebecca had been abducted.

Chapter 17

Each morning for the last month, Poe had needed to unfreeze Edgar's outside water bowl. At Herdwick Croft he brought it inside and put it under the hot tap.

Rebecca Pridmore didn't have a dog bowl. But she did have a birdbath. A *stone* birdbath that would freeze solid every night just as Edgar's water bowl did. And no way was she bringing that inside – it had probably taken two strong men just to site it. She'd have taken the hot water to it.

She'd have taken her *kettle* to it.

Every morning.

Poe imagined she boiled it, poured some into her cafetière, and then took the rest outside. He doubted it would take more than five minutes but it would be five minutes when she'd have been vulnerable. If someone was aware of one of the few routines she had, they could lie in wait and grab her when she stepped outside. And in a garden with such high walls, no one would witness it.

If he was right, the kettle was still in the garden.

'I'm popping outside, Tilly,' he said.

He found it immediately. One of the advantages of a garden stripped of its greenery was that things were easier to find. The kettle was in a small shrub near the birdbath. It was stainless steel and half-dome-shaped. An old-fashioned one that would sit on the Aga.

Poe thought Rebecca had probably dropped it when the killer

grabbed her. If it had been early in the morning he could have easily missed it in the dark.

He looked back into the bungalow. Sparkes had returned. He was talking to Bradshaw. Poe thought he'd better get back in before she showed him how to log onto the site showing where the UK's Continuous at Sea Deterrent submarines were.

'Mr Sparkes, while Tilly is busy can you give me a hand with something?' Poe said when he walked back into the main room.

The MoD man looked at him quizzically but followed him outside onto the front drive.

'I need a favour,' Poe said. 'I'm going into the back garden. Can you go and stand on the other side of the road and let me know if you can see me? If you can't, move position until you can.'

Sparkes's extra height was a bonus. If he couldn't see Poe then the chances were no one could.

Poe let himself into the back garden then walked to the birdbath. He pottered around it for about the time he figured it would take to fill it with water then returned to the back door. He repeated the process until Sparkes had had enough time to observe him from more than one position.

The back door opened and Sparkes joined Poe at the birdbath. His knees were wet and his shoes were muddy.

'Anything?' Poe asked.

'Nothing. From the main road the front wall obscures most of everything unless you're facing the driveway, and even then you can only see the bungalow. You can't see the back garden at all.'

'What about through the windows?'

Sparkes shook his head. 'No, the building's raised. All you can see is sky and the tips of the two taller trees. I walked across the road and into the farmer's field. Held a straight line all the way to the river. At no point can you get high enough to see anything other than the bungalow's roof. If she was observed in her garden, it wasn't from the front.'

Which meant the killer had most likely been able to see into her back garden. But how? The rear wall was even taller than the front. Unless he used a ladder and stuck his head over like a 'Chad woz 'ere' cartoon, Poe couldn't see how the killer could have known about Rebecca's birdbath routine.

'He could have used a drone,' Sparkes said.

'Those toy helicopter things?'

'Yes. The non-military versions are cheap enough. He could have sat in his car and operated it.'

'Tell me how they work,' Poe said.

'Assuming he doesn't have access to the ones we use, which cost hundreds of thousands of pounds, he'd have to have been fairly close. They're easy to use and most come equipped with HD cameras.'

Poe considered it. A drone *would* be one way of seeing over the wall but there was a major problem with it: Dalston was rural and that meant a big open sky. He pointed at a kestrel hovering near the river's edge.

'Look at that – it's standing out like the last leaf on the tree. A drone would be seen, and in a village like this half of them would think they were being attacked by aliens. It would have been reported.'

'What's left then?'

'I want to check the field at the rear. Maybe there's a vantage point high enough to see into her back garden. You coming?'

Sparkes said, 'Yes.'

There was no direct route from Rebecca's back garden to the fields behind it but, the day before, Poe had noticed a purpose-built stile in the dry stone wall, and a wooden public access sign a couple of hundred yards up the road.

He grabbed his binoculars from his car, changed into some walking boots and went to see what he could find.

Chapter 18

Poe didn't know what turned a field into a paddock but he knew when he was in one. It had jumps set for horse field trials. Nothing too high, suggesting it was a children's gymkhana. The grass was damp and spongy. He could see their footprints all the way back to the stile.

A flock of Swaledales watched them warily. Poe and Sparkes skirted past the sheep then turned to look at the bungalow. The high wall hid Rebecca's garden completely. The killer wasn't standing in the paddock when he watched her. He'd have stood out like a scarecrow and wouldn't have been able to see over the wall anyway.

Poe wasn't ready to give up. He surveyed the surrounding land, searching for a viable observation post. If he'd still been in the Black Watch and had been asked to set up an OP in Londonderry, where would he have felt safe?

High ground, certainly. And not in any obvious cover; obvious cover draws the eye. Somewhere less noticeable then. Poe turned his back on the bungalow. There was a wood on a plateau that looked promising. It was five hundred yards from the bungalow but with the right equipment it might have been possible to see over the wall and into the back garden.

The wood was a mixture of deciduous trees and rhododendron bushes. Tangled roots and animal tracks made the hard ground lumpy. Skinny branches let in pale light. The air was thick with the smell of decaying leaves. Poe heard the scuttle of something small and unseen. He doubted the wood was used much by dog walkers. The undergrowth was too thick and there were other, more scenic walks within easier reach.

He raised the binoculars. He still couldn't see into the garden. He *could*, however, see Bradshaw through the windows. She was alternating between two laptops – hers and Rebecca's. Poe hoped she wasn't copying anything sensitive.

'Anything?' Sparkes asked.

'I can see inside the bungalow but not the garden.'

'What about up there?' he said, pointing to the trees.

Poe nodded. If the killer had chosen a tree inside the treeline the chances of being discovered would have been negligible, even during the day. It would have to be easy to climb, though, so that meant evenly spaced, low branches. He'd also have needed a cover story in case someone had seen him, but a man of his ingenuity wouldn't have let that stop him.

It didn't take Poe long to find a tree that could be climbed without specialist gear that also afforded views of the bungalow. It was ten yards in from the treeline. He searched for more but found none.

'This is the one,' he said.

'You sure?'

Poe moved some of the top leaves at the base of the tree and grunted in satisfaction.

'I am now.' He pointed at the ground. 'The leaves underneath the fresh ones I've just moved are crushed. Someone's been standing there. And not just once.'

He then pointed at the lowest branch. It was about four feet from the ground. 'He'd have put his foot on this branch first, grabbed the one above and pulled himself up. Look at the moss.'

Some of it was missing, some of it was compressed and some had been torn and was dying. Poe took some photographs. CSI would come later and take more professional ones.

'This is a crime scene now,' Poe said. 'Can you go and get some forensic gear from my car? And tell Tilly I'll be sending her some photographs.'

When Sparkes left, Poe called Flynn and told her what he'd found.

'What's your next move?' she asked.

'I'm going to go up and have a look.'

'Are you sure, Poe? You shouldn't be climbing trees at your age. Why don't you wait until CSI get there?'

'I'll be fine,' he replied. 'I'll wear a suit and if I think I'm going to destroy evidence I'll stop.'

'OK, I'll leave it half an hour before I tell Jo Nightingale.'

Sparkes returned with the forensic suits.

Poe said, 'Thanks. I'll stay here until the cavalry arrives. Can you go and see if Tilly needs any help?'

'No problem,' he said.

When he left, Poe grabbed a branch and looked up.

Chapter 19

It was funny the way the mind made connections.

The last time he'd climbed a tree Poe thought he'd known everything there was to know about himself. He'd had a father he loved and a mother who'd abandoned him. This time he knew the man who'd raised him wasn't his biological father and his mother had left so she didn't have to see the face of her rapist grow onto the face of the son she'd chosen not to abort.

He'd known the truth for over a year but he was no further forward in his off-the-books search for his biological father. But he was looking.

Six months ago the man who raised him had unexpectedly come home. They hadn't seen each other for years and they'd had a lot of catching up to do. Poe had told him he knew the truth and the old man had broken down in tears. Poe's mother had been raped at a diplomatic party in Washington, DC. His father hadn't been there. She'd told him everything when she returned to the UK and he'd made copious notes. He kept them in a cabin he owned in New Zealand and he was on his way there now. He'd promised to ship them over as soon as he arrived.

It would be somewhere to start.

Poe avoided the branches the killer might have used and hauled himself up the tree. It was hard going but three years of having to cut his own fuel had given him wiry muscles. He was soon standing on a branch ten feet from the ground.

He faced Rebecca's bungalow and looked through his binoculars. He had a decent view of the back garden. Another six feet and he'd have the *perfect* view. He looked up, searching. A sturdy branch, about five inches thick, jutted out at 90 degrees. If he'd wanted to sit and watch Rebecca's home and back garden for any length of time, that was the one he'd have chosen. Poe picked a route so he could get above it. The tree was easy to climb and it didn't take long.

He looked down at the branch he thought the killer might have used and smiled to himself. An eighteen-inch section looked different to the rest of the branch.

Almost as if it had been rubbed smooth by someone sitting on it . . .

This was where the killer had set up his observation post. It was perfect: he'd have been able to see everything. Poe couldn't see what he'd used as his cover story in case he was observed up the tree, but apart from that he was happy with what he'd found.

Poe moved as close as he dared. The killer wouldn't have expected them to find this and that meant he could have been sloppy. Poe turned on the torch function of his mobile. He scanned the surrounding area for anything out of the ordinary and snapped some photographs to study later. Nothing jumped out.

He sent Flynn a text asking her to call it in. He needed CSI. If there was a hair trapped in a ridge of bark, they'd find it. If the killer had nicked his finger climbing and smeared blood against the tree, they'd find it. If there was any forensic transfer at all they'd be a step closer to catching him.

Poe sent Bradshaw an email with the pictures attached while he still had a decent signal. She'd put them on a laptop and enlarge them. As he was waiting for the email to send, a drop of rain hit the screen. He put his phone back in his pocket and looked up – winter in Cumbria meant five or six different types of weather a day.

And that's when he saw what the killer had brought with him on the off-chance someone had seen him up the tree.

Chapter 20

It was a kite.

And not one of the tissue paper and stick things Poe had been given as a child – this was an adult's kite. He reckoned it would have been at least six feet across when fully assembled. The string was wrapped round the trunk and a couple of branches, a few feet above Poe's head. If it hadn't rained he might have missed it.

The kite itself was tangled in among some branches and its own lines. It was black with random squares of red and purple. It had a logo on each wing, but Poe couldn't make out what they were. It was crumpled and looked smashed beyond repair. He didn't know what they were called but most of the frame tubing, and all of the supporting struts, were either broken or bent. The nylon was ripped in at least two places.

It was wedged in tight. If it had been flown into the tree by accident he'd have expected it to catch in the outer branches, not tight against the trunk like it was. It had been carried up and staged. Which made sense. That way the killer had avoided having it anywhere unrecoverable, in which case climbing a tree would be too suspicious.

Poe paused a beat before climbing again. The rain had made the branches wet and slippery and he wasn't an idiot – if he fell he'd break half the bones in his body. He should wait for it to be professionally recovered.

CSI would take their time. Probably use a cherry picker so they had a safe and stable aerial platform to work from. That would be the sensible thing to do. No one would get hurt and no evidence would be lost.

But . . . he wanted a look first.

After fifteen minutes Poe was above the kite. He was confident he hadn't touched anything the killer had. As far as he was concerned, the crime scene was still untainted.

He had a better view of one of the wing logos. It was golden but the fabric was crumped and folded over so he still couldn't make out what it was. It was probably a brand logo but he wanted to take a photograph anyway, and the only way that would be possible was if he lay horizontally above it. He'd be able to see it perfectly but, without the trunk to cling to, the branch might not be able to support his weight.

It might bend or snap and it was a long way to the ground.

Sod it, he thought. Sometimes the only way to get the job done was to literally go out on a limb . . .

Chapter 21

Poe waited in the wood for CSI and the responding detectives.

He'd called Nightingale and told her what he'd found. She'd been so pleased to have a solid lead that she forgot to be angry about how far up the tree he'd climbed.

'Thank God for Edgar's frozen water bowl,' she'd said, then hung up.

When the two detectives from Carlisle CID arrived, and Poe had handed over responsibility for the scene, he made his way back to Bradshaw. Sparkes had already left with Rebecca's laptop. Poe told her what had happened, leaving out the part where he'd slipped and fallen the last few feet out of the tree. He'd torn three fingernails and his left knee was now clicking.

As Bradshaw downloaded his photographs, she briefed him on what she'd been up to.

'I've now got copies of the hard drives of all the victims' computers, Poe,' she said. 'I'll get the contents of their phones and tablets after we've finished here. I'll need to write a program that can work across all platforms simultaneously.'

'And you can do that?'

Bradshaw shrugged. If she were the type of person to say things like 'piece of piss' she'd have said 'piece of piss'. Instead she said, 'I'll have something by the end of tomorrow. If there's an electronically recorded link between the three victims, I'll find it.'

Her computer beeped.

'The photographs have downloaded, Poe,' she said. 'What do you want to look at first?'

'The ones with the kite,' he said.

Bradshaw selected the best and enlarged it.

'See how it's been tied?' Poe said, pointing at the screen. 'He put it there so he had an excuse to be up the tree if someone saw him.'

'I agree. That's a knot at the bottom.'

'Which begs the obvious question: why did he leave it up there?'

It didn't make sense.

'Perhaps he lost his nerve when it was time to collect it? These photographs were taken from awfully high up.'

Poe shook his head. 'If there's one thing our killer has, it's balls. He's been brazenly nipping in and out of places, leaving body parts under the noses of people who'd have ripped him to shreds if he'd been caught. Climbing a tree isn't going to faze him.'

'Maybe he just saw his chance and took it,' Bradshaw said.

Poe nodded. That was more likely. If he'd been watching Rebecca's bungalow and saw an unexpected opportunity, he could have rushed across the paddock and taken her while he had the chance. It would explain why he hadn't had time to remove the kite.

A thought occurred to him. 'Which means he might come back for it . . .'

He lunged for his phone.

92

Chapter 22

Nightingale called off the hounds and arranged covert surveillance of the wood. Poe volunteered to be part of the team but she politely refused. She did, however, invite him to the planning meeting at Carleton Hall. Poe attended to see if he could change her mind. Until Bradshaw's program had finished merging and sorting the victims' information, he didn't have a lot to do.

'Keep doing what you do, Poe,' Nightingale said when he broached the subject. 'If the surveillance pays off, then great, but I like to plan for the worst and all that bollocks.'

Poe didn't reply.

'We have three teams of twelve,' she continued. 'Two cops are in a house six doors down from Rebecca's. From the top floor they have a decent view of the wood. Another two will rough it in the woods behind the one we're watching. The other eight in the team will be spread out in a net in case he runs. We have four motion-capture cameras in the wood and even though I know they're there, I couldn't see them. Everyone will have thermal imaging equipment.'

'Shifts?'

'Eight on, sixteen off.'

Poe grunted his appreciation. A twelve-twelve shift was the usual for surveillance. That Nightingale had budgeted for an eight-sixteen meant that she was in it for the long haul. Research had shown that twelve-twelve surveillance shifts became less effective after four days. Officers lost their edge. Tiredness crept in. When you were in a twelve-twelve shift pattern all you did was work and sleep.

Flynn and Nightingale began discussing budget contributions, stuff he had no interest in. Poe wandered off. It was late in the afternoon and Bradshaw had already headed back to the North Lakes Hotel and Spa. He sent her a text asking if she fancied getting an early supper.

She did. Poe jumped in his car and drove to the hotel. She was waiting for him in the lobby. Instead of the formal dining room, they elected to grab one of the leather sofas in the bar area. They were more comfy and there was less chance of being overheard.

'Can I get you anything to drink?' the barman asked.

'Sparkling water, no ice, please,' Bradshaw said.

'Same for me but I'll have ice,' Poe said.

After the barman had disappeared, Poe said, 'How's your program coming along?'

'I'm running tests now, Poe,' she replied. 'I'll put the data in tonight and I'll have early analysis this time tomorrow.'

Poe nodded. He wasn't expecting much – the victims' ages, education levels, geography and socioeconomic factors were too different for them to be linked – but experience had told him never to underestimate Bradshaw's contributions.

The lack of anything connecting the victims was irrelevant, though, as they *had* been selected. Working out how was what SCAS did, and Poe knew Bradshaw had already tasked her small team of analysts – affectionately known as the 'Mole People' due to the way they tended to blink when they went outside – with analysing victim selection criteria.

The barman brought their drinks and placed them on coasters. He also placed a bowl of peanuts in front of them. Poe grabbed half a dozen, threw them in his mouth and started crunching. He passed the bowl to Bradshaw.

'No thank you, Poe,' she said. 'Studies have found that bar

nuts can contain as many as one hundred unique specimens of urine.'

Poe stopped chewing. He spat out what he hadn't swallowed into his handkerchief.

'Thanks for the heads-up,' he said.

'You're welcome, Poe,' she replied politely.

He popped an ice cube in his mouth and crunched it to get rid of the imagined taste of urine.

'And I don't have ice in my drinks for the same reason.'

Poe froze. 'Urine?'

She shook her head. 'Coliform. It's the bacteria found in human faeces.'

Poe stared at his empty glass.

'You see, this is why I drink beer. If something's going to taste like piss then the least it can do is get me drunk.'

'I've been thinking of competitive kite flying, Poe.'

'Who hasn't?' he grumbled.

'It's a real thing,' she continued. 'They have leagues and everything. Some competitions are about precision flying where they have to demonstrate compulsory figures as laid down by the judging panel. Another discipline is a freestyle interpretation of a piece of music. This is called a kite ballet. Both disciplines can be individual, in pairs or in teams.'

'That's a weird thing to know a lot about,' Poe said.

'Jeremy, one of my—'

'Mole People.'

'—team,' she said without missing a step, 'has been flying kites since he was a child.'

'I flew kites when I was a child as well,' Poe said. 'Thing is, I stopped when I *wasn't* a child. You know, like adults are supposed to do.'

'Anyway, Mr Cranky Pants, I called Jeremy earlier—'

'Called or emailed?'

Bradshaw never spoke to people face-to-face if an electronic message would do.

'OK, I *emailed* Jeremy earlier and he told me that the kite in the tree looks very much like a stunt kite. Quite expensive as these things go.'

Poe sat up straight. This was more like it. They might have started out talking about the specific gravity content of piss in bar snacks but they were now firmly back in police territory.

'And did Jeremy say where you might buy such a thing?'

'Too many to list. He did say that the kite's logo was probably bespoke, though. Most serious enthusiasts have their own design, apparently. Because we don't have a great view of it, and because we had to leave the kite in situ, I'll have to run the photographs you took through an object-based image analysis program.'

'What's that do?'

'It will break the photograph into pixels then group them into homogenous objects. Each object has statistics associated with them, like shape, geometry, context and texture, which can assist with its identification.'

'Which means?'

'We'll get a report containing a number of composite images with likelihood expressed as percentage points.'

'The program can predict what the logo is?'

'With a percentage point indicating likelihood beside each one.'

'That's one clever program,' Poe said. 'Yours, I take it?'

Bradshaw shook her head. 'No. This is an open-source one I've adapted.'

'When we get your report we'll need to speak to someone,' he said. 'There's bound to be some boring bastard out there who knows about this stuff.'

Bradshaw shook her head again.

'So rude,' she said.

Chapter 23

When Poe stepped out of Herdwick Croft the following morning, Shap Fell looked like someone had thrown a duvet over it. Snowflakes the size of bottle tops were still falling. They had softly covered the ground, changing the harsh ancient moorland into something altogether more welcoming.

Except the trees. The stunted, thorny hawthorns that somehow eked out an existence on the moor stood out like they'd been X-rayed. Harsh black against the perfect, untouched white canvas that stretched as far as the eye could see.

Edgar yelped with joy – he loved the snow. He bounded out in a splash of white powder and had soon disappeared in new, clean surroundings. Poe had collected him last night. It wasn't convenient but the truth was he missed him when he wasn't there.

He watched the spaniel's antics for a while but Poe wasn't dressed for snow and he was soon shivering. The cold air fogged his breath, chilled his cough-ravaged lungs and watered his eyes. As soon as Edgar returned, all wet and steaming, Poe went to find something more suitable to wear. He chose layers rather than thick coats and jumpers – snow on Shap Fell didn't mean snow lower down.

He called Bradshaw to tell her he was on his way, whistled for Edgar to jump on the back of the quad – the only way of getting to and from Herdwick Croft that didn't involve walking – and set off for Shap Wells and his car.

Poe picked up Bradshaw outside the North Lakes Hotel and

Spa's reception. Bradshaw had found someone who might be able to help. He was called Sean Carroll and he was a kite nerd. He lived in Cullercoats on the north-east coast. Poe reckoned it would take an hour and a half to get there.

The previous night he'd called Nightingale and told her where they'd be the next day. She hadn't been keen – Rome was burning and she wanted SCAS drawing up profiles, not goofing off playing the fiddle. Poe privately agreed but he'd told her that Bradshaw thought it was worth doing and he'd learned never to dismiss that.

Twenty minutes later they were on the A69, headed towards Newcastle. It was a road Poe knew well and he slowed down for the fixed speed cameras and eased up to a steady eighty when the road allowed. It seemed most drivers had taken the advice on the radio and were only doing essential journeys – the road was as quiet as he'd seen it.

They were on the Coast Road and had already passed Battle Hill when his phone rang. It was Nightingale. Poe pressed the accept button on his steering wheel.

'Ma'am,' he said. 'You're on speakerphone. I've got Tilly with me.'

'How far from Newcastle are you?'

'Not too far, ma'am. We're meeting the kite dork in Cullercoats – it's a bit farther up the coast. What's up?'

'The snow's playing havoc over here. Half the county's shut and the other half has blue skies and sunshine. I'm supposed to be in Newcastle later to observe the post-mortem on Howard Teasdale but I'm still in Barrow. I'm not convinced I'll be able to get across. I was wondering if you'd be able to stand in for me?'

'What time's it scheduled for?'

'Two o'clock. Professor Doyle can delay it an hour if that helps.'

'Two o'clock works. I can't see this kite thing taking too long.'

'Thanks, Poe.'

'Sean Carroll's a kite *enthusiast*,' Bradshaw said after Nightingale had ended the call. 'He's not a dork.'

Poe grunted. He had a problem with 'enthusiasts'. As far as he was concerned, on the ladder of weird interests that eventually escalated to criminal behaviour, enthusiasts were only a rung below obsessives, and he'd seen first-hand what obsessed people were capable of . . .

Carroll was meeting them at the beach rather than his home or place of work. He was still on holiday and the weather was going to be perfect for kite flying. He hadn't wanted to waste it. He'd promised to bring everything with him.

He'd sent Bradshaw directions to the car park and said he'd be in an old Ford Transit. He hadn't supplied a colour or registration number but that didn't matter. It was the only vehicle there.

The wind was strong enough to send sand sweeping across the concrete, obscuring the bay markings, but it was no big deal. Poe parked adjacent to him.

If Poe had thought about it at all, he'd have pictured someone like Bradshaw's friend Jeremy. When the office had unofficially labelled her team the Mole People, Poe was sure they'd done it with Jeremy in mind. A pale, bookish man with thick glasses and thin fingers. Could solve fractional equations without using a calculator but had to be told to wear a coat when it was cold.

Sean Carroll looked more like a bouncer.

He was six-and-a-half feet tall, shaven-headed and, despite the cold, he only wore a T-shirt. He had hands like bunches of bananas and knuckles like walnuts. A barbed wire tattoo wrapped a bicep bigger than Poe's thigh.

He smiled warmly and shook Bradshaw's hand, his ham-sized fist dwarfing her own. When he shook Poe's, his grip was firm and dry.

'I understand you want help identifying a kite, Miss Bradshaw?' He had a strong Geordie accent.

'We do, Sean Carroll.'

Bradshaw's unusual way of addressing people didn't faze him. He nodded, reached into the open window of his van and retrieved two files. He handed her one.

'You can take this away but I'll answer anything I can now.'

'Tilly's sent you photographs of the kite and composite computer images of possible logos,' Poe said.

'She did, aye. I understand I can't see the original?'

'Sorry. No one's seen it yet.'

Carroll opened his own file and removed a sheet of paper. The language was in Dutch but there were enough pictures for Poe to recognise it had been taken from the website of a kite supplier in Rotterdam.

'I think the kite you're looking at is a Mirage Stunt Kite. Probably the XL model.'

The kite was V-shaped, a bit like a stealth bomber or a hang-glider. The colours matched the ones in Poe's photographs. Despite the page being in a language he didn't understand, he recognised dimensions when he saw them. Fully assembled, the kite had a wingspan of ten feet. He'd thought it was big but not *that* big. If that thing caught a strong gust of wind it looked like it could rip someone's arm off. Perhaps competitive kite flying wasn't as nerdy as he'd thought . . . It also explained the massive muscles on Carroll. He wondered how Bradshaw's friend, Jeremy, managed it – Poe had seen him reach for his inhaler after walking to the fridge.

The other thing Poe had no trouble translating was the price tag: three hundred and fifty euros. With the pound doing what it was, that meant it was over three hundred quid. A lot of money to leave flapping about in a tree.

Carroll put the website page and one of Poe's photographs side-by-side.

'See how the carbon frame matches here' – he pointed at the top of the kite – 'and here' – pointing at a wing.

Poe nodded. 'This is the one. What can you tell us about it?'

'Just the basics. I don't have the funds for something like this. It's a bit slower than other stunt kites, which means you have more control. It can fly in winds up to thirty miles per hour. One hundred and fifteen-foot dual Dyneema line, straight-tracking with a highly responsive—'

'Dyneema?' Poe cut in.

'It's an ultra-high molecular weight polyethylene, Poe,' Bradshaw said. 'It has extremely strong intermolecular interactions because its long chains have a molecular mass of between 3.5 and 7.5 million AMUs.'

Poe looked at her blankly.

'I guess she's the brains of the outfit, huh?' Carroll said.

'That's a peculiarly specific thing to know a lot about, Tilly,' Poe said.

'I researched kites last night. Didn't you read the document I sent you?'

'I think you already know the answer to that.' He'd skimmed it without really understanding it. Instead, he'd focused on the type of people who flew kites. What clubs they went to, what competitions they entered. It was why he hadn't been surprised that Carroll's printed webpage was in Dutch. Kites were a huge deal over there.

Cost aside, the other interesting aspect about the Mirage Stunt Kite XL was that the golden logos weren't pre-printed on the wings. Poe reckoned the kite's owner had probably added them.

'What do you know about logos, Sean?' Poe asked.

Instead of answering, Carroll led them to the back of his van and unlocked the doors. A kite rested on the bare metal floor. It wasn't the stealth bomber shape of the Mirage; instead it seemed a bit limp and lifeless.

'This is what's called a foil design. It doesn't have the rigid frame of the Mirage and it'll only take form when air enters it via the front edge vents. When it's in the sky it looks like a modern parachute instead of a hang-glider.'

He pointed at one of the logos imprinted on the nylon. 'That's what I fly under.'

It was an anthropomorphic magpie. It wore a black and white waistcoat, a black and white top hat and a bright blue morning coat. Black trousers, yellow shoes and a walking cane completed the image.

Poe wasn't a massive football fan any more – the money involved these days had sucked the charm from the game – but he recognised Newcastle United's mascot when he saw it.

'This is bespoke, I assume?'

Carroll shrugged. 'Aye, sort of. The design isn't my own – I lifted it from the Toon's website – but as far as I know, I'm the only one flying it.'

'Did you have to register it anywhere?'

'Nope.'

'So there's nothing we can check our images against?'

He shook his head. 'Kite flying's not really taken off in the UK. Not like it has in other countries.'

Poe studied the magpie. It had been attached professionally. No wrinkles, no peeling edges.

'How did you fix the logo on?'

'Silkscreen print transfers. The ones we use are designed for industrially washed work clothes. There are seven or eight companies who can do it in a three-mile radius of here alone, though.'

Poe grunted his frustration.

'Tilly's program identified a pterodactyl as being the most likely image,' he said. 'A gliding Batman was second and an eagle third. There were seven others we have to consider too.'

'Pterodactyls are flying dinosaurs from the Tithonian age of the Jurassic period, Sean Carroll,' Bradshaw said.

Carroll smiled. 'Flying kites is just a hobby, Miss Bradshaw. During the day I'm an entomologist at the Great North Museum – what used to be called the Hancock Natural History Museum; I know what a pterodactyl is.'

'Is there anyone we can ask?' Poe said before Bradshaw could respond. If she had a fault it was that she could be a bit snippy about any science that wasn't maths. She barely tolerated physicists; she wasn't going to let a biologist get the better of her.

'Best I can do is ring round some of the event organisers,' Carroll said. 'See if anyone recognises them.'

It wasn't a brilliant solution – they weren't even sure the killer flew kites competitively. Poe said as much.

'Oh, he flies competitively, Sergeant Poe. I can guarantee you that. If you just want to go in a field and turn a few loops, any thirty-quid stunt kite will do. This is a next-level kite with a personalised logo; someone will know the man who stands under it.'

Chapter 24

Poe had an hour to kill before Estelle Doyle's post-mortem. The sea breeze was clearing his lungs, so he walked down to the beach with Bradshaw and Edgar, who immediately started playing tug-o-war with a sun-bleached piece of driftwood, the spaniel's tail wagging faster than a twanged ruler. Bradshaw finally wrested the stick free, pretended to throw it, and when Edgar ran off she doubled over laughing.

Poe stood and watched. Before long his skin was coated in a light mist of brine. He licked his lips and tasted salt. Foam-crested waves lapped at his feet. He liked the North Sea almost as much as he liked the Irish Sea. It was rough and choppy, grey not blue. A British sea. Even in summer it was too cold to swim in.

He joined Carroll and watched him expertly fly his kite. With the slightest pull he had it twisting and turning and doing loop-the-loops, with another it was slicing through the air like a peregrine falcon. At all times he was in complete control.

A breathless Bradshaw joined them. Her face was red and her eyelashes were encrusted with salt. She was grinning wildly.

'Edgar's found another stick, Poe. He ran into the sea so I couldn't chase him.'

'He'll come out when he's bored, Tilly.'

'Watch this,' Carroll said. He straightened his right arm and pulled back his left. The kite dipped sharply and raced towards the sand. At the last possible moment he pulled it up. It flew three feet above Edgar's head and he launched himself into the air trying to catch it. For a few minutes Carroll flew nearer and nearer to the spaniel without ever getting close enough for him to catch it. Edgar barked in frustration.

'How did you get into this?' Poe asked.

'A few years ago I wasn't feeling very well,' he replied. 'I asked the doctor what he recommended for chronic wind and he suggested a kite. Ten years later, here I am, addicted.'

Bradshaw frowned.

'That was irresponsible,' she said. 'Excessive flatulence can be a warning sign for something serious. He should have referred you to a gastroenterologist.'

'It's a Tommy Cooper joke, Tilly,' Poe explained.

'Who?'

'Google him when you get the chance. He's one of the best comedians there's ever been.'

'I will, Poe.'

He knew she wouldn't. Other than her weird sci-fi shows, she eschewed all forms of light entertainment.

'I suppose the real reason is that I've studied insects and arachnids my whole adult life,' Carroll said, his eyes never leaving the kite. 'It seemed only natural to have a hobby that included an element of flying.'

They watched him for half an hour more but Poe could tell the thin coat Bradshaw was wearing wasn't keeping out the biting wind. He told Carroll they had somewhere to be.

The man promised he'd get back to them about the logo designs as soon as he could.

Chapter 25

Bradshaw hadn't attended a post-mortem before. Poe wasn't sure she was even allowed to. He'd leave it up to Estelle Doyle – as she'd said many times before: 'My house, my rules.'

They found a parking space close to the mortuary at the Royal Victoria Infirmary. The last time Poe had been there some building work had just begun. This time it was in full swing.

The mortuary was in the basement but the corridor he usually followed no longer existed. Instead there was a new sign and a 'You Are Here' map with their location marked with a red star. Poe memorised the new layout and, with Bradshaw in tow, set off to find Estelle Doyle's new hangout.

Part of the ongoing renovation work included the mortuary. Gone was the door anyone could walk through, the door that always had one of Doyle's trademark signs Sellotaped to the frosted window – 'Pathologists Have The Coolest Patients', 'People Are Dying To Get In Here', and Poe's all-time favourite: a straight to the point 'Go Away!' – had been replaced with an automatic, sliding glass door.

It opened with a quiet 'whoosh' as they approached. The room that used to contain the staff lockers was now a reception area.

Poe pressed the bell.

'Bit different to last time I was here,' he said.

'It smells new, Poe.'

It did. And everything looked clean and shiny and untouched.

A man stepped through a door behind the reception desk.

'Can I help you?'

Poe flipped his ID card. 'I'm here to view a post-mortem at two. One of Estelle Doyle's.'

The man took their names and asked them to take a seat. Two minutes later he was back.

'That's all fine. If you'd like to follow me.'

He led them through a keypad-protected door into the staff area.

'You ever worn a forensic suit before, Tilly?' Poe asked.

'I haven't, Poe.'

He hadn't thought so. There'd have been no reason for her to. Although she got out into the field these days, her role was still primarily analytical.

'And you won't need to wear one this time,' the man said.

'Oh, why not?' Poe said. He hoped the post-mortem hadn't been cancelled. Nightingale asking him to attend in her place had been a bonus.

'Professor Doyle has a dedicated PM room now. She's been asking for one for years and the lab she works for offered match funding if the hospital agreed to her demands. It has a bespoke, fit-for-purpose viewing area.'

Poe whistled in admiration. Doyle was in high demand. She was a partner in the private laboratory that handled most of the forensic and pathology work for the north-east, a Home Office pathologist and a highly paid guest lecturer at any university and teaching hospital who could afford her.

They had occasionally spoken of what her ideal mortuary would look like. It would have a dedicated room so that the urgent nature of forensic post-mortems wouldn't disrupt anything and it would have a new viewing area. She'd never liked the old one. It was too far away from the examination tables, the dissecting bench couldn't be seen at all and it could only comfortably fit four people. It was why she'd always insist on the SIO being suited and booted and in the room with her. If they didn't need to get changed then Doyle must have got the viewing area she'd wanted.

The man led them down a new corridor and to a door with 'Observation Area' stencilled on the frosted glass. It was a small waiting room, about ten feet by ten feet. A low table with a jug of water was in the middle. Plastic-moulded seats were stacked against the wall.

'You should stay here, Tilly.'

'I'd like to come in if I may, Poe?' she said. 'I believe seeing a post-mortem will make me a better analyst.'

'OK, but if you want to leave then do. Plenty of cops can't cope with them. There's no shame in it.'

He opened the other door in the room. The familiar smell greeted him, one he hoped he'd never get used to.

The new post-mortem room looked state of the art. It was square and designed for efficiency. The expensive fixtures and fittings were robust and easy to clean. The floor's channel gratings were in short, detachable sections so they could be removed and submersed in one of the large sinks fitted against the wall opposite. Even the ceiling looked as though it could be hosed down.

The wall on the right was lined with fridges. Poe suspected they would have doors on both sides so Doyle and her team didn't have to enter the main post-mortem room to collect their cadavers.

The observation area they were in wasn't enclosed. Instead, a tall, angled glass divider separated them from the business side of the post-mortem room. The observation area was above the dissection bench. They were so close that when Poe leaned over he could see the digital read-out on the weighing station. The observation area was spacious, at least twice the size of the previous one, and afforded excellent views of all parts of the post-mortem room.

Poe could feel air on the back of his neck. That made sense. It would be designed to flow from the so-called 'clean area' – the waiting rooms, the viewing and bier rooms – and into the designated 'dirty' areas: the body store, the PM rooms and the used instrument stores. It was the most modern post-mortem room he'd ever been in, and it was utterly cheerless.

An examination table with a hoist and adjustable lighting above it was in the centre of the room. Estelle Doyle was working on the cadaver of Howard Teasdale, the victim found in his bedsit. He looked even bigger on the slab. His pallid skin was waxy with a blue tinge. His chest and shoulders were marbled and his abdomen had a green tinge. Shrunken, milky eyes stared lifelessly at the ceiling. His bloated head was raised with a block. Poe could see a cut that started behind his ears and went over his crown, made so that Doyle could pull down the front of the scalp to expose his face, and the back to expose the skull. Removing the top of the skull with a Stryker saw was how pathologists accessed the brain.

Estelle Doyle had started without them.

Chapter 26

Estelle Doyle was bent over Teasdale's neck, dictating as she worked.

'The fatal wound measures three hundred and nine millimetres and is above the thyroid cartilage, in between the larynx and the chin. It has broken the skin in several places but not torn it.'

As she manoeuvred herself around Teasdale's head, she saw them watching her. She took her foot off the splash-proof foot control that turned the dictation system on and off.

'When I was told it was you who'd be attending, Poe, I assumed you'd be OK if I made an early start? There's a lot of Mr Teasdale to get through.'

'Not a problem.'

'And who's your little friend?' she said.

'Matilda Bradshaw, Professor Estelle Doyle,' Bradshaw replied. Already paler than a cavefish, she'd blanched even more since entering the post-mortem room. Poe didn't embarrass her by asking if she wanted to step out.

Doyle removed her safety glasses and walked over to them.

'I won't shake your hand, Matilda Bradshaw, but can we assume that if I could I would?'

Bradshaw nodded.

'I owe you a debt of gratitude,' Doyle continued. 'I gather it was you who dragged this temerarious man out of a burning building?'

Bradshaw said, 'He's my friend.'

'Temer what now?' Poe said.

'Temerarious, Poe,' Doyle replied. 'It means recklessly confident. And I gather you're also the one who made the links on the Jared Keaton case?'

'Poe and DI Stephanie Flynn do all the real work,' Bradshaw said. 'I just help with the science.'

'And what colour crayons do you use when you explain things?' Doyle said. 'I use blue. I find it calms him.'

Bradshaw giggled, then said, 'He knows more than he lets on, Professor Estelle Doyle.'

'Loyal too, Poe,' Doyle said. 'She'll do, she can stay.'

'You got your second room then, Estelle?'

She looked around and nodded. 'Thanks in part to all the additional work you've been bringing across.'

Poe said nothing.

'I'm serious, Poe. The respective boards of the lab and the RVI read the papers like everyone else. Not including this one, you've embroiled yourself in some extremely high-profile cases over the last couple of years. The exposure we got working on them helped bring in funding.'

'Happy to help then,' Poe said. 'What you got so far, Estelle?'

'Death came quickly to this man,' she said. She put her safety goggles back on and walked back to the corpse. 'Although not that much quicker than if nature had been allowed to play its hand.'

'Explain,' Poe said.

'If your killer hadn't got to him, I'd have said Howard Teasdale had no more than a year to live. He wasn't being treated for it so I assume it was undiagnosed, but he had stage-four lymphoma. It had spread beyond his lymph nodes and into his liver, his lungs and his bone marrow.'

'You think he might have been selected because he was terminally ill?' Poe said.

111

'I don't have anywhere near enough data to comment on that,' Doyle said. She peered at him over the top of her safety goggles. 'And neither do you, Poe.'

He made a mental note to tell Nightingale anyway.

'I've almost finished my examination. I'll send the full report later . . . Are you OK, Matilda?'

Bradshaw's brow was beaded with sweat. Her breathing was shallow and rapid. She couldn't take her eyes off the corpse. She nodded.

'It helps to think of this as a scientific process, nothing more,' Doyle said. 'I'm here to gather evidence and interpret it. You've done the same thing countless times only with a different cache of data. Poe tells me you're the best he's ever come across.'

Bradshaw gulped and breathed out carefully, winning the fight against the gag reflex. Doyle saying Teasdale was just evidence awaiting discovery would allow her to compartmentalise a PM she probably hadn't really wanted to attend.

'Thank you, Professor Estelle Doyle.'

'Cause of death?' Poe said.

'Asphyxiation. This is supported by a thin ligature mark and associated bruising around the neck. The strap muscles are also haemorrhaged.'

'Manner of death was garrotting, I take it?'

'Almost certainly.' She lifted Teasdale's head and turned it left, showing them the back of his neck. 'Note the small bruise on the left side of the cervical vertebrae.'

She turned the head right and showed them a similar mark on the other side.

'Where he used his thumbs as leverage when he tightened it?'

'The evidence supports that. And if you wait a moment I'll show you something else.'

She engineered the hoist into position and moved the twenty-five-stone cadaver onto its side. A faint bruise, roundish in shape and about the size of a coaster, stood out on Teasdale's mottled flesh.

For a moment Poe didn't know what he was seeing.

Doyle helped him out. 'He was a big man, Poe. Out of shape and dying but he had big muscles in his neck and shoulders.'

'The killer used his knee for extra leverage,' he said, the answer obvious when he put himself in the killer's mind. 'He put his knee against his back so he could pull harder.'

'Again, the evidence supports that,' Doyle said.

'How long to die?'

'Not long at all. Ten seconds before he was unconscious, probably dead in under a minute. And there's something else you need to see.'

Doyle picked up a remote control. A screen on the wall of the observation room flickered into life. She moved a slide under the lens of a powerful-looking microscope. At the same time, an image appeared on the screen. Doyle turned a knob on the side of the microscope and the image came into focus.

'You want to tell Poe what that is, Matilda?'

Bradshaw leaned towards the image. She pushed her glasses up her nose and squinted slightly, her lips pursed in concentration.

'It looks like carbon, Professor Estelle Doyle.'

The pathologist nodded. 'We'll confirm when the sample's back from the lab but I'm fairly certain it's industrial diamond dust.'

'Where did you find it?' Poe asked.

'Embedded in the neck wound.'

'Shit.'

Poe had heard about wire impregnated with diamond dust being used as garrottes but he'd never expected to see it in a case he was investigating. Eastern Bloc special forces were rumoured to use them. In theory, if their intended victim somehow managed to get some fingers between the garrotte and their neck, the killer could move his hands backwards and forwards and saw through them.

Garrottes couldn't easily be bought on the internet but wire embedded with industrial diamond dust was available in any hardware store. Garrottes were easy to make and they were the perfect weapon. Easy to explain, even easier to conceal. It could be wrapped around the wrist like a friendship bracelet or kept in a toolbox without arousing suspicion. Poe had even heard about one being used to hang a painting. All it needed to transform it into a deadly weapon was a couple of handles. The toggle buttons used on duffel coats were ideal.

Doyle talked them through a couple of minor points and promised to have her preliminary report with Nightingale by midnight. The full report would be available when the lab results were back.

When they were ready to go, Doyle approached the viewing area.

'Be careful with this one, Poe,' she said.

'I will.'

She removed her safety goggles and fixed him with an intense look. 'I'm serious, Poe. This man's not a street fighter; he's a stone-cold killer.'

'I said I will.'

Doyle shook her head. 'You won't. You'll try and do it yourself and, while that's worked for you in the past, it won't this time. Not with this man.'

She addressed Bradshaw.

'Miss Bradshaw, I'd be very grateful if you could curb Poe's baser instincts on this. When you do find him, remind Poe that calling in the men with guns isn't a sign of weakness.'

Bradshaw looked worried. 'I'll call them myself, Professor Estelle Doyle. Even if Poe tells me not to.'

Doyle nodded. 'Thank you.'

She turned back to Poe.

'But . . . if you do happen to come up against him, you find yourself a weapon of convenience and you put him down. You don't warn him and you don't try and play fair. He won't with you, Poe.'

'It's not like you to get spooked, Estelle. What's up?'

She smiled at him sadly. 'Alas, Poe, there are some secrets which do not permit themselves to be told.'

'What was all that gothic stuff about?' Poe said as they walked back to the car. 'She's not usually like that.'

'I've just checked,' Bradshaw replied, reading from her phone, 'and that was an Edgar Allan Poe quote she said at the end. It's from "The Man of the Crowd".'

Poe frowned. That had all been very strange.

Chapter 27

They made it back to Carleton Hall in time for the final briefing of the day. They found a seat at the back next to Flynn. Nightingale had drafted in almost two hundred officers and the incident room was hot and humid and smelly. Poe grabbed a half-empty carton of curry and sniffed it. It was a dhansak. All the meat had been eaten. He spooned down the cold, spicy lentils anyway.

Bradshaw glared at him.

'It helps my sore throat,' he lied.

She reached into her bag and handed him an apple.

'I'll have it later.'

'Now.'

He shrugged and bit into it.

'I think you're putting too much faith in the restorative power of fruit, Tilly. "An apple a day keeps the doctor away" isn't supposed to be taken literally.'

'Just eat it, Poe.'

'Will you two behave?' Flynn hissed.

Nightingale finished by updating them on how the surveillance of the kite was going. So far no one, not even a farmer, had been anywhere near the wood. The teams were rotating but it was becoming a less popular gig. Surveillance was exciting when things were happening, but when they weren't, cops could moan with the best of them.

Nightingale spotted Poe and waved him to the front. She asked if there was anything relevant from Howard Teasdale's post-mortem, and when he confirmed there was she gave him the floor.

For fifteen minutes he talked about what Estelle Doyle had found. He saved what he considered to be the most significant findings until last.

'Howard had an untreated stage-four lymphoma. It was in his lungs, liver and lymph nodes. According to Professor Doyle, he would have been dead within the year, and although Teasdale's registered sex offender status probably rules out a mercy killer, I don't think we should discount it just yet.'

Nightingale said, 'Pam, can you get warrants to view the medical records of Rebecca Pridmore and Amanda Simpson, please?'

A stern-looking woman seated near the front nodded. 'Will do, ma'am.'

Poe continued, 'The other thing you all need to be aware of is that the garrotte used to kill Howard Teasdale was impregnated with industrial diamond dust. That's an assassin's weapon. Easily hidden in plain sight, assembled in seconds and as deadly as anything you'll have come across. If you are the one who has to arrest him, take my advice and keep him at arm's length. PAVA spray is good, Tasers would be better.' He gestured towards the armed response team. 'Ideally, though, he needs two shots to the torso.'

Nightingale frowned. 'Sergeant Poe means after you've correctly identified yourself and tried to effect a peaceful arrest.'

She looked at him for confirmation.

Poe shrugged. 'I suppose, if someone's watching.'

The room laughed.

A uniformed cop on the front row wearing sergeant's stripes raised his hand. It was Nightingale's briefing and Poe let her call on him.

'Jim?'

'Have you ever seen anything like this before, Sergeant Poe?'

'DI Flynn and I have been involved in virtually all serial murderer investigations in this country for the last six years. They are all different but, up until now, they've also been a bit samey. This *does* seem different. He kills but, with Howard Teasdale at least, he does it quickly. He mutilates but he's also used anaesthetic. He selects his victims at random but he doesn't have a type. And he's a—'

A coughing fit stopped him in his tracks. When it was finished he grabbed the nearest cup and swigged it down. He grimaced at the taste and looked to see what he'd just drunk.

'Fruit tea,' he muttered. 'What's wrong with you all . . .?'

More laughter.

'And he's bold,' Poe continued. 'Best guess is that he deposited the body parts in full sight of everyone. He's calm too. If something didn't go to plan he either improvised or his contingencies were so well practised that despite operating in busy environments no one saw him, and the only cameras he's on are the ones he knew about. The kite in the tree is the only mistake he seems to have made.'

Poe paused. The room was silent, each face glued to his.

Another cop raised her hand. 'Is he finished?'

'Serial killers very rarely stop. They either get caught or they die. But this man . . . this man is dancing to a tune only he can hear. My answer is we don't know – he might be finished; he might just be getting started. We're in uncharted waters here so we're having to learn as we go.'

A palpable sense of fear and unease filled the room.

Good . . . Fear and unease were their friends right now.

'What are your plans for tomorrow?' Flynn said when the room had cleared.

'Sean Carroll says he'll get back to us tonight with information on kite logos,' Poe said. 'There'll probably be a lot of names so I'll triage then set Tilly loose on them.'

'You working here?'

'From home.'

'I'll work from there as well, DI Flynn,' Bradshaw said. 'Poe sees things my program can't.'

'OK, makes sense.'

'It does. As you said to Detective Superintendent Jo Nightingale: "He's a pain in the . . . bottom but it's like having Rebus on the f-word team."'

'Why's it always me?' Flynn said, exasperated. 'Why don't you ever remember some of the things Poe says?'

'I do, but he adds things like "Don't tell the boss that, obviously."'

Poe smiled. After a while Flynn did too. Bradshaw stared at them quizzically.

Flynn said, 'I have the morning briefing to attend and then a strategy meeting with Superintendent Nightingale and the assistant chief. I'll join you at Herdwick Croft later.'

'Not happening,' Poe said.

Flynn's jaw hardened.

'Boss, the journey from the car park at Shap Wells is dodgy enough at the best of times but with half the hazards hidden by snow or standing water it's bloody treacherous. I accept that pregnancy isn't an illness but there has to be some common sense involved.'

Poe knew his words had hit home.

'I'm just not used to all this inactivity,' she said. 'Did you know that when I did my Krav Maga exercises this morning I couldn't even touch my toes? I'm a third dan black belt and I can't touch my toes.'

Poe, who hadn't been able to touch his toes since he left the army, said, 'You've got a fully formed human growing inside you, boss. Perhaps it's OK to take it easy for a while.'

Flynn gave him a weary smile. 'OK, I'll go to my meetings then rest up for the remainder of the day. See if I can get my ankle swelling down a bit. Maybe try and get a pair of normal-sized shoes on.'

She looked down at two emerging damp patches on her blue blouse.

'Saying that,' she said, 'I'd be just as happy if my fucking tits stopped leaking.'

Chapter 28

Bradshaw arrived at Herdwick Croft while Poe was out walking Edgar. She was waiting for them when they returned. He'd told her to ring him for a lift when she got to Shap Wells. Evidently she'd fancied the walk.

Poe didn't blame her. It was cold enough to sting the eyes but the morning was beautifully crisp and clear. His cough had improved overnight. It had progressed from tickly to hacking. He still felt weak and achy but he knew he was over the worst. A pale blue sky and a white horizon stretched on forever, the snow's crust was crunchy underfoot and the standing water was covered in unbroken sheets of ice. Edgar crashed through them with sheer joy.

Bradshaw had collected his mail for him. There was another one from the council's legal services. He threw it in the wood-burning stove without opening it.

'What was that, Poe?'

'Don't worry about it,' he said. 'Come on, we have work to do.'

And they did.

Carroll had called Poe late the previous night. He'd been in contact with as many event organisers as he could but it would take time to hear back from some of them as they were still away for Christmas. He'd sent them both a provisional list just after 10 p.m.

Unsurprisingly, lots of kite enthusiasts preferred flying things when it came to choosing a logo, and the list, at over one hundred names, was already too unwieldy to be useful.

'How do you want to do this, Tilly?'

'Murder wall?' she replied.

'Murder wall,' he agreed.

Herdwick Croft was small and tat-free. Everything that was there had earned the right to be there. Poe read a lot and any wall that was appliance-free had a bookcase hugging it. Cheap and mismatched, their fibreboard shelves sagged under the weight of a diverse selection of books. Most were non-fiction accounts of serial killers throughout the ages – Poe believed there were very few original thinkers when it came to murder and the answer was often found in the past. He had several books on mythology and religion – a rich seam of inspiration for serial killers – and books written by most of the major philosophers and thinkers, from Aristotle to Sartre. He also had shelves stuffed with paperbacks – with no television he read for pleasure as well as for work.

But . . . as important as books were to him, ever since the Immolation Man case Poe had kept a section of one wall free and used Blu Tack to display documents and photographs. Seeing them together, mosaic style, offered a different perspective than going through a logically laid-out file or printout from HOLMES 2 – the major enquiry software all police forces use. Seeing photographs that would ordinarily be in different parts of the file side-by-side allowed links to be made that might otherwise be missed. The dry, pale-blue scars of previous investigations peppered the wall like Smurf acne.

Bradshaw hadn't finished dividing the wall into triage columns – their way of conducting an initial sift – when Poe's mobile rang.

It was Sean Carroll. Poe put him on speakerphone.

'This is probably nothing, Sergeant Poe, but you know how I said that tracking down the person who did the silkscreen print transfer would be next to impossible?'

'I do.'

'Well, that might have been an exaggeration. I fixed my logo on using the museum's equipment so I wasn't aware of this, but I spoke to a man this morning who said that if you want something that's going to stay on, isn't going to fade, and can be scaled up or down depending on your needs, then there's one printer that kite enthusiasts tend to use up here.'

'And?'

'And I called him for you and he told me he did a gold pterodactyl logo for a man in Cumbria two years ago.'

'He's sure?'

'He is. Says it's the only one he's been asked to do.'

Bradshaw's program had identified the pterodactyl as the shape statistically most likely to be the one on the kite. He wondered what the odds were for any other kite-flyer having a pterodactyl logo that was also gold. High, he reckoned.

'I'm going to need a name and address.'

'Ah,' Carroll said. 'We may have a problem there. The only thing he can remember is the date he sent it back.'

'He can remember the date but not the name? That seems unlikely.'

'The buyer paid cash. Posted him the outline of the design he wanted along with an envelope with six twenty-pound notes.'

'So there's no credit card trail to follow.'

'Afraid not.'

'And he can't remember his name? Does he not keep records?'

'Usually. Says it must have slipped his mind this time.'

Poe grunted. 'In other words it was a cash-in-hand job so he didn't record it anywhere.'

'A penny hidden from the taxman is a penny earned,' Carroll said.

'How did he send the logo back?'

'Logos. There were two of them. And he sent them back

the way he always does: in a padded envelope with a large letter stamp fixed to it.'

Bollocks. Their promising lead had just turned into a duff one.

'I'm going to need to speak to him anyway.'

'He's expecting your call,' Carroll said. 'But there was one more thing.'

'Go on.'

'The buyer didn't include his home address with his payment.'

'So how—'

'How did he get hold of his logos?'

'Yes.'

'The designer was given the address of a courier firm in Carlisle. They have a collection service apparently.'

Poe breathed out in relief.

Carroll's printer friend might not have recorded the name of the man who'd ordered the logos but he was damn sure the courier firm would have recorded who'd collected them . . .

Chapter 29

Poe had visited ANL Parcels before. It had cropped up during the Jared Keaton investigation. He'd found them helpful. Even so, he doubted they would simply hand over client details without a warrant.

He considered ringing Nightingale and asking her to get one of the murder team to apply for it but quickly dismissed this. The warrant would need to be creatively worded. They couldn't say the man who'd purchased the silkscreen prints from Carroll's printer friend *was* the kite's owner, and because it was still up a tree in a wood, they weren't even sure the logo was a pterodactyl. Nightingale wouldn't be able to authorise that warrant.

Luckily Poe knew a man who could help . . .

Poe had met Owen Dent at a workshop on ethics. His speciality was the legal minefield of warrants, specifically how badly worded, or downright false, warrants could be cause for future appeals. They had shared a drink and had kept in sporadic touch ever since. He occasionally helped Poe with drafting warrants.

Poe wrote a five hundred-word summary of what they thought they knew, how they had come by the information and what they wanted.

He pressed send and sat back.

It was an hour before Owen Dent responded. He asked Poe to complete a 5 x 5 x 5 intelligence assessment. It was standard practice but Poe had deliberately avoided sending one with his summary.

5 x 5 x 5 was a three-stage intelligence evaluation system. The first stage, an evaluation of the source, Poe had to score as an E: Untested. He'd never met Carroll before, and he wasn't registered as an informant. The second stage, an evaluation of the intelligence received, Poe couldn't score high either – the information on the silkscreen printing was second-hand. They'd heard it from Carroll but Carroll had heard it from someone else. The third was information on how the intelligence could be disseminated. Poe didn't care so ticked the middle box.

He asked Bradshaw to download a blank template from the NCA intranet.

He looked at the completed 5 x 5 x 5 despondently, thought of a way he could improve either of the first two ratings and decided he couldn't. Bradshaw sent it back to Dent as an attachment with the word 'sorry' in the subject line.

'Don't worry, Poe,' came the reply.

Before he could stop her, Bradshaw typed 'Thank you'.

'Here we go,' Poe sighed.

'What is it, Poe?'

'You'll see.'

Sure enough an email appeared in the inbox. 'You're welcome,' it said.

'Owen's a nice man, but he *always* has to have the last word on any email exchange.'

Email etiquette aside, Owen Dent came through for them. Within fifteen minutes of receiving the 5 x 5 x 5, he'd sent them draft wording for a warrant that he assured them pushed what they had to the very edge without going into any grey legal areas.

Poe cut and pasted Owen's words into a warrant and pressed print.

He checked his watch and said, 'I'll get this signed at Kendal Magistrates' during the afternoon sitting. You stay here and carry on working. We won't be doing anything with it until tomorrow anyway.'

'OK, Poe.'

Two hours later Poe stood on the steps of Kendal Magistrates' Court. He sucked in the cold air, then wished he hadn't when he was hit with a coughing fit. It hadn't been a straightforward application, partly due to his insistence that the courtroom was cleared of press and the public, and partly due to the lack of solid evidence.

The middle magistrate of the three, known as the bench chair, had suspected Poe was on a fishing expedition and had asked searching questions. In the end, the persuasiveness of Owen Dent's words won through and the chair begrudgingly signed a warrant to seize information from ANL Parcels pertaining to the murders of Howard Teasdale, Rebecca Pridmore and Amanda Simpson.

Poe's spine stiffened as he reread the document. He was in the game now.

Chapter 30

'Why would people get things delivered to a courier's depot, Poe?' Bradshaw said. 'Why wouldn't they get them delivered straight to their home?'

It was 7.58 a.m. and they were outside ANL Parcels, waiting for them to open. Poe could see movement inside but it was the front desk he needed. He'd seen the delivery drivers ANL employed and some of them looked as though they'd witnessed evolution happening from the start; he doubted they'd be able to identify a computer, never mind search one to find a name from two years earlier.

'Lots of people do, Tilly,' Poe said. 'Some don't like getting home deliveries in case they're out. Things go missing, neighbours deny having signed for them. Wheelie bins get raided by drug addicts, that type of thing. Easier and safer for some to just go and collect it from the depot. And some people just don't want sellers knowing their home address.'

At eight o'clock exactly, the front door was unlocked. Poe and Bradshaw were first through. The receptionist hadn't even made it back to her desk.

Poe showed her his ID and asked to see the duty manager. They were asked to take a seat.

Rosie, the operations manager Poe had spoken to the last time he'd been there, approached them. She looked worried.

'Sergeant Poe,' she said, reaching for their outstretched hands, 'what can I help you with this time?'

The last time Poe had spoken to her, he'd been checking the chain of evidence on a blood sample. He'd found her open and helpful. He hoped she'd be the same after she'd read the warrant.

She took them through to her office and asked them to wait while she checked with the CEO. ANL was a local courier firm and there was no corporate headquarters or batteries of legal departments to check with – just a woman who'd built up her business from scratch.

Rosie read the warrant out over the phone. Eventually she nodded and said, 'Thank you, Alison.'

She touched her mouse and the ANL logo on the computer screen changed to a login screen. 'Tell me what you need,' she said.

An hour later Rosie provided them with a 'collect at depot' printout for the date stated on the warrant. Thirty-two names. Addresses all over Cumbria and south-west Scotland. Bradshaw completed a quick cross-reference and confirmed none of ANL's names were on the list that Carroll had provided the day before.

'And they were *all* collected?' Poe asked.

Rosie nodded.

'What ID would you need?'

'For a missed delivery it's either the card we leave or photo ID. For parcels delivered to the depot it's always photo ID.'

'Could someone claim it on their behalf?'

'If their ID has the same surname and address then we use discretion. As long as we're sure the person signing for the parcel is who they say they are, then we try to be helpful.'

Poe nodded and thanked her. When they got back in the car he handed the list to Bradshaw.

Reducing a list of thirty-two names down to a list of one was a job for a mathematical and analytical genius.

Chapter 31

On the way back to Herdwick Croft, Poe called Flynn and updated her.

'And how did you get this list of names?' she asked.

'Don't worry about it.'

'Poe . . . what did you do?'

'All above board,' he said. 'Ask Tilly.'

'All above board, DI Stephanie Flynn,' Bradshaw said. 'Poe had to ask his friend how to lie properly on the warrant but—'

'OK, OK, I've heard enough,' she cut in. 'This list, Poe, you're sure the killer's on it?'

Now wasn't the time to exaggerate. It was a lead based on second-hand information based on an assumption that a crumpled logo, when straightened out, would be what they thought it was. And, as Bradshaw had said, surely more than one kite enthusiast would have a flying dinosaur as a logo. Nerds liked dinosaurs.

He said as much.

'OK,' Flynn said after a short pause, 'I'll pass it up to Superintendent Nightingale but don't expect her to leap up and down with excitement – this is about as tenuous as it gets.'

'It is,' Poe admitted. 'I don't think we can ignore it, though.'

'You can't,' she agreed. 'I take it you're going back to Herdwick Croft to work on reducing the numbers down from thirty-two?'

'We are,' Bradshaw replied. 'I'll use statistical correlation of criminal behaviour and some other tricks I've wanted to try for a while. I'll let Poe reduce it further by giving him a red pen.'

Bradshaw wasn't being sarcastic. The red pen method had worked for them in the past. Science could only take things so far; sometimes it needed instinct.

'Sounds like a plan,' Flynn said.

'We'll ring you every hour, boss,' Poe said. 'I take it you're with Nightingale?'

'I'm taking the day off, Poe. I've got indigestion like you wouldn't believe. It feels like I've been eating raw chillies all week.'

Poe winced. He'd heard that indigestion was probably the worst thing in the later stages of being pregnant.

'And don't ask me about my haemorrhoids.'

'I definitely won't,' Poe said, quickly revising his last thought.

'They've inflamed so much they're almost glowing. If there was a power cut I swear I could read by the bastards,' she said. 'That's something they don't tell you at the mother and baby class.'

Poe looked at Bradshaw. 'What? No questions, Tilly?'

'Are your breasts still leak—'

'Not long now, boss, hang in there,' Poe said hurriedly.

'Oh, while I remember,' Flynn said, 'Nightingale wants you both at Carleton Hall for a briefing tomorrow morning. She's bringing in an expert in semiotic studies.'

Bradshaw booed. She turned in her seat and gave Poe a double thumbs down.

'What the hell's semiotic studies?' Poe said.

'It's the pseudo-science that claims to interpret signs and symbols,' Bradshaw said. 'And it is, of course, an utter waste of time. You'd have more chance predicting the future from animal poo.'

'The Met uses someone to help decipher gang tags,' Flynn said.

'And that's who Nightingale's got, is it? This London dork?' Poe said.

'No. She has a lecturer from the university coming in,' she replied. 'He's going to talk about what the bird symbols found at the first crime scene might signify. The ones that the mug had been wrapped in.'

Bradshaw booed again.

'She's desperate, Tilly,' Flynn said.

'I'm with Tilly on this, boss. It *does* sound like a waste of time,' Poe said.

'Oh, it's a massive waste of time, Poe,' Flynn agreed. 'But she wants you there and she's running the show.'

'Fine. What time?'

'Ten o'clock.'

'We'll be there.'

'Good. And Tilly, please don't boo tomorrow.'

Chapter 32

'We'll need a new list, Poe,' Bradshaw said. 'We need to know about everyone who lives at those addresses, not just the names ANL supplied to us. It's possible that the two logos were a present for someone. The person who ordered them might not be who they were intended for.'

Poe nodded. 'And if they were a present, it could explain why they weren't delivered to the home address – they wanted them to be a surprise.'

'I'll log onto the Police National Computer and the electoral roll.'

When Bradshaw finished adding anyone who lived in the same house as those people on the 'collect at depot' list, they had a final tally of seventy names. She spent an hour doing what she called 'snap profiles' – basic information such as gender, date of birth, ethnicity, any history of criminal behaviour – then Blu Tacked everything to the murder wall.

'I'll go through it first, Tilly,' Poe said.

He started by putting a red line through all the females. Poe had seen the killer on the CCTV at Fiskin's Food Hall, and although his face had been obscured, he was very definitely male. And he'd moved like a younger man so Poe felt confident in putting a line through anyone over the age of sixty.

That left eighteen.

Two of the men in the right age range were Asian and one

was black. Nightingale's team had interviewed every member of John Bull Haulage and all the bookmen who'd been seen entering the office had been white. Bradshaw added that all research on serial killers suggested they kept to their own ethnic groups when selecting victims. Poe put a red line through them.

Fifteen.

Bradshaw took over. One of the men was in the Royal Navy, had been overseas for three months and wasn't due back until April.

Fourteen.

Another was ex-army. He'd lost an arm in an IED incident in Afghanistan. Poe crossed him off – using a garrotte needed two hands.

Thirteen.

Using a database Poe didn't recognise, Bradshaw discovered that one of the men had spent Christmas in London and was yet to return and another was an Australian who had flown back to Melbourne for the Boxing Day test match. She highlighted them both on her screen – her version of Poe's red pen.

Eleven.

Bradshaw wanted to reduce the list further by using her rudimentary profiles, but Poe stopped her.

Two hours later and Bradshaw had gone deep into the online lives of the remaining eleven. The murder wall was almost full.

Poe stared at the information she'd gathered. Some of the people on the list were active on social media, others barely touched it. Some took their online security seriously, others may as well have posted photographs of their birth certificates and bank accounts on Facebook.

His gut told him the man they were looking for would be naturally secretive, but a lack of social media presence wasn't a safe way to reduce the list further. If he was clever he'd have taken steps to blend in online. Bradshaw maintained countless social media avatars, all of which could withstand scrutiny by a third party; there was no reason their killer couldn't have done the same. A bland profile full of fluff and cat videos would disguise his secretive nature without him ever posting anything of significance.

On that basis it could have been any of them.

Eleven names.

One killer.

Chapter 33

Poe was woken by a debilitating headache. His sinuses had swollen during the night, reducing the amount of oxygen getting to his brain. He shut his eyes and tried to will the pain away. He reached out for the aspirins he kept by the side of his bed and dry crunched four tablets. He laid his head gently on the pillow and gave the drug time to work.

Turning his shower up as hot as it would go, he forced himself to stand under it until he no longer felt like he had a knife in his skull. He stepped out, wrapped himself in a towel and checked his phone. He had a text from Bradshaw.

The Mole People had found something.

Not only had they completed psychological profiles on the eleven men left on the list, they had also identified their preferred suspect.

His name was Robert Cowell. He was twenty-two years old and he lived with his sister in a rented house near the Cumberland Infirmary in Carlisle.

Poe ran downstairs, his headache forgotten, and studied his details on the murder wall.

He remembered Cowell. Yesterday he'd been close to putting a red line through him on the basis of age alone. Twenty-two seemed far too young to be such an accomplished murderer.

Poe read the Mole People's new information and didn't find it compelling. None of the usual causal factors that turned a normal person into a premeditated killer were present. He'd had an unremarkable childhood. Didn't break any records at school but didn't stand out as a dumb-dumb. He didn't play any sports, but that wasn't the big deal it had been when Poe was at school. Nerds were in vogue now. His late teens had been uneventful too. He'd taken a job at a small website development company but had left after three years to go into business with his sister who had largely followed the same life pattern.

The Mole People's analysis was that, although he was statistically their preferred suspect, Cowell was more likely to be a conspiracy theorist than a murderer. Bradshaw had calculated that there was less than a 10 per cent chance that he had the capacity to kill.

Less than a one-in-ten chance.

More than they'd had before but nowhere near enough.

Poe needed more information.

He picked up Bradshaw two hours before they were due at Carleton Hall for the semiotic studies briefing. Poe's opinion hadn't changed overnight: it was still a colossal waste of time. He'd considered using his recent bout of ill health as an excuse to stay at home and spend more time obsessing at the murder wall. See if he could squeeze any more inspiration from it. In the end he decided it would only end badly if Bradshaw attended the briefing alone.

He hadn't yet decided whether to tell Nightingale that Robert Cowell was a suspect she should look into. The way they'd narrowed down their seventy names was subjective, and the way they'd got their list was dubious. Sean Carroll's friend could well be the discerning kite flyers' printer of choice when it came to logos, but these days they could be ordered from anywhere. A man in the north-east of England *could* have designed the logo but it could just as easily have been designed by a child labourer in Bangladesh.

After Bradshaw had fussed over how awful he looked, she twisted round in her seat and shouted, 'Hi, Edgar! I've brought you some bacon.' She threw a couple of rashers through the bars of the dog guard. The spaniel gulped them down like a pelican eating fish.

'I'd have had that,' Poe muttered. He'd run out of bacon the previous night and had eaten a meat-free breakfast that morning.

'You eat too much bacon, Poe,' she said. 'Where are we going anyway?'

'We're taking a drive past Robert Cowell's house. I want to see if anything jumps out.'

'OK, Poe,' she replied, turning back round and fastening her seatbelt. 'I had a look on Google Street View and Google Maps last night. He lives in a semi-detached house in a modern cul-de-sac.'

Poe nodded. Images of Cowell's home had been included on the profile the Mole People had sent. It was a blah-blah suburban house on a family estate. The satellite image showed that the houses either side had swings and trampolines in their back gardens. That in itself didn't mean much: serial killers were almost all psychopaths, and psychopaths were the human equivalent of leaf-tailed geckos – experts at blending in. Still . . . it would have been nice if there was *something* suspicious about where he lived to take to Nightingale.

Because Poe couldn't risk Cowell spotting them as they filmed his house, he twisted the flexible arm of the phone cradle that Bradshaw had bought him and fixed his BlackBerry so it could record as they drove. Poe would drive slowly down Cowell's street, as if searching for an address, and Bradshaw would pretend to be talking to him.

Neither of them would look in the direction of his house.

Poe entered the estate and his first thought was how clean it was. Despite being twelve years old, it looked like it had only been finished the previous week. As Poe drove down the street, geometric shapes straight out of an architect's brochure flickered past the edge of his vision. The building company had tried to make each house stand out a bit by using different types of brick but the result was negligible. It seemed people no longer cared that the house they lived in had been repurposed all over the north of England. The same families living in the same design on the same type of estates.

Poe had lived like that once. Never again.

He reached the end of the cul-de-sac and used the turning circle to about-face. He waited as Bradshaw adjusted the camera before setting off again, this time at a faster pace. If anyone was watching it would appear that they hadn't found the house they were looking for and were now moving onto a different street. As they passed Cowell's house, Poe couldn't resist taking a quick glance.

The kitchen's blinds were up and Poe could see the glossy white of a fridge-freezer and the brushed steel of an oven extractor hood. He saw the same thing in the next kitchen on the street and realised that the appliances must have come with the house.

And then they were out of the estate and back on the main road. Job done. If he put his foot down they'd have enough time to review the footage before they met with Nightingale.

They found a quiet corner in Carleton Hall and Bradshaw uploaded the video to her laptop. They hunched over the screen and watched it a dozen times. Robert Cowell's house was the same as the others. Nothing stood out, nothing raised suspicion.

Nightingale walked in.

'Have you got two minutes?' she said.

They followed her down the corridor and into her office.

'No DI Flynn today?' she asked.

'She's not feeling great,' Poe said. 'She's up to date with everything we've done, though. Still making sure we stay out of trouble.'

Nightingale cracked a tired smile. She looked exhausted. Bleary, bloodshot eyes in shrunken sockets. The pallid skin of someone who hasn't spent enough time outside. Yesterday's clothes hung on the back of her door.

'You OK, ma'am?' Poe asked.

'Have you got anything for me, Sergeant Poe?'

She sounded frustrated. Poe understood why. With the surveillance of the kite, she'd called a play that wasn't working. It hadn't been the wrong play but if her assistant chief asked another force to undertake a progress review, the detectives coming in would have had eight hours sleep and be armed with twenty-twenty hindsight. Their first question would be about her effective resource strategy. A large number of detectives had been taken out of the mainstream investigation to watch the tree. So far she'd got nothing for it.

'It's possible the kite logos were provided by a printer in Newcastle,' he said. 'We don't have a name but we've tracked the parcel to a courier firm in Carlisle. We've narrowed down the list of names they gave us from seventy to eleven.'

Nightingale didn't ask how he had convinced ANL Parcels to provide their customer details. Poe suspected she already knew. Flynn had probably told her.

Poe handed her the Mole People's profiles.

'Anyone stand out?' she said after she'd flicked through them.

Poe told her that Robert Cowell was statistically their most likely suspect.

'How likely?' she asked.

'Under ten per cent.'

Nightingale frowned. 'We can only surprise him once. If we rush in now and find nothing – and let's face it he's hardly put a foot wrong so far – then he'll be out in twenty-four hours and he'll either disappear or clean up.'

'We had a look at his house this morning,' Poe said.

'Who told you to do that?' she said sharply.

'We weren't peeping through his letterbox, ma'am, we drove past quickly with a fixed camera.'

'And?'

'Nothing,' he admitted. 'Nice estate. Quiet. One of those new builds cropping up everywhere.'

'So we're back to watching the tree, hoping the killer comes back for the kite.'

Poe said nothing. At some point, no matter how hard it was, you had to cut bait. Stop throwing good detectives into a bad gig. He shuddered to think how many investigative hours had been lost watching a tree.

'You could put a team on Cowell,' Poe said.

Nightingale let out a long sigh. It sounded like she was deflating.

'I don't have unlimited resources, Poe,' she said. 'I'll need to speak to the chief. See if she can stretch the budget. She might not, though – not for a one-in-ten chance.'

Poe didn't push it. He wasn't convinced that Cowell was their man either.

Chapter 34

The expert in semiotic studies, clearly enjoying a rare moment of employment, looked like he was auditioning for Doctor Who. He wore a tweed trench coat and a scarf, and had sweeping hair he had to keep flicking out of his eyes.

It seemed the ill-health excuse Poe had thought of using was catching. Half the room was empty and the cops who were there looked tired and cranky.

'Ladies and gents,' the man said, 'my name is Spencer Maxwell and I'm an academic with an expertise in semiotic studies. Detective Superintendent Nightingale has asked me to speak to you about the pictures of Anatids that were left at one of your crime scenes—'

'Anatids?' a huge cop with a ham-coloured face and a monobrow said.

'The Anatidae are the biological family of birds that includes swans, ducks and geese. They are—'

'Well say that then,' Monobrow snapped. 'It's bad enough we've got to sit through this shit without you talking bloody Latin.'

'It's not Lat . . .'

Monobrow glared at him.

'Yes, well. Anyway, I'm here to talk to you about what these Ana . . . birds might represent to the killer. Hopefully by the time I've finished you'll be able to draw up a detailed profile of what he wants and what he plans to do next. Are there any questions?'

There weren't. There were a lot of bored faces, though. Maxwell used the silence to distribute some handouts.

'So, what is semiotics? Semiotics is anything that can stand for something else. A symbol rarely stands on its own; it is almost always part of something. To the person using the symbol – and in this case, judging by the neck to body ratio, it's almost certainly a swan – it will have significant meaning.'

A bored-looking cop on the front row stuck up his hand. 'What does a swan mean then?'

'Traditionally, swans have represented grace and white swans have represented light and purity, even the higher self. Swans also symbolise travelling to the otherworld after death. There is also the well-known fable "The Ugly Duckling", which is about transformation and fulfilling potential. That your perpetrator has chosen a *black* swan is, I think, very telling. He's letting you know that he was once pure but he is no longer. When you catch him you'll find he has been through a transformative life event recently. It is also possible that he thinks he is helping the people he's killing.'

Bradshaw folded her arms and scowled. 'What a blockhead,' she said.

'This handout is as much use as tits on a flatfish!' Monobrow snapped.

'If you don't like it, you know where the bin is!' Maxwell replied.

Poe had nodded off. The shouting had woken him.

It seemed Maxwell had lost control of the room. These weren't impressionable students, desperate for good grades and willing to put up with anything; these were hard-edged, sleep-deprived cops, most of whom had barely seen their families since Christmas Eve.

Monobrow didn't back down. He ripped his handout in half, walked over to the bin and dropped it in.

'Fuck this,' he said, before storming out and slamming the door behind him.

Maxwell turned white. Everyone else tried not to laugh. Even Bradshaw was smiling.

Poe wasn't.

Something about their exchange was bothering him. He knew what it was but he didn't know why.

It was the bin. Maxwell had told Monobrow to put his handout in the bin and Monobrow had.

Bins . . .

'Show me that video again, Tilly,' Poe whispered.

Bradshaw brought her laptop from her bag and opened it. She muted the sound and pressed play. Robert Cowell's street sped by in real time. She slowed it down.

Nothing.

No bins.

She loaded the second video, the one they'd taken after Poe had turned around.

And there it was: a solitary dark grey bin at the top of Cowell's drive. Hidden by a hedge on the way in, it had only been visible on the way out.

Poe knew what he had to do.

He stood. 'Please excuse us, Mr Maxwell.'

Bradshaw looked at him quizzically but followed him out of the room.

When they were outside she said, 'Whatever are we doing, Poe?'

'We're speeding things up, Tilly, that's what we're doing,' he replied. 'But first, we need to go and get some things from the CSI store.'

Chapter 35

'She's stuck in a loop, boss. Fixated on that kite. A literal case of not being able to see the wood because of the tree,' Poe said.

It was early the following day and he was in his car, waiting. He had half an hour before he was supposed to be in position and he'd used that time to call Flynn and tell her what he was up to.

'She doesn't have your freedoms, Poe,' Flynn said. 'You can't expect her to drop a perfectly valid line of enquiry because you want help staking out a suspect who our own profile says is unlikely to be the person we're looking for.'

'You've got a better idea?' he asked.

'I have. It's called doing analysis and supporting the investigation like we were brought in for.'

After a short delay he said, 'You give your ideas names?'

Flynn snorted. 'Dickhead. What are you and Tilly doing today?'

'Tilly's at Carleton Hall. She's taking Edgar to the dog section to play with the drugs spaniels there, and then she's heading over to a room we've set up with CSI.'

'Why?'

'I don't have anyone to look after him and the dog section very kindly said they'd—'

'Why is Tilly in a specially set up CSI room?'

'Because,' Poe said, 'I'm going bin-dipping.'

The lone bin must have been percolating in the back of Poe's mind for some time. He put down living at Herdwick Croft as the reason it had taken him so long to make the connection. He didn't have a bin collection. Initially he hadn't requested one, as he'd wanted to keep as low a profile as he could. And now the council had found him, providing a bin service would have undermined their position that Herdwick Croft wasn't a legal dwelling. Poe could have used it in the civil case – an 'if the council collect my bins then they must also recognise it as my home' kind of thing. Like a smellier version of *Miracle on 34th Street*.

Instead, whatever rubbish he couldn't burn he bagged up and took to the council tips.

But . . . when he'd lived in Hampshire he *had* had a bin service. And there were a few idiosyncrasies associated with British rubbish collections that he hadn't forgotten. And even in the environmentally friendly age of recycling, where you were expected to root through your garbage like Great Uncle Bulgaria, separating one lot of shit from another lot of shit, there was one golden rule: the first person to put their bin out was a knob.

And there was always one. One household who ignored the never-enforced rule about what time you were allowed to put your rubbish by the kerb. Poe knew there were reasons to put your bin out the day before collection: you weren't going to be home until after bin day; you didn't like dragging them out in the dark; you liked annoying your neighbours . . .

A lone bin at night often meant that the rubbish had been collected but the bin's owner hadn't been home yet to put it away. But a lone bin in the morning meant that someone was going against bin etiquette, because if it had been bin day, *all* the houses would have had bins outside. In Poe's experience, a lone bin in the morning meant that bin collection was the following day.

That meant that right about now, Robert Cowell's bin was sitting on the edge of his drive, waiting to be collected. Where Poe could legally grab the contents without the need for a warrant.

Or at least he thought he could. In the same way that the term 'implied consent' allows the police to enter gardens and driveways and postmen to deliver the mail, Poe believed that anything in a wheelie bin was classed as 'disclaimed'. Admittedly, it was a grey area, and ultimately a judge would decide whether it had been gathered legally. Anything in a wheelie bin was the property of the council anyway – it was where the authority to issue fines came from when the wrong rubbish was put in the wrong bin.

Despite being sure he was acting within the law, Poe was being extra cautious. The bin men were collecting Cowell's rubbish on his behalf. He and Bradshaw had visited CSI the day before and signed out three extra-large paper evidence bags. Three feet by one and a half, they were the same size as a standard bin liner. Poe had agreed to meet the crew that serviced Cowell's road in the nearby hospital car park to make sure they understood what it was he was asking of them.

He had considered doing a shift with them but he'd been convinced otherwise. Notwithstanding the insurance issues, no one thought Poe would be able to hack it. And he was minded to believe them; living the life he did at Herdwick Croft had made him lean and wiry, but the men and women who dragged heavy wheelie bins for a living had muscles like cables.

There was another more important consideration: the killer could have been observing the investigation. If he had, then he'd almost certainly have seen Poe. If Cowell was their man, Poe dressing as a bin man would set off all sorts of alarms.

An accident at the Hardwicke Circus roundabout had brought rush hour to a standstill and the refuse vehicle was running late. It was why he'd had the time to call Flynn. He had thought of floating it past Nightingale as well but decided it would be better to seek forgiveness than ask for permission. Flynn would tell her anyway but he'd left it late enough so he couldn't be stopped.

Poe needed to be proactive. He couldn't just sit around and hope the killer made a mistake and collected his kite. His brain wasn't wired that way. Would his life be easier if it was? Undoubtedly. He didn't enjoy feeling like he was under permanent attack but it was a price he'd learned to pay a long time ago.

As expected, his mobile rang. It was Nightingale. He was saved the decision of whether or not to answer by the rumbling and metal clanking of a lorry. Ten seconds later the refuse vehicle rounded the corner and parked beside him.

Poe jumped out to greet them.

The shift supervisor was a small, mean-looking man called Ben Stephenson. He was sucking on a cigarette like it was an exhaust pipe. Poe felt the power in the man's grip when they shook hands.

The crew gathered round Poe as he talked them through what he needed.

'I can't tell if he's at home,' Poe said, 'so we have to assume he is.'

He handed Stephenson the three evidence bags. He took them without looking.

'I don't know how you usually do things but if you park up short when you get to his house, he won't be able to see the back when you transfer his rubbish into my evidence bags.'

The refuse truck was rear loading. The crew dragged the bins to the back then a mechanical arm hoisted them in the air and tipped the contents into the vehicle's well. By parking up short Cowell shouldn't be able to see what was happening.

'And he's definitely a tax dodger?'

'That's what we're trying to find out.'

It was the only lie he'd told.

'I need you to video it,' Poe said, handing Stephenson a camera he'd bought the day before. 'From the moment the bin is collected to the moment the evidence bags are sealed. We can't have him claiming you lot planted evidence.'

One of the men, a brute with a face like an Easter Island head, grunted. Poe was under no illusion what would happen to Cowell if he made an accusation against this lot.

They agreed to meet back at the hospital in an hour. Poe wished them luck.

Chapter 36

Poe smiled in satisfaction as he watched the video Ben Stephenson had shot.

The refuse truck crew had done a sterling job. Robert Cowell was obsessively neat and his wheelie bin contained no loose rubbish. It was all tied up in kitchen bin bags. It had taken the crew seconds to lift them out and seal them in Poe's evidence bags. They'd even gone through the motions of putting the bin on the truck's mechanical arm to put it through the disposal cycle. Poe hadn't identified a single thing he'd have done differently.

As a token of his appreciation, he handed each of them a crate of beer and a bottle of whisky.

'Just nail the cheating bastard,' one of them said.

'We will,' Poe replied.

Poe returned to Carleton Hall where Bradshaw and a CSI technician waited for him. With a video recording everything, the first evidence bag was emptied onto a forensic groundsheet on the floor. Before they had a chance to start rooting through the rubbish, Nightingale walked in. She was annoyed, but not angry, that he'd gone behind her back. She checked Ben Stephenson's video and agreed they had an unimpeachable chain of custody.

'I'll come back in a couple of hours to see how you're getting on,' Nightingale said. 'Call me if you find anything.'

Poe looked at Bradshaw when she'd shut the door.

'You ready?'

She was poised with her laptop, ready to analyse or go deeper into anything they found.

'I feel dirty, Poe,' she replied.

He nodded. He did too. And not just because he was knee-deep in greasy takeaway boxes, stinking chicken carcasses and bloodied disposable razors. Reverse-engineering the lifestyle of a suspect by going through their discarded rubbish was a window into their most intimate secrets. Poe didn't care what the law said; it *was* an invasion of privacy.

'Can't be helped,' he said. 'This is the other part of police work, Tilly. The part the public never get to see.'

'It's very smelly,' she said.

Poe nodded. He'd been trying not to breathe through his nose since the bag had been emptied. Carlisle City Council operated a once-a-fortnight household rubbish collection so some of the stink was two weeks old.

The CSI technician recorded each individual piece of rubbish Poe picked up. Poe didn't know what he was looking for, only that he'd know it when he saw it. To that end he didn't have a system – he just dove in and worked his way through.

To clear space and to keep the air as fresh as possible, Poe worked on the organic matter first. Other than confirming Cowell had a healthier diet than he did, it didn't reveal anything useful. He soon had most of it bagged up again. Before long, the fetid stench of sour milk, mouldy vegetable peelings and rotten eggs faded.

Next he worked through what he considered normal house-hold trash. Milk cartons, empty crisp packets, paper tissues – the kind of things he had in his own bin at Herdwick Croft. This took a while longer as each piece had to be recorded, examined and catalogued. After an hour he took a break to change his gloves. He sniffed the soiled ones he'd discarded.

'You don't see this on the recruitment posters, Tilly: join the police and poke around someone's rubbish. Try not to stick your finger through a bag of week-old dog shit while you're at it.'

'Yuk,' Bradshaw said, her nose wrinkled. 'I didn't even know he had a dog.'

'I didn't either.' He sniffed the discarded glove again. 'But that's definitely shit.'

After a cup of tea they walked up to the dog section to see Edgar. He seemed to be enjoying himself. The springer spaniels were on an unstructured play session and there was no dog better at playing than Edgar. He yelped with excitement when he saw them both. A dog handler threw in a punctured football and Edgar lost interest as he joined the scramble to reach it first.

'Charming,' Poe said.

Back in the CSI room, Poe suited up and opened the next evidence bag. Bradshaw took up station at her laptop. So far he hadn't passed her anything. He hoped to soon. He was tired of being sweaty and grimy, and he was tired of looking through stuff that had no bearing on anything. So far his gamble wasn't paying off. He decided to sod logic and just stick his hand in until he could pass her something to examine.

His hand touched some papers. They must have been at the bottom of the bin as they were stuck together and stained with tea or coffee. Poe handed them to the CSI technician who separated and photographed them before passing them to Bradshaw.

For an hour they worked their way through the second of the three evidence bags. Bradshaw kept up a steady stream of chatter as they did. He suspected it was keeping her mind off the smell. She asked him what Flynn might call her baby. Poe had no idea. He still couldn't get his head around the idea that his boss would soon have an infant to care for.

'I think they should call him Bruce if he's a boy and Diana if she's a girl. They'd be cool choices.'

'They wouldn't happen to be superhero names, would they?' he said.

No answer.

'I bet they are.'

Again, no answer.

Poe looked up but Bradshaw wasn't listening.

Instead she was poring over images on her laptop screen. What looked like the lens and clip from a small head-torch were slotted over the end of her iPhone. A lead connected the phone to her laptop.

'What's that on your phone, Tilly?'

'It's a macro lens, Poe,' she said without looking up. 'It transforms the camera into a digital microscope. I've been able to take detailed photographs at times twenty-one magnification.'

'Of?'

But she was back in her mind again, oblivious to the outside world. Poe kept quiet and let her work.

Eventually she raised her hand and punched the air in triumph.

'Yes!' she said.

And then she told him why.

And everything changed.

Chapter 37

Poe had once been asked why the police made arrests so early in the morning. He'd replied that it was common sense – that dawn was the part of the day when the suspect was most likely to be home.

And officially there were other reasons.

That early in the morning, the door crashing down under the weight of battering rams gave the police an advantage over sleepy suspects. There was less chance of wits being gathered and evidence being flushed away. An offender known to be violent was less likely to be so when only wearing underpants. And finally, dawn raids caused less disruption to everyone else on the street.

But mainly the police did dawn raids because they'd *always* done dawn raids.

Poe had attended the midnight briefing for the arresting officers and given a short talk on how they'd honed everything down to this one suspect. The men and women in the room didn't care about that. They were uniformed cops whose only involvement in the case would be executing the arrest. They were much more interested in what he knew about Robert Cowell.

Was he known to carry weapons?

Yes. A garrotte.

Anything else?

Probably. No one went straight to the garrotte. A garrotte was something you eventually got to. It was the end of a killer's journey into weapon proficiency, not the beginning.

Would he run or would he fight?

Poe didn't know.

Could they expect anyone else to be in the house?

Probably his sister.

And after that it was all about the logistics. The crash team were in charge and they ran the show. Poe was told he could attend but only as an observer . . .

Which was why he was in his car, engine running to keep warm air circulating, just two streets away from Robert Cowell's cul-de-sac.

He'd been there for an hour and a half already, when the blackness was absolute and the air felt refrigerated. He'd sat silently and sipped his coffee, fingers tracing the swirling steam rising from the hole in the cardboard cup's plastic lid. The coffee was long gone. The taste nothing but a memory, the lingering smell now almost imperceptible.

It was starting to get light – more a sensation than anything tangible. The birds knew first, of course, their chirps provoking many more. Melodious choruses without structure or pattern. Poe smiled. Anything seemed possible at dawn. It was a new day, a fresh page waiting to be written on.

A burst of static came over the radio he'd been given. It was followed by a series of quiet instructions. Confirmations really. Everyone knew what they were doing at this point.

Poe checked his watch.

The arrest team was ready.

'Go! Go! Go!'

Police officers are like greyhounds: they have a natural chase instinct.

If a member of the public runs, even one they have no interest in, the average cop is going to put their head down and take after them.

So, when Robert Cowell's sister jumped out of the bedroom window and ran, three cops sped after her. She was half-awake and dressed only in a T-shirt and knickers – the chasing cops were fully awake and flowing with adrenaline. The chase didn't last long.

Poe followed all this on the radio. Excited instructions yelled. Shouted requests for updates. And finally calm.

'Suspect in custody, ma'am,' a voice said. Poe recognised him as a sergeant from the briefing.

'CSI to me, please,' Nightingale replied. 'Oh, and Poe, if you're listening, you can come in as well.'

A cop with a clipboard was already controlling egress and access to the house. The vans carrying Robert Cowell and his sister, Rhona, had already left. They'd been taken to Durranhill, Cumbria's newest and most ridiculous-looking police station.

Poe suited up and signed into the outer cordon. Nightingale was waiting for him.

'He was awake but he didn't resist,' she said.

'And the sister?'

'She ran, as you might have heard. We don't know why at this stage.'

Neither of them stated the obvious: that they might have been in it together. A brother and sister killing spree unlike any seen before in the UK.

'What do you think?' Poe asked.

'Oh, he did it,' she replied. 'And she either knew or she assisted him.'

Poe raised his eyebrows.

'There was a bit of a fuck up,' Nightingale admitted. 'Robert was being escorted out of the house when the cops returned with Rhona.'

'And they spoke,' Poe said. He didn't phrase it as a question.

'They did. Well, she did at least. She shouted "Don't say anything" before anyone could stop her. Luckily the cops on Robert muffled his reply.'

Poe considered this. In the grand scheme of things a successfully executed arrest where no one was hurt wasn't a bad exchange for one small mistake.

And it also looked like the Mole People had been right: Robert Cowell *was* their killer.

The next question was why?

Chapter 38

There were four people in the room: Robert Cowell and his solicitor on one side of the table, Poe on the other. Bradshaw sat in a chair in the corner. Nightingale hadn't been keen for a civilian to sit in on an interview but she hadn't had a choice: Bradshaw was the only person who fully understood what she'd found.

Bradshaw was nervous. Poe knew why: her filter between thought and speech had improved over the last year but she still blurted out things. She didn't want to let anyone down.

Poe had chosen the smallest and drabbest interview room available. He wanted Cowell to feel cramped and claustrophobic. Wanted him feeling as though the walls were closing in on him.

Poe stared across the table.

Although he knew that they mutated and evolved, Poe was forced to admit that Robert Cowell was the most unlikely serial killer he'd ever come across. A stringy bundle of nerves, he was tall and heron-like and paler than Bradshaw. He had arms like noodles and a voice like a cartoon mouse. His hair was dyed black and held in a low ponytail. He looked like the kind of man who'd had nosebleeds as a child.

And he was terrified. Fidgety. Sweating. His rapid, blinking eyes were looking at anything but Poe. Far cry from the brazen killer they'd been chasing.

Cowell's solicitor was a grey-faced man named Jon Lear. He was frowning.

Poe thought he knew why. So far, everyone Lear had dealt

with had been wearing a uniform or a suit but Poe was wearing jeans and a jumper and Bradshaw was wearing cargo trousers and a superhero T-shirt. Black Panther this time. He must have realised they weren't Cumbrian cops but he didn't yet know who they worked for.

Poe planted his elbows on the table like they were fence posts.

'It's been a while since I've spoken to someone whose life is in more of a mess than my own,' he said.

Poe laid down a photograph of the kite. As soon as Cowell had been taken into custody, CSI had recovered it and fast-tracked the lab work. The photograph on the table had been taken when the kite had been removed from the tree and straightened out.

'This is your kite, yes?' Poe said, pointing to the gold ptero-dactyl logos.

Cowell picked up the photograph. His brow furrowed. Before Lear could stop him, he said, 'Where did you find it?'

'We'll get to that soon enough. Is it yours, Robert?'

'It looks like it.'

'When was the last time you saw it?'

'A few weeks ago. I had it outside drying and it was stolen.'

Poe nodded. He'd anticipated this response – it was the only explanation available to him. They'd found photographs on Cowell's computer of him flying it and his prints and DNA were all over the frames, grips and fabric.

'Did you report the theft?' Poe said. 'A kite like that doesn't come cheap, I understand.'

Cowell shook his head. 'At first I thought my sister had hidden it. Trying to stop me practising before a meet. She's done it before but she always returns it.'

'But she didn't this time?'

'No. I was in the process of buying a new one. I was in

Manchester a couple of days ago actually. Rhona and I stayed overnight and visited a few shops.'

That explained why his bin had been left out early: he hadn't been home to put it out at the normal time. The unprompted mention of his sister reminded Poe that she'd run but Robert hadn't. He was tempted to go off script and see if he could find out why.

Before he'd entered the room Poe had been watching Rhona Cowell's interview on the monitor. When the police had broken down their door, she hadn't long been out of the shower and her dark hair – beaded and braided close to her scalp in a style Bradshaw said was called cornrows – was still wet, like damp rope. The hair at the back of her neck clicked whenever her head moved. She had perched on the chair catlike, with her legs tucked under her and out of sight. Her smile was lazy and confident, like she was the only one who understood the punchline. Even in the shapeless forensic suit she was wearing, Poe could tell she was a beguiling woman. High cheekbones and clear skin. A natural beauty, the kind most often associated with supermodels from Nordic countries.

Unlike her brother, she had taken her own advice and said nothing. Not a word, not even to confirm her name.

Poe decided to leave it for now. Why she ran could wait until he had more leverage.

'Do you know where we found your kite?' he asked Cowell.

He shook his head.

'For the tape, please.'

'No.'

Poe upturned another photograph. This time it was the kite in situ. Not one of the rough-and-ready ones he'd snapped with his BlackBerry, this was a professional one taken by a CSI photographer on a raised platform.

'It was up a tree in a wood on the outskirts of Dalston. Does that ring a bell?'

'No.'

Poe turned over the next photograph. It was a close up of lines tangled around the trunk. A knot could be clearly seen.

'To me it looks as though it's been tied up there. Would you agree, Robert?'

Cowell nodded.

'For the tape.'

'I agree. It does look as though it has been tied up there. What's this have to do with me, though? I told you, my kite was stolen weeks ago.'

Poe showed Cowell more photographs. This time they were of the view taken *from* the tree. One of them was a long-range shot of Rebecca Pridmore's back garden.

'And would you also agree that where this kite had been tied to the tree offered a perfect view of this house?'

'I would.'

'So what would you say if I told you that the owner of this house, a woman called Rebecca Pridmore, was murdered just before Christmas?'

Cowell's eyes widened. His mouth opened.

'Murdered?'

'And mutilated.' Poe rooted through the file and showed him a photograph of Rebecca's fingers on the carpet tiles at John Bull Haulage.

Cowell clamped his eyes shut.

'These were left under the Christmas tree in an office in Carlisle. They were found on December twenty-fourth.'

Poe tucked the photograph away. Showing disturbing crime scene photographs, even to the perpetrator, could be viewed as intimidation if done excessively.

'Unpleasant, isn't it?' Poe said.

Cowell's solicitor frowned. 'I assume you think whoever put my client's kite up that tree is also responsible for this murder?'

'Absolutely we do.'

'And my client absolutely denies having had anything to do with any of this,' Lear said. 'I would draw your attention to his earlier statement about the kite's theft . . . Robert, are you OK?'

Cowell had gasped. He couldn't tear his eyes from the top photograph on the pile. It had been exposed when Poe had picked up the one above it, the one of Rebecca's fingers.

It was a photograph of the Secret Santa mug – the one with #BSC6 printed on the side. And for some reason it bothered Cowell far more than its gruesome predecessor.

He began trembling. His breath became ragged.

'OK, this has gone on far enough,' Lear said. 'I need a consultation break.'

Chapter 39

'My client has explained that his kite was stolen some weeks ago and this is therefore circumstantial evidence at best,' Lear said after the interview had recommenced. 'Now, I assume from your informal dress code that the pair of you are with some specialist unit? Why don't you cut to the chase and show us the real evidence?'

Poe watched Cowell for a moment more.

'As you wish,' he said eventually. 'Tilly, you're up.'

Bradshaw stood and moved to the seat beside Poe. As they'd practised, she waited for him to introduce her.

'This is Matilda Bradshaw. She's a civilian analyst with the National Crime Agency. She's here to explain some technical evidence.'

Bradshaw smiled and gave Cowell a small wave. 'Hello, Robert Cowell.'

Cowell returned it. He looked confused.

'I gather you like computers,' Poe said. 'Miss Bradshaw likes computers too. Please listen carefully as what she's about to explain gets to the very heart of why we're here.'

Bradshaw cleared her throat. 'Thank you, Detective Sergeant Washington Poe. Robert Cowell, I'm here to explain how laser printers work.'

'I know how laser printers wor—'

Poe had never been able to stop Bradshaw explaining science; Cowell stood no chance. She simply carried on talking. It was possible she hadn't even heard him.

'When you press print, your computer sends millions of bytes of information to a chip in the printer where it is converted into a two-dimensional image. The photoreceptor drum, positively charged with static electricity, begins to turn and, as it does, laser beams hit it millions of times forming the image of whatever has been sent to it.'

Bradshaw removed a diagram of a printer and pointed out each part.

'Each spot on the drum the laser hits has its positive charge turned negative. This attracts the positively charged toner powder. Another process puts a stronger negative charge on the paper and when it is passed over the drum, the toner jumps across before being fused on at two hundred degrees Celsius. Do you understand, Robert Cowell?'

Cowell nodded. Poe did too, even though he didn't.

'And here's the thing,' Bradshaw continued. 'Because each photoreceptor drum has its own unique, microscopic flaws, they can be treated like fingerprints. Under magnification we can match a drum to a document.'

There was no reaction. Cowell was either a very cool customer or he hadn't realised what he'd thrown away.

Bradshaw brought up blown-up segments of the four A4 pages that had been used to wrap the Secret Santa mug. She arranged them so Cowell could see. She then pointed out the imperfections in the black swan images.

Each document had identical visible blemishes. A scratch that bisected the black swan logo in the top-right corner, what looked like a patch of dust covering two of the logos in the middle and a bubble that could be seen on a logo near the bottom.

Bradshaw had told Poe that the photoreceptor drum would have had many more blemishes but they could only be seen on the parts of paper that had logos printed on.

'I am told that these four documents all coming from the same printer is non-interpretable evidence, Robert,' Poe said. 'Would you like to comment?'

Cowell shrugged, which Poe took as a no.

'Show him the next document, please, Tilly,' Poe said.

Bradshaw placed a single sheet of A4 on the table. It was a printer test-page. The kind used to isolate problems between computer and printer. It was all square and circles and *lorem ipsum*, the dummy text used on documents and brochures when the real text isn't yet available. Parts of the page were in colour and parts were in black and white. Small font, big font, small circles, big circles – the entire page was filled. It was stained, in an evidence bag and, up until that morning, had been in Robert Cowell's bin.

It didn't take long for Bradshaw to point out what was obvious to them all: the imperfections on the test-page stood out like they'd been highlighted. There were more of them as there was more ink on the page, but the imperfections she'd identified on the documents wrapping the Secret Santa mug were all present.

'They match, don't they?' Poe said.

Cowell looked at him in confusion.

'I'll recap for everyone. The documents used to wrap the mug that contained Rebecca Pridmore's fingers match the document we found in your bin, the kite you say was stolen was found in a tree overlooking her back garden and when the police raided your house this morning your sister ran and then told you to say nothing.'

Poe turned to the solicitor.

'Do you think a jury will find that circumstantial, Mr Lear?'

Lear said nothing.

'Tilly, please show Robert the documents recovered from the next two crime scenes.'

Bradshaw laid out blown-up segments from the A4 pages found at the church and Fiskin's Food Hall.

'This was found on Christmas Day at a crime scene in Barrow,' Poe said, pointing to the document from the church. He then pointed at the one found in Fiskin's Food Hall. 'And this was found on Boxing Day at a crime scene in Whitehaven.'

Bradshaw indicated how the flaws on the photoreceptor drum had left corresponding marks on the two documents.

'You can see that a different photoreceptor drum was used on both these documents,' she said. 'They *do* have blemishes but they match neither those on the printer test page that Poe found in your bin nor the ones that wrapped the Secret Santa mug.'

'So why show us them?' Lear said.

'I'd pay attention,' Poe said, 'because you ain't gonna believe this.'

Chapter 40

'When Miss Bradshaw matched the flaws on the document found in your client's wheelie bin to the flaws found on the paper used to wrap the Secret Santa mug, she was using what's called a passive printer identification technique,' Poe said. 'It means the marks are unintentional. A by-product we're happy to exploit. But, and I could scarcely believe this when she told me, there's another printer identification technique and this one isn't passive, it's active. It's called yellow dot tracking and it rendered redundant all the steps Robert had taken to make it look like the three murders were the work of three separate killers.'

'What the hell is yellow dot tracking?' Lear said.

'I'm glad you asked,' Poe said. 'Tilly?'

Bradshaw turned over seven photographs and laid them out in a row.

'These images are heavily magnified sections of each of the seven A4 pages connected to this case,' she said. She pointed at the first four. 'These are from the pages used to wrap the Secret Santa mug.' She pointed at the next two. 'These are from the documents found at the church and the food hall. The last one is the document Poe found in your wheelie bin.'

Cowell and Lear both leaned in.

Lear looked up first, his face showing the same level of confusion Poe's had when Bradshaw had explained it to him earlier.

'What are we supposed to be looking at?' he said.

'Yellow dot tracking is an active technique where traceable

data is explicitly and covertly embedded within the body of a document,' Bradshaw said. 'The dots are arranged in grids and are printed in a regularly repeating pattern across the whole page. Each grid can encode up to fourteen seven-bit bytes of tracking data. They are embedded into each document about twenty billionths of a second before printing commences. They can only be seen under blue light or under a microscope.'

'You're kidding?' Lear said. 'What about privacy laws?'

'It's been around since the 1980s, Jon Lear. No laws are being broken and the public don't have a right to be informed. Most of the major manufacturers use active printer identification techniques.'

Lear shook his head in disgust. 'This is absolutely unacceptable.'

'Hate the game, not the player, Mr Lear,' Poe said.

Bradshaw opened her laptop. 'I scanned and magnified all seven photographs. The software needed to separate the colours, which would enable us to examine the blue channel in isolation, hasn't arrived yet so the yellow dot tracking just look like flecks of dust. But, when I do this,' – she typed a series of commands and superimposed the seven images – 'you can see that the pattern on all seven documents is identical.'

'What are you saying?' Lear said.

'You know what we're saying, Mr Lear,' Poe said. 'The documents used to wrap the mug, the ones found in the church and the food hall, and the one found in your client's bin, all came from the same printer. Robert tried to disguise this by changing drums for each murder but yellow dot tracking is embedded into the printer's software – it cannot be cheated.'

Lear made some notes.

'I would like to confer with my client, please.'

Poe stood. Bradshaw did too.

'Take your time. You have a lot to discuss.'

Cowell was sweating and shaking when they resumed. He looked subdued, his solicitor looked grim. Poe thought Cowell probably wanted to talk but Lear had overruled him. Poe didn't blame him; he was just doing his job. Even when caught red-handed – and with the kite, photoreceptor drum flaws and yellow dot tracking, Poe reckoned Cowell almost had been – remaining silent and letting the solicitor talk was invariably the best legal strategy.

'When did these murders occur, Sergeant Poe?' Lear asked, pen poised over his notebook.

'We only have a rough timescale with the fingers in the Secret Santa mug,' Poe replied, 'but we know that the fingers were left in the food hall on Boxing Day as Robert was caught on CCTV, and we're fairly sure when the fingers were left in the church in Barrow.'

Lear looked up from his scribbling. '*Fairly* sure?'

'We think Robert mingled with the Midnight Mass congregation on Christmas Eve, found somewhere to hide when it finished then let himself out when the caretaker came in on Christmas Day morning to—'

'*After* Midnight Mass?' Cowell said. He shook his head violently. 'No, that's not fair. That's not fair at all!' He began breathing through his nose, fast and loud like an angry bull.

'What's wrong, Robert?' Lear said.

'Bitch! Bitch! FUCKING BITCH!'

Before Poe could stop him, Cowell had leant back and then smashed his face onto the table. He raised his head, his nose spurting blood, and, with even more force than before, did it again. Poe heard the crunch of bone. When he raised his head this time, his nose was mushy and his eyes were unfocused.

He reared back for the third time, readying himself for one final act of self-harm.

Poe launched himself across the table and bear-hugged him.

Chapter 41

'So he still hasn't been charged?' Nightingale said.

'We didn't get that far,' Poe said. 'He wigged out as soon as I mentioned Midnight Mass.'

Nightingale had missed the latter parts of the interview and wanted to hear what had happened first-hand. Cowell was still in hospital. He'd been patched up and psychiatrically assessed.

'I've just heard from his solicitor,' Poe continued. 'He's being discharged in an hour. You want me to continue?'

'Please,' Nightingale said. 'Keep pushing him. I want this boxed off today so we can start building an airtight case against him. His sister too, if she's involved. There has to be a reason she told him to keep quiet. She might be calm and collected now but she wasn't when she was arrested, I can assure you.'

'Can you send me a link to her most recent interviews?'

'I will. I don't know how useful they'll be, though; she's still barely saying a word. Even her solicitor is getting pissed off.'

'Cheers. I'll take a look anyway.'

'How's DI Flynn?'

'Duvet day.'

'I'm not sure she should still be here.'

'You going to tell her?'

Nightingale laughed. 'Do I look stupid? Ah, here's DC Coughlan. Dave, do you have a minute?'

It was the hulking detective, the one with the monobrow who'd stormed out of the pointless semiotics briefing.

'Ma'am,' he said, eyeing Poe with suspicion.

'Can you make sure Sergeant Poe is given access to all the Rhona Cowell interviews?'

'Yes, ma'am.'

He lumbered off. They both watched him go.

'DC Coughlan hasn't been with us long. He's hardworking and trustworthy,' she said. They watched as he tried and failed to key in the right sequence to the interview suite's security pad. 'But he's not one of our deep thinkers . . .'

Poe sat for an hour and watched the last Rhona Cowell interview. The detective had laid down the same information that Poe had laid in front of Robert. Rhona didn't react to any of it. Even when she was told about the yellow dot tracking and how her brother had been linked to three murders.

His BlackBerry alerted him to an incoming call. It was Bradshaw. Poe muted the sound and tapped the accept button.

'Hello, Poe. How are you feeling?'

'I'm fine, Tilly. What's up?'

'Robert Cowell is back from hospital.'

'His solicitor with him?'

'I think so. I'm just passing on the message, though. I think they're ready for you.'

Poe didn't answer.

'Poe?'

Poe stared at the screen. He unmuted the sound and rewound it ten seconds. Played it again.

Did it one more time to be sure.

'Tilly, I've seen something odd.'

Cowell had broken his nose when he'd headbutted the table. The ugly, beaklike metal splint he was wearing made him look like RoboDuck. His eyes were bloodshot and his sockets were puffy and yellowing.

'My client is not prepared to talk about what happened earlier,' Jon Lear said. 'We'll put it down to stress and move on.'

Poe ignored him. Solicitors didn't determine the parameters of interviews. Especially after what he'd just seen. He opened the laptop Bradshaw had set up for him. It was prearranged to start when the evidence in the church had been laid before his sister. The same bit of evidence that had caused Robert to lose it.

'I don't intend to make you sit through the whole interview but, rest assured, up until this point your sister hasn't reacted to anything put before her. Now, please watch.'

Poe pressed play.

The interviewing detective said, 'The only time your brother could have put these fingers in the font was after Midnight Mass but before the caretaker came in at 6 a.m. on Christmas morning. That's a pretty narrow window. We want to know how much you knew.'

Poe made them watch it three times.

'When I put this to you earlier, Robert, you had a . . . psychiatric episode and, although your sister's reaction wasn't so extreme, she *did* react.'

Barely . . .

Rhona Cowell had smirked. On its own it wouldn't have meant much, but in the context of what had happened with her brother, it was everything. The timing of the church crime scene meant something to them both. Poe was sure of it.

He just didn't know what.

'Your sister reacted to the same thing you did, Robert, almost to the second,' Poe said. 'It's only a smirk but it's the only time she's shown any emotion at all.'

That wasn't entirely truthful. At the end of the interview Rhona Cowell had also spoken. It was little more than a mumble and even with the sound turned up full he hadn't been able to make it out. He was waiting for the interview transcript, although the detective who'd been observing had told him it was 'just some hippy-dippy bullshit about staring into her soul and seeing the truth'. Poe would wait and read the transcript but he couldn't see how it would be relevant. The only reason the detective had mentioned it at all was because it was the one and only time she'd opened her mouth.

'The Midnight Mass evidence isn't the first time you've reacted to something, though, is it, Robert?' Poe said.

Cowell looked up, confused.

'You didn't react when we showed you your kite and, other than revulsion, you didn't really react when we showed you a picture of Rebecca Pridmore's fingers on the carpet at John Bull Haulage. But you *did* react when you saw the mug the fingers came in. The mug with hashtag BSC6 written on it.'

Cowell slumped in his chair and began biting his lips.

'You see, hashtag BSC6 has cropped up at every crime scene, Robert,' Poe continued. 'You've seen how it was written on the Secret Santa mug at John Bull Haulage and you've seen how it was inserted into the hymn board at the church and fixed like a price tag at the food hall.'

Cowell was watching him carefully.

'We don't know what hashtag BSC6 means.' He met Cowell's eyes and didn't break contact. 'But I think *you* do.'

For a moment the two men stared at each other.

'Am I right, Robert?' Poe said.

Cowell nodded slowly, his eyes glued to Poe's.

'And are you finally ready to tell me?'

Cowell nodded again.

173

Chapter 42

Despite the late hour the incident room was packed tighter than two coats of paint. Detectives and uniformed cops, civilian staff and press officers had squeezed themselves into a room meant for a quarter of their number. Even Shirley Becke, Cumbria's chief constable, was there. It was hot and humid. A background of excited chatter filled the air. It faded when Nightingale stood up.

'Robert Cowell has admitted to competing in something called the Black Swan Challenge,' she said. 'It's an escalating contest where tasks are set by an as yet unknown administrator. I'm going to ask Tilly Bradshaw from the National Crime Agency to take you through the next bit. She's the one who put it all together.'

A nervous Bradshaw made her way to the front. She looked down at Poe on the front row and waved. He gave her a thumbs up. This was the largest crowd she'd been asked to brief and she wanted to do well. She said she was representing SCAS. Poe knew she'd be fine if she stuck to the science. It was the audience participation he was worried about.

'Hello, everyone,' she said. 'My name is Matilda Bradshaw and I'm a civilian analyst with the Serious Crime Analysis Section. We are part of the National Crime Agency.'

The room stayed silent.

She nervously adjusted her glasses then checked her PowerPoint presentation. She clicked her handheld remote and the screen changed into a black swan.

'The Black Swan Challenge, or hashtag-BSC, isn't, as Detective Superintendent Nightingale has just said, an online escalating challenge game, it's actually a sophisticated control and manipulation scheme aimed at vulnerable people.'

Nightingale frowned and glanced at the chief constable.

'It cannot be found except by those who have been told how to find it,' Bradshaw continued. 'And it's not new.'

A click and the black swan disappeared. A blue whale replaced it.

'The Blue Whale Challenge,' Bradshaw said. 'Believed to originate in Russia, it was a series of tests, one a day over fifty days, that ultimately groomed the victim into committing suicide. The full number is disputed but it is believed that over one hundred vulnerable people killed themselves in Russia alone.'

The image on the monitor changed to a list of tests.

'The first few tests on the Blue Whale Challenge seem easy, don't they?' she said. 'The first is to cut a blue whale symbol into your hand and send a picture to the game's administrator. It doesn't even have to be deep. It's all about demonstrating commitment to the game. The next is even easier. All you have to do is get up at four o'clock in the morning to watch horror films and listen to death metal. The third is cutting yourself along a vein.'

Bradshaw clicked her remote and the Blue Whale Challenge task list image disappeared. A diagram of the human brain replaced it.

'These instructions can be sequentially classified as the psychological principles of induction, habituation and preparation. Induction is ensuring the victim commits to the Blue Whale Challenge by psychologically rewarding compliance and admonishing disobedience. In a vulnerable person, particularly one who hasn't had a lot of positive reinforcement, this can be a powerful, sometimes even addictive, motivator.

'The habituation instructions are designed to interrupt the

victim's usual sleep pattern, which, combined with the constant exposure to horror films and songs about death and suicide, leads to dysregulation of the orbitofrontal cortex. This of course is the part of the brain that regulates emotional decisions—'

Dave Coughlan, the detective with the monobrow, stood and said, 'What is this nonsense?'

Nightingale turned in her seat. 'I beg your pardon, DC Coughlan?'

'This is that semiotic briefing all over again, ma'am,' he said. 'We're sitting here like social workers when we should be out looking for the bastard behind it all.'

'And how do you propose we do that?' Nightingale snapped.

Coughlan said nothing.

'This is a briefing on how a person can be remotely manipulated into committing murder,' Nightingale continued. 'It's important, so either sit down and shut up or leave the room.'

'If it's that important shouldn't we get someone normal to do it then?' he muttered.

There were a couple of titters but probably not as many as he'd hoped.

Poe's jaw hardened but he remained seated. A year ago a remark like that would have reduced Bradshaw to tears and him to violence. These days, though, insults seemed to bother her about as much as farts bothered dogs. And her beguiling honesty meant she flipped most of them anyway.

'Don't get angry, Detective Constable Dave Coughlan,' Bradshaw said. 'Not everyone has the intellect for complex briefings like this.'

Coughlan reddened. 'And what makes you think I don't have the intellect? You don't even know me.'

Poe turned in his seat. 'She's a profiler, dickhead. She'll have been analysing your speech patterns, non-verbal communication and mannerisms since the moment she met you.'

Bradshaw nodded enthusiastically. 'And also Detective Superintendent Nightingale told Poe that you aren't a deep thinker.'

The room erupted into laughter.

Coughlan scowled but eventually said, 'I'm sorry.'

'That's OK, Detective Constable Dave Coughlan, Poe doesn't understand complex briefings either. He doesn't even know how to use his new BlackBerry. He was trying to send me a text last week but all I received was empty speech bubbles.'

Poe grimaced. Bloody NCA, always changing things. He'd only just got used to his old phone.

'It was like having a conversation with a fish,' she added.

More laughter.

Nightingale stood up.

'OK, settle down. I know cracking a case can feel like the last day of school but may I remind you all that we haven't finished yet. We don't know who is behind all this and we don't know why.' She sat down. 'Miss Bradshaw, please continue.'

'Dysregulation of the orbitofrontal cortex is perhaps better known as brainwashing, DC Coughlan,' Bradshaw said, picking up where she'd left off. 'The final psychological principle in the Blue Whale Suicide Challenge is preparation. This is simply desensitising the victim to pain and harm, which in turn gradually erodes their survival instincts. After completing forty-nine tasks, when given the fiftieth – to jump off a high building and take your life – it doesn't seem such an impossible choice.'

'That's it?' Nightingale said. 'That's all it took to make these kids kill themselves?'

Bradshaw shook her head.

'I believe that when selecting victims, the administrator will have looked for four preconditions: bad life experiences, unwanted isolation, depression and a borderline personality disorder. Unfortunately, young people, whose neural pathways haven't yet fully developed, tend to unwittingly share these characteristics on social media. We have a saying in SCAS: there are some things that can only be shared with a psychiatrist and one hundred thousand people on the internet. It means that the most vulnerable young adults are easily identified by the predators out there, which in turn makes them even more vulnerable.'

'It's a chicken and egg thing,' Coughlan said, eager to make up for his earlier outburst.

Bradshaw looked at him blankly.

'You know, what came first – the vulnerability or the person making them vulnerable.'

'Indeed,' Bradshaw said. 'But what does that have to do with a chicken?'

'It's a saying. What came first, the chicken or the egg? It's an unanswerable question.'

'The chicken came first, obviously,' Bradshaw said. 'The proteins found in eggshells can only be produced by hens.'

Laughter.

'Really?' Coughlan said. He turned to Nightingale. 'I've changed my mind, ma'am, I'm *glad* she's on our side.'

'Sit down, Dave,' Nightingale replied.

'But . . . but why?' someone at the back said. 'What's in it for the administrator?'

'The only person convicted of administering a Blue Whale Challenge game is a Russian called Philipp Budeikin. He claimed he was cleansing society and that his victims were nothing more than biological waste.'

'And do you believe that?' Nightingale said.

'I don't. I've studied his profile and I think Philipp Budeikin was an intelligent young man who had failed to build any connections with anyone. He developed his methods and honed his manipulations until eventually he felt like God. He had the

178

power of life and death over people. That's why he did it. He was simply an evil man.'

'Why have I not heard about this?' the chief constable asked. Poe stood.

'Couple of reasons, ma'am.' He held up a finger. 'First, there haven't been any Blue Whale attributable deaths in the UK.' He held up a second finger. 'And two, everyone did what we would have done: downplayed it to discourage copycats.'

'So it might not even be real?'

Poe shrugged. 'Opinions are divided.'

'What do you think?'

'I think that when the Russian investigative newspaper *Novaya Gazeta* reported that one hundred and thirty child suicides took place in a six-month period, almost all of them were in the same internet group and they were all from good families.'

'Jesus . . . And that's what we have, a sicker version of Blue Whale?'

Bradshaw changed the screen.

#BSC6

'The Cowells certainly thought so,' Bradshaw said. 'I believe they were selected because of their intense sibling rivalry, which, to anyone who knows where to look for these things, is discoverable online. Robert Cowell says that after they were sent an invitation they ended up daring each other to play. Hashtag BSC1, the first Black Swan Challenge task, was to commit a low-level act of vandalism. Robert destroyed a tree in a local park and his sister went one better and slashed a police vehicle's tyre.'

'And that's it? It escalated into murder?' Nightingale said.

'No, Detective Superintendent Nightingale,' Bradshaw said. She changed the screen again. A chatroom exchange appeared.

'This is where the Black Swan and Blue Whale Challenge differ. Whereas administrators in the Blue Whale Challenge manipulated their victims using the psychological techniques I mentioned earlier – induction, habituation and preparation – the administrator in the Black Swan Challenge simply used blackmail. This is a screenshot of an exchange Robert Cowell had with him. As you can see, when he logged on for the next task, he was told that malware had been inserted into his computer and that he had to keep playing or all his files and personal information would be made public. I've run a diagnostic check and, although there *was* no virus, Robert Cowell clearly believed there was.'

'What was it he needed to stay secret?'

'That's just the thing, Detective Superintendent Nightingale: I couldn't find anything on his computer that would make Robert Cowell susceptible to blackmail.'

'Nothing?'

Bradshaw shook her head.

'So why did—'

'His perception is his reality,' Poe said. 'Even if he didn't have anything on his computer he could have been blackmailed over, he obviously thought he did.'

He and Bradshaw had already had this discussion. He privately agreed with Nightingale – that someone with nothing to hide couldn't be easily threatened – but she'd persuaded him that vulnerable people didn't have the same cognitive processes as him.

'And that was enough to blackmail him into committing murder, was it?' Nightingale said, shaking her head. 'Please tell me it's not that easy, Miss Bradshaw.'

'I can,' Bradshaw replied. 'The administrator also applied similar techniques to Blue Whale. Between each challenge, which got progressively more serious, he had them watching videos. Instead of horror films though it was war crimes, beheadings and executions. Instead of desensitising them against pain and the fear of death, he desensitised them against violence and the consequences of violence.'

'What were the other challenges?'

'We've prepared a briefing pack, ma'am,' Poe said, 'but essentially the second and third were more of the same. Nuisance stuff mainly. It wasn't until the fourth challenge that it started to get serious . . .'

Chapter 43

#BSC1, 2 and 3 had been low-level offences, annoying to anyone directly involved, but although they were on the wrong side of criminal behaviour, they weren't on the wrong side of public opinion.

#BSC4 changed all that. When Robert Cowell had told Poe what he and Rhona had done, it had taken every ounce of willpower he had not to slap him in front of his solicitor.

Instead he'd called a break and walked up to the dog section to see Edgar. As he'd stroked the spaniel's soft ears, he thought about what Cowell had told him. Had it been enough to set him on the path to murder?

Although he knew he might be biased, Poe thought if someone was capable of stealing a wounded soldier's prosthetic limb they were probably capable of anything . . .

The Cowells had travelled across the A66 to Catterick Garrison and made their way to Phoenix House, the recovery centre run by Help for Heroes. Posing as family members they'd tricked their way into the hydrotherapy pool where Robert had stolen the trans-femoral prosthetic leg of a Royal Marine who'd had an above-knee amputation after stepping on a landmine in Helmand Province. Rhona had recorded him. The video was on the cloud and Cowell gave Poe the password.

As Cowell described posing for a selfie with the leg outside Phoenix House before discarding it in a ditch on the A66, Poe's grip on the edge of the table tightened until his knuckles turned white. A marine's independence, fly-tipped like a piss-stained mattress. Willpower aside, if Cowell had smirked once, or allowed his expression to be anything other than conciliatory, Poe didn't think he'd have had it in him not to launch himself across the table and pull his face off.

'Anyway, I've called North Yorkshire Police and they have a report on file,' Poe told Nightingale. 'Rhona Cowell still hasn't said anything of substance but Robert has signed a statement saying they were both involved so you should be able to bring charges against them both. Even if she denies it, you can hear her egging him on in the video.'

Nightingale nodded in satisfaction. Although Robert Cowell wasn't going anywhere, things hadn't been quite as clear-cut for Rhona. They suspected joint enterprise but without evidence she could easily have walked. The theft of the marine's leg changed all that. Rhona Cowell had more chance of finding a one-ended stick than making bail.

'What was the fifth challenge, Sergeant Poe?' the chief constable said.

'What was the fifth challenge, Robert?' Poe had asked.

Cowell's cheeks flushed. He swallowed a couple of times.

'We played a joke on someone,' he said.

Poe took some details then stopped the interview. What Cowell had described wasn't a joke; it was the abduction of a child. Poe checked with the detective inspector observing. There *had* been an abduction. A five-year-old girl called Lucy had been taken from Chance's Park in Carlisle. Although she'd been returned unharmed a few hours later, there was still an ongoing police investigation.

The cop leading the abduction investigation was called Rachael

Carrigan-King. Poe had known her when he'd been with Cumbria Constabulary. She was a solid, no-frills detective inspector. She'd asked to see Poe before she went in to speak to Cowell.

'Is he full of it?'

Poe had shrugged. 'Hard to say. He's cooperating now but that could be him attempting to condition us before he starts denying the more serious stuff.'

'Do you believe he abducted my victim?'

'I believe Robert and his sister abducted someone. Rhona Cowell isn't talking but Robert has already admitted they stole a Royal Marine's prosthetic leg and I've confirmed that offence took place. A DC from North Yorkshire is on his way now to interview him.'

'It must be my victim then,' Carrigan-King had said. 'Lucy's our only open abduction investigation.'

'And she wasn't harmed?'

'Not at all. She was taken from Chance's Park on Wigton Road. She'd been chasing a dog and her mum wasn't paying attention. Lucy said that a man with a long coat gave her some sweets then just drove her around in his car. Dropped her off at Houghton Hall Garden Centre. She was only gone three hours. Didn't even know people were looking for her.'

They'd chatted for ten more minutes, then spent half an hour reviewing the interview footage.

It took forty-five minutes for Carrigan-King to get everything she needed. Cowell hadn't held anything back. Hadn't tried to minimise the impact his actions had had on Lucy's family, the wider community and the already stretched resources of the police. Didn't offer any mitigation. Just told her that he and his sister had been forced into doing challenges and abducting a little girl had been the next one.

Chapter 44

'Surely there's a point where the blackmail threshold is passed,' Nightingale said when Poe had finished.

He knew what she meant. Whatever it was on his computer that Robert didn't want made public – and Bradshaw still hadn't found anything – it couldn't possibly be worse than the offences he was committing to keep it private.

'Ordinarily I'd agree with you, ma'am,' Poe replied. 'But I think there was also some sibling rivalry at play, and by this time our man had successfully subverted any moral code that either of them had left. It seems implausible but the evidence is compelling – when it came to the sixth challenge they were both willing participants.'

'What does he say about the murders?'

Poe invited Bradshaw to take the room through the final challenge.

'Thank you, Poe,' she said. She sent another image to the monitor. 'This is a screenshot that Robert Cowell took of a conversation he had with the site administrator. It took place in an untraceable private chatroom.'

She blew up a section of dialogue near the bottom.

SITE ADMIN: THIS IS YOUR FINAL TASK. DO THIS AND YOU'VE SUCCESSFULLY COMPLETED THE BLACK SWAN CHALLENGE.

RC: WHAT IS IT THIS TIME?

'Robert hadn't replied when he took this screenshot so we don't know how he responded,' Bradshaw continued.

'And it's hardly subtle,' Poe said. 'Kill a stranger? Tilly and I were expecting something a bit more . . . I dunno, psychologically complex.'

Bradshaw nodded. 'This instruction has none of the induction, habituation or preparation associated with Blue Whale.'

'It did the job, though, it seems,' Nightingale said. 'I gather he's denying the murders?'

'Absolutely,' Poe replied. 'Said that as soon as he saw the final challenge he took a screenshot then turned off his computer. Claims he hasn't had any contact with the site administrator since then.'

'Why didn't he come to us?'

'He couldn't. Not without his other crimes being exposed.'

'Convenient,' Nightingale said. 'And he's still claiming his kite was stolen?'

'He is.'

'What about the printer test-page you found in his bin?'

'He has no explanation for it. Didn't even try to account for it.'

'He didn't try to shift the blame onto his sister?'

'No. Said that she's innocent as well.'

Nightingale turned to the chief constable.

'I think we're in a good position to take it to the CPS, ma'am. We have enough to charge Robert Cowell with murder. We'll charge Rhona with abduction but keep investigating her.'

The chief constable said, 'Poe, you were in the room with him – what are the obvious sticking points?'

Poe considered the question for a few moments.

'I don't know why he killed three people when the instruction

186

was just to "kill a stranger" and I don't know why he used different methods to amputate the fingers. If the yellow dot tracking didn't link him directly to all three murders I'd have said that the Cowells weren't the only people playing the Black Swan Challenge.'

'Could Rhona Cowell be behind all this?'

'I thought that, ma'am, but if she is, why expose herself?' Poe said. 'She's almost certainly going to prison for the abduction.'

The chief constable nodded. 'Anything else?' she said.

'I'd like the printer,' Poe replied. 'Cowell's defence is going to be that he's being framed – it's his only option – and by saying his kite was stolen he's already sowing the seeds for that. If we find the printer we negate a large part of his strategy.'

'Where are we on tracing this administrator, Tilly?' Nightingale said. 'Tell me you have some good news?'

'No, Detective Superintendent Nightingale,' she replied. 'He's used his own websites to host the chatrooms in which he spoke to Robert Cowell and presumably anyone else playing the Black Swan Challenge. This is the URL for one of them.'

She brought up a fresh screen.

dhwehi234o8757o4632obf.onion

'I'm assuming that's a dark web address?'

Bradshaw nodded. 'They all are.'

'You said he used more than one?'

'It was like a game of whack-a-mole. He would use a site for a limited period of time then shut it down. As soon as he did, another would immediately go live.'

'What's that "onion" thing at the end of the URL?'

'That's the TOR extension. It's how he hosts his websites.'

'TOR?'

'The Onion Router. It's free software that enables anonymous communication. TOR directs internet traffic through thousands of relays, which makes it difficult to trace the user's location. He hosted all his Black Swan Challenge chatrooms on the TOR Network.'

Poe didn't pretend to understand what Bradshaw was saying but he silently cursed the dark and deep web – the 96 per cent of the web that wasn't discoverable with standard search engines such as Google. Living at Herdwick Croft, he had every sympathy for anyone wanting to protect their privacy, but as far as he could tell, the dark web was just a marketplace for weapons, drugs, hitmen and indecent images of children. And now serial killers by proxy had started using it. As if their job wasn't hard enough already.

'You said difficult to trace, not impossible?' Nightingale said.

'I can normally trace the user's IP address using TOR entry and exit points but in this case all we ended up with was this.'

Bradshaw reached down and retrieved a paper evidence bag. One of the brown ones with a clear window. It contained a flat piece of electrical equipment.

'This is a single-board computer,' she said. 'It is basically a computer where all the components it needs to be functional have been built into a single circuit board. It has microprocessors, storage and memory. Single-board computers are normally embedded into larger devices like ATM machines, cash registers and medical equipment, but anyone can buy one. They are not expensive. The model in the evidence bag can be bought online for under thirty pounds.'

Bradshaw changed the image on the monitor again. The exterior of a scruffy-looking guesthouse appeared on the screen. It looked like the type that specialised in the transient and hard-to-house population. It would be skimming money from their housing benefit and would have police officers there every other week.

'This is on the outskirts of Carlisle. I traced this single-board computer to a bedroom on the top floor. It had been plugged in, connected to their free wi-fi network then hidden under the floorboards. It was recovered not an hour earlier. The guesthouse owner had no idea it was there.'

Nightingale had already been briefed on this part but she asked the question for the benefit of those who hadn't.

'And this is as far as you can trace?'

'It is. He managed it remotely for a short period of time then moved on to the next one he'd hidden. After he'd finished with this he remotely factory reset it, so we are struggling to recover any digital evidence. I have traced five computers in total. I understand detectives and CSI teams are recovering the remaining four as we speak.'

He'd been clever and chosen guesthouses on the outskirts of town as CCTV didn't cover them and, unlike the bigger hotels, their wi-fi networks weren't protected by security systems such as guest portals, firewalls or logging systems. Bradshaw said that they could have been placed there at any time and, as long as they remained plugged into a power source, could remain there indefinitely. Nightingale had a new line of enquiry but Poe didn't think the man they were now hunting would be careless enough to leave actionable evidence at any of the locations.

'I suppose it's possible he still has single-board computers he hasn't brought online yet?' the chief constable said.

Bradshaw nodded. 'And we have no way of knowing how many. He could have been planning this for years and they can be anywhere in the world. The five we located were in Carlisle but the sixth could be in Mumbai.'

Nightingale stood to address the room.

'Thank you, Miss Bradshaw, and thank you, Sergeant Poe. Are there any questions before we move on to tasking?'

There weren't.

Poe stayed behind to talk to Nightingale. To his surprise, Flynn joined them. If she had managed to rest, the effect was negligible: she still looked tired and swollen. She was wearing trainers so big it looked as though she'd stolen them from a clown.

'Boss? What you doing here?' Poe checked his watch. It was coming up to 10 p.m.

'Tilly's briefed me on what's going on.' She turned to Nightingale and said, 'Ma'am, I hope you don't mind but this is potentially a national public safety issue and I need to get involved. It's contained in Cumbria for now but it might not stay that way.'

'I could do with the support to be honest, DI Flynn,' Nightingale replied. 'What do you need from me?'

'I've arranged for Poe to meet someone in Public Health for Cumbria first thing tomorrow. Apparently he's the council's lead on Blue Whale. I'm happy if you want to send someone with him.'

'I will, thanks.'

Flynn turned back to Poe. 'Before I forget, someone called . . .' – she reached into her pocket and read a note written on North Lakes Hotel stationery – 'Melody Lee rang for you.'

'Unusual name,' he said.

'You not paid your tab at Rouge, Poe?' Nightingale asked.

He laughed. Rouge was Carlisle's only pole-dancing club. 'She leave a message?'

'Just a mobile number and a request that you ring her ASAP.' She passed the information across.

He glanced at it. It was a strange number. Thirteen digits instead of eleven, it also began with 001 instead of 07. It wasn't a UK mobile, that much was clear.

'I'll call her later,' he said, tucking the note into his pocket.

Chapter 45

The meeting with Public Health was scheduled for nine-thirty the following morning and Nightingale insisted that Poe call it a night. He offered perfunctory resistance but, in truth, he was glad to get away. His bones felt tired – payback for the long hours and cheap coffee – and his mind felt like a spreadsheet with too many tabs open. A meal, a walk in the snow with Edgar followed by a full night's sleep would see him reinvigorated. He said goodbye to Flynn and Bradshaw, collected Edgar from the dog section and headed home.

Robert and Rhona Cowell remained in his thoughts as he manoeuvred the BMW X1 through the deepening snow, the winter tyres and four-wheel-drive torque ensuring he fared better than most other road users. He thought Rhona was probably equally as involved as Robert and, although they made good suspects, a lot of unanswered questions remained. Neither of them looked like criminal masterminds, and although Poe knew that few crimes made complete sense, even if they were dealing with the two luckiest pinheads alive – bumbling clowns who'd somehow defied the odds and pulled off three almost perfect murders – nothing explained why they'd pumped two of their victims full of anaesthetic while one had simply been dispatched on the spot.

They were still missing something.

The weather had cleared and, with a Cumberland sausage and a potato in the oven, Poe took Edgar for a walk along his boundary walls. Herdwick sheep would use them as shelter and they'd occasionally get stuck if the snow drifted. More than once he'd had to drag them out by their feet.

He walked the length of the dry stone wall that served as the demarcation between his and Victoria's land. It was free of trapped animals. He was about to head home when he heard something. The idling engine of a quad.

He turned to the noise and saw two headlights. It seemed that Victoria had been having one last check as well.

'Washington,' she said, when he popped his head over the wall, 'what are you doing out so late?'

'Same as you by the looks of it,' he replied.

'You couldn't give me a hand, could you?'

Poe leaned over.

A large Herdwick lay on its side, its foot wedged in a gap in the wall. Poe couldn't imagine how it had managed to get like that. It was trembling, which was unusual for the breed. Although they were prey animals, Poe's experience of Herdwicks was that they wore the label lightly. The ones that hung around Herdwick Croft either ignored Edgar completely, or, if he was being particularly annoying, charged him – a reminder that he was a daft spaniel and they had heads designed for butting.

'It's not fully grown,' Victoria continued. 'We must have missed it when we gathered the fell last year.'

Poe looked again. What he'd initially thought was a large sheep was in fact a young sheep weighed down with a fleece heavily matted with snow. The reason for its distress made sense now – if it hadn't been gathered the previous lambing season it was possible that Victoria was the first human it had had contact with.

Poe climbed over and grabbed it securely around the midriff, making sure he kept clear of its thrashing head. While he held it steady, Victoria worked on freeing its leg.

It didn't take long with the two of them. The Herdwick limped off without a backward look.

'Thanks,' Victoria said, blowing on her hands to warm them. 'You OK? You look tired.'

He shrugged. 'We have a bad one.'

'Do you want to talk about it?'

'Not yet.' He sometimes offloaded to Victoria – she'd proved a useful sounding board in the past – but now wasn't the time.

'How are you managing with Edgar?'

'Not great,' he admitted. Edgar had been passed from pillar to post these last few days.

'Shall I take him?'

He looked at the spaniel. He'd jumped the wall and was sitting on the back of Poe's quad. He'd obviously remembered there was a Cumberland sausage roasting in the oven.

Poe sighed. 'I suppose you'd better.'

Poe walked back to Herdwick Croft alone. He'd miss Edgar but, although the spaniel had enjoyed the beach and the time he'd spent in the dog section, it wasn't fair to push it. He was an energetic dog and needed constant exercise. Far better he was on Victoria's farm for a while.

The rescue of the trapped Herdwick meant he was home half an hour later than he'd planned. His baked potato resembled a prune and the sausage was black and crispy, more charcoal than pork. He threw the former and ate the latter. Never in his life had he thrown away a Cumberland sausage.

He briefly considered cooking another but decided that he needed sleep more than he needed food.

Poe woke eight hours older. Sunlight pushed through the slats in the window shutters – a new sensation for him; he was usually up before dawn. He'd slept in because Edgar wasn't there, licking his face, reminding him that morning meant breakfast. He had another headache, not as ferocious as the bastard of the other day, more a dull throb than bone-splitting agony. He didn't even reach for the analgesics.

He got up and stepped under the shower, initially blasting himself with ice-cold water before turning it up way higher than was comfortable. He stood motionless as the scalding jets stung his skin and cleared his mind.

As the hot water flushed his system, Poe visualised what he wanted to do next. There wasn't an obvious role for him. They had their killers and the hunt for the Black Swan Challenge administrator would start and finish online. Now that she knew what she was looking for, Poe didn't doubt that Bradshaw would find a way to track him down.

He'd ask Nightingale if he could join the team she had going through the guesthouses where the single-board computers had been hidden. Poe didn't think for a moment that the site administrator would be caught that way but at least it was police work.

After he'd got out of the shower and towelled himself dry, he checked his phone for messages. There was a text from Bradshaw reminding him to take the vitamin pills she'd bought him and one from Flynn saying she wouldn't be in until later. There was also a missed call from a withheld number, probably someone from Carleton Hall reminding him about the meeting with the council's Blue Whale expert.

He thumbed Bradshaw a reply confirming he'd taken the pills and that he'd have weird-smelling urine for the rest of the day. He sent another to Flynn telling her everything was in hand and he'd call her if there was anything she needed to know.

The missed call he couldn't do anything about.

Chapter 46

An online, challenge-based murder game taking place in Cumbria required a countywide multi-agency response. Public Health, the agency charged with protecting and improving the nation's health, would lead but all agencies would be involved: the children safeguarding board, the adult safeguarding board, the police, schools, probation, everyone. A press strategy would be needed too. The pros and cons of sharing it with the public would be discussed and agreed.

The pros being that parents, schools and social care agencies could identify vulnerable kids and adults and put interventions in place.

The cons being copycats. In Bridgend, Wales, after a spate of young people had hanged themselves, the media had been accused of glamorising suicide and triggering more. So much so that the police had to ask them to stop covering it. They'd become part of the problem.

Poe was glad the decision wouldn't fall on him. There were no good choices, only bad ones.

Poe arrived at Carleton Hall with ten minutes to spare. The road to the M6 had been slow going but the gritters had been out overnight and the motorway had been clear.

Before he could get out of his car someone rapped on his window.

It was Dave Coughlan. Poe opened the door. If there was going to be trouble he wanted to be standing.

'What's up, DC Coughlan? I'm sorry about Tilly's deep-thinker remark. It shouldn't have been made public.'

Coughlan shrugged. 'You're going to the meeting with me today. Might as well go in my car – you have a parking space, I don't.'

Poe grabbed his bag.

'Lead the way.'

Coughlan, like most low-ranking cops at Carleton Hall, had more abandoned his car than parked it. It was half under a tree, half on the road, and nearer Cumbria Fire and Rescue Service's head-quarters complex than his own. He drove an aging, mud-spattered Volvo with new and faded Guide Dogs for the Blind stickers on the bumper and on the rear window.

'Your friend Matilda seems to speak without thinking,' Coughlan said when they were on the M6 and heading for Carlisle. 'I'm surprised she got a job with the National Crime Agency, given how corporate they are.'

'I wasn't at SCAS when she applied but as I understand it she corrected seven questions on the entrance exam,' Poe said. 'The NCA might have an image to protect but it also recognises a once-in-a-generation mind when it sees one. If they'd knocked her back the intelligence services would have snapped her up in a heartbeat.'

'She's that good?'

'Best I've ever seen.'

'Where were you when she joined?'

Poe checked to see if he was taking the piss. He wasn't.

'I was suspended for eighteen months. I'm surprised you didn't hear about it – I was a cause célèbre up here for a while.'

'I haven't been in Cumbria long.'

That was right. Nightingale had said as much.

'Which force were you with before?'

Coughlan glanced at him. He seemed irritated by the question.

'I wasn't. I'm a late entrant officer.'

There was no longer an upper age limit in the police recruitment process so Coughlan could have joined any time. Poe put him to be in his early forties. Although it was the right age for a mid-life crisis career change, Poe wondered if there was a story behind the decision to join at the age most cops had one eye on retirement.

'What did you do before?'

'Bit of this and that.'

Poe was spared asking an awkward follow up when his phone beeped. It was a text from Bradshaw. She wanted to know if he'd be back for lunch. By the time he'd replied, Coughlan had found one of Carlisle's rare on-street parking places. It was close to where their meeting was: the Citadel, the immense oval towers that in the 1800s had been used as assize courts and a prison, and until recently had been used as county council offices. They were impressive and it was a shame their purpose was now so mundane.

Poe had been to many boring meetings and the one concerning the Black Swan Challenge easily made his top twenty. It was clear that no one understood what it was, didn't understand why kids would want to play and didn't have a clue what to do.

The last ten minutes had been a back and forth between someone from Public Health and a squat woman with a pudding-bowl haircut from probation. Poe suspected they were rehashing a long-running power play.

He was saved from further silliness by his phone vibrating. He looked at the screen. It was a withheld number, probably the same one from that morning. He excused himself and left the room.

'Hello,' he said, when he was in a quiet corner.

'Sergeant Poe? This is Special Agent Melody Lee. I'm with the FBI.'

The woman with the peculiar name who'd been leaving him messages.

'The FBI have been trying to get hold of me?' Poe said, nonplussed.

'I have.'

'I'm sorry I haven't had a chance to call you back, Special Agent Lee. I haven't found the time yet.' Poe thought it sounded better than telling her he'd forgotten.

'That's OK, Sergeant Poe,' she drawled. 'I can't tell you how glad I am to speak to you.'

She pronounced her 'I' as 'aah' and her 'can't' rhymed with paint not aunt. Poe reckoned she was originally from one of the southern states, maybe Louisiana or Mississippi.

'How can I help you, Special Agent Lee?'

'Can you tell me about the case you're currently working on?' she said.

'Can you tell me about the case *you're* currently working on?'

Silence.

'I didn't think so,' Poe said.

More silence. This time he relented.

'Look, why don't you tell me what this is about? I can then decide if I'm in a sharing mood.'

She did.

And when she'd finished, Poe had to re-evaluate everything he thought he knew . . .

Chapter 47

'What I'm about to tell you is not the FBI's formal position,' Special Agent Melody Lee said. 'This is my theory, and repeatedly voicing it is why, instead of being in DC, I'm in South Dakota investigating the crap that goes on in the oil-producing region of the Bakken.'

'I'm listening,' Poe replied. 'You're not the only person in this conversation who's held a minority opinion before.'

'You know that the FBI has liaison officers with all the world's major law enforcement agencies, right?'

'I do.' He didn't but, as a national agency, it was definitely the type of thing the NCA would be involved in.

'For a while now I've had a standing request for our liaison officers to look for cases with . . . certain peculiarities. Yours is the only one I've found.'

'Peculiarities?'

'I need to give you some context,' she said. 'A few years ago, when I was with DC's violent crime task force, we had a series of seemingly unrelated assaults that crossed state lines. "Happy slapping", you guys might still be calling it. Initially we thought it must be a gang initiation ceremony we weren't aware of, but when we eventually caught a couple of assailants they were good kids, not the usual gangbangers at all.'

'What did they say?'

'Not much. By the time we got anywhere near them they'd

lawyered up and taken the fifth. Eventually one of them agreed to speak to me off the record. She told me a right yarn.'

'Go on,' Poe said.

'She said she'd been playing an online dare game and it had gotten a bit out of hand. Started with silly stuff but the final dare had them assaulting a stranger.'

'She admitted it?'

'Before her asshole lawyer stopped her.'

'I'm assuming you're not ringing because of an assault?'

'I'm not. Predictably, one of the victims died.'

'You get the perpetrator?'

'We did. A sailing jock from Georgetown, guy named Stuart Wilson. He'd already played the game twice and the assaults had resulted in minor injuries – little more than a busted lip and a cricked neck. But with the third he went too far, beat the guy to death.'

'He admit it?'

'Came clean about the two assaults. Denied all knowledge of the homicide. Said that he'd logged into the chatroom but the site administrator wasn't there.'

'Anyone buy that?' Poe said carefully.

'Not really. We assumed he'd found himself up dime alley with just a nickel in his pocket. Admitting the misdemeanours but denying the homicide was the only play he had left.'

'Was the evidence solid?'

'Irrefutable,' Melody Lee said. 'Kind of stuff that gives the DA wet dreams. Overwhelming physical evidence and, if you knew what you were looking for, you could also follow everything online.'

'What was the physical evidence?'

'Victim's blood in the grooves of his sneakers.'

'Just the sole?'

'Yes.'

'How did the victim die?'

'This is the thing: he was kicked and punched to death.'

'So there should have been blood on the toe areas and spatters on the laces and eyelets as well.'

'Exactly. But there wasn't.'

'How did the prosecution explain that away?'

'Convinced the jury that he'd almost succeeded in scrubbing off the blood. Claimed it was more evidence of his lack of remorse.'

'So he'd washed them but forgotten to check the treads?'

'You can see why I had doubts.'

'You said you're in South Dakota. Even I know the Badlands are a punishment posting. No way did you risk your career on a pair of trainers that may or may not have been scrubbed.'

'I did not.'

'What else did you find?'

'The make-up of the victims,' Melody Lee said. 'The nine who were assaulted were about as random as you could get. Two students, a bank clerk, a couple of store workers. An old lady getting off the bus.'

'And the one who died?'

'On the face of it there was nothing special about him either.'

'And the face of it was as deep as the FBI were prepared to dig, I take it?'

'They had their man, they had their evidence and they had their motive. They'd have liked a confession but they were happy with everything else. It was a slam-dunk case for the DA and, because Stuart Wilson was from a wealthy family, he could show he wasn't soft on the Washington elite in an election year.'

'So what was it about the victim that worried you?'

'Not so much him as his business partner,' she replied. 'He'd tried to buy out the victim the previous year but their business was growing and the sum he offered was half of what it was worth. A death clause in their partnership contract meant that the victim dying in a random mugging game was extremely fortuitous.'

'You're thinking this was a hit. That the random victim wasn't random at all? Someone hid a murder in the carnage of a happy-slapping game?'

'That's why I'm in the Badlands,' she said.

'It's a bit thin.'

'The victim's business partner had taken one hundred thousand dollars out of his checking account that he couldn't account for. Hid behind his lawyer who got onto the DA, who didn't want his nice, easy conviction complicated. Shut me down.'

Poe grunted in annoyance. He frequently butted heads with people intent on taking the path of least resistance. If he didn't already live in Cumbria, he'd have been sent there years ago. Cumbria was the Badlands of the UK.

'I met with Stuart,' Melody Lee continued. 'He's a sweet kid. Made a bad choice but he swears blind he didn't kill anyone and that he's being set up as a patsy. And his girlfriend, who'd sworn she was with him the night of the homicide, had backed off when the DA threatened her with joint venture. Made him look as though he'd tried to construct an alibi. His parents are taking civil action against her but it doesn't matter; the damage is done. He was found guilty of second-degree murder. The DA asked for a deterrent sentence and the judge came through. He's currently looking at another ten years before he can be released. I doubt he'll make it.'

Poe said nothing for several moments. 'What was the game called?' he said eventually.

'White Elephant.'

'Challenge?'

'Yes! The White Elephant Challenge. How the hell could you know that?'

Poe breathed out slowly. They were way past the point where the coincidences could be ignored.

'Sergeant Poe,' she urged. 'What aren't you telling me?'

'Our game is called the Black Swan Challenge,' Poe said.

'So *that's* what the BSC stood for!' Melody Lee yelled. 'I god-damned knew it was the same thing!'

'The similarities are remarkable,' Poe admitted.

'And look, this asshole can't help fucking with everyone when he names these goddamned games. Always puts in some double-entendre shit.'

'Explain.'

'Do you know what a white elephant is, Sergeant Poe?'

'It's an unwanted gift. One you don't feel you can throw away.' Poe had Bradshaw's pasta maker firmly in mind when he said this.

'It's been appropriated to mean that, yes, but the original meaning goes back to the days of the Siamese kings, way before Siam was renamed Thailand. Apparently, if an underling or rival angered the king, they might be presented with a white ele-phant as a gift. Ostensibly a reward, because of their tremendous housing and feeding costs, they were actually a shrewd form of punishment. More often than not, caring for a white elephant drove the beneficiary to financial ruin.'

'You think the killer was telling everyone that the game was actually a punishment?'

'I do. Also it was probably a way to let the person who'd hired him know that the victim dying was down to him and not just some crazy coincidence.'

'What's that have to do with a black swan, though? I've not heard of that term relating to anything other than the Australian bird.'

'It's a metaphor for high-profile, hard-to-foresee events that, nevertheless, after the fact are rationalised to have been predictable and therefore preventable: nine eleven is a classic example. No way could anyone have figured out we'd be attacked like that, but afterwards there were hearings and shit and good people lost their jobs.'

'So, if your game was a punishment, ours is . . . what, some sort of completely unpredictable seismic-sized event?'

'I dunno, Sergeant Poe, but I think at the very least you need to be looking past what you think you have, and consider that everything that's happened so far has been carefully choreographed.'

Poe sighed. He wasn't convinced but neither was he ready to dismiss it.

'Why don't I tell you what's going on over here, Special Agent Lee?' he said.

Poe spent fifteen minutes summarising the events leading to the discovery of the Black Swan Challenge.

He finished with, 'One victim was left in situ, the other two are still unaccounted for. Two fingers were taken from each victim, one ante-mortem and one post-mortem. The two missing victims had both been anaesthetised.'

'Anaesthetised? That's some fucked-up shit you've got going on over there, Sergeant Poe.'

'Tell me about it.'

'And you think this asshole's not operating remotely?'

'We know he's been here as the single-board computers were all placed locally. When is up for debate. My IT specialist says they could have been there for months, years even.'

'Do you have anyone for the murders yet?'

'A brother and sister.'

'And let me guess. They both copped to things you hadn't even known about but vehemently deny murdering anyone.'

'Pretty much,' Poe admitted.

'How'd you identify them?'

Poe was about to say 'good police work' but managed to stop himself.

'There was . . . evidence,' he said carefully.

'Solid?'

'Yes.'

'But not easily found?'

'No. We had to work for it.' I had to climb a bloody tree, he almost added.

'So you were more likely to have faith in it.'

Poe said nothing. The thought had crossed his mind a couple of times. Human nature meant that evidence you worked for tended to be trusted more than evidence that came easily.

'What did you have?'

'A kite we traced back to the brother was found in a tree overlooking one victim's house and a piece of paper found in his bin matched documents left at the deposition sites.'

'Careless of him.'

'It was.'

'Maybe *too* careless.'

'As I said, there are similarities,' Poe said.

Melody Lee sighed. 'Sergeant Poe, I think it's about time I told you about a man who calls himself the Curator . . .'

Chapter 48

'It didn't even start as a rumour,' Melody Lee said. 'More like the rumour of a rumour. I'd picked up this guy outta Boston on a racketeering charge and he tried to sweeten the DA's deal with some bullshit story about a fixer for hire. Calls himself the Curator because of the way he goes about his business. All long-arm. Never gets involved directly so he can't be caught via traditional law enforcement methods. He supposedly uses online tools to manipulate vulnerable kids into doing what needs to be done.'

'He's a contract killer?' Poe said.

'He didn't think so. He claimed that this guy was more of a problem solver. For the right price he offers bespoke solutions to whatever mess you've gotten yourself into. Manipulates a hacker into planting kiddie porn on the computer of the man who dumped you, fixes a DUI by getting some kid to burn down the lab storing the blood sample. That type of thing. Even if the person is caught, there's no link back to him. And therefore absolutely no way back to the person who hired him.'

'Murders?'

'I only know of my happy-slapping case but, if he does exist, I doubt it's the first time he's fixed a problem that way.'

Poe said nothing. As implausible as it sounded, why couldn't there be someone like that out there? An evil *Jim'll Fix It* as it were. He rephrased that in his mind: *Another* evil *Jim'll Fix It*.

'Anyhow, this racketeering asshole said he'd tried to get in touch with him regarding his own problems but hadn't been able to. The DA didn't buy it and he ended up flipping to make sure he didn't die in jail. But what he told me stuck. I think it was the lack of specifics that caught my attention.'

'You thought that your businessman might have hired him?' Poe said. 'Started digging?'

'Not officially. But yes, I started digging.'

'And?'

'Not much,' she admitted. 'I did find corroborating anecdotal evidence but no one had details.'

Poe paused a beat. It sounded a bit far-fetched. He said as much to Melody Lee.

'That's what I thought,' she replied. 'But the stories *were* consistent. And eventually a theme emerged. This guy can't be contacted. This guy contacts you. That's why I think he's managed to stay under the radar. I think he monitors the sites where these things are discussed and then does his own research into potential clients. He's very selective, very discreet. Everything's done remotely and the two parties never meet. All payments are in untraceable cryptocurrency; all communications are encrypted and on disposable devices.'

'You think he's the puppet master. Identifies the target then manipulates vulnerable or impressionable kids to murder for him?'

'I think he does get the kids to do some nasty shit but, for the bigger jobs, all he's really doing is setting up a patsy.'

'And he does the actual hit himself?'

'I'm convinced of it. He identifies the one he likes for it then plants the evidence. It explains how the blood was only on the sole of Stuart Wilson's sneakers. I figure he collected some from the murder scene and put it somewhere he knew Stuart Wilson would come into contact with it. His stoop, probably.'

'Stoop?'

'What you guys call the steps in front of your houses, I guess. Stuart Wilson must have stood in it.'

'And even if you found traces of it on the stoop you'd assume the forensic exchange was shoe to stoop, not stoop to shoe.'

'Exactly.'

Poe considered what she'd told him. Although it sounded a bit conspiracy theory-ish, a fixer for hire *did* explain some of the doubts he was beginning to have about the Cowells as serial killers.

There was one major flaw, though.

'None of our victims are linked, Special Agent Lee,' he said.

'You're sure?'

'We are.'

'Is it possible he's hiding the real motive for one murder in the chaos of a serial killer investigation?'

One of Nightingale's cops had already floated that theory. Poe didn't think so and explained why.

'I can't see any of our victims being the target of a hitman. One was a young girl working in a shop, one was a recluse and one held a minor position with the MoD.'

'How minor?'

'She was a contracts manager. Probably all I can say. I'm told she didn't have access to any sensitive information.'

'Damn,' Melody Lee said.

Her sense of disappointment was palpable.

'Can I ask why you didn't tell any of this to my senior investigating officer?' Poe said.

She didn't respond.

'You tried, didn't you? And either no one would listen or someone called afterwards and discredited you.'

'I haven't spoken to anyone actually. I wanted to, of course. Even raised it with my SAC.'

'SAC?'

'Special agent in charge. He forbade me from contacting the British police. Said I'm no longer considered . . . credible.'

'So . . .?'

'So why did I contact you?'

'Yes.'

'My understanding is that you're a fed, not local police. Sanctimonious prick shoulda been more specific.'

Poe grinned. The ability to misinterpret clear instructions was a much-underrated skill in his opinion.

'I'm going to have to pass this on to my SIO, though,' he said. 'If it helps, I'll say that I contacted you.'

'Appreciate that, Sergeant Poe.'

A thought occurred to him.

'How'd you get hold of my phone number?'

'Your name's flagged on one of our databases.'

'It is?'

'Actually, it's your father who's flagged but, as you're law enforcement, you are too.'

'What's my dad done?'

'He was recently asking about a diplomatic party his wife attended in the seventies. Upset a few people.'

Poe came over all cold. He hadn't heard from his dad since the end of the Jared Keaton case. They'd discussed his parentage, how his biological father had raped his mother while she was attending a party in the British Embassy. How he'd raised him as his own because Poe's mother hadn't wanted to be around when he started looking like the man who'd raped her. He'd told Poe he'd see what he could find.

Clearly he'd meant it.

'We about done, Special Agent Lee?' he said. 'I need to ring the boss.'

'I think so,' she replied. 'You have my number. Call it any time.'

'I will,' Poe promised.

'And be careful, Sergeant Poe – if I'm right, the Curator's death for hire.'

Chapter 49

Poe was back at Carleton Hall. He'd just finished telling Nightingale and Flynn about his conversation with Melody Lee and her theory about a problem solver called the Curator. It was clear Nightingale already knew.

'She's a kook, Poe,' she said. 'Her supervisor called me after she'd asked him for permission to get in touch. Said that, despite being told not to, she'd probably try anyway. Said she's an anti-authoritarian discipline case.'

'You should marry her, Poe,' Flynn said.

'She has this whacked-out theory there's a bogeyman out there, Steph,' Nightingale continued. 'But really she just got far too involved in a case. Her supervisor says the perpetrator's family groomed her to the point she became convinced of their kid's innocence. Instead of believing the evidence, she went and found an alternate theory that *fitted* the evidence.'

'Did they look into her claims, though?'

'They had to. She'd filled in some form that made it official. They launched a multi-state investigation but found no evidence to support it. They are satisfied that justice was served in the happy-slapping case.'

'She did have a compelling story,' Poe said. 'And the evidence she queried didn't make sense to me either.'

He didn't know why but he felt as though someone should stick up for her.

'You know what they call her over there?' Nightingale said.

'Nothing good, I suspect.'

'Spooky. After Fox Mulder in *The X-Files*. Sees conspiracies everywhere. She's on her final chance now but I suspect she's blown it by contacting you. My advice is that you leave it alone, Poe. There is no bogeyman out there.'

Taking Nightingale's and the FBI hierarchy's advice and leaving it alone was undoubtedly the sensible thing to do.

They had physical evidence tying their suspects to the three murders, neither of them had alibis and one of them had already admitted to some serious offences. With the search for the Black Swan administrator taking place in cyberspace, the rational thing to do would have been assisting Nightingale and her team as they built their case against the Cowells.

That would have been the sensible thing to do.

But that was reactive thinking and Poe wasn't built that way. The possibility that their administrator was Melody Lee's Curator was now playing on a loop in his mind and he knew from past experience that the only way to get rid of it was to satisfy himself that the claims were baseless.

So, instead of taking Nightingale's advice, he went and found Bradshaw.

'Poe, what are you doing?' Nightingale said.

They were in the small room they'd been assigned while they were going through the contents of the wheelie bin. Poe was re-watching the part of the interview where Robert Cowell had headbutted the table. Jon Lear, his solicitor, had tried to explain it away as a reaction to the situation but Poe didn't think that was right – Rhona Cowell had reacted when the same bit of evidence had been put before her as well. Not as extremely, but she *had* reacted.

Bradshaw was checking their computers. The Cowells knew

their way around them so would be adept at hiding things, she'd told him. She would find everything but it was going to take time.

'Just want to be sure, ma'am,' Poe said.

Nightingale leaned against the doorframe. He didn't blame her for not coming into the room; it still smelled, which was probably why it had been empty. She didn't look angry.

'DI Flynn warned me about this, you know.'

'About what?'

'She said that there'd come a point in the investigation where you'd start doubting the evidence and convince yourself you'd got it wrong.'

'Did she now?'

'She explained it's your failsafe and that I'd be well advised to listen to you when it happens. Said that if I leave you alone for a bit you'll come round eventually.'

'She have anything to say if I don't come round?'

Nightingale grinned and nodded. 'She said, "Fuck him, he's a sergeant and you're a superintendent."'

'Sounds about right.'

'You got an angle?'

'Not really,' Poe admitted, 'but this is bugging me. Rhona and Robert both reacted to the same bit of evidence. He smashed his face into the table and she sort of smirked. If you watch it's almost at exactly the same point. Other than that I don't have anything to go on.'

'I can't spare any personnel but let me know if you need help.'

'Will do,' Poe replied. 'How are the interviews going?'

The duty inspector had already authorised a twelve-hour custody extension and Poe knew Nightingale was working on getting a magistrate to increase it to the maximum of ninety-six hours. As much as PACE allowed, the Cowells were being interviewed around the clock.

213

'Robert's still protesting his innocence and, apart from the "look into my eyes" comment, Rhona's continuing to say nothing.'

'"Look into my eyes"? I thought she'd said, "Stare into my soul and see the truth"?'

'I've spoken to the interviewing detective and it was definitely eyes she said, not soul. Why, is that important?'

'Don't see how it could be. I'll take a look anyway.'

'OK, keep me informed?'

'Will do.'

Poe clicked the link for the relevant Rhona Cowell interview and scrolled to the place where the evidence about Midnight Mass had been put to her. She definitely reacted at the same time Robert had. He dragged the curser along the progress bar at the bottom of the screen until he'd found the part where she'd spoken.

He turned up the sound.

It was muffled, and in the official transcript would no doubt be recorded as 'inaudible'. Nightingale had been referring to her detective's *unofficial* notes. The ones that would be on HOLMES and the file but not used in any charging decisions.

Poe tried to watch Rhona's lips to see if he could see the words being formed but, as she was staring into her lap when she spoke, he could barely see her mouth at all. He watched it a couple of times but nothing leaped out.

He dragged the progress bar back to where she'd smirked. She'd smirked and Robert had become distressed. Why?

And in every interview he'd watched she'd remained in full control. So why did she bother speaking at all? It didn't make sense. She hadn't even confirmed her name, but for some reason she asked the cop to look into her eyes and see some sort of divine truth?

Poe played it again.

'Tilly, what's wrong with this picture?' he said.

He played it for her.

'I don't know, Poe. What's bothering you?'

'She's not looking at the detective when she tells him to look into her eyes. She's not even looking at the camera.'

'So?'

'So, who's she speaking to?' he said. 'Asking someone to look into your eyes but looking away from them while you do is plain weird, don't you think?'

Bradshaw frowned then looked at the laptop she'd been working on. It was Robert's. It was connected to her own by a thick cable. A program was running on both of them.

She pressed a button and killed it. The desktop image, the one he used as a background, reappeared on Robert's laptop. It was a close-up photo of him and Rhona posing next to a kite-flying trophy. They were both smiling.

'I wonder . . .' Bradshaw said. 'What if we have this all wrong, Poe? What if she wasn't being figurative when she said, "look into my eyes", what if she was being *literal*?'

Ten minutes later Poe called Nightingale.

'Ma'am, we have a big problem,' he said.

Chapter 50

Nightingale glared at the wall monitor as if it was personally responsible for the disastrous turn the investigation had just taken. She'd wanted her senior team briefed but, given what Bradshaw had uncovered, Poe had insisted on it being a small and select group for now. There was only Nightingale, the chief constable and the assistant chief of operations.

'Talk me through it,' the chief constable said. Given the about-turn they'd all experienced, she seemed ready to take a more hands-on role. She wasn't blaming Nightingale – she'd been following the evidence like everyone else – but it was clear she no longer wanted to hear things second-hand.

'There was a hidden folder in Robert Cowell's laptop,' Bradshaw said. 'The link to it was embedded in a single pixel in the desktop background photograph he was using.'

'It was in his sister's eye, to be precise,' Poe added.

'People can hide files in images without specialist software?' Nightingale said.

'If you have a decent steganography tool, yes,' Bradshaw said.

'And what was in this folder?'

'He'd been spying on his sister for years,' Poe said. 'There are thousands of photographs and videos of her.'

'Naked?'

'Not just naked. There are lots of her masturbating and a fair few of her with various men.'

'Dirty bastard,' the chief constable said. 'Well, at least we can

216

add voyeurism to his charge sheet. I'm assuming he'd hidden cameras in her bedroom and bathroom?'

Poe shook his head. 'All the videos were handheld and almost certainly filmed on a mobile phone. He was standing outside her bedroom door when he recorded some of them.'

'She left her door open when she was having sex?'

'I'm fairly certain she knew she was being filmed and left it open deliberately, ma'am. In at least two of the videos she's looking directly at the camera. In one of them she winks at it. She must have also known where Robert hid them on his laptop. It explains the cryptic message in her interview. When she said look in her eyes to see the truth, as Tilly worked out, she was being literal.'

'She got off on it?'

Poe nodded. 'Probably loved the power she held over him. It explains why he seems so conflicted over her. Obsessed with her but hates her too.'

'That's messed up,' the chief constable said.

Poe agreed. Robert and Rhona Cowell certainly put Flynn's rivalry with Jessica into perspective.

'Sergeant Poe thinks this is what the Black Swan site administrator threatened to make public,' Nightingale said.

'Having that in the public domain *would* be a powerful motivator,' the chief constable agreed. 'I'm not seeing a problem, though. All this does is confirm what we thought: that he was being blackmailed into playing Black Swan. What haven't I been told yet?'

'Tilly?' Poe said.

'I've run every diagnostic tool I have and neither the phone he used to film Rhona Cowell nor the laptop itself have had their date and time stamp altered.'

'So?'

Bradshaw reddened and brought up a video on the monitor.

'This is one of two videos shot the same night. This is the first and it starts just before midnight.'

It was a still of two people having sex. A shaven headed man covered with black tribal tattoos lay on his back. Rhona Cowell straddled him.

Bradshaw pressed play then turned her head so she didn't have to watch.

Rhona Cowell began to vigorously thrust her hips back and forth, her hands reaching behind her as she grasped the man's thighs for support. After a minute, Rhona turned her head and looked directly at the camera. She held her gaze for a moment before smirking. She then shut her eyes, arched her back and climaxed. The video ended.

'That's *really* messed up,' the chief constable said again.

Bradshaw right clicked the video file. A menu appeared. She scrolled down and clicked 'Get Info'. A detailed page appeared on the monitor. It had information on the kind of file, its size, where it was located on the hard drive, and finally, at the bottom of the page, when the video had been created . . .

'No,' Poe said. 'This is what's messed up.'

He pointed at the date and time stamp.

'Robert was filming his sister having sex on Christmas Eve. The video begins at 11.52 p.m. and ends forty-three minutes later at 12.35 a.m. Tilly has it being logged into the hidden folder at 2.16 a.m. The second video was filmed at 3.06 a.m. and lasts for thirty minutes. It was logged just before 4 a.m.'

'But if he was watching his sister then, how could he have been . . .?' The chief constable didn't finish her sentence. Poe reckoned she was beginning to understand Nightingale's anger.

'How could he have been hiding in among the Midnight Mass congregation at a church on the outskirts of Barrow-in-Furness?'

The chief constable nodded.

'Obviously he couldn't, ma'am.'

'So either someone else is involved or your Special Agent Melody Lee is right: Robert *is* being set up as a patsy.'

'And there's still someone out there, killing people to an agenda we haven't come close to figuring out . . .'

Chapter 51

After the chief constable and the assistant chief had left to form a media strategy, and Bradshaw had left to log the evidence with the High-Tech Forensic Crime Unit, Nightingale and Poe talked around the edges of alternative explanations.

'It's possible Robert *didn't* hide among the Midnight Mass congregation. That he filmed his sister then drove to Barrow and found a way to break into the church after the service had ended.'

'It's possible,' Poe agreed.

'But you don't think so?'

'I don't, ma'am. From Carlisle it's the best part of a two-hour drive to Barrow and, even if he had left as soon as he'd filmed the second video, he wouldn't have had time to do what he needed.'

'He could have left the fingers before Midnight Mass, I suppose,' Nightingale said unconvincingly.

'And no one noticed two fingers in the font?' Poe said. 'The font that everyone in the congregation had to walk past.'

'Fair point,' she said. 'So, you think Robert would have rather gone to prison for murders he hadn't committed than show us the videos he'd taken of his sister?'

'I absolutely think that,' Poe said. 'It also explains his "bitch" remark – he had the means to exonerate himself but he knew that he couldn't use it.'

'So when it became apparent that Robert wasn't going to reveal that he'd been filming her, she decided she'd better help him out.'

'Getting herself out of a jam in the process.'

'What do we do now then?' Nightingale asked.

'I'd take the Cowells out of play and charge them for the abduction of the little girl. They'll be safe and secure and we'll know where they are.'

'And then what? If there's no link between the victims there's nowhere to start.'

'Not true,' Poe said.

'Go on.'

'If we accept the possibility that we're dealing with Melody Lee's Curator, then we also have to accept the possibility that he's hiding one murder in among three. We need to go deep into their lives, *really* deep. Maybe one of them did something that forced someone into hiring a hitman.'

'That's an awful lot of data to crunch.'

'I have just the person for that,' he said.

DC Dave Coughlan had gone from antagonist to Bradshaw's biggest fan.

He'd set them up in a well-equipped, stench-free room off the main incident room. It had views of the old air ambulance helipad and fields beyond full of lowland sheep picking out what little grass hadn't been covered by the recent blanket of snow.

A large-scale, detailed map of the county covered one of the walls. Another was filled with press clippings, photographs, reports and documents. It was a more formal version of the murder wall at Herdwick Croft. Poe had seen these before in complex investigations. Wily SIOs would set aside a room, always near the main incident room, where cops could wander in with a brew and view things in a less pressurised environment. Sometimes this sparked a memory or helped someone make a connection. Poe immediately felt at home.

Within an hour the first lot of new data had arrived. Phone, credit cards and bank records for the victims had been accessed and Bradshaw busied herself with running it all through one of her existing analytical programs.

The door opened and Coughlan entered. He'd brought back a selection of snacks from the canteen vending machine. Crisps, dry sandwiches and Kit Kats. He put them on the table then wandered over to the murder wall.

Poe tucked in.

Bradshaw looked on in disgust. 'Poe, you're like a seagull: you'll eat anything.'

'Squawk,' he said through a mouthful of cheese Quavers.

'I thought I'd told you that you had to eat five bits of fruit . . .' She stopped and frowned at the screen on her laptop.

'That can't be right,' she said.

'What?'

'Nothing. Just checking something.'

Five minutes later she picked up her mobile, scrolled down her contact list and called someone.

'Malcolm Sparkes, this is Matilda Bradshaw from the National Crime . . . oh, you remember me?' She covered the phone with her hand. 'He remembers me, Poe!' She removed her hand and continued, 'I'd like you to tell me if Rebecca Pridmore had access to a car we don't know about . . . yes, please, to the email address I gave you.'

She hung up and Poe looked at her.

'I'm sure it's nothing,' she said.

Knowing that it was pointless asking her to voice unproven theories – she'd tell him only when she had something concrete – Poe picked up an egg and watercress sandwich and joined Coughlan at the murder wall. He stared at it while he chewed on the stale bread and the claggy filling, the egg congealing on the roof of his mouth.

Poe reread the victim summaries. Tried to will a new thought into his head. The only one he could summon, though, was that the differences between them couldn't have contrasted more.

Amanda Simpson was a no-frills working-class girl. Happy. Optimistic. Active circle of friends and a boyfriend she adored. She had a full employment record but it was obvious she worked to live rather than lived to work. She frequently changed jobs but stayed in the retail sector, mainly clothes shops.

Rebecca Pridmore was the polar opposite: she lived to work. Her career was everything, and although she didn't appear to be ruthlessly aggressive, she obviously loved what she did and took it very seriously. Despite Bradshaw's mysterious phone call to Sparkes, Poe had dismissed her as the favourite to be the 'one murder that counted'. She *did* have access to sensitive information, and while a bad report from her might send the share prices of some multi-billion-dollar private defence contractors plummeting, Malcolm Sparkes hadn't been worried and he undoubtedly had information he wasn't sharing. If the MoD were convinced she hadn't been killed because of her work then, for now at least, Poe was too.

Poe moved on to the third victim.

Howard Teasdale. Fifty years old and fat. A self-employed web designer. Despite living on the top floor of a townhouse, he was a poster-boy basement dweller. The inventory of his possessions would have kept teenage boys wanking for years. Despite not being allowed to access the internet for pornography, he had every category there was saved onto his computer: Asian, BDSM, fisting, lesbian, threesomes, amateurs, gay, everything. Nothing illegal. If he was still into children, he was no longer sating it online.

Of the three victims, Howard was currently Poe's favourite. He spent his life online and was the type of person who'd stick his nose into the darkest corners of the web. Had he stumbled across something he shouldn't have?

Poe sighed. It could have been any of them.

Or all three as it turned out . . .

Chapter 52

'You're now saying the three victims are linked?' Nightingale said.

'We are, ma'am,' Poe replied.

Poe had taken Bradshaw's findings straight to Nightingale's office. He'd brought along Bradshaw to explain it and Coughlan to stop him gossiping. Nightingale would want a lid kept on the new information, at least until she'd decided what to do with it.

Her office was roomy with a decent-sized conference table. Manuals and force policies were neatly arranged on her bookcase. Her desk had a computer, an empty in-tray and a photograph of her family. The coasters on the conference table were corporate, as were the mugs from which they were drinking. Other than that it was bare – it was an office to work from, not one to enjoy being in.

Bradshaw was about to begin when Flynn walked in. Coughlan stood and offered her his seat. Poe winced; Flynn hated chivalry in all its forms but, to his relief, she accepted gratefully. She took off her shoes and began massaging her feet.

'Tilly's found something, I gather?' she said.

'She has,' Poe said.

Bradshaw hadn't had time to put together a presentation. She flicked through some papers until she found the ones she wanted.

'These are Howard Teasdale's credit card statements. I've looked at the last six years. He had his shopping and takeaways delivered and everything else came from Amazon or other specialist online providers. His social life is entirely on social media.

His main activities were gaming and collecting pornography. Other than his court appearances for possessing indecent images of children and the subsequent sex offender's course he was forced to attend, he rarely left his flat.'

She pulled out one of Teasdale's statements and put it face up on the table. She'd highlighted a number of transactions.

'Except, that is, for a two-week period in September three years ago. As you can see, there are several purchases in Carlisle, sometimes in the morning and sometimes in the middle of the day. Food and drink mainly. He ate at KFC six times. There are also daily receipts for train tickets.'

'And it wasn't work related?'

'No, Detective Superintendent Nightingale. For that two-week period Howard Teasdale worked on his web design business in the evenings. Whatever he was doing in Carlisle, it wasn't work.'

'Could have been any number of reasons,' Coughlan said.

'I agree, Dave Coughlan, but it *was* an anomaly and that's what I look for – things out of the ordinary.'

She rifled through the documents again, this time pulling out a bank statement. It was Amanda Simpson's. It looked like she had one of those interest-free basic accounts designed for people with low credit scores. She'd have been able to deposit and access her money but she wouldn't have had an overdraft facility.

'I couldn't find train ticket payments for Amanda Simpson, but given that she had a car that's not surprising. She doesn't use her bank card to pay for petrol so that was no help, but what I did find was this.'

She pointed at a single highlighted line on the bank statement. It was an outgoing payment to Accessorise in the Lanes Shopping Centre in Carlisle. Bradshaw had cross-checked with the store's records and Amanda had bought three hair scrunchies, whatever they were.

'For at least one of the days Howard Teasdale was in Carlisle, so was Amanda Simpson,' Bradshaw said.

She turned over another document. This time it was an HSBC Premier Account statement belonging to Rebecca Pridmore. Sure enough there was a payment made in Carlisle in the same two-week period. Again, Bradshaw had checked with the store: it was a blouse from Marks and Spencer.

'Carlisle's the only city in Cumbria,' Nightingale said. 'Travelling from the south of the county to shop there is hardly errant behaviour, especially for a fashion-conscious young woman. And Rebecca Pridmore lived on the outskirts anyway. She'd have visited most weeks. I go in most weeks and I live in Appleby.'

Nightingale seemed disappointed. But then again, she didn't know what they knew yet.

'I'm not saying that Rebecca and Amanda popped in to do some shopping, Detective Superintendent Nightingale, I'm saying that they all spent the same two-week period in Carlisle.'

The room went silent.

'You'd better explain, Tilly,' Poe said.

'Weekends excepted, Howard Teasdale went to Carlisle every day in that period. The train receipts are conclusive.'

She opened her laptop and turned it so everyone could see the screen.

'Amanda Simpson was working at an independent clothes shop. This is her annual leave card. As you can see, she booked time off for the same two weeks that Howard was in Carlisle.'

'And Rebecca Pridmore,' Nightingale said, 'was she on leave at the same time?'

'She wasn't, Detective Superintendent Nightingale. Her leave record shows she spent two weeks in Portugal in July and a week in Paris in November that year. Her bank statements support this.'

'But . . .'

'But I don't think she was at work, either.'

She brought up Rebecca Pridmore's credit card statements for the preceding six months.

'Travelling from Dalston to BAE systems in Barrow-in Furness is a daily journey of one hundred and sixty-eight miles. Taking a median working month of twenty-one point seven five days that's a monthly commute of three thousand six hundred and fifty-four miles.'

'No wonder her marriage was fucked,' Flynn muttered.

'According to the manufacturer's website, the average miles-per-gallon for her Range Rover is twenty-nine to forty-four on a motorway. The fuel tank capacity is just less than twenty gallons so if we assume an average miles-per-gallon of thirty-six and a half she would have to fill up every four days. Which is supported by what her bank statements say. Sometimes it's five days, sometimes it's four.'

'But she didn't fill up in the two-week period we're interested in?' Flynn said.

'Not once.'

'And if she only needed her car to drive from Dalston to Carlisle, which is what . . . five miles?'

'Six.'

'Twelve miles a day for two weeks. Easily done on a full tank.'

'Easily,' Bradshaw agreed.

'Car sharing?' Nightingale asked. 'Don't BAE encourage it? Part of their corporate responsibility policy.'

'They do,' Bradshaw replied, 'but it's unlikely in this case. Rebecca Pridmore had a highly classified job and she usually made phone calls while she drove. I called Malcolm Sparkes to see if she'd had access to a car we didn't know about. She hadn't.'

'Anything else, Tilly?' Nightingale said. She'd gone from sceptical to convinced right about the same time Poe had when Bradshaw had explained it to him half an hour earlier.

Bradshaw brought up a different image.

'Her phone records. BAE have a strict policy on mobile phones. They don't allow them inside. Very few exceptions and Rebecca Pridmore wasn't one of them. As you can see' – she pointed at the list that was far too small to read – 'she only ever made calls before and after work.' The next image came up. 'But in the two-week period we're interested in she made calls and sent emails at all sorts of times.'

'So she wasn't on leave and she wasn't at BAE,' Nightingale said. 'She could have been working from home, I suppose. Maybe she was ill?'

Bradshaw shook her head. This time when the image changed it showed three sets of phone records, side-by-side.

'The thing is,' she said, 'there were times during that two-week period, sometimes for hours at a time, when none of the victims used their phones.'

'OK, that *is* weird,' Nightingale admitted.

'And that's not all,' Bradshaw said. 'When one of them eventually used their phone, the other two invariably did as well, within minutes of each other. Amanda Simpson would usually check her social media pages and send some texts, Rebecca Pridmore would send emails or make phone calls and Howard Teasdale would play online games or look at pornography.'

'OK, that's too much of a coincidence to ignore,' Nightingale said. 'Can we locate where they were by their phones?'

'Too long ago, Detective Superintendent Nightingale. That's why we don't have information on what was in the texts or emails. There's no depth to these reports. It's to do with data protection and how long companies can hold on to our information.'

'OK,' Nightingale said. 'This is a job for the main investigation team. I'll flood Carlisle with cops and photographs of the victims. Someone will remember something.'

Poe wasn't so sure. It was three years ago and Carlisle was a transient city. He thought they needed to go bigger.

'What about *Crimewatch*?' he said. The popular BBC programme that reconstructed major unsolved crimes in order to jog the public's memory had helped catch some of the country's most notorious villains over the years. Poe had seen the policy for submitting crimes to the programme on Nightingale's bookcase.

'*Crimewatch* doesn't run any more, Poe,' Bradshaw said. 'It became redundant at the same time linear television did. Other than major sporting events, we rarely view live television; the trend is to record and watch later.'

'Tilly's right,' Flynn said. 'By the time viewers were getting round to watching it no one was on the phone lines any more.'

'The jury was out on how effective it was in the shire counties anyway,' Nightingale added. 'It tended to work best in metropolitan areas with high-density populations. Lots of potential witnesses.'

Poe froze.

'I need to make a phone call,' he said.

'Why?'

'I think the Curator's real . . .'

Chapter 53

'I think the three victims were on jury service,' Poe said. 'That's why they were in Carlisle at the same time.'

Nightingale stared at him. 'Explain,' she said.

'DI Flynn is getting our director to put pressure on Her Majesty's Court and Tribunals Service to release the names of jurors but I'll talk you through it.'

He held up a finger.

'One: crown court's in Carlisle and jury service lasts for two weeks.'

He held up a second finger. 'Two: Tilly's checked with the MoD and they don't require employees to take leave for jury service, which explains why Rebecca had nothing on her leave card. Howard was self-employed and Amanda *did* have to take leave.'

'And when court's in session you have to have your mobile switched off,' Nightingale said.

'You do, ma'am,' Poe said. 'It also explains the irregular times their phones were switched back on. In a crown court trial the jury are often dismissed while a point of law is being discussed. If it's going to be a while, the usher will allow mobiles to be used while they're in the jury room.'

'And because you have to hand them in while you're deliberating,' Nightingale added, 'it explains the longer period they were all off at the end.'

Poe hadn't considered that. He nodded as another piece of the puzzle fell into place. 'And finally, although you can't serve on a jury with a criminal conviction, the trial period predated Howard Teasdale's sex offence.'

'All trials are public record,' Nightingale said. 'I assume you've formed a theory on which one they were on?'

'There were a few during that two-week period but one in particular stands out. I think you'll remember it, ma'am.'

'Why's that?' she asked. 'Who was on trial, Sergeant Poe?'

'It was Edward Atkinson.'

Nightingale gasped.

'Oh my God. The man . . .'

'The man in the mask,' Poe confirmed.

And then the room went quiet.

Chapter 54

'The Curator exists then,' Flynn said.

'Seems that way,' Poe said. 'Too many similarities for it to be a coincidence.'

'And who the hell is Edward Atkinson? Why's he called the man in the mask?'

After Director of Intelligence Edward van Zyl had confirmed that Howard Teasdale, Rebecca Pridmore and Amanda Simpson had been on the jury for the Edward Atkinson trial, it had been organised chaos. People had phone calls to make. The rest of the jury had to be identified, located and made safe.

They'd assembled in a corner of the incident room. Nightingale had only just returned. She looked exhausted. Coughlan put a steaming mug of coffee in front of her. She sipped at it gratefully.

'Ma'am, do you want to tell DI Flynn who Atkinson is?' Poe asked.

'You do it,' she replied, her mobile pressed against her ear. 'I'm trying to get your lot to tell me what his new name is.'

'You weren't informed at the time?' Poe asked, surprised.

She shook her head. 'You know what happened. Can you blame him? If it had been me, I know I wouldn't have wanted . . . hello, this is Detective Superintendent Nightingale from Cumbria Constabulary; I'd like to speak to your operations manager, please . . . yes, I'll hold.' She turned to Flynn and said, 'I'd better take this in my office.'

After she'd left, Flynn asked again, 'Who the hell is Edward Atkinson?'

'I was working for SCAS when it happened but for a while Edward Atkinson was the most hated man in Cumbria,' Poe said. 'He worked for a waste management and recycling business. One of those companies who securely dispose of the hazardous materials some industries create.'

As he spoke, Bradshaw was typing furiously. 'J. Baldwin Limited? Based in Workington?'

'That's the one,' Poe confirmed. 'Companies paid them to collect their hazardous waste. Atkinson's job was to uplift their acids, alkalis and phenols and transport the waste back to their depot outside Distington. Sometimes it was safely disposed of, sometimes it was reconditioned and sold.'

'Something went wrong, I take it?'

'Human nature,' Poe said. 'Atkinson had had a late collection and by the time he returned to the depot it was shut. When that happened, he was supposed to call the duty manager who would come out and unlock the disposal unit. They would then get rid of whatever he'd collected together.'

'What happened?'

'Atkinson was going on holiday the next day and he hadn't wanted to wait. So, instead of calling the duty manager and safely disposing of the five drums of contaminated acid he'd collected, he falsified the logbook to say he'd returned to the depot at 4 p.m. He then emptied everything onto some nearby waste ground. By the time he got back from holiday, two children had lost their sight and another had chemical burns on more than twenty per cent of their body.'

'Oh my goodness,' Bradshaw said. 'That's awful.'

'Pretty much how everyone in Cumbria saw it. The Environment Agency charged him with unauthorised disposal of waste and, as it was a category one, deliberate offence, he was potentially looking at three years. The CPS charged him with a section twenty GBH.'

'Grievous Bodily Harm?' Flynn said. 'How did they get away with that?'

'There were culpability issues. The CPS argued that no reasonable person would illegally dispose of dangerous chemicals in a place where children were known to play.'

'Still, it was a brave charging decision.'

'It was in part driven to appease the local community and in part to appease the police. One of the children who lost their sight was the son of a police officer.'

'You said "the man in the mask". What was that about?'

'That's when the case took an even darker turn,' Poe said. 'Atkinson pleaded not guilty and it went to a full trial. He claimed that he *did* ring the duty manager. That the CEO's son came and unlocked the gates for him. Took the material from him and told him that he'd dispose of it himself and that he should get away and start his holiday.'

'Did the defence provide any evidence?'

'None. The logbook was a key part of the prosecution's trial strategy. It had been tampered with to look like Atkinson had returned from his rounds earlier than he did, before the disposal unit needed a duty manager to unlock it.'

'So why . . .?'

'Why did he go not guilty? The defence's theory was that the CEO's son didn't know how the disposal unit worked. They suggested that, rather than humiliate himself in front of the staff by seeking help, he just dumped it and hoped no one would notice.'

'And the jury were buying it?'

'Nope. Not even a little bit.'

'So?'

'About three days before the scheduled end of the trial, something awful happened. Atkinson had been getting death threats.

He'd reported them to the police and they'd said they'd have someone intermittently drive by his house.'

'Seems light,' Flynn said.

Poe nodded. 'Very light. Anyway, on the morning in question, someone with a sense of irony threw concentrated acid at his face. Right outside the court.'

'Ouch.'

'The perp handed himself in and got sent down for GBH with intent. He got out a year ago. Nightingale's got him in the cells already.'

'Possible suspect?'

'Not if I remember him correctly,' Poe said. 'Bit of a fuckwit. Impressionable. Mainly did it for the kudos.'

'What happened to Atkinson?'

'In hospital for months. Had nearly forty operations. Skin grafts, experimental surgery, everything. Nothing really worked, though, and he had to wear this burn mask twenty-four hours a day to keep his scar tissue moist.'

'And the trial?'

'The first was declared a mistrial because of his injuries. It was almost a year before they were ready to go again. Different jury this time, obviously. *Our* jury. Same overwhelming evidence but the jury couldn't agree on a verdict and it was hung. The prevailing theory was that some of them were swayed by what had happened to him. Apparently he was a pitiful sight in the dock. The CPS elected not to pursue a third trial and Atkinson walked free.'

'What a clusterfuck,' Flynn said.

'Gets worse,' Poe said. 'Within a year of the hung jury two things happened: Atkinson tried to hang himself and a whistle-blower came forward.'

'*Tried* to hang himself?'

'Messed it right up. Ended up with an incomplete spinal cord

235

injury. He's now in a wheelchair for the rest of his life. Has feeling below the waist but no movement.'

'And the whistleblower?'

'He was more of a co-conspirator really, but he said that, at the behest of the CEO himself, he'd amended the logbook so it looked like Atkinson had tried to cover his tracks. He also said that J. Baldwin Limited had been illegally dumping hazardous material on the waste ground for months while they waited for one of their disposal units to be repaired.'

'So he *wasn't* guilty?'

Poe shook his head.

'Poor sod,' Flynn said.

'Not poor,' Poe said. 'He sued J. Baldwin and won a seven-figure sum. He then went after the police for not taking his protection seriously—'

'Had they?' Flynn cut in.

'I honestly don't know. I *do* know that they settled with him. A big pay out.'

'They were worried about the optics? Thought that it'd look like they'd deliberately ignored Atkinson's concerns because a Cumbrian cop's kid had been blinded?'

'Probably.'

'So where is he now?'

'That's just the problem,' Poe replied. 'And it's why Superintendent Nightingale's on the phone to our lot as we speak – Atkinson's a protected person . . .'

Chapter 55

The UK Protected Persons Service, previously called Witness Protection, was formed in 2013. Regionally delivered by the police but coordinated by the National Crime Agency, Poe had never had active involvement with them other than attending mandatory briefings. All he knew was that people would be removed from the area of threat and relocated to a different part of the country – sometimes even abroad – where their lives were rebuilt with new identities.

UKPPS operated in great secrecy and on a closed computer system. It could only be accessed by sitting in front of a UKPPS terminal with a complex set of passwords and identifiers.

Even Bradshaw couldn't beat a system like that.

Poe seriously doubted that Nightingale would have much luck getting Atkinson's new name. And, as the best tool at UKPPS's disposal was putting distance between the protected person and the problem area, Poe also doubted that Atkinson, whatever his name was now, would be living anywhere near Cumbria anyway.

Nightingale's face was sourer than a Scottish banana.

'No joy?' Flynn said.

She shook her head. 'Not a credible threat. Wouldn't even confirm he was on the scheme.'

'But we already know he is.'

She shrugged.

An admin assistant popped her head round the door. She

waved a folded bit of paper and Nightingale beckoned her in. She read it.

'Think this'll change their mind?' she asked, handing it to Flynn. 'We've tracked down one of the jury members and he says that Howard, Rebecca and Amanda were the three dissenting voices who went for not guilty.'

'I think it'll make them dig in further,' Poe said. 'From their perspective, the fewer people who know, the safer he is. Any ideas on how the Curator identified members of the jury?'

'We have,' Nightingale said. 'Apparently, one of the jury gave a paid interview to the press a year or so ago. We think this might have been the killer's way in. We've arrested the juror but he's refusing to speak. His neighbours say that he recently bought a new car, though. It looks like he might have been paid to reveal the identities of the jurors who went for not guilty.'

'Reckless bastard,' Poe said. 'What about Atkinson's barrister and solicitor? And the judge?'

'All safe,' Nightingale confirmed. 'Everyone else remotely involved in the hung jury has covert protection in case someone makes a move against them. If we're lucky we'll catch him in the act.'

Poe didn't think they would but it was worth a try.

'And the CEO's son?' he asked. 'The one who was actually responsible for blinding those kids?'

'He's out of prison and we're looking into him but it's a long shot. The civil action that Atkinson and the families took, along with the massive fines they received after the Environment Agency prosecution, bankrupted the company. Made them social pariahs, so they haven't been able to restart. I can't see how they could afford someone like the Curator.'

'When do we think this all started?' he asked.

'Why?'

'Because the whistleblower's bothering me,' Poe said. 'If this is a plan a long time in the making then Atkinson's exoneration should have changed things. The Baldwins should be the targets now. But they're not. So it either *didn't* change things or this isn't what we think it is.'

'You're thinking this might not be revenge for what happened to those kids, it could be revenge for what happened to the Baldwins?'

'Why not?' Poe said. 'When J. Baldwin went bankrupt people will have lost money. That's hopefully a much smaller pool of suspects.'

Nightingale made a note.

'There's a third option,' Flynn said. 'Someone who has held on to their hatred. Nurtured it to the point that new information wasn't going to change things.'

'Belief perseverance, it's called,' Bradshaw said, the first time she'd spoken in a while. When cops were talking cop stuff she tended to hover in the background.

'Which is?' Nightingale said.

'It's when a belief is maintained despite new information that definitively contradicts it. And it isn't just restricted to people with low levels of education. In the 2009 paper "Experimental Studies of Belief Dependence of Observations and of Resistance to Conceptual Change", Moti Nissani and his wife Donna did an experiment on nineteen PhD students. They were all given a flawed formula on how to determine the volume of a sphere. They were then given a measuring container to check their results. Eighteen of the nineteen refused to believe the measurements, despite their empirical observations.'

'How's that different to what I said?' Flynn said.

'I quoted actual research, DI Flynn,' Bradshaw replied. 'You guess—'

'Tilly, you're getting right on my fucking tits,' Flynn snapped. 'Are they still leak—'

'How common is it, Tilly?' Poe asked before things had a chance to escalate.

'Common enough not to rule it out, Poe.'

'Bollocks,' Nightingale said. 'If we can't rule it out then I need to look at both suspect pools: people who either didn't respect the lack of a guilty verdict or didn't believe the whistleblower, *and* people who have a grudge against Atkinson because of what happened to J. Baldwin. I need more resources and we're already stretched thin. I'm going to need a new budget meeting.'

'While you're trying to get blood out of a stone, ma'am, I'm going to get an address for Atkinson.'

'How on earth are you going to do that?'

'By playing to my strengths.'

'Which are?'

'Politics, obviously,' Poe grinned.

Nightingale put her head in her hands and groaned.

'We're all doomed,' she said.

Chapter 56

'It's more than a credible threat, sir; I think there's now an inevitability to it,' Poe said.

Poe was speaking to Edward van Zyl, the director of intelligence and his ultimate superior. He'd called him on his personal mobile and van Zyl had known him long enough to know he only ever did that when it was serious.

'UKPPS are happy with his security,' van Zyl said.

'I'm not. My FBI contact says the Curator might have been behind that death the US Marshals had in their witness protection programme last year. If he can breach their systems, he can certainly breach ours.'

Melody Lee had said no such thing. Poe didn't like lying to the director but it was the lie he needed to hear. He knew that van Zyl wanted to help and Poe's job was to give him the cover to do so.

Van Zyl didn't respond.

'I also think we have a unique opportunity,' Poe continued, 'not only to catch a very dangerous man, but also to elevate the NCA's standing in law enforcement globally.'

'Appealing to my vanity, Poe?'

'If I thought it would work on you, I would, sir. No, but apart from my source, the Yanks don't believe he exists. If we can prove he does, not only will we have one up on the FBI, they'll be desperate to speak to him. It'd be nice to have them owing us a favour for once.'

Like anything else, international law enforcement worked on relationships and favours as much as it did protocols and intelligence-sharing agreements. An FBI favour in van Zyl's back pocket would be a valuable thing to have later down the line.

'I'm listening,' he said.

'We get the name and we go in gently. Set up covert surveillance and wait for the Curator to find him.'

'We can't leak Atkinson's name, Poe.'

'We won't need to, sir. If the Curator is half the adversary I think he is, it won't take him long to get it.'

'Honestly, Poe,' Bradshaw grumbled, 'when are you going to realise that vegetables won't kill you?'

'It's only a sandwich,' he protested. 'And I need to build up my strength.'

'It's a loaf of bread stuffed with meatballs and cheese.'

They'd gone to a local café while they waited for van Zyl. Bradshaw had ordered the five-bean salad and he'd ordered the meatball sub, extra Monterey Jack, extra jalapeños. He pulled out a bit of limp lettuce and held it up.

'See, it's got salad in it.'

Bradshaw put down her fork. She looked troubled.

'DI Flynn was cross with me before, wasn't she, Poe?'

'She's cross with everyone right now, Tilly. My advice is don't worry about it. It's a symptom of what she's going through, not a reflection of what she thinks.'

Bradshaw thought about that for a moment then nodded decisively.

'OK, I shan't worry about it.' She started eating again.

'But you might want to stop asking her about her leaking . . .'

His phone rang. Van Zyl's name was on the caller ID. He answered it.

'Sir?'

'Poe, how soon can you get to a secure laptop and an internet connection?'

'Is that thing secure, Tilly?' Poe said, pointing at her MacBook.

'It is, Poe.'

'What about the café's wi-fi?'

'Not at the minute. If it's important I can hijack it and make it secure. It will mean everyone else will lose their connection, though.'

Poe looked round. There were half a dozen people still in the café. Four of them were reading and another was on a tablet. The sixth was staring into space like a weirdo.

'Do it,' he said. 'Give me a minute, sir . . . how long, Tilly?'

She held a finger in the air while she fiddled about on the Mac's trackpad.

'Done,' she said.

'We're up and running, sir,' Poe said.

After Bradshaw had given van Zyl her details he said, 'Someone's going to call you now.'

He then hung up.

Two minutes later the videoconference icon on Bradshaw's laptop began flashing.

Chapter 57

'Edward Atkinson is now called Ian Carruthers,' Poe said to the small team he'd been authorised to brief. 'And he wasn't ghosted somewhere new, he's still living in Cumbria.'

There was a burst of muttering. Atkinson being in their area wasn't just surprising – it gave them a whole new set of problems, one of which was resourcing. Nightingale and the assistant chief exchanged a worried glance. They'd just won a hard-fought increase in their budget – now they were going to need even more.

'When I called, I was told this information was classified,' Nightingale said. 'Why were they happy to tell you, Poe?'

'I explained how there would be certain . . . political advantages to the NCA being involved in this arrest,' Poe said. 'Ultimately, though, the only reason they released the information is that they aren't actively involved any more. Atkinson accepted a new identity and then opted out of the scheme altogether. As you know, it's voluntary.'

'Why would he do that?'

Poe didn't know for sure but he could guess.

'I think it was because they wanted to move him out of Cumbria,' he said. 'Miles on the map is the best tool UKPPS have at their disposal, but he's lived here all his life and you know what home birds Cumbrians are. And because of the compensation he received from the police and the civil action, he wasn't short of money.'

'So he decided to arrange his own protection?' Nightingale said.

'Sort of . . . He bought an island.'

The resulting silence wasn't unexpected. Poe had had exactly the same reaction. The only people who owned islands were whacky billionaires and Bond villains.

'An island?' Flynn said eventually. 'An *actual* island?'

'Well, not all of it,' Poe said. 'But most of it. Montague Island. It's one of the Islands of Furness.'

He hadn't known much about the islands so Bradshaw had researched them on the way back to Carleton Hall. They were all situated off the Furness Peninsula and 20 per cent of the district of Barrow's population lived on them, almost all on the largest island, Walney Island.

Walney was eleven miles long but less than a mile wide. It was crescent-shaped, like a quarter moon. Although it was officially the windiest lowland site in Britain, it pinched up against the mainland and formed the Walney Channel that protected the islands that sat within it from the ravaging Irish Sea. At low tide, most of them could be accessed on foot, carefully and under the guidance of someone who knew where the quicksand and deep channels were. Piel Island, with the popular Ship Inn whose landlord was officially the 'King of Piel', was a particular favourite with tourists.

Montague Island, the island that Atkinson owned most of, was outside the Walney Channel, although it was still accessible on foot. Just. It was farther out to sea and the tide didn't stay low for as long as it did in the sheltered areas of the channel.

Poe had never heard of it. According to Bradshaw, like the nearby Sheep Island, an isolation hospital had been built on it in 1892. *Unlike* Sheep Island, Montague Island's had been used. In 1894, a plague ship had attempted to berth at Devonshire Dock in Barrow. It was carrying Chinese labourers needed for the construction of Royal Navy warships. It had suffered an outbreak of typhus en-route. It was redirected to the isolation hospital on

Montague Island where care was given. Twelve Chinese labourers died and their unmarked graves were still at the western end. Bradshaw said that it was rumoured that the island's rats still carried the virus. It was all nonsense, of course, but that, and the exposed, isolated nature of the island, explained how Atkinson had been able to purchase so much of it.

The assistant chief of operations was called Pete Nippress. He was a big man with a nose like a baked potato. He'd transferred in from Greater Manchester so Poe only knew him by reputation. He was well liked and known to be supportive of the cops on the ground.

'Do the NCA have any preferences on how this situation with Atkinson is handled?' he said.

'I think they'd prefer something low-key.'

'Use him as bait?'

'At the minute we have an advantage: the Curator probably doesn't know that *we* know who his primary target is. We have a unique opportunity to catch him in the act. If we go in mob-handed we'll tip him off and Atkinson will spend the rest of his life looking over his shoulder.'

Nippress turned to Nightingale. 'Jo, the NCA can piss off – this is your op, what do you want to do?'

'I'm sorry, Poe, but I can't risk Atkinson's life that way,' she said. 'I'll dispatch two detectives to transport him to Barrow nick. I'll be waiting for him when he arrives to explain what's happened. By then I'm hoping I'll have authority to put something more suitable in place. We don't know how long this will last but he's disabled and he can't stay in the nick for more than a night. We're not geared up for it.'

'I'll get you what you need,' Nippress said.

'It may be moot anyway,' Poe said. 'According to the person Tilly and I spoke to, Atkinson hates Cumbria Police. Really hates them. Blames them for everything, from the botched investigation that led to his arrest, to the acid attack – even the failed suicide attempt that put him in a chair. He bought the island to get as far away from everyone as he could.'

'You don't think he'll come back to the nick?' Nightingale asked.

'I don't think a couple of cops rocking up with even more bad news is going to change his mind about you. I think he'll tell them to fu . . . to go away.'

'Even when we tell him he's in danger?'

'UKPPS reckon no one knows he's there. Monthly deliveries come in by boat and he has a private doctor on-call if he needs one. He never leaves the island and he never has visitors. Montague Island is barren, privately owned and very dangerous to walk to so they don't get the tourists that Piel, Sheep and Roa Islands get.'

'Still . . .'

'I agree with you, ma'am,' Poe said. 'I think he is in danger. UKPPS's assertion that no one knows he's there is flawed. No one knew he was there while no one was looking for him. But if someone puts the word out . . . He's in a wheelchair and he either still wears a mask or he has a face that's basically one big scar; someone will know of him.'

'So?'

'I don't have an answer for you,' he said. 'I'm just saying I don't think he's going to be amenable to the shock and awe approach. I think you're going to have to be more subtle.'

'What do you suggest?'

Poe grinned. 'Do you own a pair of wellies, ma'am?'

Chapter 58

Despite Poe's misgivings, Nightingale planned to send two detectives out to Montague Island immediately, tasked with bringing Atkinson back to the mainland. They hadn't been told why, only that he was at risk. As the tide was in, the North West Police Underwater and Marine Unit, a collaboration between six of the northern constabularies, were taking them out.

She'd then sent SCAS home with instructions to meet on Walney Island at 7 a.m. the next day. Poe had gone home and slept soundly all night.

Poe arrived at Snab Point on Walney Island at 6.30 a.m. It was where the majority of walks across the Walney Channel to Piel Island departed from and, as they were trying to blend in, it made sense to start where everyone else started.

Nightingale had arrived before him and she was in a foul mood. She'd been up all night coordinating her response to the new threat but she hadn't had much luck. It had been after midnight when she'd driven across the bridge that connected Barrow Docks with Walney Island and by then Poe had already been proved right: Atkinson had thanked the two detectives she'd sent ahead but had politely asked them to leave his land. Without contradictory instructions, and as they hadn't been read in on who he actually was, they'd done as he asked and returned to the mainland with the marine unit.

'Rough night?' Poe said as he handed her a coffee.

She stamped her feet in frustration. The tide in the Walney Channel was too high to walk across but too low to sail. She paced up and down the shoreline, straining her eyes to see the mist-shrouded Montague Island in the distance, oblivious to the seawater ruining her shoes and the wind buffeting her hair.

'What's he playing at, Poe?'

'He's still angry, ma'am.'

'Well he doesn't own the whole island,' she snapped. 'I've a good mind to surround him with a ring of blue steel. Patrol cars, command tents, air support, the works. Now we've identified the risk it's indefensible not to take robust countermeasures.'

Poe knew she was just blowing off steam. He didn't blame her. Whether Atkinson liked it or not, protecting him was her responsibility. Someone not wanting protection didn't absolve her of the obligation.

As Nightingale continued to fume at the tide, at the two detectives and at Atkinson himself, Poe found himself tuning her out. He wandered across to the white sign emblazoned with 'Danger' in big red letters. It warned against soft sands and incoming tides, and that using a mechanically propelled vehicle on a Site of Special Scientific Interest was strictly prohibited. The waves that lapped at its base were neither gentle nor urgent. They moved with force but died and retreated, leaving nothing behind but sea foam. Poe found something Zen about the tide. Watching something being controlled by a planetary satellite hundreds of thousands of miles away put things into perspective.

Barrow-in-Furness had never scored well on any of the health and wellbeing indicators, despite being set among some of the most striking scenery in the UK. Low self-esteem, high unemployment, low levels of entrepreneurship and a poor sense of identity all contributed to the feeling that Barrow was marking time, waiting for something to happen.

However, despite being linked by road, Walney Island had a

different zeitgeist altogether. It was wild and rugged and, to Poe, felt like it was straining to get away from the mainland. As the violent wind took hold of his coat tails, making them crack like a snapped towel, Poe tucked his head into his chin and wondered how many people had stood before him on the same bit of land, shielding their faces against the elements as they squinted at the bleak horizon, pondering a life beyond the Irish Sea. Somewhere exotic, where the sun warmed your back and the air cleared your lungs. In a country where no one lived farther than seventy miles from the coast, he suspected the urge to get in a boat and go exploring was a uniquely British thing.

Nightingale stomped up. Her shoes were ruined and her trouser legs were sodden and muddy. The wind was beating her hair into her face and blowing it above her head. Her eyes looked gritty and tired.

'I'm booking into a local hotel,' she said. 'Going to grab an hour's kip if I can. Will you, Tilly and DI Flynn want rooms? We could be here a while.'

Poe looked across at his car. Earlier, Bradshaw had taken three steps into the stinging wind and said, 'Blimey'. She'd immediately got back in the BMW and turned up the heating. So far she'd steadfastly refused to get out, saying the sea air would damage her computers. Flynn was arriving later in her own car.

'Probably just the two,' he said. 'I'll commute.'

She nodded. 'We'll be able to walk across in two hours apparently. As you weren't with Cumbria when he was attacked, and you're not with Cumbria now, I'm hoping he might find your presence a bit more palatable.'

'Not a problem,' Poe said. 'Do we have a guide? It's a dangerous walk.'

'I spoke to someone who takes tourists from here to Piel Island. He'll take us across the first time. After that we'll just have to work something out. Until we've found this bastard, I'm putting officers on that island whether Atkinson likes it or not. The marine unit reckons there's only one place a boat can dock – if we watch that and the route in on foot I think we can ensure no one gets on the island who shouldn't, while keeping the low profile you wanted.'

Poe nodded. As an ex-infantryman, he knew that observation posts were all about location, not boots on the ground. Choose the right position and one person and a pair of binoculars could cover tens of miles of ground. At sea it was even easier as the only thing you had to contend with was the curvature of the earth.

He walked back to his car and rapped on the window. A startled Bradshaw lowered it an inch.

'What is it, Poe?'

'Superintendent Nightingale is booking you and the boss into a hotel,' he said. 'Take my car and get checked in. Get a wi-fi signal and start working on who might have hired this prick.'

'What will you be doing, Poe?'

He looked at the retreating tide.

'Me? I'm going for a walk . . .'

Chapter 59

The close-growing lichen that covered the rocks above the tide-line made them look as though they had been sprinkled with curry powder. They were slippery and Poe trod carefully. If Bradshaw heard he'd gone arse over tit he'd never live it down. Gradually, the muddy inlet they followed petered out and became tide-smoothed sand, the dark brown kind that never really dries out, and the going got easier.

It wasn't obvious at what point they left the saltmarsh on Walney Island's Snab Point and stepped onto the bed of the Irish Sea. Judging by the way the jelly-like sand was moving underfoot, sucking at his walking boots, Poe reckoned it had been fifteen minutes earlier.

The sand was wet and flat, an environment best suited to crabs and burrowing shellfish. Other than the odd bed of ugly black seaweed, there was no vegetation whatsoever. The gritty sand didn't even glisten, dulled as it was by the blanket of cloud overhead.

Their guide was called John and he'd been taking tourists to Piel Island for almost thirty years. He had a shock of white hair, a nut-brown face and wore boots stained with salt.

'We'll skirt around Sheep Island, take the usual route towards Piel Island for half an hour then bear right towards Montague,' he told them. 'You should be able to see it soon.'

Nightingale's plan was to speak to Atkinson then head back to Walney Island where a command centre was being set up. The two plain-clothed cops she had with her didn't look happy that they'd be standing the first post.

'Dunno why the gutter rats couldn't have loaned us one of their X5s,' one of them muttered, using the derogatory term for traffic cops.

The other replied, 'White-hatted bastards wouldn't want to get mud on their shiny—'

'Shut it!' Nightingale snapped.

John the guide chuckled. 'Can't drive to Montague Island, son. Piel, yes, if it's low tide and you have a four-by-four and follow the markers, but Montague, not a chance. Even when the tide's fully out it's surrounded by water.' He pronounced it 'watter'.

He paused to look around as if searching for something.

'You see that brown thing sticking out the sand over there?' He pointed towards a dark misshapen tangle of metal that Poe had assumed was a piece of flotsam. 'That's what's left of the last idiot who tried to take a short cut.'

Poe looked closer. It wasn't marine debris; it was the skeleton of a vehicle – a campervan by the looks of it. It was half buried in a sandbank. The only thing not yet stripped away by the sea was its frame, which was now a mass of bubbling rust. During high tide Poe suspected the van would be fully submerged and become a haven for some of the smaller sea creatures, the same way shipwrecks were for lobsters and moray eels farther out.

'The locals wanted it moved,' John continued, 'but it serves as both a warning and as a navigation tool. We'll see a few of these on the way to the island. The world's full of fools who think they can race the tide.'

Poe stepped forwards to take a closer look.

'I'd stop there if I was you,' John said. 'See that sign beside the van? The white one encased in erosion-resistant concrete?'

'I see it.'

'That's telling you there's quicksand in that area. Get stuck in that and you're in trouble.'

Poe shuddered. Since he was a child he'd had an irrational fear of drowning in quicksand, a legacy of too many cheesy westerns in which the struggling cowboy sinks, leaving only his hat behind. He'd mentioned it to Bradshaw once who, true to form, had explained the science behind it. Something to do with reduced friction between sand particles, meaning it couldn't support the weight of a human. She'd said it was a myth that you could drown, though – eventually the particles would rearrange themselves.

'I thought you couldn't drown in quicksand,' Poe said.

'You can't. But it will trap you until the tide comes in. How long can you hold your breath, Sergeant Poe?''

Poe rejoined the small group.

After forty minutes they skirted past Piel Island. Despite the encroaching gloom, the ruins of the fourteenth-century castle, built by the Abbot of Furness to guard Barrow against pirates, were clearly visible. Another slice of Cumbria's impressive history.

Nightingale said, 'Jesus, that's bleak.'

He turned to where she was looking.

Montague Island, hidden until then by Piel Island and the inclement weather, was now visible.

Poe stared at the place Atkinson had chosen for a home. Nightingale was right: it was bleak.

Chapter 60

Montague Island, half a mile from the southern tip of Walney Island, sat outside the protective windbreak that Walney afforded Barrow and everything inside the channel.

Poe reckoned if Montague had been sand and soil based like the others it would have eroded away eons ago. Instead it was a craggy outcrop, steep-sided and aggressive looking. It was the type of island that deserved a lighthouse even if there was no strategic need for one. A less hospitable coastline Poe couldn't have imagined. Jagged fingers of barnacle-covered rock, jutting out in no discernible pattern, greeted them in the same way defensive spikes greeted advancing cavalry in medieval times. The pier that the marine unit had docked against the night before extended into the sea on mussel-encrusted stilts. It cast an ominous silhouette in the early morning light.

There was a small beach to the right of the pier and the rocks. Half a dozen small boats had been hauled onto the dunes to ensure they didn't float away when the tide returned. Poe assumed it was how the islanders coped with their isolation. Rather than rely on deliveries, some of the islanders sailed to the mainland for their provisions.

Steps had been carved into the rocks beside the pier and the party headed towards them. John the guide had been right: despite the tide being fully out, a ring of shallow water formed a natural moat all the way around the island, and although it was no more than a foot deep, no one stepped onto the island with dry feet.

'Montague Island, ladies and gents,' John said, after they'd helped each other up the treacherously slippery rock steps and onto drier land. 'The pier and the land up to that boundary fence' – he pointed to a sun-bleached structure made of crudely assembled driftwood – 'is public land. Everything else is privately owned and you'll need permission to enter. The people on the far side of the island have right of way so I suppose you'll be OK passing through to visit the man you want.'

The area designated as public land included the outline of what had been the isolation hospital. Poe wandered over to have a look. He suspected it had been dismantled and the stone used to build the island's homes. What remained looked like rows of broken teeth.

On the way back he glanced in the boats that had been pulled onto the small beach. The one on the end had a lobster pot tucked under the seat. Shaped like a miniature Nissen hut, it had a one-way 'funnel' entrance and was lined with rocks so it wouldn't blow away. All the other boats were empty.

He rejoined Nightingale.

'How long do we have, John?' she said.

Their guide reached into his jacket and handed her a folded document.

'That's the tide timetable for Piel Island. There isn't one for Montague as no one comes here. Low tide was at ten past eight and we set off then.' He checked his watch. 'It's taken us an hour and fifteen minutes to get here and the next high tide is at one-forty. We'll need to leave here by midday to be safe. Any later than that and you'll have to wait until the next low tide this evening.'

Poe checked his own watch. It was 9.30 a.m. In two and a half hours they'd have to leave.

Two and half hours to convince Atkinson that they were there to save his life.

Montague Island had its own microclimate. Cold air from the

Irish Sea was forced up the steep cliffs where it mixed with the island's warmer air, forming unstable clouds.

According to Bradshaw, the island was ten acres in size, the same as five football pitches. It was egg-shaped and rose out of the sea like a door wedge. The eastern side, the side with the pier and steps, was the lower side. The west side ended abruptly with sheer cliffs.

Like Snab Point on Walney Island, it was also a designated Site of Special Scientific Interest, partly because of the grey seals that frequented the western rocks and partly because of the small colony of natterjack toads that had made their home in the dunes on the more sheltered eastern side, the same dunes that housed the islanders' boats.

No sheep were allowed on the island but the grass was kept short by the well-established colony of rabbits. Glistening droppings and a series of holes gave away the warren's location. Poe wondered how deep the burrows were. Not as deep as they'd have liked, he suspected; it looked like they'd only be able to dig a few feet before they'd hit the island's bedrock. Then again, rabbits were invasive pests and could adapt to all but the harshest environments.

There were six houses on the island. They were all squat and drab and rain-lashed. According to their guide they were only occupied during the summer months. Atkinson's building was the oldest. It had originally been the administrative building for the isolation hospital and was situated away from the others on the west-facing side of the island, the opposite side to where they'd landed.

To get there they had to cross land belonging to two other houses. The boundary of each primitive-looking property was delineated by the remains of a dry stone wall network. With livestock no longer allowed on the island, it seemed it wasn't just the hospital that had been requisitioned as building material.

It started to snow but, despite it being cold enough, it wasn't lying. The ground was far too salty. Poe had expected it to be squelchy and soft but it wasn't, it was dry and solid – Montague Island was obviously fast draining. The short grass was tough and springy and easy to walk on.

John stayed on the public land and the two cops got on with ensuring the properties on the eastern side of the island were definitely unoccupied. Poe and Nightingale made their way to the western side where Atkinson lived.

The complete absence of man-made sound was eerie. Gulls and terns squabbled and squawked and the wind whistled through the rocks and crevasses but otherwise it was peaceful. Poe could see the attraction. He removed his BlackBerry, turned around and snapped a pic. He attached it to a text and sent it to Bradshaw.

A red exclamation mark appeared beside it. He checked for a signal.

Nothing. Just a 'No Service' message where the bars should have been.

Nightingale saw him staring at his phone.

'No signal?'

'Not even one bar,' Poe replied.

'It's a dead spot apparently. The two clowns who came out last night said exactly the same thing. Their radios barely worked. They said it was why they came back without checking in with me.'

Bradshaw would worry – she'd read stories of people drowning in the Walney Channel trying to reach the islands – but there was nothing he could do. He doubted Atkinson would have a landline. Doubted it would be possible to even *have* a landline this far out.

'There it is,' Nightingale said.

Poe looked up.

Chapter 61

Edward Atkinson lived in a recently extended bungalow of unevenly sized grey stones, the same type as the remnants of the island's hospital and dry stone walls. It had a slate roof and crouched low in a grassy embankment near the steeply sloping cliffs. Before its extension, it had been shaped like a shoebox. A central door bisected two salt-pocked windows no bigger than a tabloid newspaper. The annex was newer and windowless. It had been constructed with the same stone but it hadn't yet weathered the elements for one hundred and thirty years. A chimney topped it all, a thin, silver trail of smoke curling from the flue before being whipped away by the wind.

It looked like Atkinson had spent a chunk of his settlement money renovating the bungalow before he moved in. Whereas the other houses had grass and weeds pushing up against the walls, Atkinson's had smooth, wheelchair-friendly paths and ramps. The equipment they'd seen beside all the other houses – equipment Poe recognised from Herdwick Croft: septic tanks, water pumps, gas bottles and the like – were all there but arranged so that they could be managed by someone sitting down.

Making Herdwick Croft a viable place to live had been a challenge for Poe; he had nothing but admiration for someone who could make a go of it in an even harsher environment while confined to a wheelchair.

Nightingale rapped her knuckles on the sturdy door. There

was no bell and no knocker. There was a keyhole and after waiting a minute she leaned down and looked through it.

'Anything?'

'Key's in the door but I can't hear anything,' Nightingale said. She sounded concerned.

'You stay here, I'll have a wander round the back.' Something didn't make sense. Everything about the bungalow was wheelchair friendly but the doorframe hadn't been widened and the keyhole hadn't been lowered. Why spend all that money only to scrimp where it mattered?

Unless it *didn't* matter . . .

Poe skirted around the side of the bungalow, sticking to the smooth tarmac of the path. As he rounded the corner, a rush of sea wind caught him in the face making his eyes water. When they'd cleared, two things were apparent: what they'd assumed was the front of the bungalow was actually the back, and the reason Edward Atkinson hadn't answered his door was because he wasn't inside.

From the back, Atkinson's house was as drab and unwelcoming as the rest of the houses on the island; from the front it was jaw dropping. The builders he'd hired had excelled themselves.

A stone terrace, thirty yards by fifteen, ran the length of the bungalow and beyond. It stretched all the way to the cliff edge. Raised, weed-free flowerbeds were set into the low wall that bordered the terrace. Poe had no doubt that come spring they would be a riot of colours and scents. A place to enjoy the breeze, the sun and sea spray.

At the far end of the terrace a brick barbecue and a pizza oven were fixed into the wall, both at an accessible height for someone in a wheelchair. A neat pile of chopped wood was stacked under a covered lean-to. Poe hadn't seen any trees on the island and assumed Atkinson had the same problem he had: having to buy in his fuel – a small price to pay to live in such a raw and beautiful environment, though. Terracotta pots containing hardy plants were positioned to catch the sun, but otherwise the terrace was clutter free.

Wheelchair-sized observation areas had been cut into the wall at regular intervals. Atkinson would be able to admire the view from any direction he wanted. In decent weather the Isle of Man would be visible. Today, though, Poe could only see as far as the Walney Wind Farm. With over one hundred turbines, it was one of the largest offshore wind farms in the world.

Poe peered over the edge of the terrace wall. The cliffs weren't as sheer as they had appeared from a distance, and he could see down to the grey seal colony basking on the rocks below and, because the bungalow sat on the top of an inlet, he could also see the land either side. A grim-looking graveyard dominated the bluff on the right. Poe wondered if it was for the islanders or whether it was where the Chinese labourers had been interred. Probably the latter; the gravestones were too uniform to have been spread over a period of time.

Poe watched a wave crash into the rocks below and, although it bothered the seals about as much as the fat content in sausages bothered him, it did send up a cloud of sea spray that caught the wind. Poe felt it on his face. He wiped it off with the back of his hand.

Atkinson didn't move.

He was in his wheelchair, pushed up against one of the more central viewpoints, his back to the bungalow. Poe wasn't surprised to see he had a powerful build – he knew how hard he had to work at Herdwick Croft and Atkinson had double the work with probably half the number of working muscles. A weak man couldn't manage a property like this. Atkinson was probably stronger than he was.

He had a pair of binoculars raised to his eyes and he was staring out to sea.

'I saw a minke whale yesterday,' he said without warning and without turning round. His voice was muffled. 'I've been waiting to see if it's still here.'

'Really? I didn't think they came this far,' Poe said.

Atkinson said nothing for several moments. 'You lot just won't take no for an answer, will you?'

'I'm not the police, Mr Atkinson.'

He sighed and lowered the binoculars into his blanket-covered lap. 'So, who are you then?' With practised efficiency, he pushed one wheel, pulled the other and did a neat one-eighty.

And Poe got his first look at the person they called 'the man in the mask'.

Chapter 62

Poe had attended surveillance courses throughout his career, and the one lesson that had stuck was to look beyond the moustache, the long beard, the silly hat. A man robs a post office wearing a pair of horn-rimmed spectacles and the human condition meant that that would be all the eyewitnesses would remember. Ten people would describe the same person differently but they'd all be able to tell you what his glasses looked like.

He'd assumed he was above all that. That when he looked at people, he *really* looked at them. But, right then, if anyone had asked him the colour of Atkinson's hair, he wouldn't have been able to tell them – all he could see was the mask.

Bradshaw had sent him a link so he'd known what to expect but seeing it for the first time was still a shock. It was clear plastic and moulded to fit the contours of Atkinson's acid-ravaged face. It started at his hairline and ended an inch or so underneath his chin. It extended to his ears and had a hinged jaw, which explained why his voice had been muffled.

He could see the hypertrophic scarring underneath, the result of an overgrowth of collagen, the fibrous protein that forms part of the body's supporting tissue. The network of scars were thick and white and awful. It looked as if Atkinson's face was covered with caul fat, the lacy membrane of a pig's abdomen that encases butcher's faggots.

The inert plastic mask applied direct pressure to the face and helped flatten out the non-elastic collagen fibres and reduce the livid purple hues. Bradshaw said it would be OK to take it off for short periods of time, although it would get uncomfortable – the mask caused sweat to build up on the face, which kept the scarring moist and flexible.

'I'm sorry,' Poe said. 'I thought I'd have done better.'

He stepped forward and offered his hand. It wasn't taken. 'I'm Washington Poe. I'm with the National Crime Agency and I really need to talk to you.'

'So talk,' Atkinson said.

'Can I bring Detective Superintendent Jo Nightingale round? She's police but she's good people, I promise you.'

'You know what Cumbria Police did to me?'

'I do and I'm sorry. All I can say is that neither me nor the super had anything to do with it.'

Atkinson shrugged. 'Five minutes. Then I want you off my property.'

Without another word he wheeled himself up the ramp, through the modern French doors and into the cottage.

Poe walked round to what they'd assumed was the front of the bungalow. Nightingale was still peering through the keyhole.

'He was whale watching,' Poe said. 'He's not happy but he's agreed to give us five minutes.'

'What's he like?' she asked.

'Pissed off. And don't stare at his face. We won't get away with that twice.'

Much like Herdwick Croft, most of the bungalow was open-plan. The French doors led into a large living area. A wood-burning stove filled with glowing embers warmed the room. The floor was stripped pine and the walls were whitewashed. The furniture was minimal and functional and there were wheelchair friendly routes between everything. No tight corners or narrow gaps between chairs. Two of Atkinson's walls were fitted with

264

bookcases and every chair in the room had a quality reading lamp beside it. No prizes for guessing what he did in the evening.

The room and its fittings had been designed well: nothing was out of reach for a man sitting down. The doorframes Poe could see had been widened and the doorknobs lowered, the floor was obstruction free and there was ample space to turn a wheelchair. Poe assumed the kitchen and bedrooms were equally as accessible.

Nothing was cheap either; it was all high-quality stuff. The kind you have when you spend most of your time at home. Poe would have liked a look around the rest of the bungalow. He felt an affinity with Atkinson and his way of life and thought he could probably learn from him.

There was a gap between two low tables and Atkinson reversed into it. It looked to be where he sat when he wasn't using one of the reading chairs. Poe didn't want to sit without being invited, but he didn't want to stand over Atkinson either. Lesson one, day one of the interviewing victims and witnesses course was get down to their eye level.

Nightingale forced the issue by taking a seat. Poe got the feeling she was still annoyed that Atkinson had sent her officers back with a flea in their ear the night before. He reluctantly took the seat opposite her.

'Mr Atkinson,' Nightingale said, 'my name is—'

'Not you, him,' Atkinson said, clipping her sentence. 'I won't talk to Cumbria Police. He said you were a nice person and I won't have you standing outside in this weather but while you're in my house you won't speak.'

Nightingale stared at him. Eventually she shrugged.

'Fine,' she said.

'Mr Atkinson,' Poe said, 'we have reason to believe that your life's in danger.'

Atkinson's expression didn't change. Poe wasn't sure if it could underneath the mask.

'Out here?' he said. 'I hardly think so.'

'Nevertheless.'

'Why, though?'

'We don't know. We think because of the court case.'

'I was cleared of all wrongdoing and even if I hadn't been' – he gestured at the wheelchair and at his face – 'I've paid a steep enough price already.'

'We believe this threat is credible.'

'I imagine they all do to Cumbria Police. They won't want to mess up again.'

'Can I tell him, ma'am?' Poe asked Nightingale. They needed Atkinson to start taking things seriously and at the minute they were getting nowhere.

Nightingale nodded.

'Mr Atkinson, on Christmas Eve two severed fingers were found wrapped in a Secret Santa gift in Carlisle. On Christmas Day two more were found in the font in a church in Barrow. The last pair was found on Boxing Day. They'd been put into the deli counter at a food hall in Whitehaven. Each pair came from a different victim. The victims are all dead.'

Atkinson stared at him.

'All the victims have now been identified, although only one body has been recovered. We think you've been selected as the fourth and final victim.'

'What makes you think that? I don't bother anyone out here. I rarely see anyone. The court case is over.'

'Because of who the three victims were.'

When Atkinson spoke his voice was muted. 'Who were they?'

Poe glanced at Nightingale.

'Tell him,' she said.

'They were the three jurors who voted not guilty at your trial,' he said gently.

'Oh no,' Atkinson cried, his hand going to his mouth. As much as it could, his face blanched.

Poe pressed on.

'The killer is ruthless, resourceful and well-funded and, although your being alive proves he hasn't yet located you, we believe it's only a matter of time before he lands on Montague Island. Superintendent Nightingale has over two hundred police officers working this case and we are no nearer to identifying or catching him.'

'But . . . but why?' Atkinson said. 'What possible motivation could he have?'

'Superintendent Nightingale is following several lines of enquiry, one of which is that someone who lost everything when the waste management plant went bust hired him.'

'Someone from J. Baldwin is trying to kill me?'

'It's possible they've hired the services of this man, yes. We're watching them, of course, although whoever's behind this is not our primary concern right now. The most pressing matter is to find the killer before he finds you. That's why Superintendent Nightingale sent out officers last night and why we walked across the sand flats this morning.'

'What makes you think he'll be able to find me, though?' Atkinson said. 'Witness protection changed my identity to Ian Carruthers. Everything's registered under that name. There's nothing on the island under the name of Edward Atkinson.'

'I don't want to appear rude, Mr Atkinson, but you don't exactly blend in. How long do you think it'll take a determined and resourceful man to find out where the man in the mask lives?'

Atkinson gave it some thought.

'A long, long time,' he said eventually.

Chapter 63

'Let me explain,' Atkinson said. 'The builders who renovated my bungalow did so under the guidance of the architect. None of them met me and I didn't move in until after they'd left. I purchased the land via email and under my witness protection name. You haven't been on the island long but I can assure you, everyone here fiercely protects their privacy – I haven't seen or spoken to any of my neighbours in years and during the colder months none of them are here anyway.'

'Even so—' Poe said.

'My provisions are brought in by sea and left on the terrace,' Atkinson continued. 'I do not meet with the people who deliver them and the account is settled monthly under the name Carruthers. I have a handyman on retainer in case I need assistance but I've never had to call upon his services. I don't meet with these people out of any concern for my security, you understand, but because I'm hideous. South Cumbria is not a progressive place and I will not become an object of curiosity. And don't forget, I could be anywhere in the world. The money I got from Cumbria Constabulary and from J. Baldwin was not inconsiderable – to any right-minded person, an isolated and inhospitable island off the coast of Barrow-in-Furness would be the last place to look for a man in a wheelchair.'

Poe conceded he had a point.

'This is a safe place for me to be, trust me.'

Nightingale, who'd hadn't spoken for a while, said, 'Be that as it may, Mr Atkinson, now I've identified you as being at risk I have a statutory duty of care. I realise we fucked that up spectacularly last time and I appreciate we're the last people you want to see, but I promise you, we're not going anywhere. If I have to put fifty police officers on and around this island I will. I would rather have your cooperation but I don't actually need it. This is an active murder investigation and putting you under surveillance is a legitimate tactic.'

Atkinson let out a lisping sigh. He shrugged and said, 'I can't stop you from using the island's public land but I will *not* have Cumbria Police on my property. If I have to, I'll go to the press.'

Nightingale was about to protest but Atkinson raised his hand to stop her.

'However, I can see a compromise is needed. How about this: as Mr Poe isn't Cumbria Police, I will allow him to stay with me until this thing's resolved. Is this agreeable?'

Atkinson and Nightingale negotiated for ten minutes. They finally agreed that Poe could rotate with Flynn if she were up for it. Nightingale had been reticent about allowing a heavily pregnant woman to take on the task but agreed that the decision was Flynn's, not hers.

'I'll start now, ma'am,' Poe said. 'Can you call DI Flynn for me when you get back? See if she's OK with what we've agreed?'

'You can email her if you want,' Atkinson said.

'You have the internet?' Poe said, surprised.

Atkinson's scars distorted as he smiled. 'We have an arrangement with the wind farm company. The wi-fi network they use to remotely access the turbines passes over our heads and they let us piggyback on it. One of the perks of living out here.'

'I'll email her when you've gone, ma'am,' Poe said. 'She'll want to do her bit, though – she's been feeling left out recently.'

What he *wanted* to say was that a team of oxen with freshly peeled root ginger jammed up their arses wouldn't be able to drag her off the next boat.

Nightingale nodded. 'I'll leave one of my officers at the pier. We can cover the whole island with just two people that way. The detective coming back with me will leave his radio with you so you can keep in touch with each other.'

It was a good plan. With Poe and Flynn on Atkinson's land covering the western approaches, and Nightingale's cops on the public land covering the east, the island would have all-round surveillance. No one was getting on or off without being seen.

'I'll rotate my officers each high tide,' Nightingale said. 'The marine unit can bring them in. I assume you'll want to do longer shifts, given you'll be indoors?'

'I'm happy to do twenty-four hours,' Poe replied, 'but it'll depend on the boss. She might bring someone up from Hampshire if this is going to drag on. Spread the load.'

'And Tilly?'

'She'll stay on the mainland and keep working.'

Nightingale said she'd have armed response units on Walney Island, ready to be rushed across should either of her two lookouts request assistance. She'd also see if it were feasible to have another armed response unit permanently at sea.

'I'll set up a dedicated and permanently staffed email address in case you can't get through on the radio. Send details if you can, otherwise 999 will be enough to trigger an urgent assistance response. That OK?'

Poe nodded. It would have to be.

'We good then?'

He ran through everything. Securing the island was like a military op and, although it had been a long time since he'd worn khaki, he couldn't think of anything they'd missed. They had a 360-degree line of sight, and they'd soon have a way to call in reinforcements.

'We are,' he said.

He hoped he was right.

Chapter 64

When Nightingale left, Poe got the wi-fi password from Atkinson and emailed Flynn. He told her that he would stay on the island until high tide the following morning. After that he'd need to be relieved.

As he'd expected, she confirmed she'd share the work with him. The exact words in her email were: 'Poe, I'm more than capable of sitting on my fat arse with a pair of binoculars.'

Nightingale must have called as soon as she'd found a signal as Flynn already had the tide timetable. She'd land at approximately eight o'clock the next morning.

He then sent a quick email to Bradshaw letting her know where he was and when he'd be back. She sent him a link to something called 'WhatsApp' and asked him to download it. It was some sort of internet-based free messaging service she said would be quicker than email. Poe did as he was told.

With his admin done, he told Atkinson he was going to check the perimeter. What he really wanted to do was make sure the cop Nightingale had left at the pier was doing his job.

He needn't have worried. The cop saw Poe before he saw him. He'd found a sheltered gap between two boulders and had fashioned his waterproof coat into a poncho-type shelter. He was out of the fine drizzle but wasn't sacrificing his tactical advantage. Poe spoke to him for a minute and they agreed that they would both patrol the island's perimeter at least once every two hours. Nothing regular that someone could use against them.

Satisfied Nightingale hadn't left him with a duffer, Poe made his way back to Atkinson.

He was back on his terrace, a full cafetière and two mugs on the wall next to him. He gestured for Poe to join him.

'I want to have a look inside first,' Poe said. 'Get my bearings.'

'OK,' Atkinson said, picking up his binoculars and staring out to sea again.

Poe let himself in through the French doors. So far he'd only been in the living room. There was a door to his left, which he assumed led into the annex Atkinson had arranged to be built, and a door on the opposite wall. He opened the door on his left first.

The door led into a short hallway with two additional doors. Poe stepped through and opened the nearest one.

It was Atkinson's bedroom. The bed was large with space either side. An over-bed pole hoist to help him with sitting up, getting in or out or simply changing position was the only nod to Atkinson's disability. Two fitted bookcases hugged the walls either side of his bed. They were ornate with raw bark edges. Poe picked up a couple of books. *Moby Dick* and one of Wainwright's pictorial guides, a first edition by the looks of it. If he hadn't been there to work he'd have taken a seat and read it in one sitting. He reluctantly put it back.

The bedroom had a door that Poe assumed was an en suite.

It was. A wet room rather than a traditional bathroom so there was nothing that Atkinson had to climb into. There was a large rainfall showerhead above. A handheld one in an adjustable holster was set halfway up the shower rod, about head height for someone sitting down. There was a wheeled shower chair in the corner. Presumably Atkinson transferred onto it so he didn't get his wheelchair wet. The toilet had handrails either side and the sink was set at a lower height.

Poe walked back through the bedroom and into the hallway.

The other door opened into a treatment room. An examination table, the kind used in GPs' surgeries, was in the middle of the room. White cupboards covered the wall. Poe opened them. They were full of things related to Atkinson's acid burn. Ointments, bandages, antibiotics and spare masks. Atkinson didn't need to leave the island for medical treatment – he could do it all himself.

Poe went back to the living room. By process of elimination, the other door would have to be the kitchen. He was right.

It was a decent sized, well-equipped room. At the far end was another door, the un-widened one that Nightingale had knocked on earlier. Poe could see it hadn't been opened for a long time.

Everything in the kitchen was at an accessible height. It was clean but not so clean it looked unused. Judging by the pots and pans attached to low-hanging ceiling-hooks, Atkinson could cook. A packet of coffee beans and a grinder lay next to a modern kettle. They reminded Poe that he was thirsty.

It was time to join Atkinson on the terrace.

Chapter 65

Poe's landscape changed over the course of a season, Atkinson's over the course of a minute. When he picked up the scalding black coffee the sky was a colourless sheet; by the time he'd taken a few sips, the sun had cracked through the cloud cover and the seascape was transformed.

The choppy waves refracted the light; turning the sea into a glittering pool that Poe couldn't drag his eyes from. He'd never lived near the sea, had always thought it a bit too busy, a bit too much sensory overload, but the view from Atkinson's terrace was mesmerising. No wonder he'd been sitting out there.

Poe didn't have to ask Atkinson why he lived here – he knew. A few years back he'd been in much the same position: a tabloid pariah, the cop who'd taken the law into his own hands. Instinctively he'd sought isolation and inaccessibility. He'd found what he needed on Shap Fell.

Atkinson had taken his self-imposed exile even further. Poe was awestruck by his commitment. At Herdwick Croft if Poe needed civilisation he could pop into Shap Wells Hotel for a meal or a pint, or drive into Kendal and beyond. On Montague Island, in a wheelchair, Atkinson had put down roots impossible to dig up.

'Nice coffee,' Poe said.

Atkinson raised his mug in acknowledgement. 'I spend serious money on it. Jamaican Blue Mountain. Get it shipped in, literally, from a specialist in York.'

Poe had heard of Jamaican Blue Mountain coffee but he'd

274

never expected to taste it. Only a limited amount of the bean was grown each year and most of it was sent to Japan or used to make coffee liqueur. It was smoother and less bitter than any coffee he'd tasted before – the kind of brew you could drink all day without getting a caffeine-induced headache.

Taking the expensive coffee as a cue, Poe said, 'How much did all this set you back?'

'The land or the modifications?'

Poe shrugged.

'The house cost me a quarter of a million.'

'Seems expensive?'

'Cheap, actually. The island's a designated SSSI so there are limitations with how it can be developed. Made it unattractive to prospective buyers and the owner was struggling to sell it. And, because the old admin building is responsible for the upkeep of the graveyard, the surrounding land couldn't be sold separately.'

'You own the graveyard as well?'

Atkinson nodded. 'It's consecrated land so it's virtually worthless. It can't be built on and, as the graves are all designated as infectious, they can't be exhumed.'

'The island's an SSSI because of the seals and toads?' Poe said, remembering Bradshaw's briefing.

'And the marsh harriers,' Atkinson said. 'We have a nesting pair and some of their chicks from previous years still visit.'

'Wow,' Poe said. He'd never seen a marsh harrier before. He lived too far from the coast and they weren't particularly well established in Cumbria as it was. 'Is it the marsh harriers that control the rabbit population?'

Atkinson raised what was left of his eyebrows.

'I live in the middle of Shap Fell,' Poe explained. 'We don't have a huge rabbit problem there, partly because they're competing with sheep for food and partly because of predation from the air. Lot of buzzards.'

275

'The marsh harriers *do* take some of the smaller rabbits,' Atkinson agreed. 'Buzzards take a few and we occasionally get golden eagles, but by and large the rabbits manage themselves. It's a small island and food isn't abundant. Enough to sustain a small warren but not much else.'

They stopped talking and finished their drinks. Atkinson refilled their mugs.

'Anyway, I was limited with how much work I could do,' he continued. 'Inside, I could do what I wanted, but I needed permission for any material changes to the building. In the end the extension was granted as I was able to prove I needed a dedicated and sterile treatment room.'

'I saw it,' Poe said. 'Pretty modern.'

'Chemical burns burn deep and cause problems for years. They require ongoing treatment that I wasn't prepared to travel for. I have private doctors but they needed somewhere to work.'

'How often do you need treatment?'

'Not as much as I did. I need new masks every few months as the shape of my face changes as the scarring flattens, and they need to take biopsies to see how much the nerves are regenerating. Everything else I can pretty much do myself.'

Poe drained his mug and looked wistfully at the empty cafetière. Given how expensive the coffee was he didn't feel comfortable asking for another pot to be made.

'I don't know much about the actual attack,' Poe admitted. 'I haven't had time to read up on it yet.'

'Not much to tell. The man who did it was fuelled by alcohol and fabricated tabloid headlines. Fake news we'd call it now. His next-door neighbour was a jeweller and he broke into his chemical store. Stole a bottle of the nitric acid he used for etching. Waited outside court for me one day and threw it at my face.'

Poe grimaced.

'At first I thought it was urine,' Atkinson continued. 'Then,

276

when I felt my face burning, I thought it was boiling water. It wasn't until I felt my skin melting that I knew it was acid.'

'It didn't get in your eyes?'

'I'd instinctively covered them with my arm. It's why I had to have skin from my thigh grafted onto my forearm. But it's also why I can still see.'

'It must have been very painful.'

'It was until it wasn't. Acid keeps burning until it's removed and by the time someone had thought to douse my face with bottled water it had already eaten through my pain receptors. My face may look like a melted candle but it wasn't that painful for the first few months, not until the nerves began to regenerate. That's when the real discomfort started. I still feel it now.'

'The mask helps?'

'It does. Keeps the scarring moist and supple. I keep it on when I'm outside as the salt in the air isn't brilliant for it. I tend to take it off at night now.'

Poe wanted to keep talking. While they were outside he could delve deeper into Atkinson's life *and* keep an eye on the western approaches to the island. A win-win situation. It was possible that someone from Atkinson's past had hired the Curator. Someone unconnected to J. Baldwin, someone who became incensed by the verdict and subsequent payout.

He'd only find out if he got to know him better and, like reconnaissance, time spent on intelligence gathering was seldom wasted.

Chapter 66

Poe had been on a lot of stakeouts and most of them had been boring and uncomfortable. Countless hours spent on bruised estates stripped of hope and ambition. All cracked pavements and broken lives. Estates where the only things that flourished were the weeds and the far-right recruiters, where the only splashes of colour were the gang tags.

He remembered one he'd been on before things had got technical. He'd been driven into position in the boot of a clapped-out Vauxhall Cavalier. He'd then spent eight hours staring through a strategically placed crack in the brake light. At one point the target of their investigation had actually stopped to relieve himself against the side of the car. To this day, every time he saw a Vauxhall he smelled piss.

This wasn't one of those stakeouts. This stakeout was a joy to be on. If he ever did something as unlikely as take a holiday, Montague Island was the kind of place he'd choose to go. The scenery was outstanding and ever changing, the wildlife remarkable and the coffee excellent. And the sea air was doing wonders for his chest. He could breathe properly again, the first time in weeks.

When the cop on the other side of the island emailed to say his shift was coming to an end and his replacement was in sight, Poe couldn't remember the last time twelve hours of nothing had passed by so quickly. He hadn't moved much for the last eight and it felt like his bones had rusted. He didn't care.

He stood, stretched his legs and arched his back. Worked out the major kinks. A bit of stiffness was a minor price to pay.

He walked over to meet the new cop in case it was someone he hadn't met yet. Two people, strangers to each other, patrolling an island in the dark was how blue-on-blue accidents happened.

The outgoing cop had his eyes glued to his binoculars. He was frowning.

'What's up?' Poe asked.

'There's someone else with my replacement,' he replied, passing the binoculars over.

Poe raised them to his eyes and burst out laughing.

The rigid-hulled inflatable boat – the RIB – carrying the incoming cop did indeed have an extra passenger. It was Bradshaw. He didn't need to ask why she'd made the trip across the Walney Channel. He was her friend and, as long as she had access to the internet, she would always want to work where he was.

Even if it meant crossing a choppy body of water, apparently. By the looks of things, she hadn't enjoyed it. She was wearing two lifejackets and a woollen hat. She had a stiff but determined expression on her face. She was even paler than usual. Despite the boat only being in a few feet of water she clung to the gunwale like ivy on oak.

Poe walked to the end of the pier and caught the rope the marine unit cop threw him. Never having been a Scout, he tied it with the only knot he knew: the reef knot. Right over left and under, left over right and under. Gave it a tug to tighten it. It'd do; it wasn't his RIB.

'Hi, Poe,' Bradshaw said. 'I've never been on a boat before.'

'You don't say?'

'I saw a shark,' she added.

'I *told* you, it wasn't a shark, it was a bloody harbour porpoise!'

the marine cop snapped. He looked like he'd had the journey from hell.

'Can't you swim, Tilly?' Poe said.

She looked at him blankly. He might as well have asked if she fancied suckling pig for dinner. He reached down and helped her onto the pier.

The replacement cop disembarked without his assistance. She introduced herself before removing her lifejacket and throwing it back onto the RIB. She handed Poe a small canvas bag.

'For when it gets dark,' she explained.

He pulled the Velcro straps and looked inside.

'It's a thermal imaging monocular,' she continued. 'Courtesy of Detective Superintendent Nightingale.'

Poe nodded in appreciation. No one was getting on the island now.

'Can I have my lifejackets back, please?' the marine cop said to Bradshaw.

'No, you may not.'

He muttered something under his breath. It sounded like 'Why me?'

'I intend to wear them any time I'm outside,' Bradshaw said.

'No you bloody aren't. They're part of the boat's manifest.'

A spirited exchange of ideas followed, one the marine cop had no chance of winning. In the end he gave up and compromised: Bradshaw could keep one as long as he got it back.

'What do you want a lifejacket for anyway?' Poe asked as they made their way to Atkinson's bungalow.

'I've read the weather reports, Poe – I don't want to drown if I'm blown off a cliff.'

'It's the rocks you'll have to worry about, not the Irish Sea.'

She stopped in her tracks.

'I need a helmet then,' she said. 'I wonder if the boat driver has one.'

It was pointless explaining he was joking. He waited while she made her way back to the pier. She returned two minutes later.

'Any luck?'

'What a rude man,' she said.

Chapter 67

To his surprise, Atkinson and Bradshaw hit it off immediately.

'He speaks my language, Poe,' she said.

Bradshaw had a working knowledge of several languages including Klingon and Elvish. Atkinson, with nothing but books, a computer and a Netflix subscription to keep him company, was no doubt just as geeky as she was.

'What language is that, Tilly?'

'Computers, silly.'

'Oh. Here, grab these mugs and take them outside, can you?'

They were in Atkinson's kitchen. Poe was making more of that wonderful coffee; Bradshaw was making something green and awful called matcha tea.

When they were seated, and after Poe had checked in with the cop on the other side of the island, they got down to more intelligence gathering.

'Can you think of anyone who might want to cause you harm?' Poe said. 'Someone we might not automatically think of.'

'I can't, no. And I get what you're saying, but I don't think it's anyone from J. Baldwin. It wasn't a publicly listed company and my understanding is that when they filed for bankruptcy they lost everything. I don't see how they could have afforded this Curator of yours.'

Nightingale was chasing down the financial angle but Atkinson made a fair point. According to Melody Lee, the Curator didn't come cheap and no one involved in the company had that type of cash any more. Not unless they'd hidden it offshore somewhere.

'What about the families of the children who were injured?'

'I can't see them having the motivation – the court case against J. Baldwin was iron-clad.'

Iron-clad and compelling, Poe thought. It had removed all doubt about Atkinson's culpability. But if it wasn't someone from J. Baldwin, and it wasn't someone whose children had been chemically burned, who was left? Who else had been damaged by Atkinson's hung jury and subsequent exoneration?

'Do we know if anyone's career was damaged, Tilly?' Poe said. 'Someone in the police, maybe? It was high profile and the chief constable in those days was our old friend Leonard Tapping. No way he didn't find a suitable scapegoat.'

'I'm not sure we've looked at that, Poe. I'll check now.'

She removed her mobile and began typing.

'You won't get a signal here, Tilly,' Atkinson said.

'We'll see about that.' She scurried off inside.

Poe turned back to Atkinson.

'What about the islanders?'

'Here?'

Poe nodded.

Atkinson shook his head. 'We're not a community, Mr Poe, we're a gathering of hermits. The people who live here aren't the type to commit to time-consuming machinations like this. They might get into the occasional argument with the supply boat but otherwise we avoid human contact at all cost.'

Bradshaw was standing on a chair waving her mobile in the air as she searched for a signal. Despite being indoors she was still wearing her lifejacket and woollen hat.

'What a bunch of weirdos,' she said.

Chapter 68

It had been an interesting night. Poe had felt like a gooseberry at times. Bradshaw and Atkinson had talked non-stop about computers and Netflix and movies and books. If she'd been able to get a signal on her mobile she'd have probably moved in with him.

So Poe had done what he was there to do: he'd watched.

He'd watched the sea disappear under the moonless night and he'd watched it reappear as dawn struggled through the murky clouds, shockingly bright but only in comparison to the Stygian darkness it had followed. He'd watched the seals slip into the freezing water and he'd watched them return to eat their catch on the slippery rocks. And he'd watched the clouds tighten and the first flecks of snow float weightlessly down – colourless confetti landing silently on the terrace before melting into nothing.

But most of all he'd watched the approaches to the island.

He doubted a boat could dock on the western side but he wasn't taking any chances. Everything about this case had been unlikely and, now that he'd spent almost twenty-four hours there, slipping unseen onto an island with 360-degree surveillance somehow no longer seemed impossible.

Atkinson wheeled himself out to hand Poe another coffee. Instead of going back inside to Bradshaw he took up the position beside him, the light snow sticking to his mask and shoulders like dandruff.

After a few moments Bradshaw joined them.

'Why did you try and kill yourself, Edward?'

Poe noted Bradshaw's use of his first name. She'd been calling him Mr Atkinson up until then. He wondered what had changed.

'Have you ever suffered from depression, Tilly?'

'I haven't.'

'I have,' he said. 'Had it bad and couldn't see a way out. I didn't have the mask at that point and I was in too much pain to sleep naturally. I could either take the pills that turned me into a zombie or stay exhausted. I wanted to be alone but I couldn't stand the silence.'

'It sounds like you had post-traumatic stress disorder, Edward,' she said.

Poe thought the same. It wasn't just returning veterans who suffered from PTSD. People had developed it after being involved in something as simple as a traffic accident. An acid attack certainly passed the threshold.

'I saw a shrink,' Atkinson said. 'He suggested PTSD but his solution was more medication. I started drinking heavily. By the time I was ready to end it all I was drinking two bottles of Jack Daniel's a day.'

Bradshaw, who'd never had an alcoholic drink in her life and therefore couldn't comprehend how quickly it could become a crutch, said, 'There's one unit in every ten millilitres of alcohol and Tennessee sour mash has an alcohol content of forty per cent. If we assume a standard bottle holds one litre' – she looked up and did some mental arithmetic – 'that's four hundred millilitres of alcohol, which means forty units a bottle. You were drinking eighty units of alcohol a day, Edward.'

'That many? I didn't reali—'

'And the recommended weekly alcohol allowance is fourteen units.'

Atkinson said nothing. Neither did Poe – he was trying to work out his own weekly intake. Although he was nowhere near where Atkinson had been, the uncertainty surrounding his future at Herdwick Croft had seen him drink more than usual. Probably best not to tell Bradshaw.

Atkinson shrugged it off. 'I knew it was too much but all I saw was a future devoid of meaningful moments. Drinking myself to death didn't seem like such a bad thing.'

Bradshaw didn't have an answer to that. Her unique view of the world meant she sometimes struggled with empathy but she seemed to understand that now wasn't the time to continue a lecture on safe drinking levels.

'Anyway,' Atkinson continued, 'it was taking too long and after a particularly difficult night I decided I didn't want to go on. I strung two bedsheets together and tied them to the top of the banister. Tied the other end round my neck and stepped off.'

'What happened, Edward?' Bradshaw said. 'If you'd ended up with lesions on the neck area of your spinal cord you'd have been a tetraplegic not a paraplegic – paralysed in four limbs rather than the two.'

Poe grimaced at the lack of tact. Atkinson smiled.

'Shitty builders happened, Tilly. The banister fell apart and I fell fifteen feet. The base of my spine hit the bottom of the stairs. Ended up paralysed from the waist down. Instead of ending my suffering I trebled it.'

'You were sectioned?' Poe said, knowing he had been.

Atkinson nodded. 'All in all it was a bit of a shit year.'

'It must have worked, though.'

'Not even a little bit. All they had was second-rate therapy and first-rate liquid coshes.'

'So . . .?'

'Some of the compensation money came through and a doctor came up from London with a mask. The pain stopped about the same time I could afford to remove myself from everyone and everything. A land agent bought this place for me. I spent a lot of money making it accessible and getting the terrace right and, while I'm not exactly happy, I can at least see a path to old age.'

Poe nodded. Finding peace wasn't an attainable goal for most. That Atkinson had stared into the abyss, no, *stepped* into the abyss, and survived was a remarkable testament to human endurance. He redoubled his commitment to keeping the man safe.

'Do you want some more coffee, Mr Poe?' Atkinson said.

'No more for him, thank you, Edward,' Bradshaw said before Poe could say yes. 'He has virtually no fibre in his diet. If he's not careful he'll end up with an impacted—'

Poe didn't want to know what was going to get impacted and fortunately for him the tide agreed.

His radio crackled. It was the cop at the pier.

'Your replacement's here,' she said.

Chapter 69

Flynn, her balance compromised by an eight-month-old baby bump, was holding onto the rail of the RIB as tightly as Bradshaw had the night before. Her belly was so big that the lifejacket wouldn't fasten and she wore it loose, like an unbuttoned waistcoat. Poe suspected there'd been quite the discussion before she'd been allowed to sail.

He grunted in satisfaction when he saw her companion. It was Dave Coughlan. The big cop might not be a deep thinker but he seemed solid and unflappable. Poe doubted he'd scare easily. It would be one less thing to worry about while he was on the mainland.

Poe, Coughlan and the cop Coughlan was replacing all helped get Flynn off the boat. The snow still wasn't settling but it had made the pier treacherous. She glared at them all but eventually allowed herself to be manhandled.

'We'll never talk about this, Poe,' she said when she was on dry land.

The marine cop threw up her bag and Poe caught it.

'Come on, boss,' he said. 'While Tilly's going through her ridiculous marine safety drills I'll take you across and introduce you to Atkinson.'

'You sure you're up to it, boss?' Poe said. 'There's no shame in sitting this one out. I'm more than capable of doing another shift. Allow you time to get some NCA replacements up here.'

Flynn snorted. 'You looked in a mirror lately? You've got eyes like a racing dog's bollocks. Go on, get yourselves home. I need you rested and I need Tilly helping Nightingale track down whoever's behind all this.'

Poe nodded. She was right.

'I'll see you in two tides' time then. Round about this time tomorrow, I expect.'

With Flynn safely ensconced on the terrace of Atkinson's bungalow Poe jogged back to see Coughlan.

'I don't care what she says,' he told him, 'you radio check every fifteen minutes and—'

'That's not what she said on the way over—'

'Look into my eyes, Dave,' Poe said, staring at him. 'Every fifteen minutes. I'm not having her go into labour and not getting the help she needs because she's too stubborn to ask.'

'Every fifteen minutes,' he agreed.

'And you do a visual check on the hour.'

'You do know she outranks me.'

'Everyone outranks you,' Poe replied, 'but I'm a sergeant and sergeants are always right.'

Coughlan grinned. 'Radio check every fifteen minutes and a visual check on the hour it is then.'

'You'll pass on these instructions to your replacement?'

'I will.'

'Good man,' Poe said, handing him a bit of paper. 'Here's Atkinson's wi-fi code – if Flynn gives you any shit email me or Tilly. One of us will be awake.'

The boat ride back was uneventful and they were soon on the road. Bradshaw had refused the offer of a hotel on Walney and had instead booked a room at Shap Wells, the hotel nearest to Herdwick Croft. She wanted to carry on working.

Poe knew he should sleep, that the time he'd stolen by

overindulging in Atkinson's coffee would soon demand a heavy price, but he was still jittery and wide awake. He'd work until his body told him to stop then get some sleep. He wanted to get at least six hours before his next shift on the island.

A grey sky leached colour from the land. Even the snow seemed muted, more off-cream than the brilliant white of the previous day. It wasn't falling heavily and Poe only needed his windscreen wipers on intermittent. Bradshaw's Mole People had already sent information on how the Atkinson case had ruined a handful of police careers. She was trying to read it but the hot air coming from the heaters, combined with the caffeine-free night she'd had, meant her eyelids were drooping.

He was about to tell her not to fight it when his BlackBerry finally picked up a signal again. It started to vibrate like crazy as missed calls and texts from the last twenty-four hours came flooding in. He passed it across to Bradshaw and asked her to see what was happening.

She blinked wearily. 'You have three missed calls, Poe. All from the same number. They haven't left a voicemail.'

'I disabled voicemail,' he said.

She looked at him.

'Someone disabled voicemail for me,' he admitted. 'Can you ring it back? It'll come through on the car's speakers.'

Bradshaw pressed return call.

'Hello,' a sleepy voice said.

'This is Detective Sergeant Washington Poe. I think you've been trying to get in touch with me.'

'Ah, Sergeant Poe,' the voice drawled, 'how y'all been doing over there?'

It was Special Agent Melody Lee.

Chapter 70

Melody Lee wanted an update. Poe told her what they knew – that with her prompting they'd been able to see the part of the story the Curator had tried to hide. That they now knew who his final target was.

'So you don't think he knew that this Cowell dude had the hots for his own sister?'

'I don't, no. Tilly says there was no malware on his computer so he couldn't have known that Cowell had a video that exonerated himself. Tilly also says it's possible he'd only intended to set Cowell up for the Rebecca Pridmore murder and had other Black Swan Challenge players in mind for the other two.'

'But the yellow dot tracking tied him to all three,' Melody Lee said.

'Exactly. And when the video of his sister having sex cleared Cowell of the murder he'd been set up for, it inadvertently cleared him of them all.'

'That's some complicated shit you've got going down there, Sergeant Poe,' she said. 'You'll keep me informed?'

'I will.'

'Good luck then. And be careful: I've found that when you think you've figured out what the Curator's up to, you're normally exactly where he wants you to be.'

'Why did she have to say that, Tilly?' Poe said. 'It'll be all I can think of now.'

Poe was worried and he didn't know why. Montague Island was secure. Completely locked down. Flynn was watching the western approaches, Coughlan was watching the east. Now they had thermal imaging equipment, anyone approaching the island would stand out like dog balls. Armed cops were on standby, ready to be rushed wherever they were needed.

'What are we missing, Tilly?'

'I can't think of anything, Poe,' she said. 'Apart from the Curator's identity and the name of the person who hired him, of course. Other than that we have the complete picture.'

He nodded. They *did* have the complete picture.

And that was the problem. In a case this complicated there still should have been one or two things that didn't make sense.

'I'm calling Nightingale,' he said.

'It's been too easy,' Poe said.

'*Easy?*' Nightingale replied. 'This has been the most challenging case I've ever worked.'

Nightingale was about to go into a briefing with the chief constable so she couldn't give him long.

'Has it, though? Really?' Poe said. 'It's been shocking and distressing, but think about it: from the moment I found that kettle, which wasn't exactly hidden, each clue took us nearer to where we are now. There are no gaps. We didn't have to make any leaps of faith. There's just an unbroken line of evidence leading directly to Edward Atkinson and Montague Island.'

'None of the evidence was easy to find, though, Poe.'

'Exactly.' He paused. 'What made us trust it, ma'am?'

'Because it was compelling,' she said without hesitation.

'No.'

'No?'

'Something more primitive than that. Something intrinsically cerebral.'

'I'm listening.'

'Psychologically, we're predisposed to rely on evidence more heavily if we've had to work hard for it. And, as you say, we had to work hard for everything we found, but it *was* there. The trail never went completely cold. I think that other than Tilly's yellow dots, everything we've uncovered so far we were meant to uncover. It's almost as if he wanted us to get to Atkinson first.'

'Oh shit,' she said. 'Is it possible he hasn't been able to find Atkinson after all? That he deliberately allowed us to identify him so we'd lead him there? All he has to do is follow someone involved in the investigation. Me, probably – I've been doing daily press conferences.'

Poe had already considered and dismissed that.

'Someone this resourceful would have been able to track him down eventually,' he said. 'And even if he was struggling to find him, he must have known that once we'd identified who his target was, you'd do exactly what you have done: make the island impregnable. With just two people we have three hundred and sixty degree coverage. Armed response is on permanent standby and the marine unit can get them on the island in minutes. It looks like security is lax but it's an illusion – it's actually very thorough. No way is he getting to Atkinson now. His best chance of success was always to stay covert.'

'So what's this really about, Poe?'

'I don't know and that's what worries me.'

Chapter 71

The sky was the colour of lead. Unbroken, unblemished cloud stretching as far as the eye could see. Serious clouds for serious weather. The Met Office had issued a yellow warning for snow and Poe did what he always did with their alerts: he added a colour. Shap Fell always got an extreme version of Cumbria's weather and although the snow was light now it was only going to get heavier.

Bradshaw had insisted on coming back to Herdwick Croft. She said they still had work to do and he knew better than to argue. His quad would be able to cope with the snow so at least she wouldn't get stranded – the treads on the tyres were an inch and a half deep. Even so, he took it slowly, tested every dip for drift, and got back to Herdwick Croft fifteen minutes later than he usually did.

As soon as they were inside Poe boiled some water and fired up the wood-burning stove. He'd had enough coffee but he made Bradshaw a mug of nettle tea. She accepted it gratefully.

'Where do you want to start, Poe?' she said.

Poe had been arguing with himself for more than an hour and he still had no idea who would win.

'I feel like I'm the idiot who's peeped through the letterbox and thinks he's seen the whole house, Tilly. No way someone this clued in doesn't know we've identified his target, so either he has contingencies, or us being there was part of his plan all along.'

'But what could that plan be, Poe?'

Poe stood still and tried to untangle his mind. None of it felt right, some evidence contradicted other evidence – it was like trying to solve a Rubik's Cube that fought back. Every suspect they'd identified, every clue they'd uncovered, when put under the lens looked like a square peg in an oblong hole. It fit but it left obvious gaps.

So it was the gaps that he focused on. It was there he thought he'd find the answers. The *real* answers, not the faux-answers they were being drip-fed. And they had enough information so they wouldn't be far away – intangible for now, but only a prompt away from instant recall. Like remembering the words to a long-forgotten song when the guitar thrums out the opening riff.

Poe didn't know who had fallen asleep first. He suspected he had. He remembered he and Bradshaw talking themselves into a loop. How the Curator seemed to want them on the island but while they were there Atkinson was untouchable. The more they talked about it, the less sense it made. Eventually Poe had sat down and yawned.

His collar was now damp with drool, his head felt as though it was stuffed with marshmallows and his mouth was parched. He checked his watch. It was almost 6.30 p.m. There'd be another high tide soon and Coughlan's shift would be ending. He'd send him an email. The grizzled cop had promised to pass on his instructions to check in on Flynn to his replacement, and he wanted to remind him.

Poe stood, stretched, walked over to the sink and turned on the tap. By the time he'd filled his glass Bradshaw had woken. She'd been curled at the end of the couch, in the place Edgar usually slept.

'What time is it, Poe?' she yawned.

'Late. Nearly half-six. Let's get you back to Shap Wells. We have an early start tomorrow.'

Bradshaw nodded tiredly and rubbed the back of her neck. When she'd gathered what she needed, Poe opened his front door.

'Fuck,' he said.

Because that was the thing with Shap Fell: when the weather turned, it turned quickly. The snow, falling like confetti two hours earlier, was now a swirling white vortex. The word blizzard seemed inadequate. It was more arctic tundra than Cumbrian fell out there, the type of weather that made statistics out of ill-prepared tourists. The type of weather that made statistics out of experienced mountaineers . . .

Driving back to Shap Wells would be a mistake. Potentially a fatal one.

He told Bradshaw and she nodded.

'I'll sleep on the sofa,' Poe said, 'you can have the bed. I've got some potatoes I can bake. Hop in the shower; the storm will blow itself out soon but we might as well get comfy in the meantime.'

'OK, Poe.'

Before long he could hear the shower running above him, the first time he had – he'd never had an overnight guest before. Up until now, if the shower was on, he was standing under it.

While the potatoes baked and Bradshaw showered, Poe stood in front of the murder wall. He reread the documents. All of them, even the ones that couldn't possibly be relevant. When the prompt came, it was often from the most unlikely source. The unguarded remark, the unconnected thought, the smell that brought back a memory that ignited something deep in the recesses of his mind.

Poe stared at the wall for twenty minutes but nothing happened.

If there *was* a prompt, it wasn't on the murder wall.

A noise made him look up. Bradshaw was at the top of the stairs. She was wearing his dressing gown and had a towel wrapped round her head. It was the most feminine thing he'd seen her do. She was red-faced and glowing. The shower had washed away most of her fatigue.

'You have wonderful water pressure, Poe.'

It was true. He did. And the water, drawn directly from the ground, was about as pure as it was possible to get.

'The bakies have another twenty minutes. I don't know if I have any vegan stuff to go on them but you're welcome to anything you can find. I'm having black pudding, but I'll cook it.'

Poe climbed the stairs and got undressed. The wood burner was doing its job and the croft was cosy. If he didn't have a guest he'd have got into bed and slept through to the morning. He stepped under the shower, readjusted the head after Bradshaw had lowered it, shut his eyes and lathered his hair with shampoo.

And deep in his mind something stirred. He stopped washing his hair. Poe knew his mind was like one of Bradshaw's bespoke computer programs: it never stopped processing what it had read. What it had heard.

What it had seen . . .

A memory surfaced, one that felt so real it was as if he'd stepped back in time.

His eyes snapped open as he made connection after connection, each bit of evidence now slotting neatly into an unfolding nightmare. Melody Lee's words filled his mind: 'When you think you've figured out what the Curator's up to, you're normally exactly where he wants you to be.'

Poe had made a terrible mistake.

Atkinson wasn't the target.

He was the bait . . .

Sixty miles away on Montague Island, Stephanie Flynn looked out to sea, her eyes tired and gritty – a by-product of staring through thermal imaging equipment for hours at a time. She was currently sheltering from the blizzard under the lean-to

Atkinson used to keep his logs dry. It wasn't a perfect view but she was confident no one could approach her side of the island without being seen.

Her feet were swollen but so far she'd managed to stay on them. She was starting to agree with what Poe was clearly too scared to say: that she shouldn't be at work. That she should have started her maternity leave a month ago. It had been stupid to keep going for as long as she had.

She'd see this shift through, then ring Director van Zyl when she was back on the mainland. Tell him she was going on leave and that he needed to cough up some NCA officers. There was a building full of them in Manchester. She knew he'd comply with her request. When it came to maternity leave, van Zyl was firmly in the Poe, Zoe and Bradshaw camp. She'd only been putting it off to annoy her sister. If Jess said cake was nice, Flynn would never eat it again – it was just the way it was between them.

A noise made her turn.

Her eyes widened in shock.

'You!'

'Me,' the Curator agreed.

He then punched her in the face.

Chapter 72

'We leave in one minute!' Poe shouted, racing down the stairs to get Bradshaw.

She looked at his expression, nodded once and ran up the stairs to get dressed.

Good girl. No messing about, no asking why.

Poe tried to call Nightingale.

'Pick up, pick up,' he urged.

Nothing. Not even a dial tone.

He checked the screen. It said, 'No service'.

'Shit!'

He didn't waste time trying again. Signals going down were a common occurrence around Shap at the best of times and entirely predictable in extreme weather. He knew he wouldn't get a signal until he was nearer a different cell-phone tower.

He gathered everything he could think of for what was going to be a dangerous journey to Shap Wells. He was confident that if he could reach his car then he could make it to the M6. As the only motorway in Cumbria it would still be open and, if the weather in the south of the county wasn't as bad as it was in Shap, he'd be able to get to Snab Point on Walney Island within an hour.

He grabbed his coat and pulled on his boots. They had thick treads and wore well. He only had one pair of gloves and he'd have to give them to Bradshaw. He took the stairs three at a time and ran into his bedroom, yanking a pair of green army socks out of his chest of drawers. They were heavy and woollen and would work as mittens in an emergency. He stuffed them into his pocket. As he left his bedroom, Bradshaw emerged from the bathroom, fully dressed, a determined but scared look on her face.

'What's happening, Poe?'

'I'll tell you in the car but I think DI Flynn's in trouble, Tilly. Serious trouble.'

She set her jaw and her myopic eyes turned to steel.

'I'm with you all the way, Poe.'

A mile from Herdwick Croft and the quad slowed then stopped. Its wheels span without gaining traction.

He always had a shovel in the back in case he became an 'unexpected item in the boggy area' but the tyres were useless in snow this thick. He could spend fifteen minutes digging the quad out only to get stuck again a couple of yards farther on.

He turned to Bradshaw, shielded his eyes with his arm and shouted above the noise of the storm.

'We're stuck, Tilly! We're on foot from here.'

She tightened the straps on her satchel and zipped up her jacket so it covered the lower part of her face. She nodded.

Poe bent his head, narrowed his eyes until they were almost shut and started walking.

The quad had taken them a mile, so Poe reckoned another mile on the same bearing would bring them to Shap Wells. He was worried, though. The swirling white dust had hidden his usual landmarks and he'd already veered too far to the left.

Bradshaw, lagging five yards behind him, was in danger of becoming part of the landscape – she was already little more than a crude outline of a human. He stopped and waited for her. Knew that if they were separated she'd get lost and freeze to death.

He removed his coat, took off his jumper and put his coat back on. He passed her one of the jumper's arms and took hold of the other.

'No arguing, I'm tethering you to me.'

No doubt like his own, her face was red raw. Although she was frightened, she smiled and gave him a double thumbs up. He knew she would keep going or die trying.

With the snow stinging his exposed cheeks and the wind's savage blasts cutting through his sock-mittens and into his bones, Poe headed off in what he hoped was the right direction. He could barely see farther than his breath.

For ten minutes they slogged on, their feet crunching the snow and their breath fogging the air. They forced their way through snowdrifts and jogged down the side of slopes protected from the wind. Bradshaw was breathing heavily but so was he. The cold air was burning his lungs and, although he was used to physical activity, his recent illness had weakened him more than he'd realised. He was soon wheezing. Bradshaw, who had never knowingly exercised, didn't complain once. Each time he caught her eye she smiled and gave him another thumbs up. He took strength from her.

He put his head down and kept going.

A tug on the jumper they were using as a tether made him turn. Bradshaw was pointing at something. He looked but couldn't see anything. His eyes were permanently watering. Bradshaw's were dry, probably because her glasses were shielding them from the worst of the wind. For once she could see farther than he could.

'There's the hotel, Poe!' she yelled into his ear.

He strained but could see nothing.

'You lead, I'll follow,' he told her.

With renewed purpose they headed off again.

Chapter 73

With a fixed bearing to walk towards, they finished the last half mile in good time and were soon in Poe's X1, heater on full, edging out of Shap Wells Hotel. The wind was blowing the snow off the tarmac and into the gorse and bracken and his winter tyres and four-wheel drive were more than a match for the steep road leading up to the A6.

They were soon on the relatively quiet M6 and, as they had moved off the high ground of Shap, the weather began to ease. It was still snowing but at least visibility was above zero. Poe tried Nightingale again but there was still no service. He pressed his foot down hard on the accelerator and the BMW responded.

Sixty.

Seventy.

Eighty.

He kept it there, as fast as he was willing to go in these conditions. Anything above would be reckless and he had Bradshaw to think of as well as Flynn.

'What's happened, Poe?' Bradshaw said. 'Why is DI Stephanie Flynn in trouble?'

He told her what he knew.

When he finished he glanced across. Bradshaw was trying out the words. Silently, as if she wouldn't believe them until she'd tested them on herself.

'But why, Poe?'

He told her what he thought. Couldn't believe what he was

being forced to say. It was horrific but it was the only thing that worked all the way to the end.

When he was done, she looked at him and then at the dashboard.

'So why are we going so slow?'

He pushed his foot to the floor and they watched the speedometer hit one hundred and keep moving clockwise.

He tried Nightingale again. This time he got a dial tone.

'Poe?' she said. 'Everything all right?'

He told her what he knew. She didn't interrupt.

When he'd got to the end, she said, 'Let me get back to you.'

Five minutes later she rang back. Her voice was hoarse, as if she'd been yelling instructions. She was outside now and on the move. She had to shout to be heard.

'What the hell's going on, Poe? We can't raise DC Coughlan or DI Flynn!'

Poe nodded grimly.

'And let me guess: DC Coughlan volunteered to do an extra shift?' he said.

Nightingale paused. 'How the hell could you know that? I've only just found out myself. He radioed to say he would do a double. My inspector saw no reason not to let him.'

Poe said nothing.

It was happening now.

Chapter 74

Nightingale had called in armed response but Poe's worst fear had been realised: the tide had only just started to come in and it wasn't yet deep enough for them to take a marine unit RIB across the Walney Channel. They were stranded at Snab Point for at least another hour.

'Try not to worry, Poe. The storm's playing havoc with our comms,' Nightingale said. 'It might not be what you think.'

But it was, he knew that. Knew that Nightingale knew it too.

'We can't get a chopper in the air but armed response will get across as soon as the water's deep enough,' she added. 'Hopefully they'll be in—'

Poe ended the call. He indicated and left the M6 at junction 36. When he was on the Barrow road he turned to Bradshaw and said, 'Find a way to get us onto that island, Tilly.'

While Bradshaw worked Poe said nothing and did nothing. He didn't beat a drum on the steering wheel and he didn't fidget in his seat. He didn't sigh and he didn't ask her how she was getting on. He drove and kept quiet. Bradshaw had an impossible task and she needed silence.

He glanced across.

She had her laptop open and she was doing maths, her fingers dancing across the keyboard, her lips pressed together in concentration.

Five more minutes passed.

'There might be a way, Poe,' she said, 'but you're not going to like it.'

She told him.

She was right. He didn't.

Poe drove into Barrow ignoring the speed restrictions – the storm had cleared the town anyway – and headed towards the dock area. Bradshaw wanted him going no slower than fifty miles an hour at this point.

A traffic light ahead of him turned red. A cab and a silver Audi stopped for it. Poe didn't. He swerved round them and carried on.

'Yeah, yeah,' he muttered when a car coming the other way sounded its horn.

He was soon in the dock area.

Bradshaw was glued to her laptop, plotting their progress.

'How we doing?'

'It's going to be tight, Poe,' she said. 'We can't afford to stop.'

The phone rang. Poe pressed the answer button on the steering wheel, his eyes never leaving the road.

It was Nightingale.

'Where are you, Poe?'

'Just crossing the bridge to Walney Island.'

'We're assembled at Snab Point,' she said. 'The marine unit has agreed to leave in less than ideal depth conditions. They estimate an hour. You can't go with them but I can get you on the second boat.'

Poe said nothing. He turned left off the bridge and sped south along the promenade on Walney Island. He was soon through the isolated village of Biggar and had a clear run along Mawflat Lane. The worst of the storm either hadn't reached Walney yet or it had already passed. A weak moon offered pale light through

305

cracks in the low cloud. Poe grunted in satisfaction. It should be enough for them to see Montague Island's silhouette.

Walney was eleven miles long but the distance between the bridge and Snab Point was less than five. Poe ignored the unsuitability of the road and the conditions and put his foot down again. Bradshaw kept her eyes on her computer.

'I'll be at Snab Point soon,' Poe said. 'Stay on the line.'

'Why?' asked Nightingale.

Poe ignored her.

'How we doing?' he whispered.

Bradshaw shrugged.

Even if he hadn't been to Snab Point before, Poe wouldn't have needed directions to find it. The air was flashing like a rock concert. Nightingale had called in the cavalry. There were at least twelve police cars, two of which Poe recognised as armed response vehicles. They all had their blue lights on.

He slowed as he approached them. He had to. He could see Nightingale on her phone, her neck craning to see where he was. He flashed his headlights.

'I see you,' she said. 'Park where you can and we'll get you kitted out. Everyone's wearing a stab-proof vest.'

Poe said nothing.

He had no intention of wearing a stab-proof vest.

He had no intention of stopping . . .

Chapter 75

Bradshaw's solution had been simple.

Simple but reckless, the type of thing *he* usually came up with.

The tide was coming in too fast to drive across but it wasn't yet in far enough for the marine unit to get an RIB afloat.

Bradshaw's answer was to drive out into the Walney Channel as far as the tide would allow, abandon the car on the sand flats and then do the rest on foot. A variation on what they'd done with the quad on their way to Shap Wells not an hour before.

She said the maths worked. If they were in luck, and if it wasn't an aberrant tide, there was a 60 per cent chance they wouldn't drown. Unfortunately there was a 100 per cent chance he would lose his car to the Irish Sea and a zero per cent chance he'd be able to make a claim on his insurance.

Poe trusted Bradshaw's maths and, as he couldn't see another option, instead of following Nightingale's directions to park and collect a stab-proof vest, he accelerated past her, ignored the shouted instructions and the warning signs about not driving on a Scene of Special Scientific Interest and drove straight into the sea . . .

'Poe!' Nightingale screamed into her phone. 'What the hell do you think you're doing?! Get back here now, that's an order!'

'Sorry, ma'am,' he said, 'this is an NCA operation now.'

'Poe, you listen to—'

He ended the call. He hadn't enjoyed that. He had a great

deal of respect for Nightingale and would have preferred to do as she asked.

He turned to Bradshaw.

'Just you and me now, Tilly.'

'We'll get there in time, Poe,' she said.

As soon as he was into the Walney Channel proper, when grass ended and the sand started, Poe slowed down and engaged the four-wheel drive function. Speed wasn't their friend any more. Speed would get them stuck before they'd reached where Bradshaw had calculated they could abandon the car and still have enough time to get to the island without drowning. She told him he had to keep to a steady twenty for as far as he could but he kept it at thirty while he dared. Tried to build a bit of a safety margin.

It was a surprisingly smooth ride.

Poe was scared. Terrified even. He glanced across at Bradshaw, still staring at her laptop screen, and drew strength from her again. If she could face the incoming Irish Sea and whatever lay at the end, then he damn well could. He set his jaw and, fighting every instinct he had to go faster, found the courage to slow down.

Sheep Island was now in his rear-view mirror and Piel Island was coming up straight ahead. Poe bore left. Two minutes later Montague Island came into view. It was already surrounded by water. At least fifty yards.

Poe reckoned they still had half a mile to go and the BMW felt sluggish as the wheels dug into the wet sand.

He slowed to ten miles an hour.

'We might have to swim the last bit, Poe,' Bradshaw said.

'Tilly, you *can't* swim,' he said.

'It can't be difficult,' she said. 'I'll just paddle like Edgar does.'

Poe ignored her hopelessly naive remark.

'Why didn't you tell me we'd have to swim the last bit?'

She folded her arms and ignored him.

'Because you knew I'd kick you out before I drove into the sea,' he said, answering his own question.

He raced through his options. Decided he didn't have any. Sending her back was a death sentence, as was leaving her with the car. Even if she could swim, the Walney Channel was treacherous when the tide came in.

She would have to come with him.

The BMW juddered, then stopped. Poe selected reverse and tried to ease out of the rut he'd created. Managed to move back a few inches. Selected forwards and tried rocking the car out.

Nothing.

'You ready to get your feet wet?' he said to Bradshaw.

She grabbed a plastic bag and wrapped her laptop in it before stuffing it into her rucksack. She removed her Converse trainers and put them in too.

'It'll be easier to walk barefoot,' she said. 'Simple physics.'

Poe had nothing he needed to take with him. He left his keys with the car in case the unlikely happened and one of Nightingale's cops was able to salvage it.

By the time they got out of the car the water was already lapping at their feet.

Chapter 76

Poe fixed his eyes on the horizon and forced himself to keep moving forwards. He was exhausted. The cold dead sand shifted with every step. It sucked at his boots and tested his laces to their limits. After a hundred yards his jeans were soaked through and felt like they'd doubled in weight. After two hundred yards it felt like his boots were encased in concrete. He was sucking in air harder than he thought possible, his ribs heaving in and out like bellows, but he couldn't seem to fill his lungs. His thigh muscles were trembling and he was close to a major cramp.

And it was cold.

The water was stealing the little heat he'd recouped in the car. His feet were numb and he had pain in his fingertips. His teeth were chattering and his whole body was violently shaking.

Bradshaw wasn't faring much better. Her hair was plastered wetly against her head and her lips had a blue tinge.

She gave him a fierce smile.

He'd worried she'd slow him down but the reverse was true – because he was wearing heavy jeans and she was wearing light-weight cargo pants, he was slowing *her* down. And she'd been right: it *was* easier to walk barefoot. Where Poe's thick hiking boots meant he had to pull his feet out of the wet sand step-by-step using brute force, she was breaking the suction just by wiggling her toes.

Cramp ripped up his hamstrings. It was excruciating and the

pain brought him to his knees. He screamed but forced himself to get up and wait for it to pass. Eventually it did.

'Are you OK, Poe?'

'I'm fine,' he said, massaging the back of his legs. 'Come on, we're nearly there.'

The tide was laced with sea foam and Poe knew that was because it was moving faster than before. It was surging at knee height and the weight of the water was almost enough to topple him.

In front of him Bradshaw fell, and for a moment disappeared from view. Poe couldn't move any faster. By the time he reached her she was up and on the move again, not even stopping to cough out a mouthful of seawater.

'Tilly!' he yelled. 'Five more minutes!'

He could see the pier. Could even make out the stone steps to the side.

The current he was bracing himself against changed direction slightly and, because he wasn't paying attention, it caught him unawares.

He fell.

Bradshaw struggled on ahead, oblivious to what had happened.

His head went under the water and the world went silent.

Chapter 77

Poe struggled to his hands and knees, vomiting salt water. He couldn't get to his feet. Each time he tried the weight of his wet clothes sucked him back down. And each time he tried, the weaker he became.

He felt dizzy.

He knew this was how people drowned in the Walney Channel. The tide came in slowly, lulling you into a false sense of security, but before you knew it, it had drained you of every ounce of strength. And once you were down it kept you down.

He thought of Flynn. Tried to extract one last bit of moisture from the well. Fell back again. Shouted in frustration.

A thin arm grabbed him under his shoulders. Began pulling.

'Come on, Poe!' Bradshaw yelled. 'Don't give up now!'

With one final heave he put everything he had into his legs and forced his body out of the foaming surf. Bradshaw steadied him before he could topple back over.

'We'll hold on to each other, Poe! DI Flynn needs you rather than me – my job is to get you onto that island.'

Poe nodded, too exhausted to speak.

By the time they reached the pier and the adjacent steps carved into the stone, they were wading rather than walking. Another five minutes and they'd have been swept out to sea.

Bradshaw wanted him to go up first but Poe refused. Once he was up he wasn't sure he'd be able to get back down.

He held her by the hips as if he was footing a ladder and steadied her as she climbed. One final push on her backside and she was up. She immediately turned and offered him her hand. Poe wasn't taking any chances; he went up like Edgar would have done: on all fours.

He looked round. The natural alcove that acted as the observation point for the eastern side of Montague Island was empty.

Dave Coughlan was nowhere to be seen.

Poe gingerly got to his feet. He felt wobbly and he couldn't feel his fingers and toes but that was to be expected – in the last hour they'd been caught in a snowstorm and had been wading in the Irish Sea.

Bradshaw was shivering so much it looked like she was vibrating. She needed to get some heat back in her. He removed his sodden jacket and wrapped it round her shoulders. It was better than nothing.

'Put your shoes and socks back on then start moving, Tilly,' he said. 'I don't think we were in long enough to lose core body heat so we should be able to generate the warmth ourselves. Watch me.'

Poe blew on his hands to get the blood pumping again then stuffed them in his armpits. He jogged on the spot and jumped up and down a few times to demonstrate.

Bradshaw copied him.

'What are we going to do now, Poe?' she said through chattering teeth.

And that was the question. The one that constant movement and panic had allowed him to put off.

Just what *were* they going to do now?

'You need to stay at the pier, Tilly. Armed response will be here soon and they won't know where they're going. You'll need to guide them in.'

She folded her arms in defiance. 'Estelle Doyle said you

weren't to try to do anything yourself, Poe. She said he's not a street fighter like you, he's a stone cold killer.'

'I'll be careful,' he said.

'She said that calling in the men with guns isn't a sign of weakness. I think you should wait.'

'It's right that you should have second thoughts, Tilly, and I don't want to do this any more than you but I'm not sure we have enough time.'

'You need a weapon then.'

She was right; he needed something. People who knew how to use a garrotte knew how to use other weapons.

His car was kitted out for winter with a shovel and rope in the boot. There was even a small pickaxe. He wished he'd had the foresight to bring it. What he'd give for a pickaxe handle right now. Like a baseball bat but with a lump of metal on the end.

He thrust his hand in his pockets – in an emergency he could use his keys. Grab the main bunch to put some weight in his fist – like holding a roll of ten-pence pieces – and leave one or two poking out between his fingers to act as a knuckleduster. A fistful of keys jabbed into the sensitive muscles around the eyes would spoil anyone's day.

'Bollocks,' he said. He'd left his keys in his car.

He wondered what Bradshaw had in her bag. She had a laptop and it was a Mac and made of metal. He certainly wouldn't want to get cracked on the side of the head with one. He dismissed it. You could maybe start a fight with one but he doubted you could end one. It was too unwieldy.

His thoughts raced back to his time in the army and a day spent in the classroom discussing improvised weapons. The difference between a thing and a weapon was intent, the instructor had told them. He'd explained that when the police began searching football hooligans at the turnstiles they'd had to find new ways of getting weapons into the ground. They'd had to *improvise*. So,

314

instead of knuckledusters and coshes, they brought newspapers into the stadiums. Once inside they folded them until the newspaper was a wedge-shaped club. Bash someone with a Millwall Brick and they didn't get up for a while.

Poe looked down.

He didn't have an improvised brick but he didn't need one. He was standing among a pile of rocks.

Big rocks. Small rocks. All potential weapons. Primitive but effective. Probably the first weapon in the history of the human race.

He picked one up and tested it in his hand. Swung it a couple of times. It would have to do.

Bradshaw watched him. He expected her to tell him that hitting someone with a rock was wrong. It was, but he'd rather have a rock and not need it . . .

'Do you still have those green socks, Poe?'

He stared at her. Knew she wasn't being Bradshaw this time, she was trying to help.

'In the jacket you're wearing.'

Bradshaw reached into the pockets and removed one. It was wringing wet.

'Did you do physics at school? Specifically the relationship between acceleration and velocity?'

He was about to shake his head. Tell her he didn't have a clue what she was talking about.

But all of a sudden he did.

Chapter 78

Poe had the eye of an ex-infantryman and he'd already plotted an approach that got within fifty yards of Atkinson's bungalow without him having to leave dead ground – ground that couldn't be seen from the western tip of the island. Unless someone had watched him arrive on the island he'd be approaching under cover. Even with his aching muscles the dash across the last fifty yards would take no more than fifteen seconds.

It was tempting. It really was.

But . . . he wasn't a soldier any more; he was a police officer. And police officers didn't skulk around in the bushes; they walked up the garden path and knocked on the door.

And right now, Poe needed to be a police officer.

The moonlight was pale and delicate and, although it painted the island grey, it was more than enough to navigate by. The grass was wet and quiet underfoot. Poe took the route he'd taken previously. He passed the outline of the isolation hospital and he passed the five empty cottages. He startled the same rabbits and they bolted into the same burrows.

This time he didn't turn to see if they'd reappeared after he'd passed.

His eyes never left the bungalow.

He was soon stepping over the remnants of the dry stone wall that marked the border of Atkinson's land. The front of the bungalow, the side Atkinson never used, was in full view, all neglected and forlorn.

The wind dropped and the island became shrouded in silence. Poe could hear his own breath. He was panting and it was nothing to do with the struggle to get there.

He felt very alone.

Being a police officer had installed in Poe the belief he had the inherent right to knock on any door he felt like, at any time he wanted. It didn't mean he had to rattle a bucket of spoons at the same time, though. He walked the final fifty yards quietly and with caution.

Poe ignored the unused front door and instead followed the wheelchair-friendly path around the side of the building. He paused before he reached the stone terrace. Took a deep breath and gathered his thoughts.

It was possible he was wrong. That Nightingale was right and the storm had knocked out the police communications the same way the cell-phone tower had been silenced. That Coughlan *had* fancied the overtime and he was on the island patrolling somewhere.

Nightingale's armed response would be on the island in thirty minutes. Officers who would bring guns to a garrotte fight. All he had was a rock and an untested theory.

The sensible choice was to wait.

But then he thought about Flynn and his resolve hardened. He wasn't certain there was a threat against his friend, only that there was the possibility of a threat.

It was enough.

Poe stepped round the side of the building and onto the stone terrace.

It was empty.

He didn't hesitate. Marched straight up to the French doors and tried the handles.

Locked.

He banged on the wooden frame, rattling the glass. Waited ten seconds. He looked round for something to break the window. Saw a terracotta pot he reckoned he could just about manage to lift. He was about to pick it up when a noise turned his head back to the inside of the bungalow.

Atkinson had wheeled himself to the door, a look of confusion on his face.

'Can you open the door, Mr Atkinson?' Poe said loudly.

Atkinson reached forwards and turned the key, opened the door and reversed his wheelchair to let him in.

'Where's DI Flynn?' Poe barked.

Atkinson's eyes widened.

'What's up, Sergeant Poe? You're scaring me.'

Poe stepped inside.

'Where is she?' he urged.

'She's with DC Coughlan,' Atkinson said. 'He said he had something he needed to show her. Wouldn't say what it was. Why, what's happened?'

Poe nodded.

He then reached into his pocket, unfurled Bradshaw's weapon and smashed it down onto Atkinson's hand.

Chapter 79

The Curator screamed, his right hand ruined.

Poe didn't hesitate. He swung the improvised cosh again, this time aiming for his other hand. Can't use a garrotte if you don't have the use of your hands.

The army sock with an orange-sized rock inside was wildly inaccurate, though, and he didn't have the element of surprise for the second blow. The Curator was already moving and, instead of his hand, the second blow caught him on the shoulder. Poe heard a bone break and watched as his left arm went limp.

Despite this, he managed to launch himself out of the wheelchair, a calculating look on his face. He jabbed at Poe's throat with his ruined right hand. Poe dipped his head and the man's broken fist bounced off his chin.

Poe stepped back and for a moment the two men stared at each other, panting. Poe had a problem: the cosh was an impact weapon and didn't have a stun setting – if he hit him on the head he risked killing him and, while that was less important than Flynn's safety, he needed to know who'd hired him.

He remembered Bradshaw's rushed instructions: 'Using a sock will lengthen the weapon. Even a small acceleration at the centre will create massive velocity at the other end.'

Poe shortened the length of the sock to about six inches. Enough to put him down but hopefully not enough to kill him. It was guesswork but it was all he had.

The disadvantage of the shortened weapon was that he'd have

to get in closer and, while the Curator had a broken right hand and an unusable left, he was still a dangerous man.

But right now, so was he.

Poe charged forwards, swinging the cosh ahead of him in a figure of eight pattern, driving the Curator back against the back wall where there was no escape. He aimed for his head again. The Curator threw up his right arm to protect himself.

The rock shattered his elbow.

He screamed again, both arms now hanging limply by his side.

It had been short and violent but as a fight it was over.

'OK, OK!' he shouted. 'No more! I've had enough.'

Poe stared but saw nothing but defeat in his eyes. He didn't care – there was no honour in what had just happened, no code of conduct, no points deducted for style. All that mattered was that he finished it.

He heard a noise at the French doors.

Bradshaw was standing in the doorway. She was holding a piece of driftwood no bigger than a headmaster's cane. She looked terrified but determined.

'Freeze, dirtbag!' she shouted.

Poe looked at the Curator.

'What she said.'

He then stepped forward and clubbed him on the side of the head.

And this time he did go down.

Poe had to secure the Curator before he could search for Flynn. He ripped a reading lamp from the wall socket and used the cable to bind his legs. Used another to tie his hands behind his back. He used a third to tie him to the wheelchair he'd been squatting in.

'Put your stick down, Tilly,' Poe said.

Bradshaw said nothing. Just looked at the man on the floor

and the blood coming from the compound fractures in his hands and elbow. She was trembling. He needed to keep her busy.

He walked up to her and gently prised the stick out of her cold hands.

'Let's go and find DI Flynn, Tilly.'

Bradshaw tore her eyes away from the devastation on the floor and nodded. She looked at the Curator.

'OK, Poe,' she said softly. 'But if this man has killed DI Stephanie Flynn I . . . I don't know what I'll do to him.'

'If the boss is dead, Tilly, this bastard's going in the sea.'

Poe stood and headed into the guts of the bungalow. He ignored the bedroom and en suite and headed for Atkinson's treatment room, hoping he wasn't too late. He tried the door but it was locked.

He didn't bother searching the Curator for the key – he walked back five paces and ran at it shoulder first. The flimsy internal door was no match for his anger. It tore from its hinges and fell inwards.

Poe stepped over the splintered wood and in a single glance understood why the female victims had been abducted and why there'd been anaesthetic in their blood.

He understood everything . . .

Chapter 80

It was worse than anything Poe had dared fear.

Flynn was lying half-naked on the treatment table. She was stony pale and wasn't moving. A blue hygiene towel covered her midriff and groin. It was soaked with blood. Too much blood.

A purple bruise covered one side of her lifeless face. Two empty bags hung from an IV stand at the top of the treatment table. Stained tubes ran from them to the cannula taped to the back of her hand. One bag had contained blood; the other had contained a clear liquid. Possibly a sedative, possibly an anaesthetic.

Poe rushed over and pushed two fingers into Flynn's neck. She had a pulse. It was faint and rapid but it *was* there. Her eyelids fluttered and she let out a small groan but didn't wake.

Poe knew he had to check her wound but he didn't want to look under the blue hygiene paper. He'd never be the same once he had. He knew what he'd see.

And he also knew what he wouldn't see.

He had no choice, though – the price of being able to do the things that others wouldn't is that sometimes you had to do the things that others *couldn't*.

He heard a noise behind him.

'Is DI Flynn alive, Poe?'

Bradshaw had followed him into the room.

'She is, Tilly.' He used his body to shield her view of Flynn. 'Can I have my jacket back, please?'

Bradshaw slipped out of it and handed it to him. He laid it over Flynn's upper torso.

'Don't look, Tilly.'

He didn't wait to see if she was averting her eyes. She'd either take his advice or she wouldn't. He lifted the blue hygiene paper and saw what he'd dreaded seeing.

Bradshaw gasped.

He turned. She was ashen, her hands clamped to her cheeks. Poe pulled Bradshaw close and hugged her.

'Poe,' she sobbed. 'Where's DI Flynn's baby?'

Chapter 81

Instead of the maternal bump they'd grown used to, there was an eighteen-inch vertical slash. The deep wound stretched from Flynn's navel to her groin. It was seeping but encrusted with dry blood. It had been crudely stitched together with what looked like catgut, all thick and black and awful.

Poe could see the scalpels the Curator had used to open her up and the three-inch needle he'd used to close her. A semi-professional job, competence achieved through practice. Special Agent Melody Lee was right; it *was* a black swan event. The motive for Rebecca and Amanda's abductions, impossible to understand at the time, now all too obvious.

But where was Flynn's baby?

His eyes were drawn to the bin in the corner. It was the kind found in doctors' surgeries all over the country. Moulded plastic with a push-pedal to open the lid. Cheap and easy to clean.

The lid was smeared with blood.

Poe stopped breathing. He began shaking. His mouth turned to sand. The blood pounded in his ears, drowning out all other sound. He didn't want to open the lid. Didn't want to see what was inside. But if he didn't, Bradshaw would have to.

And that was unacceptable.

The walk to the corner of the room was the worst thing he'd ever had to do. It was only seven steps but it felt like seven thousand.

He stepped on the pedal but didn't dare look. Nothing

happened. It was broken. If it were a GP's surgery it would have to be replaced. Atkinson wasn't bound by the same rules.

He'd have to lift the lid himself.

He reached out but withdrew his hand. Found he didn't have the courage. He turned and saw Flynn lying on the table. An involuntary groan escaped his lips.

Bradshaw grabbed his arm and steadied him. 'I'll open it, Poe.'

She was trembling as well, her eyes wide and scared. She'd do it. He knew she would. Just so he wouldn't have to, Bradshaw would confirm what they both knew.

She was so much stronger than he was.

He shook his head. Knew he couldn't let that happen. Bradshaw was one of life's innocents. True evil had never really touched her. If he allowed her to open that bin the world wouldn't be as nice a place tomorrow.

And if Flynn were ever to get over this she'd need Bradshaw's uncomplicated view of the world. That couldn't happen if she looked in that bin.

He took a deep breath, reached down and lifted the lid.

Poe frowned. The bin was full of bloody tissues and cotton wool and swabs. He reached inside and moved things around until he was sure.

There was no sign of Flynn's baby.

Chapter 82

'Wake up!' Poe said, slapping the Curator's head.

Nothing.

His face was grey and clammy, his breathing rapid and shallow. Poe opened his eyelids and saw his dilated pupils. He was in shock. Probably needed urgent medical attention.

He didn't care; he needed answers.

Bradshaw was still in the treatment room. She wouldn't leave Flynn's side now. That suited Poe given what he was about to do.

He tapped the bone sticking out of the Curator's elbow with the tip of his finger.

His eyes fluttered open. He moaned.

'Do you believe me when I say I'll do what it takes?' Poe said calmly.

'I do,' he grunted.

'Where's the baby?'

He told him.

Ten minutes later and Poe was quivering with barely suppressed rage. His face was grimmer than a carved mask.

'Who hired you?' he said. His voice was low and ominous.

'I don't know. Anonymous.'

'What did they pay you to do?'

He shook his head.

'You're going to tell me. It's up to you how much pain you want to endure before you do.'

Poe tapped the protruding bone again. A bit harder this time.

'If I have to, I'll pull this out of your fucking arm.'

The Curator said nothing.

Poe gripped the bone.

'OK! Stop!'

And so he told Poe what he'd been hired to do. All of it. He spoke flatly and without emotion. When he'd finished it took every ounce of Poe's willpower not to grab a scalpel and open up his throat.

Instead, he leaned into the Curator's ear and spoke for five minutes, his voice never getting above a murmur.

When he'd finished, Poe said, 'Are we in agreement?'

The Curator nodded.

'We are.'

Chapter 83

Poe stood alone in the hospital room. He hadn't been in one quite like it before. He'd ended up in a private ward after the Immolation Man case but that had been because his burns had been so susceptible to infection. But whereas his had been sparse and functional, Flynn's was . . . well, Flynn's was an example of what money could buy.

It was light years away from anything available on the NHS.

It was larger than Poe's croft, a light and airy room with views of the landscaped garden, an ornamental lake and the rolling Cambridgeshire countryside beyond. Warmly wrapped patients took strolls or rested on one of the many benches and seats. A lone gardener tidied one of the raised flowerbeds.

Poe didn't know if Zoe or Flynn's sister was paying for it, but whoever it was they were getting their money's worth. The monitoring equipment was state of the art, sleek and polished and expensive-looking. The en suite was modern with a bath, a shower and a bidet. There was even a guest room off to the side.

It was spotless and dust-free. No lemon-scented disinfectant to strip the inside of the nostrils, just the pleasant and fragrant bouquet of lavender.

A fifty-six-inch 4K television hung on the wall. Instructions on how to access Netflix, Sky and Amazon Prime were in the welcome pack Poe had read. A Bose sound system and DVD player were on shelves underneath the TV.

Fresh flowers in expensive vases and original watercolours completed the décor.

The room had everything.

Everything that is except a patient. There was an ominous space where the bed should have been.

Flynn had been in surgery when he'd been driving down. She was now in recovery. He'd been there for two hours and so far hadn't spoken to anyone he knew. Someone had brought him a pot of coffee and a selection of pastries. Poe had eaten the lot then worried they hadn't all been for him.

He picked up what passed for a hospital menu. It was simply an instruction for Flynn to write down what she wanted and, after her consultant had reviewed it, the ingredients would be sourced and it would be freshly prepared.

It was blank.

Of course it was blank.

Flynn wasn't going to be hungry. Not for a long time.

He'd brought flowers. The NHS no longer allowed them on their wards. Something to do with the water being a breeding ground for bacteria. This hospital had the staff to do regular water changes, though, and flowers were encouraged.

Until he'd been forced to spend time in one, he hadn't understood the purpose of flowers in hospitals. Although they made the room look pretty and smell nice, that wasn't their primary purpose. They were there to remind the doctors and nurses that patients weren't just units, there to be fixed and sent home. They were humans, and humans needed more than technology and medicine to get better. They needed to feel alive again.

Flowers were essential to the healing process.

Even the bed didn't squeak.

A smartly dressed orderly wheeled in Flynn. He was followed by a doctor and two nurses. Jessica, Flynn's sister, and Zoe, her partner, brought up the rear. They looked dog-tired, worse than he did, and he wouldn't have thought that possible.

The orderly manoeuvred Flynn's bed into the gap and the nurses fixed it to the machines. One of them handed her the remote control that raised or lowered the bed, then left the room.

Poe smiled at Flynn. She ignored him. He wasn't sure she'd even registered who he was.

She seemed to be radiating heat. Her skin glistened like warm cheese. Her lips were cracked and hollow sockets framed her bloodshot eyes. Her face was still bruised. She looked small and vulnerable.

It wasn't a look he recognised.

'My baby?' she said to no one in particular. 'Where is he?'

There was no strength to her voice and it came out as a half whisper, but it was manic nonetheless.

For a moment no one spoke.

Eventually Zoe stepped forwards. She took hold of her hand.

'He's coming, Steph,' she said. 'You remember? The nurse is feeding him.'

'Oh, yes,' Flynn replied, relaxing back against the pillow. 'That's right. I'd forgotten. The nurse is feeding him.'

The room descended into silence.

Flynn broke it.

'Why is the nurse feeding him?' she said, tears rolling down her face. 'Why aren't *I* feeding him?'

'You can't, Steph,' Zoe said gently. 'Not just yet. You've been through a terrible ordeal and your body has stopped producing milk. The doctor says it shouldn't be long before your system reboots, though.'

'Here's the little scrapper now,' one of the nurses said.

Another nurse walked into the room and headed to the bed. She handed Flynn a small bundle swaddled in blankets and a bonnet.

The bundle sighed. Poe could see a wrinkled face, eyes tightly shut. His heart missed a beat. The last time he'd seen him, he'd been in a canvas bag on Edward Atkinson's bed.

Wet and red and covered in vernix, the greasy substance that protects the skin from amniotic fluid, he'd been alive but only just.

Poe had got there just in time. The doctors he'd spoken to said that a baby born before the thirty-seventh week of pregnancy would ordinarily need specialist support if it were to survive for more than a few hours. The marine unit had rushed Scrapper and Flynn to Furness General Hospital. While Scrapper was being assessed in the neonatal unit Flynn was undergoing emergency trauma surgery. The Curator had also been taken there and, for a while, all that had separated the three of them were walls and armed guards. Zoe had flown Flynn and Scrapper down to the private hospital as soon as they were stable enough to leave.

Flynn hugged her son. A look came over her face. The transformation was immediate and remarkable.

She no longer looked small and vulnerable.

She looked fierce, like a lioness protecting her cub.

'Hi, Poe,' she said, refusing to look away from her son's face. 'Where's Tilly?'

Poe waited for the nurse to attach the finger-clip that monitored her vitals before he replied.

'Still in Cumbria. She's going through the Curator's computer. I'm hoping to hear from her soon.'

'Tilly will untangle it all,' Flynn said.

'She will,' Poe agreed. She almost had. He was waiting for a text to say she was ready to brief him.

'It's funny, Poe,' she said, 'but you don't realise how many people you hate until you have to name a baby.'

He smiled. 'I can imagine.'

'Zoe wanted to call him Washington but I said it's a foolish name.'

'He's been through enough already,' he agreed.

Flynn laughed as a tiny hand grabbed her finger.

Zoe leaned in and kissed her. She straightened and said, 'Washington, can I have a word?'

'Poe,' Flynn croaked. 'He prefers Poe.'

'Poe, then, can I have a word?' She gestured towards the guest room.

'Of course.'

'Jess, can you join us?'

Flynn's sister nodded. So far she hadn't said a word. Her distraught look changed to one of resolve.

After Zoe had gently shut the door, she turned and said, 'Why did Edward Atkinson want to steal our baby?'

Poe shook his head. 'Edward Atkinson didn't want to steal your baby, Zoe.'

Both women frowned.

'Explain,' Jessica said.

'Edward Atkinson's dead,' Poe explained. 'Whoever the Curator is, and Tilly says she'll ID him soon, he killed Atkinson and took his place on the island with the express purpose of luring Steph there.'

'But how?' Zoe said.

'The how is easy. Montague Island is deserted during winter and he had the place to himself.'

'His scars, though, how did he fool you all?'

'Rigid collodion,' Poe said. 'It's a readily available special effects liquid used in the film industry. It wrinkles any skin it's applied to. With a bit of practice it's not difficult to create a scarring effect. And underneath one of Atkinson's burn masks . . .'

'It was enough to fool everyone.'

Poe nodded.

'But . . . but why?'

'All I know is that . . . under duress, he admitted to being paid to remove Steph's baby before it went full term. The details had been left to him and the Black Swan Challenge is how he chose to do it. It's a variation of something he's done before in the States.'

'Human traffickers?' Zoe asked. 'Some fucked-up plan by someone who couldn't conceive naturally?'

Poe shrugged. 'Probably. He was to get further instructions when it was done.'

Jessica stared at him. 'You don't think that, though, do you?'

'There are easier ways to steal a baby,' he said. 'I think this is personal. I think this wasn't just about stealing a baby, this was also about punishing Steph.'

'That fucking job of hers!' Jessica growled.

Zoe's hand went to her face.

'Oh my God,' she said. She slumped onto the guest room's bed. Jessica sat down and held her. For a moment the two women drew strength from each other.

'Right, I'm getting some private security up here,' Jessica said. She tapped a number on her phone and held it to her head. 'James, I need you to get me the name of a reputable private security firm. One of those that only hires ex-special forces, that type of thing.'

She listened.

'No, I'm fine.'

She explained what she wanted and then listened for a bit longer.

'Thank you,' she said. 'And James, I want them here within the hour.'

Poe nodded in satisfaction. His phone beeped. It was a text from Bradshaw telling him that she was ready to brief him and he should get back to Cumbria.

'I have to go,' he said. 'I'll be back as soon as I can.'

'Do you think he'll talk?' Jessica said.

'Depends what Tilly's found, I suppose. We'll know soon enough. He won't be in hospital much longer.'

'How is he?'

'In a pretty bad way actually. Eight broken bones in his hand, a shattered elbow, a fractured shoulder blade and dislocated socket. Oh, and a ruptured testicle.'

'Your doing?'

'The ruptured testicle wasn't. I don't think he got it all his own way. He might have caught Steph unawares but her training in Krav Maga has given her excellent reflexes. Given how close we came to being too late, I reckon the knee to the balls she gave him saved the day.'

Zoe smiled at that.

'Good,' she said. 'And what about you? Will you come out of this OK?'

'The official version of events will be kind to me,' he assured them. 'I know it will, as I'll be writing it.'

He checked his watch.

'Look, I can be back in Cumbria in five hours. If you keep your phones on I'll let you know anything the second I know it.'

'Make it four hours, Poe,' Zoe said, throwing him a set of keys.

Poe caught them.

'What's this?'

'There's a Range Rover in the car park,' she said. 'Your director told us what you did. We know we can never repay you but Jess and I can certainly replace the car you lost.'

'You didn't have to do that.' He then lied and added, 'The insurance will cover it.'

'You deliberately drove it into the sea. The insurance most definitely will not cover it. And anyway, it's now registered in your name. If you don't take it you'll start racking up parking charges.'

Poe didn't know what to say. He settled for, 'I'll keep it for now but only because of that shite thing the hire car company gave me.'

'Leave the keys here and we'll get someone to return it,' Jessica said.

Flynn was sleeping and he saw no reason to wake her. Within seconds he was striding down the corridor.

He was at the front door when a voice called him back.

It was Zoe.

She had run to catch him.

'One more thing, Poe,' she said. 'I know all about you. I know the things you've done and I know you'll not rest until you find the person behind this.'

'I'll find them,' he confirmed.

'And when you do,' Zoe said, her eyes monstrously calm, 'you kill them. Do you understand me, Poe? You find the person who did this and you fucking kill them.'

Chapter 84

Poe had thought his X1 was a smooth ride but the Range Rover was something else. It ate up the two hundred and fifty miles to Cumbria silently and in no time at all.

He was soon turning into the car park at the back of Barrow police station. The Curator was still under armed guard in Furness General Hospital but would shortly be on his way.

Nightingale and Bradshaw met him as he got out of his car.

'How's Detective Inspector Stephanie Flynn, Poe?' Bradshaw said immediately.

The stress of the last forty-eight hours had caused her to revert to using Flynn's full, formal address. It was a habit she'd tried hard to break over the last year.

'Out of surgery and she'll make a full recovery.'

'And the baby?'

'Doing well. The nurses have named him "Scrapper".'

Bradshaw silently mouthed the name.

'I don't like it, Poe.'

'Zoe wants to call him Washington.'

'Yes!' she said. 'That's a marvellous idea!'

'Nice wheels,' Nightingale said. 'The NCA must have a different pay scale to us country plodders.'

Poe smiled and patted the warm bonnet.

'It's a misguided present and I'm not keeping it. Where are we?'

Bradshaw passed him a folder.

'Almost everything you need is in there, Poe,' she said. 'I've circumnavigated most of his security but, as he knew what he was doing, there are parts I need a password for. There are also things he'll have done in live chatrooms that aren't recoverable.'

'Estelle Doyle's completed the post-mortems on Rebecca Pridmore and Amanda Simpson, I take it?'

'She asked me to tell you that you're a reckless idiot, but yes, she worked through the night and finished this morning,' Nightingale said.

She handed him a thin file. Probably just summary sheets. The full reports would follow. 'You have a messed up mind, Poe. It's exactly as you said. He *had* practised on them, right down to the crude stitching.'

A search of the island with ground-penetrating radar had found that there were more bodies in the old isolation hospital's graveyard than there were headstones. The real Edward Atkinson had been interred on his own land, in the grave of a Chinese labourer. The bodies of Rebecca Pridmore and Amanda Simpson were in adjacent graves. Dave Coughlan had been found alive, but only just. He had bruising to his throat and had been zip-tied to a cast-iron radiator in one of the empty properties. Other than someone grabbing him from behind he had no recollection of what had happened. Nightingale said he'd make a full recovery. Poe didn't doubt it – he was as tough as teak.

'And the other thing?' he asked.

'Came through an hour ago.'

'Good,' he said. Now he didn't have a compound fracture to threaten him with, he needed a different type of leverage.

He made to go inside, stopped and turned.

'Do we have a name for him yet?'

Nightingale nodded.

'The one he's using at least. Tilly found it on his laptop and my team found a passport. It was in the same name.'

'And?'

'He's ex-army intelligence,' she said. 'Left under a cloud at the rank of captain. He's called Oliver Hartley-Graham.'

'What's his story?'

'Dishonourably discharged after he was caught passing on details of future troop deployments to the Chinese. Left the country and never came back. At least not under his real name.'

Oliver Hartley-Graham looked like a man who'd been hit with a rock in a sock after having his testicles ruptured by a woman fighting for her life. He was wearing surgical shorts and a dressing gown. His face was so dry and flaky from the repeated use of rigid collodion that it was hard to tell what he actually looked like.

Poe's cosh had broken his left clavicle, or collarbone. Although it was a neat break and would be left to heal naturally, Oliver Hartley-Graham would need a sling to support the weight of his left arm for a couple of months.

His right arm was a different matter.

When Hartley-Graham had protected his face with it, his elbow had taken the full force of the rock. As well as the broken bone, he also had damaged nerves and blood vessels. He'd been in surgery for six hours. The plaster he'd have to wear for months ran from his shoulder to his hand and he'd never be able to lift his arm above his head again.

And that wasn't the worst injury. Because Poe's first blow had hit Hartley-Graham's hand while it was on the arm of the wheelchair, he had significant crush trauma. As well as compression fractures to all four fingers, three of his fingertips had burst under the pressure.

He also had a head wound. The one he'd sustained when Poe clubbed him unconscious so he could find Flynn. Although there'd been no lasting damage, the bruise on his right temple had spread into his eye sockets. His right socket was stained yellow and had swollen shut. The left was open but not by much more than a squint. His nose had been set as straight as it could be, but it would always whistle when he breathed through it.

Hartley-Graham was seated in a wheelchair. This time he needed one. He shifted in the seat and winced when he did. Poe suspected he was going to be in pain for a long time.

His solicitor was seated beside him. She was called Lauretta Notman. She was from a local firm. The Barrow cops who knew her said she was tough but fair. She was dark-haired and wore a trouser suit, not unlike the ones Flynn used to wear before the pregnancy caused a wardrobe change.

She was pulsating with anger.

Poe ignored her. She would soon be irrelevant. Instead he locked eyes with Hartley-Graham and wordlessly reaffirmed that the agreement they'd reached in those final minutes on the island still held. Poe was confident it would; it was in neither of their interests for it to get out.

'So, you're the Curator, are you?' he said, reading from his file. 'A man who couldn't be in more shit if he'd jumped into a swimming pool filled with shit.'

Hartley-Graham said nothing.

'I don't often use the word ghoulish,' Poe continued, 'but in your case I can't actually think of another.'

He picked up a document and pretended to read it.

'You were a captain in the British Army and you're now a hired killer,' he said. 'Your mother must be so proud.'

'My client will not be saying anything, Sergeant Poe,' Notman snapped, clearly not used to being ignored. 'We have prepared a statement, which you can read now or later.'

She slid a two-page document across the table.

Poe let it fall to the floor.

'I think there's been a misunderstanding, Mrs Notman,' he

said. 'This is a Cumbrian case and I am no longer involved in it. Superintendent Nightingale's team will be along soon if you still want to talk statements and assault charges. No, I'm here in a *liaison* capacity.'

Poe opened his file and retrieved a document. He didn't offer it to Notman. Not yet.

'My colleague Tilly, who you met on the island, Oliver, broke most of the security on your laptop in under two minutes. We have your files, we have your Black Swan Challenge blueprints and we have the bitcoins you were presumably paid in.'

Bradshaw had found over two million pounds' worth of the cryptocurrency on Hartley-Graham's laptop. She was trying to trace its origins but she wasn't hopeful. She'd explained that he'd probably used random people to withdraw small amounts of his fee from his employer's digital wallet, giving them a reasonable cut when they did. Tracing the person who'd hired him via his payment would be impossible.

Poe continued, 'I understand that, unless you give us the password, it will take specialist software to open the rest of it. Proprietary software, which I'm told is only available from the laptop's manufacturer.'

Notman frowned, unsure where Poe was going.

'Anyway, I digress. If I may, I'd like to talk about an American called Stuart Wilson and a game called the White Elephant Challenge. Do you remember Stuart? He's the rich college boy you thought would make the perfect patsy.'

Hartley-Graham shifted in his seat. Poe knew he hadn't expected to hear that name so early.

'I know you remember him. You're an intelligent and well-organised man, Oliver – there's no way you set someone up unless you think you know all about them.'

Poe opened his file and put on his reading glasses.

'But this time you got it wrong. Stuart Wilson *was* from a

wealthy family, and on the face of it, they weren't going to garner much public sympathy. They'd got rich investing in the construction of Iran's liquefied natural gas export facilities. As the self-declared sworn enemy of the United States, at best, anyone managing to do business there is seen as an opportunist.'

'Are you going somewhere with this, Sergeant Poe?' Notman said.

Poe ignored her, kept his eyes on Hartley-Graham. He was watching Poe now. Curious and nervous.

'And this is the thing you missed. Because of his success, Mr Wilson, Stuart's father, was in delicate but advanced negotiations to provide safety equipment for some of the state-owned oil and gas sector.'

Hartley-Graham said nothing.

'And that caught the attention of the US intelligence agencies,' Poe continued. 'They were very keen for this to happen. I'm not privy to all the details, but apparently they'd asked for some backdoors to be slipped in. Backdoors that would have allowed some of the American three-letter agencies unfettered access to raw data they'd previously struggled to get anywhere near.'

'Spit it out, Sergeant Poe!' Notman snapped.

'OK then, I will. Long story short is that your stunt with his kid caused Mr Wilson to pull out of the Iranian deal. He needed time and money for his son's court case. I also suspect he wasn't feeling the love for his government right then either.'

Poe slid a piece of paper across the table.

'We've shared what evidence we have with them and told them that Stuart Wilson was set up. The Americans are now taking the view that you deliberately sabotaged this Iranian deal.'

Hartley-Graham swallowed hard.

'On the face of it, it's a pretty reasonable interpretation of the facts,' Poe said. 'And, as you'll be aware, in this day and age, to the Americans suspected terrorism *is* terrorism.'

'I'm not a terrorist,' Hartley-Graham whispered. He knew what was coming. Knew his options had become binary, neither of them good. He would have to deal.

'I can see you've fast-forwarded to the next song. I've just passed Mrs Notman what's called an "intention to apply for extradition". The United States want you brought there under the Patriot Act.'

Poe paused while they read it.

When they'd finished, he said, 'You have a simple choice to make, Oliver: where do you want to be prosecuted? In the UK for four murders or in the States for terrorism. I'll be back in ten minutes. Read that extradition document. It's real, it's happening now.'

He stood and left the room without a backwards glance.

Chapter 85

Nightingale and Bradshaw had watched the interview on the monitor. Bradshaw's eyes were ringed with fatigue but she was still staring unblinking at the screen. Oliver Hartley-Graham had almost killed everyone she cared about.

'You did well in there, Poe,' Nightingale said.

Poe grunted his thanks. He wasn't taking plaudits until he knew who was behind it all. Hartley-Graham was someone's employee. If he didn't find out whose, Scrapper Flynn would never be safe. It didn't matter how many ex-special forces people Jessica Flynn hired, a resourceful person would find a way through. They only had to be lucky once, Scrapper had to be lucky all the time.

Poe couldn't have that.

'You think he'll talk?' Nightingale said.

'He'll talk.'

'You seem sure.'

'You should have seen how quickly he gave up the baby's location when he thought I was going to pull on that protruding bone,' Poe said. 'He has no tolerance for pain. The thought of being waterboarded will terrify him. He'll do anything to avoid extradition and the only way he can do that is to ensure he's convicted of the crimes he committed in this country. Hope that if he's ever released he'll be too old to be of interest to the Yanks.'

'You're not worried he'll come after you for assault?'

Poe shook his head.

'You don't think he'll press charges?'

'No idea. I'm just not worried. I've gone through it over and over again and I firmly believe it was the only option I had. Oliver Hartley-Graham might be clever and organised but at the end of the day he's a contract killer. Taking him down was the only way to save the boss's baby. It isn't always, but my conscience is clear on this occasion.'

He didn't add that there was another reason Hartley-Graham wouldn't press charges, one Poe could only discuss with the person who'd hired him. It would happen soon, he hoped.

Nightingale nodded. 'You're a disobedient bastard, Poe, but the chief constable agrees – under the circumstances you had no choice. Cumbria won't be seeking to press charges and, unless they receive a complaint, neither will the CPS.'

Director van Zyl had been in touch, too. He'd been calling about Flynn but he'd also told him that there would be no internal investigation on the actions he'd taken. When Poe had driven into the Walney Channel, jurisdiction was . . . unclear. It was a Cumbrian investigation so it was their case. But, an officer in the National Crime Agency had been in imminent danger and Poe had been within his rights to go to her aid. In the end common sense had prevailed and the whole thing was put down as a learning experience. Van Zyl and the chief constable would deliver a joint paper on it at a meeting they were attending in April.

'If you'd waited for the tide to come in with the rest of us we'd have missed him by thirty minutes,' Nightingale continued. 'He and DI Flynn's baby would have docked at the Isle of Man and caught a flight to mainland Europe. We wouldn't have known where to start looking for him. We wouldn't know what he looked like and we wouldn't have had his name.'

Poe already knew this. Bradshaw had found Hartley-Graham's private charter details and subsequent travel plans on his laptop. If he'd got off Montague Island he'd have been gone for ever.

'Hey, guys, get over here,' Bradshaw said. 'Something's happening.'

Hartley-Graham and his solicitor were having a heated argument. Notman looked to be reasoning with him. As best he could given his extensive injuries, Hartley-Graham was waving her away.

'Looks like you're on, Poe,' Nightingale said.

Poe retook his seat. It was still warm.

The detective constable with him completed the formalities. It would be the last time she'd speak. Poe was in charge from now on.

'I'd like to cooperate, Sergeant Poe,' Hartley-Graham said.

Poe said nothing.

'I have three conditions,' he continued. 'One, my solicitor is legally absolved from all consequences. This is my decision and she has advised against it.'

'Noted,' Poe said. 'If Mrs Notman draws up the relevant paperwork, you can sign it before she leaves the building.' He turned to the solicitor. 'Is this acceptable?'

She nodded and visibly relaxed.

'Two,' Hartley-Graham said, 'I'll give you everything you want but I have to be prosecuted in this country.'

'I'll do everything I can to make sure you spend the rest of your life in a British prison,' Poe said, 'but if I think you're lying, or lying by omission, I'll take you to the bloody airport myself.'

'Fair enough.'

'What's your third condition, Mr Hartley-Graham?'

He tried to smile. It came out as a grotesque grimace.

'I want to know what I did wrong.'

'The criminal who doesn't make mistakes is yet to exist,' Poe replied, 'and you didn't have the discipline to stay in role . . .'

Chapter 86

It's sometimes the smallest thing that cracks a case.

Dennis Nilsen's blocked drains.

The BTK Killer sending a traceable floppy disc to a television station.

The Son of Sam's parking ticket . . .

Small mistakes, unimaginable consequences.

In Hartley-Graham's case it had hinged on whether it had been Bradshaw or Poe who'd been first in the shower after the snowstorm had trapped them at Herdwick Croft.

If it had been him then Hartley-Graham and Flynn's baby would have disappeared without a trace and the murders of Edward Atkinson, Rebecca Pridmore, Amanda Simpson and Howard Teasdale would have remained unsolved.

But he hadn't gone first. Bradshaw had.

And she wasn't as tall as him . . .

'The shower,' Poe said. 'I recently had a guest, and for the first time since it had been installed someone had lowered the shower on the shower rod. They aren't as tall as me, you see. That was your mistake. If you'd stayed in role and used the shower chair like Edward had, you'd be a free man. But you didn't stay in role. You wanted to stand in the shower and you raised the shower-head accordingly. When I readjusted my shower, it reminded me I'd seen witness marks on Atkinson's shower rod that were way too high for a man sitting down. You'd put the shower back to where Edward had put it but it still left marks where you had it.'

'That was it? You got the whole thing from a shower head?'

Poe shrugged. Of course that hadn't been it. Until he'd brought everything together it was just one more thing without any context. But . . . when he put it alongside a trail of bread-crumbs that had been difficult but not impossible to follow, and Melody Lee's warning that when you thought you knew what the Curator was doing he had you exactly where he wanted you to be, it had all pointed to a complex but brilliant plan to isolate a single person.

'I knew it couldn't have been me you were after,' Poe said. 'You'd had me alone for a whole night and hadn't made a move. And me being the target didn't explain the female abductions or the anaesthetic we found in their blood. That suggested there was a medical angle and her pregnancy made DI Flynn the obvious choice.'

Notman was staring, open-mouthed. Poe felt like leaning over and pushing up her lower jaw. Hartley-Graham said nothing.

'It was enough for me to think that she could be at risk anyway.'

Hartley-Graham nodded thoughtfully.

'But I was only sure when I confirmed that DC Coughlan had asked to do a double shift on the island. You could only escape at high tide but you couldn't risk being on the water when the marine unit brought in DC Coughlan's replacement. They'd have discovered what you'd done and, as it's a four-hour journey to the Isle of Man, they'd have chased you down. No way could you outrun one of their RIBs. No, the only way it could be done was if you had that tide cycle to yourself, and the only way you could achieve that was if you found a way of cancelling DC Coughlan's replacement. I assume it was you and not him who radioed in volunteering for the overtime?'

Hartley-Graham nodded. 'It wasn't difficult. No one wanted to do a long shift out there. I'd spent twenty-four hours with you so knew the callsigns and frequencies. The detective inspector I spoke to was delighted Coughlan wanted to stay on.'

'It's time for you to try and avoid black sites and Guantanamo Bay now, Mr Hartley-Graham,' Poe said. 'Give me your password.'

Chapter 87

After Bradshaw had confirmed the password was valid, Poe went back into the interview.

'Tell me what happened. Just the highlights this time.'

'I'm a problem solver,' Hartley-Graham said. 'Under my Curator alter ego I approach wealthy individuals and offer them a way out of whatever trouble they've managed to get themselves in. Until this job I have always sought out my clients. I research them, and when I'm convinced it's safe to do so I offer a bespoke solution.'

'This client approached you?' Poe said.

Hartley-Graham nodded.

'They did. At first, I was sceptical. There are a lot of cops out there working full time on this type of crime. It wasn't until I was authorised to add one million pounds' worth of bitcoin into my digital wallet that I sat up and took notice. My client said there would be another million if I took the job and a million more after its successful conclusion. I couldn't turn down three million pounds. I set up an impenetrable firewall between the two of us and opened a dialogue.'

Before he continued, Poe flashed Hartley-Graham a warning look. Reminded him what they'd agreed on the island about what he could and couldn't say.

'What did they want?'

'Revenge.'

'For what?'

'I didn't ask.'

'This revenge was in the form of stealing DI Flynn's baby?'

'And to make it clear to her that it was because of something she'd done at work. The wound's crude stitching was to be her permanent reminder.'

'But you hadn't yet had instructions on what you were to do with the baby once you were off the island.'

'I hadn't,' Hartley-Graham confirmed. 'I presume a buyer was lined up.'

The NCA were already putting every case Flynn had been involved in under the microscope. As Poe understood it, some potential grudge holders had already been dragged out of their beds.

'Talk me through what you did. I want to know how you got from the Black Swan Challenge to performing illegal surgery on an NCA officer.'

'First, I had to make sure that DI Flynn worked the case. That wasn't as easy as it seemed. SCAS have cracked some high-profile cases recently and you're in high demand from all the territorial police forces. A single weird murder wouldn't guarantee your involvement. But a series of weird murders? In Cumbria? The locals would definitely bring in you, Sergeant Poe. And why wouldn't they? A respected resource right on their doorstep. And once you were involved then DI Flynn would be too. Maybe not immediately, but eventually. I was told she wouldn't be able to help herself. Even if it meant staying at work longer than she should.'

'You used her stubbornness against her?'

'I did.'

Poe bit down his reply. This interview was all about delicately threading a needle.

'So you dreamt up a scenario involving a revenge plot against Edward Atkinson?'

'I found a bunch of vulnerable kids online and convinced them I'd installed malware on their computers. Most of them didn't care and I let them go.'

'Robert Cowell cared,' Poe said.

'He did. I don't know what it was he didn't want me to see but it was enough for him and his sister to commit a couple of nasty offences. After that it was an easy enough thing to steal his kite and put it near one of the victims' houses, somewhere you'd eventually find it. That would start you off on the path that would lead to the one person who linked the three murder victims. And once you'd *made* that link it was only a matter of time before you ended up with me on the island.'

'How the hell did you find Edward Atkinson, though?' Poe said. 'Even the chief constable hadn't been told where he lived.'

Hartley-Graham frowned in confusion.

'I didn't *find* Edward Atkinson, Mr Poe,' he said. 'I happened upon him. Until I landed on that island I'd never heard of the man.'

Realisation dawned on Poe. 'You simply found an isolated location and constructed a narrative around it.'

'I'd been told that it was empty during the winter months,' he said.

'Because, apart from Edward, none of the other islanders live there full time,' Poe said.

'Exactly,' Hartley-Graham said. 'Edward didn't advertise his presence there so it was a bit of a surprise when I stumbled upon him. But, after . . . talking to him, I quickly realised I could turn this to my advantage.'

'You improvised the whole thing,' Poe said.

'It's what I do,' he said. 'One way or another I'd have found a way to get Miss Flynn on the island when I needed her there. All you need is a good story, Sergeant Poe. People will follow a good story anywhere and Edward Atkinson's, as sad as it was, was compelling.'

'Correction. It's what you *did*.'

'Did,' he agreed. 'Anyway, I practised the surgery on the two women. Neither of them were pregnant, but they had wombs obviously. I got Amanda Simpson's surgery wrong. Didn't use enough anaesthetic and she woke before I could finish closing the wound. Struggled so much I nicked her ovarian artery and she bled out.'

Poe knew all this. Estelle Doyle had confirmed it during the post-mortems.

'The second procedure went well. I was able to open and close Rebecca Pridmore without too much mess. I didn't need to get it exactly right. I just needed the surgery to be survivable.'

Poe's fist tightened. He stood up. He needed a break.

Chapter 88

Bradshaw leaned in and rested her head on his shoulder.

'Will DI Flynn be all right, Poe?'

'I don't know, Tilly. I really don't. She's resilient and she's tough but something like this changes a person. It has to.'

Although Bradshaw was using her glasses as a hairband, her candyfloss-hair was all over the place. Her eyes were hollow and empty. She was close to tears but was holding it together. He suspected it was for his sake. She knew he had to go back in.

'I think DI Flynn *will* be back at work one day,' she said as if she'd come to a decision.

His phone rang.

It was Special Agent Melody Lee. Bradshaw had sent her everything they'd found relating to the White Elephant Challenge and she'd promised to ring with an update.

'Stuart Wilson's legal team have filed an emergency briefing,' she said. 'I'm told the DA won't contest it. He'll be out soon. Our DC field office has already arrested the man who hired the Curator to set up Stuart. He's lawyered up but we have him. It was exactly as I said – he had his business partner murdered so he didn't have to buy him out at full value. The family will be in touch personally at some point but I've been told to thank you, Poe.'

'Glad it worked out,' he said.

They chatted for a while longer but Poe wasn't really interested. He was glad for the family, of course he was, but he had bigger concerns right now.

Melody Lee picked up on it.

'Are you OK, Poe?'

Poe dodged the question. He was far from all right. He'd taken on a burden, and although he was the only person that could, he knew it would weigh heavy over the coming weeks, months, even years . . .

'What about you?' he asked. 'Must feel nice to be vindicated.'

'I have some things to finish up here but I'll be back in DC by the end of March.'

'I'm glad for you.'

'Any time you need a favour, just pick up the phone.'

Washington Poe, named after the city his mother was raped in . . . The city Special Agent Lee would soon be heading to.

'I *do* need a favour,' he said.

'Already? That was quick.'

He told her what he wanted.

'That's it?' she said.

'That's it,' he said. 'I just want the names of everyone who attended that diplomatic party in Washington.'

Melody Lee paused a beat.

'Is this official or personal?'

Poe said nothing for several moments.

'Personal,' he said eventually. '*Very* personal.'

'Well, then may God help them.'

Chapter 89

'I want specifics now,' Poe said.

He wasn't sure he could cope with much more but he owed it to Flynn. If there was something in the details, one little clue to the identity of the person who'd hired Hartley-Graham, it had to be him who heard it.

So Hartley-Graham told him.

Told him that he had modelled both the White Elephant Challenge and the Black Swan Challenge on the suicide game Blue Whale. Hid some single-board computers locally then kicked it all off.

'I suspect that Robert and Rhona Cowell were in so deep that if I'd actually told them to kill Rebecca Pridmore, they'd have done it. I didn't leave clues at the two other murders but once you'd learned about the Black Swan Challenge I assumed you'd think you were looking for two other murderers. I wanted you to think there were others out there and Atkinson was their final challenge. I know you found out about me but the end result was the same: you and DI Flynn still had to protect Edward Atkinson.'

'What if I hadn't noticed the kite?' Poe asked. 'Or the printer test page you'd planted in his bin?'

'I had contingencies to make sure you ended up at Robert Cowell's house.'

'Let me guess: an anonymous phone call?'

'Something like that. You'd have found the document I

planted in his bin eventually. If you missed that one, I'd have planted another.'

Poe had thought the Immolation Man was the ultimate puppet master. Hartley-Graham took things to the next level. They'd all danced to whatever tune he'd played . . .

Hartley-Graham said that, while they'd been running around Cumbria and the north-east, he'd been getting used to Atkinson's medical mask and spending time in his wheelchair. Immersing himself in his new legend.

'How long did you keep him alive before you killed him?' Poe asked.

'Four days,' Hartley-Graham replied. 'I needed to become him. That could only happen with an in-depth interrogation.'

'Something you learned in army intelligence.'

Hartley-Graham nodded. 'I then found a guy who'd been on the jury. He did some stupid interview with the press a year ago. I paid him ten grand for the names of the not-guilty jurors.'

Poe didn't say anything. Nightingale's team had already charged the man who'd leaked the names.

He told Poe how he'd practised with the rigid collodion, the solution used on actors to create the effects of scarred skin. Played about with different shades until he had the look of an acid-attack survivor. He explained that by the time Poe arrived on Montague Island, he'd been using it so much that his skin was wrinkled and puckered even when he wasn't wearing it.

Poe asked how he kept his client up to date with his progress. As he'd expected he didn't understand any of Hartley-Graham's technical explanations. It didn't matter – Bradshaw was watching and would provide him with any supplementary questions. He wrote everything down anyway, mainly so he didn't have to look at him.

Something he said made him pause.

Something about his client's username. He'd said it was anonymous earlier, but he hadn't actually told him what it was.

He asked him to repeat it.

Hartley-Graham did.

Poe wrote it down then underlined it.

It was a number.

8844.

He tapped it into his phone. In less than a second Google returned over seventeen million results.

8844 was a form used by the IRS, the American tax authorities.

It was a Lego helicopter set.

It was part of the genomic sequence for a protein found in a human chromosome.

'This username, is it randomly generated?' Poe said.

'No. The user chooses their own.'

'So there'd be nothing to stop someone from calling themselves say . . . James Bond or Basil Fawlty?'

'Nothing at all. Obviously no one uses anything that could identify them. It's why random number streams are so popular.'

'A bit like numbered bank accounts?'

'I guess.'

Poe stared at the number. He underlined it again.

8844. Why did it seem familiar?

He reviewed where he'd been recently. Nothing jumped out. He went back further.

Into last year.

Poe went rigid. He caught his breath. Blood pounded in his temples. Hartley-Graham was saying something he couldn't hear. The other cop in the room was looking at him strangely.

Poe didn't care.

It couldn't be.

It didn't make sense.

Only it did . . .

When he teased it all out, in the worst way imaginable,

it absolutely *did* make sense. In fact it was the only thing that could.

'I was told she wouldn't be able to help herself . . .'

That's what Hartley-Graham had told him. That 8844 had said that Flynn wouldn't be able to help herself. She'd get involved in the case even when she should be on leave.

He forced himself to breathe normally. He kept his expression neutral. He needed to be careful. Along with what Hartley-Graham had told him on the island, Poe was in a whole new thing now.

Because if he was right nothing was going to be the same again.

For any of them.

Chapter 90

It had turned midnight and Poe sat alone in a dark room.

Waiting.

Thinking.

The darkness was his friend. It was where the answers were. No matter how hard they tried to hide, he knew he'd always be able to track them down in the darkness. In the shadow of a blizzard he'd uncovered the Curator's plan and on the cold, black island he'd listened as he described what he'd been paid to do.

All of it.

Not just the sanitised account he'd allowed Hartley-Graham to say to camera.

And the sanitised account being the *only* account was now Poe's primary concern. Because the *un*-sanitised account was the most horrific thing he'd ever heard of. It would stay with him for ever. He'd try, but this wasn't something that would fade with time.

So he waited.

No plans, no intentions.

Just counting down the time until the lights would go on.

A noise focused his attention on where he knew the door was. Someone was trying to get a key in the lock.

Fumbling. Unsteady.

Drunk . . .

The door opened and they stumbled in. The lights snapped

on. Poe blinked. Twice. He didn't allow himself the luxury of a third.

'Washington,' a glassy-eyed Jessica Flynn slurred, 'what are you doing here? How did I get in?'

She giggled.

'I mean, how did *you* get in?' She waved her hand. 'Doesn't matter. Good that you're here. Drink? I'm having one.'

'I'm good, Jessica.' He remained seated.

'Party pooper.'

Jessica lurched over to the polished wooden bar and opened a bottle of wine. Clumsily poured it. More fell on the floor than in her glass.

'I need some air,' she said. She opened the floor-to-ceiling windows that overlooked the car park. She stepped outside and peered over the balcony. 'I don't see your new Range Rover down there, Washington.'

Poe didn't respond.

She stepped back inside and collapsed onto the couch. Half her wine slopped out.

'Balls.'

Poe said nothing.

'What's happening with the . . . the . . . you know, the case thingy?'

'We have a name for the Curator. He's called Oliver Hartley-Graham.'

'And the organ grinder?'

'We have a decent lead,' Poe said. 'A few years ago Stephanie helped convict a paedophile. He died in prison. Last year his daughter won the lottery. The financial adviser the lottery company appointed helped her invest in bitcoins. It's how Hartley-Graham was paid. Cumbria are investigating.'

'S'good,' Jessica said. 'Sounds promising.'

'It does.'

'What you doing here anyway?'

'I'm on my way to see Steph. Thought I'd pop in to see you first.'

He held up the keys to the Range Rover.

'I can't accept this,' he continued.

'Why not? You earned it. My little sister would be deaded or something and baby Flynn would be in the Middle East by now if you hadn't gone all *Starsky & Hutch* on us.'

'Actually, Scrapper wouldn't be in the Middle East.'

'Well, Russia then. You're the policeman, how am I supposed to know where trafficked babies end up?'

'Not Russia, either.'

'Where then?' she snapped.

'I've been keeping something back from everyone,' Poe said. 'Something Hartley-Graham told me on the island. Something he *only* told me. I made a deal with him there and then that if he didn't mention it, *I* wouldn't mention it.'

'And what was that?'

'That he wasn't to wait for instructions on what to do with Steph's baby.'

'He wasn't?'

'No, because he'd already had them.'

'So what *was* he supposed to do?'

Poe stared at her for several moments. Watched her carefully.

'He was to kill it,' he said quietly.

Jessica took a drink of wine. 'Bullshit,' she said.

'He was to record himself disposing of the body,' Poe continued. 'Somewhere it could never be found. On receipt of the recording his client would release the last payment.'

Flynn's sister said nothing. She seemed to be sobering up, however.

'Hartley-Graham planned to dump Scrapper in the Irish Sea, halfway between Montague Island and the Isle of Man.'

'And you believe this Oliver Hartley-Graham? He was probably just trying to shock you, Poe.'

'I believe him.'

'Then you're a bigger fool than I thought.'

'Am I? Explain this then: why was there an untethered lobster pot full of rocks in the boat he planned to escape in?'

'I have no idea, Poe. Perhaps he was trying to catch lobst—'

'He told me he'd been instructed to feed Steph's baby to the crabs, Jessica.'

He paused. Wanted to see if the mental image elicited a response.

It didn't.

'I threw the lobster pot as far into the sea as I could,' he said. 'I then gave everyone a more palatable version of the truth. No way can Steph ever know.'

'This is a nice story, Poe, but I'm getting another drink,' she said. She tried to get up but fell back down.

'Why'd you do it, Jessica?' He didn't raise his voice. Kept it neutral. He could have been asking why she preferred green-topped milk to red-topped.

'Have a drink, Poe!' she said. 'Everything's OK when you've had a drink.'

Poe stood. He walked over to the mountaineering wall. The altar to her obsession. He stood in front of one picture in particular. It was next to her pride and joy: the Tenzing Norgay mountaineering axe. The photograph was of a group of Chinese mountaineers sitting around a fire at a base camp. All mugs of tea and smiles. It had been taken in 1960 and documented the country's first successful Everest attempt.

'This is where you went wrong,' he said, pointing at the photograph. 'If you hadn't tried to be clever, if you'd used a randomly generated username, who knows, we may never have caught up with you.'

Jessica Flynn looked thoughtful.

'But you didn't, did you? You chose the height of Everest according to the Chinese.' He pointed at the photograph's annotation. 'The Chinese don't accept the official height of 8848 metres. They believe the height should be to the top of the rock, not the top of the snow. The Chinese say that the official height of Everest is 8844 metres. Like it says here.'

Jessica's eyes narrowed.

'That's it?' she scoffed. 'You came all this way with a silly little number?'

'Tilly did the odds for me. The chances of someone choosing a random four-digit number that corresponds with the one in your flat is . . . how did she put it? . . . statistically unlikely.'

It was the first lie he'd told. He hadn't involved Bradshaw in this. He hadn't involved anyone.

Jessica waved him away. 'I don't care what the odds are, it's a coincidence. I live in a rented apartment and occupy a minor position in an investment bank, where the fuck am I supposed to get three million pounds from?'

Her words hung in the air. Poe could almost see them.

For several moments neither of them spoke. Poe could hear the television in the apartment below.

'I didn't tell you the Curator's fee was three million pounds,' he said quietly.

'I . . . I assumed, what with you saying all those things you said he'd been asked to do, that's about what his fee would be.'

Poe said nothing. Just stared at her.

'Makes no difference, though,' she said. 'The facts remain the same. I can't be the person who hired him because I *don't* have three million pounds.'

Poe reached into his inside pocket. He withdrew a sheaf of documents. He put on his reading glasses and read from the top one.

'Thing is, Tilly tells me that a lot of people who invested in bitcoin in the early days made staggering amounts of money. Money that was never declared and is almost untraceable.'

'Is that all you have? A theory about bitcoin?'

Poe shook his head.

'I researched your bank,' he said. 'You're not quite the put-upon corporate drone, are you, Jessica? Far from occupying the relatively junior position you claimed on Boxing Day – you're actually a senior vice president. Something to do with mergers and acquisitions, whatever that is. It also says here that although your bank *did* own this apartment, they sold it three years ago when they moved their property investments out of the UK and into mainland Europe. Part of their Brexit preparations apparently. It was bought for cash by an offshore company. *That's* who you rent it from.'

He turned the page.

'And about your Tenzing Norgay axe,' he said, gesturing towards the mountaineering display in the corner of the room, 'the one you claim is a replica. According to this, Christie's in New York sold the original at auction last year. It went for hundreds of thousands of dollars. I have a friend in the FBI now and she did some digging. Guess what she found?'

Jessica shrugged.

'It was bought by the same offshore company that owns this apartment.'

Poe looked at her over his reading glasses.

'Is this all a coincidence as well, Jessica?'

She held his gaze for a few seconds then smiled.

'Busted,' she said. She pouted, put on a squeaky, cute voice. 'Jessica's been a very naughty girl.'

'Yes, you have,' Poe said.

'So what happens next?'

'You're going to tell me why. You're going to tell me why you paid to have your own nephew killed.'

'You seem to know everything, why don't you tell me?'

'OK, I will,' he said. 'I think this started with you being told you had Addison's disease.'

'Does it now?'

'Because, although you told me you had been diagnosed with it, you didn't tell me *how* you were diagnosed with it. But I think I can guess. You're a mountaineer. A very good one by the looks of it. You've climbed all over the world but the one climb you haven't done is Everest. And until you have it's like a pebble in your shoe. Even if it isn't hurting you know you'll have to take it out at some point.'

Jessica scowled.

'You decide to go for it. You start planning. You don't want to be part of an organised tour so you assemble a team to go with. How am I doing?'

Jessica shrugged again and spilled more of her wine. She got up and refilled her glass.

Poe continued.

'But then, weeks before you're about to set off, your little sister turns up. She's been trying to get pregnant and she now knows why she's struggled. She has Addison's disease and because it can be hereditary it means *you* might have Addison's disease. You get yourself tested and, all of a sudden, your expedition is off. Stephanie's dream of having children was the end of your dream of climbing the only mountain that matters.'

Jessica glared at him.

'So you sought redress,' he said. 'As sick as it sounds, you thought it was only fair. A dream for a dream.'

He stopped talking.

Jessica Flynn threw back her head and roared with laughter.

'You think this was about the baby? Fuck the baby! This was about respect. Respect and the fact that my uppity sister gives me none. I'm her big sister and that should mean something. It

365

should *count*. She used to look up to me, used to rely on me. I'm worth millions; she didn't even have enough money for her IVF. Zoe had to pay for it.'

Poe watched her carefully. She was behaving unpredictably and, although she was drunk, she'd be formidable if things turned violent.

'I make decisions that affect the stock market, whereas she's a nobody in a nothing job. A fucking servant. And she has the gall to look down on me? Where's the respect? Where's the fucking respect! How dare that fucking carpet muncher be happy? Why should she have everything while I have nothing?'

Poe looked at the apartment he was in. The expensive décor. The beautiful fittings. An original slice of history sitting on a plinth.

'All this means nothing if she isn't jealous!' Jessica shrieked.

Poe stood. Easier to move.

'Sit down!'

Poe didn't.

'You wanted your little sister back,' he said, finally understanding. 'You knew she'd spend the rest of her life searching for a baby she could never find. It would have consumed her. It would have ruined her relationship with Zoe. She'd have had no choice but to come back to you. She'd need your money to keep searching. She'd be back under your control again.'

'And it would prove I'd been right all along. Being a police officer is a ridiculous job. So, yes, I paid someone to kill her baby. Big deal. I was going to make amends by setting up a foundation. I thought it would be nice if we could look for the baby together. We could have been a family again.'

Poe knew there and then that what she'd done had stripped her of her sanity. There would be no reasoning with her now; she'd been staring into the abyss for far too long.

He also knew he had no proof. The evidence could be on her

laptop but he doubted it. With unlimited resources she'd have used a throwaway to communicate with Hartley-Graham.

All he had was a story.

Jessica reached the same conclusion.

'Show me your handcuffs,' she said.

'I'm sorry?'

'Your handcuffs. Show them to me.'

Poe didn't move.

'That's what I thought,' she smirked. 'You're not here officially. If you had a shred of proof my door would have been kicked in and a bunch of dickheads in white suits would have searched this place top to bottom. And by the way, there's nothing to find. Nothing to find means there's nothing you can do. All you have is a number my solicitor will explain away without even trying.'

'I don't need proof,' he said softly.

'What are you talking about, you fucking idiot? Of course you need proof. No proof, no case.'

She walked over to her front door.

'I'd like you to leave now.'

Poe didn't budge.

'I don't need proof, not when I have a *story*. I'm going to see Stephanie now, Jessica. I'm going to sit her down and I'm going to tell her everything.'

Jessica glared at him.

'Now, I know Stephanie pretty well but I'm not her sister. So I ask you this: who do you think she'll believe?'

'You wouldn't dare,' she hissed. 'It would destroy her.'

'It will,' he nodded. 'But not as much as always having to look over her shoulder. Not as much as always wondering if her child is safe.'

Poe was used to violence but Jessica wasn't used to *being* violent. He could read the warning signs as easily as if she'd shouted her intentions, so when she screamed and threw her empty glass at him, Poe ducked under it easily. He heard it smash against the exposed brickwork behind him. Jessica vaulted the couch and sprinted to the mountaineering wall. She snatched the Tenzing Norgay ice axe from its plinth.

She didn't hesitate. Spinning round, she charged him, her face contorted with fear and hatred.

Because she was drunk, and because he'd been expecting it, as Jessica reached him, Poe twisted out of her way. His movement was subtle, little more than a feint, but it was enough. The swing of the ice axe whistled past his nose and Jessica stumbled past him.

The momentum kept her moving.

Out onto the balcony.

Where the top of her thighs hit the metal railing.

And like a tree being felled, she slowly toppled over.

But, as drunk as she was, she was still a mountaineer. She whipped out her arm and the tip of the axe dug into the floor of the balcony, tearing an inch-deep gouge out of the polished oak floor.

The silence was sudden and all consuming.

Poe stepped out and looked down. Jessica was hanging from the axe, swinging gently like a condemned man hanging from the gallows.

'Help me,' she pleaded. 'I don't want to die.'

'No, you wanted your sister's baby to.'

'I'm sorry. I'll tell her everything. I promise. Just help me up.'

'Swear on your nephew's life?'

Jessica nodded before she realised what he'd said.

'Yes, you're sorry now but it won't last,' Poe continued. 'It might take a year, it might take five, but at some point your resentment will build up again. While you live, Stephanie's child will never be safe.'

'Fuck you then, Poe. I'll get back up myself.'

She grunted and started swinging. Rocking really. Tried to build enough momentum to get a foot on the balcony ledge. With a foot *and* a hand she'd have the two points of contact any decent mountaineer could self-recover from. Poe watched. She came close a couple of times but she was drunk and quickly tired. Her mountaineering discipline kicked in and she stopped to conserve energy.

Her hands, wet with sweat, slipped on the axe's shaft and panic gripped her. She glanced down. Saw only concrete and death in her future.

'They'll know you were here,' she gasped. 'Your fingerprints will be all over my apartment.'

Poe shrugged. 'I was here Boxing Day. Of course my fingerprints will be here.'

'Please,' she begged. 'Don't let me die.'

Poe stared at her.

'You wrote this ending, not me,' he said.

And without another word he turned and stepped back into the room. Picking up the keys to the Range Rover he quietly left her apartment. It was late, and although he could hear movement he didn't see anyone. He made his way down the fire exit and walked across the road towards the country lane where he'd parked the car.

By the time he reached it the screaming had started.

Author's Note

Unfortunately, the Blue Whale Suicide Challenge is real. It probably started in Russia, but most countries have reported anecdotal evidence of its reach. And the underpinning psychology that Tilly explains is real as well. It's a scary world when someone who has nothing more than a damaged mind and access to a computer can manipulate kids and other vulnerable people, who sometimes live on the other side of the world, into doing these awful things. Read about it, if you haven't already. Educate yourself so you can spot the warning signs.

Yellow dot tracking is real, as well. Sixteen years as a probation officer rammed home the offenders' code that snitches get stitches, and, believe it or not, your printer *is* a tittle-tattle. So, if you're planning on posting something brown and smelly to Number 10, you'd better use someone else's printer if you want to add a typed message. Preferably belonging to someone who's annoyed you recently.

Now, a quick word of caution. Although the Walney Channel and the Islands of Furness are real, Montague Island is most definitely not. And, although you *can* walk to Piel Island when the tide is out (although you should never try this without a guide), please don't try to walk to Montague Island – you will drown in the Irish Sea. And, whilst I appreciate this might feel heavy-handed, please remember hotels have to put stickers on their hairdryers that say 'Please do not use in the shower' . . .

And finally, for all the pedants out there, I'm fully aware

that describing Walney Island as being quarter-moon shaped is technically incorrect. The correct term would have been 'waxing gibbous', but I used more accessible language. Please forgive me. Also, I hope you're aware that knowing the meaning of waxing gibbous is the reason you don't have any friends. If you feel as though you can't let this go, please do write a letter. But don't send it to me.

Acknowledgements

Lots of people to thank, not a lot of energy to do it.

In no particular order:

My wife and soulmate, Joanne. Not only do you go through the final draft and hunt out those stubborn little typos, you – and I really don't know how you do it – put up with someone who's such a constant chatter of shit. I know I wouldn't like to live with me.

David Headley (and just so we can all feel a bit inadequate here, let's list his jobs, shall we? Agent, bookseller, publisher, festival organiser . . .) for his friendship, guidance, and enthusiastic championing (and selling) of Poe & Tilly and Fluke & Towler, both nationally and internationally. You're a good man, David.

Everyone at DHH Literary Agency and Goldsboro Books, not least Emily Glenister, for all your support and kindness. And beer when I visit.

My editor at Constable, Krystyna Green, for being so awesome. And for letting me have the ending I wanted in this book. Let's see how long we can keep this racket going for, shall we? I reckon I have a few left in me if you have?

Sarah Murphy and Hannah Wann for their patience and good humour. Like Joanne, I don't know how you put up with me.

Martin Fletcher and Howard Watson, both of whom prove that you *can* polish a turd. Martin helps me see the wood when all I've been able to see is the trees, and Howard makes wot I write more good. And Howard also manages to make sure I'm not contradicting myself from what used to be book to book, but now includes series to series. Don't know how you do it, Howard, but I'm glad you do.

From the start of my journey with Constable, one thing about the books that has really caught readers' eyes is the covers. Every single one (from *The Puppet Show* to the recently refurbished Fluke series) has been absolutely spectacular. So take a bow, Sean Garrehy – you are seriously talented. And I'm sorry you missed your train after the *Black Summer* launch. Next time we'll be more sensible. Promise. ;-)

Rebecca Sheppard, a desk editor like no other, who, in the chaos of multiple drafts, last-minute inserts, last-second edits, and simple buffoonery on my part, manages to stay calm, organised and makes sure everything that needs to happen, happens.

My proofreader, Joan Deitch, for doing the most underrated but arguably most important job in the process – checking the final proof before it goes to production. And with someone like me, who scatters words around like rice at a wedding, it can't be easy. Thank you for your diligence.

Beth Wright and Brionee Fenlon, publicity and marketing respectively, for putting Poe & Tilly into the hands of so many readers it's indecent. And Beth, I'm sorry you had to hear the Mick Herron story . . .

And to everyone else at Little, Brown who has worked on Poe & Tilly in whatever capacity. It's a privilege to be published by such an eminent house and one I'll be eternally grateful for. Thank you.

And last on the editorial side, Angie Morrison, my beta reader. Although your enthusiasm for Poe & Tilly is limitless, your advice is still measured and considerate. It's also invariably correct.

Brian Price and James Grieve (Emeritus Professor in Forensic Medicine) must get a mention for explaining the science behind 'vital reaction' – how a pathologist can tell if a finger has been amputated pre- or post-mortem. You guys are gross, by the way.

Andy Atkinson (who I suspect will be getting acknowledgements in all future books, as well, and who is almost certainly regretting ever meeting me), for his advice on how someone might go about hosting a website anonymously. I'm sure he loved explaining the difference between the deep and dark web, firewalls, single-board computers, logging systems and how bitcoin works . . . We speak different languages, Andy, but you found a way to dumb it down enough for me to understand it.

Fiona Sharp, bookseller extraordinaire. You have the energy of no one else I know, and I know David Headley. I'm sure if you badger Beth long enough, you'll get your #TeamTilly tote bag eventually. Let me know if you want her home phone number . . .

Paul Musgrave and Mike Conefrey, Public Health Cumbria, for their insight into what the county's response might be if a game like Blue Whale or Black Swan took hold up here. Scary stuff.

L.J. Morris gets a nod. I killed him off in the previous book but he was still good enough to help me out with some of the technical details of how submarines are built and their contracts managed. Sorry, Les, I do of course mean Ships Submersible Nuclear Ballistics: Dreadnought Class . . . Dork.

Bob and Carol Bridgestock, the awesome R.C. Bridgestock, helped enormously with the legality of grabbing evidence out of dustbins. Thanks, guys.

And so to the whinging b******s, those people who insist on being thanked, even though they did jack s**t. In order of decreasing relevance they are:

Ted Montague, who thinks lending his surname to a

fictional island near where he lives is more than enough to get an acknowledgement. It isn't, Ted, it really isn't. You're actually in here because our shared love of sarcasm made those dull probation managers' meetings go that little bit faster.

Stuart 'I've been your friend for forty years' Wilson is in here because I can't be bothered to listen to him whine for a whole year. Yes, I know you carefully explained the difference between Swaledale and Herdwick sheep, but that nugget of gold didn't survive the first draft due to how mind-numbingly dull it was. If you want a real acknowledgement, come up with something more interesting. I'll see you in the pub.

Likewise, Crawford Bunney, who seems to think that getting an advance copy of every book somehow entitles him to get his rather silly name in the back. It shouldn't. And I'll see you in the pub too.

My niece, Katie Douglass, got a mention in *Black Summer* as she'd helped with a science issue. For some reason, that means my other nieces (and one nephew) think they should have had a mention as well. I keep telling them, become a nerd like Katie and one day you might be able to help me with something. So Sam, Joe, Rosie and Chloe, not a chance, I'm afraid.

My Uncle John gets a mention for leading with 'What's happening with the TV stuff?' EVERY SINGLE TIME he phones. And for buying more of my books than my entire family put together (if there are any authors reading this, tell him your book might become collectible – he'll buy hundreds of copies), despite never having read a single page.

See you all in a year.

Mike

Enjoyed *The Curator*?
Read on for a special preview of book four in
M. W. Craven's Washington Poe series . . .

Dead Ground

Chapter 1

The man wearing a Sean Connery mask said to the man wearing a Daniel Craig mask, 'Bertrand the monkey and Raton the cat are sitting by the fire, watching chestnuts roast in the hearth.'

Which was as good a way as any of getting someone's attention.

'OK,' Daniel Craig said.

The men wearing George Lazenby and Timothy Dalton stopped what they were doing to listen. Pierce Brosnan, with his headphones on and his laptop spitting out complex instructions, was oblivious to everything but the vault door and the Diebold three-keyed timer and combination lock in front of him. Roger Moore was outside in the van.

'Bertrand tries brushing the coals aside but he's scared of burning his hand,' Sean Connery continued. 'But he wants those chestnuts and he doesn't want to wait for the fire to cool. Instead, he persuades Raton to scoop them out, promising him an equal share.'

'And the cat does?'

'He does, yes. Raton moves the red-hot coals and picks out the chestnuts one by one. And each time he does, Bertrand gobbles them up. Eventually a maid disturbs them and they have to flee. Raton gets nothing for his pains.'

Timothy Dalton was Sean Connery's man, but the rest were Daniel Craig's. George Lazenby was *his* muscle, Pierce Brosnan was *his* technical guy and Roger Moore was *his* wheelman. As crew leader, Daniel Craig felt he should be the one to ask the obvious question.

'Why are you telling us this?' he said.

'No reason,' Sean Connery said. 'It's a fable adapted by the French poet Jean de La Fontaine. It's called "Le Singe et le Chat" and it's about people sacrificing others for their own ends. The saying "cat's paw" comes from it.'

'It's an idiom, actually,' Timothy Dalton said, 'not a saying.'

Sean Connery turned and glared at Dalton. The mood in the vault's anteroom changed. It had been tense; now there was an undercurrent of menace.

'What part of "You do not speak, ever" didn't you understand?' he said, his voice low.

Under his mask they sensed Timothy Dalton blanche. Daniel Craig glanced at the Bonds in his crew and shrugged. Sean Connery was paying and he paid well. If he wanted to talk about monkeys and cats and chestnuts and humiliate his own man then who were they to stop him?

The anteroom descended into silence.

Pierce Brosnan broke it.

'We're in,' he said.

Few banks offer a safety deposit box service these days. The vault that the Bonds had broken into was one of several purpose-built facilities belonging to a specialist provider. It had cutting-edge security, but a combination of offsite hacks and Pierce Brosnan's onsite safecracking skills had rendered them redundant.

At least until the backup systems kicked in.

'How long?' Sean Connery said.

'We've had eighteen minutes, twenty seconds,' Daniel Craig replied.

He glanced at the watch on the inside of his wrist. They still had plenty of time.

The vault was rectangular, fifteen feet by thirty, and had a low ceiling. It was lit by neon lights. A steel table was fixed to the wall opposite the door. Safety deposit boxes stretched from floor to ceiling on the two longer walls. The boxes were suitcase-sized at the bottom and got progressively smaller as they reached eye level and above.

The CCTV cameras were working but had been fixed so they were on a sixty-minute delay. The staff monitoring the vault would see what they were doing, but not for another hour.

'We'll start here,' Timothy Dalton said.

Sean Connery had hired him to evaluate the boxes' contents and he was keen to contribute. So far he'd been a passenger. He made a move to one of the larger boxes.

'Not that one,' Sean Connery said, removing a piece of paper from his pocket. He read out a serial number: 9-206.

The Bonds spread out and searched for the box. George Lazenby found it. It was at head height and was one of the smaller boxes.

'Mr Brosnan, if you will?' Daniel Craig said.

Pierce Brosnan studied the lock. The vault's door had been a challenge but, as no one should be in the vault unsupervised, the security on the boxes was perfunctory, little more than cylinder locks. He pulled a snapper bar from his bag: a locksmith tool specially designed to break and open cylinder locks. It took less than a minute. He put the snapper bar back in his bag and stepped away.

Sean Connery opened the small door. The safety deposit box was empty, as he'd been told it would be. Under his mask, he smiled.

'Never mind,' Dalton said. 'We have hundreds more to check.'

'Actually,' Sean Connery said, 'we're not here to make a withdrawal.'

'We're not? Well, what *are* we doing?'

'Making a deposit.'

Sean Connery pulled a snub-nosed revolver from his waist-band, pressed it against the back of Timothy Dalton's head and pulled the trigger.

He was dead before he hit the polished floor. A cloud of pink mist hung in the air where his head had just been. The vault smelled of cordite and blood.

And fear.

'What the hell!' Daniel Craig snapped. 'No guns, I said! We don't carry guns on jobs.'

'You know what's always bothered me about that fable?' Sean Connery said. He held the gun by his side but it was clear he'd use it again if he had to.

'Enlighten me,' Daniel Craig said, tearing his eyes from the twitching corpse.

'There was no mention of what happened next. No mention of what Raton the cat did to Bertrand the monkey *after* his betrayal.'

Daniel Craig looked at the corpse again. It had stopped moving.

'This man betrayed someone?' Betrayal was a legitimate motive in the circles he moved in.

Sean Connery said nothing.

'Dalton was a shit Bond anyway,' Daniel Craig said, looking at his watch. 'We done?'

'Almost,' Sean Connery said. He removed something from his pocket and placed it on the lip of the empty safety deposit box. He spent some time making sure it was in the right position.

'Now we're done,' he said.

And with that, the Bonds left.

Thirty minutes later, alerted to a robbery in progress by the security company monitoring the vault's CCTV, the first police officers arrived.

But all they found was a corpse cooling on the floor and a ceramic rat looking over it . . .

Chapter 2

Detective Sergeant Washington Poe usually hated attending court. He found the bureaucracy and the subservience to idiots in wigs archaic. He hated being at the beck and call of barristers and he hated the way cops were universally viewed with suspicion when they gave evidence. He hated that so-called experts were allowed to pull apart decisions made in a fraction of a second.

But most of all he hated that when he attended court it meant someone had been failed. A family would never see a loved one again. A woman would never trust a man again. An old man would never leave his house again.

There were many reasons to hate being in court.

But not this time.

This time he was attending as the defendant.

And he planned to enjoy it.

His case was being heard at the Carlisle Combined Court, a modern building in the centre of the city. Its only nod to the past was the Grade II listed statue of the nineteenth-century Member of Parliament who'd dropped dead outside. Poe approved of statues like that. He wished there were more of them.

The district judge, who had lost patience with him a while ago, tried again.

'I must impress upon you, Mr Poe,' he said, 'I know this is only a civil matter but I strongly advise you to get *legal* representation. I'm sure your friend is' – he checked his notes – '"as clever as Stephen Hawking's wheelchair" but what happens here today cannot easily be undone.'

'Consider me advised, your honour.'

'And it's been explained that refusing legal representation is not grounds for a later appeal?'

'It has.'

The district judge had jowls like a bulldog and an unsettling resemblance to Rumpole of the Bailey. Tufts of hair sticking from his ears made it look as though furry animals were burrowing in them. He peered at Poe over his half-moon spectacles. Poe stared back.

'Very well,' he sighed. 'Mr Chadwick, you may proceed.'

The council solicitor got to his feet. Small and moustached, he was an officious-looking man, the type who would take the minutes at Neighbourhood Watch meetings.

'Thank you, your honour.' He opened a thick manila file and picked up a summary sheet. 'The facts in this case are not in dispute. Almost five years ago Mr Poe legally bought land on Shap Fell from a Mr Thomas Hume. This land—'

'Mr Hume is now deceased, I understand?'

'Regrettably that is the case, your honour. Mr Hume was the legal owner of the land and he was well within his rights to sell it to Mr Poe. This land included an abandoned shepherd's croft.'

'The building in question?'

'Yes, your honour. We understand that Herdwick Croft has been there since the early 1800s. It has recently come into the catchment area of the Lake District National Park. The position of the local planning authority is that the croft has been a designated heritage asset since 2005, and therefore cannot be modified without the express permission of our office. Herdwick Croft's original owner was informed of this designation.'

'Mr Poe, would you like to interject?' the judge said.

Poe looked at the person beside him. She shook her head.

'No, your honour,' he said.

'You're aware that challenging the heritage-asset status of the croft is one of the few legal avenues you have left at this point?'

'I am, your honour. Although to be fair, I was unaware of Herdwick Croft's status when I bought it. Thomas Hume must have . . . forgotten to tell me.'

Poe felt, rather than saw, someone stiffen in the public gallery. He knew that Victoria Hume, Thomas's daughter, was there to support him. She felt responsible for her father's duplicity despite Poe reassuring her she wasn't. Poe hadn't completed the usual legal checks prior to handing over his cash and he was now paying the price.

'As a serving police officer, I'm sure Mr Poe will be aware that ignorance of the law is not a legal excuse,' Chadwick said.

Poe smiled. He had hoped he'd say that.

Chadwick spent ten minutes detailing the modifications Poe had completed at Herdwick Croft: the roof he'd fixed; the borehole and pump he'd installed to provide fresh running water; the septic tank he'd buried; the generator and how it supplied power. In short, everything he'd done to make the croft modern and comfortable. Even his beloved wood-burning stove got a mention.

When Chadwick had finished the judge said, 'And how was it you came to be aware of Mr Poe's modifications?'

'Your honour?'

'Who told you, Mr Chadwick?'

'A concerned citizen, your honour.'

'That wouldn't be the member for Oxenholme, would it?'

Chadwick didn't rise to the judge's bait.

'How we came to find out about the modifications is not the business of this court, your honour.'

Poe knew the judge had got it spot on though. The man who'd informed the council about his unauthorised restoration project was a former police officer, a direct-entrant detective chief inspector called Wardle. They'd butted heads during the Jared Keaton case. Wardle had double-downed on the wrong line of enquiry and it had cost him his career. He had since left the police and was now pursuing his new calling: local politics. Poe turned in his seat, half-expecting to see him sitting in the public gallery but, other than Victoria Hume, the benches were empty. It didn't matter, if it hadn't been Wardle it would have been someone else. Poe collected enemies the same way the middle class collected Nectar points.

'Get on with it then, Mr Chadwick,' the judge said.

The local authority solicitor spent another ten minutes detailing the planning regulations Poe had fallen foul of. After two minutes Poe had drifted off.

He'd had an extended stay at Herdwick Croft recently. The Serious Crime Analysis Section, shortened by everyone to SCAS, hadn't had a major case since the Curator and, given how that had ended, no one was looking for a new investigation. The director of intelligence, Edward van Zyl, had given everyone involved a month off.

The break had done Poe good. The Curator case had almost broken him, physically and mentally, and he'd got off lightly compared to some. He'd enjoyed spending time at home. Most days he'd packed some food in a rucksack and headed on to Shap Fell. Just him and Edgar, his springer spaniel, and thousands of sheep.

'How's DI Flynn?' he whispered to the woman beside him. Stephanie Flynn, SCAS's detective inspector, had given birth during the case and it hadn't been straightforward. She was still off sick and he wasn't sure she'd be coming back.

'Shush, Poe!' the woman whispered back. 'I need to hear this.'

Poe returned to his thoughts. Even when it concerned his own future he didn't have the type of brain that could listen to legal arguments for more than a minute. He made a mental note to call

Flynn later. He'd avoided speaking to her recently – it brought back bad memories, for both of them he suspected.

'Are you ready to respond, Mr Poe?'

Poe blinked. Chadwick was back in his seat and everyone was looking at him.

He stood up.

'Am I right in understanding that the local authority is seeking a court order to compel me to return Herdwick Croft to the condition it was in when I bought it, your honour?' Poe said.

'That's correct. Are you ready to respond?'

Poe looked at the person on his right. She nodded.

'I am, your honour.'

'And despite her not having a legal background, you're confident your colleague is up to representing you, Mr Poe?'

'She is, your honour. You may trust me on this.'

He sat down. When he'd lived in Hampshire he'd had an address. Now, he had a home. To protect it, he was willing to fight dirty.

And what he was about to do was as dirty as it was possible to get.

'Over to you, Tilly,' he said.

CUT SHORT

M.W. Craven

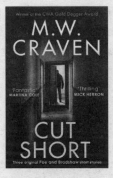

**THREE BRAND NEW SHORT STORIES FROM THE WINNER OF
THE CWA BEST CRIME NOVEL OF 2019 AWARD**

In **The Killing Field**, Poe and Bradshaw are having breakfast, wondering how to spend the rest of their holiday, when their presence is requested at a Cumbrian airfield. An airfield that, during the 2001 foot and mouth crisis, was known as the killing field . . .

In **Why Don't Sheep Shrink?,** a global pandemic forces Poe and Bradshaw to self-isolate together. Things don't go well. They're bickering and on the verge of falling out until Poe finds an old case file: a locked room mystery he's been mulling over for years. Step forward, Tilly Bradshaw . . .

Dead Man's Fingers sees Poe, Bradshaw and Edgar, Poe's English springer spaniel, enjoying a picnic at a nature reserve. When Edgar chases a rabbit, and Poe and Bradshaw chase after him, they stumble upon a twenty-year-old mystery: a mystery that couldn't be solved until now . . .

BORN IN A BURIAL GOWN

M. W. Craven

**THE FIRST GRITTY THRILLER IN
THE AVISON FLUKE SERIES BY M. W. CRAVEN**

Detective Inspector Avison Fluke is a man on the edge. He has committed a crime to get back to work, concealed a debilitating illness and is about to be made homeless. Just as he thinks things can't get any worse, the body of a young woman is found buried on a Cumbrian building site.

Shot once in the back of the head, it is a cold, calculated execution. When the post-mortem reveals she has gone to significant expense in disguising her appearance, Fluke knows this is no ordinary murder.

With the help of a psychotic ex-Para, a gangland leader and a woman more interested in maggots than people, Fluke must find out who she was and why she was murdered before he can even think about finding her killer . . .

BODY BREAKER

M.W. Craven

**THE SECOND DARK AND TWISTED THRILLER IN
THE AVISON FLUKE SERIES BY M. W. CRAVEN**

Investigating how a severed hand ends up on the third green of a Cumbrian golf course is not how Detective Inspector Avison Fluke had planned to spend his Saturday. So when a secret protection unit from London swoops in quoting national security, he's secretly pleased.

But trouble is never far away. A young woman arrives at his lakeside cabin with a cryptic message: a code known to only a handful of people – and it forces Fluke back into the investigation he's only just been barred from.

In a case that will change his life forever, Fluke immerses himself in a world of New Age travellers, corrupt cops and domestic extremists. Before long he's alienated his entire team, has been arrested under the Terrorism Act – and has made a pact with the Devil himself. But a voice has called out to him from beyond the grave. And Fluke is only getting started . . .